one summer in
arkansas

one summer in
arkansas

marcia kemp sterling

Archelaus Press

*In recognition of the Steels and Lockes,
Scots-Irish Protestants who made their way
to the Arkansas frontier to read the law,
preach the Word and till the red clay earth*

chapter one

Again I saw that under the sun the race is not to the swift, nor the battle to the strong, nor bread to the wise, nor riches to the intelligent, nor favor to the skillful; but time and chance happen to them all. For no one can anticipate the time of disaster. Like fish taken in a cruel net, and like birds caught in a snare, so mortals are snared at a time of calamity, when it suddenly falls upon them.

—*Ecclesiastes 9:11*

The late afternoon Texas sun was streaming through large plate glass windows, illuminating rows of worn red plastic seats where dozens of sweaty, baggage-laden passengers waited for the 6:15 flight to Riverton, Arkansas. Downstairs from the main terminal of the Dallas/Fort Worth International Airport, the remote corridor provided access to small towns across the South via short regional flights. In contrast to the bustling concourse above, the mix of passengers reflected unique small-town demographics, each lounge signaling the flight's destination by the dress, accent and bearing of the assembled travelers.

As Lee Addison approached the cramped waiting area for Gate 19F at the end of the corridor, he was overcome with a visceral feeling of claustrophobia.

Though boarding would not begin for half an hour, Lee preferred to stand. He dropped his briefcase near the wall and opened the *New York Times* he'd picked up in San Francisco that morning. He skimmed the latest headlines about the Gulf War as his ear acclimated to the pitch and inflection of the voices around him speaking in the familiar idiom of his childhood.

This would be his last chance to spend a summer at home before starting work. During law school, he had spent summers editing law review articles and interning at some of San Francisco's finest law firms, firms engaged in a lively competition to attract the best students from the best schools—team building in the wine country; lunch at Greens with a hiring partner, watching the bright midday sun melt the last remnants of fog hanging off the Golden Gate Bridge; all-hands meetings late into the night with the city's top investment bankers.

With each passing year it had become harder to find time to make the trek back to Arkansas. But his mother wasn't getting any younger, and she had pleaded with him to spend this summer at home, promising litigation experience at Riverton's leading law firm. And his sister, M.J., younger than Lee by eight years, was struggling. Maybe quality time with her big brother would help her through an awkward adolescence.

"Lee Addison?"

The salutation was jarring and not just because he had been deep in thought. After three years of hearing the emotionally neutral voices of California, the sweet sing-song intonation in the greeting felt like an invasion of privacy.

He looked up to see a smiling and cosmetically perfect face framed by an ash-blonde hairdo heading in his direction. The woman seemed vaguely familiar.

"How in the world are you? It's been forever since you've been home, hasn't it?"

She extended her hand. "Peggy Phillips. From high school. Do you remember me?"

He did, but not well. He remembered an active, cheerful girl, one of dozens similar in demeanor and appearance who inhabited the fading recollections of his adolescence. But the wholesome pink-cheeked exuberance of seven years ago had hardened into a more intentional look.

"I noticed you a couple of times at the Club when you came home from college. But after you broke up with Annie, you seemed to have dropped off the face of the earth."

He would have preferred this time to himself, time to adjust to the sounds and rhythms of the South, to ease into memories of his childhood and mistakes of his youth. *Annie.* Did he really have to go there, this many years later, even before he boarded the plane to Riverton?

The classmate from high school didn't appear to notice his discomfort.

"I don't see much of the old high school crowd," she continued. "You know how it is. Once you're past those years, you don't want to go back."

Peggy had a way of raising her pitch at the end of every sentence, leaving Lee unable to distinguish between statements of fact and questions.

"When did we graduate? '83? God, has it been seven years? I work in sales for Lawton Tires, you know, out on New Hampton Road? Travel all over the place—Austin, San Antonio. But my biggest clients are here in Dallas. I get over here all the time. Stay at the Hilton downtown. Great dance clubs. Nothing like Riverton, believe me.

"I don't know if you remember, I married Larry McFee right after we graduated. He walked out on me a year later. Found somebody else. I was devastated. So was my whole family. Daddy had spent every penny they had on that big wedding. I couldn't have made it through that year without my covenant group at church.

"Oh God, Annie moped around town for years after you dumped her. Everybody was talking about it. She wouldn't have anything to do with men, period. But, believe me, there were plenty of people who were not sorry to see it happen. Annie Rayburn had always gotten everything she wanted. Above it all, you know. I don't mean to put her down. I always liked Annie."

Hearing this secondhand version of his own life story told by a woman he scarcely knew was unsettling.

"By the way, I hear your younger sister has been getting into trouble. She used to be shy. I don't really know her, but I've seen her a few times at the Club. Y'all aren't much alike, are you? God, aren't you glad we're past that stage? I don't mean to butt into your family affairs but…listen, if she would ever consider coming with me to Sunday night worship out at Lakeside Baptist, I would be more than happy to come get her. Seriously.

"Anyway, Lee, you probably want to be left alone to read your paper. Sorry to butt in on your privacy. I couldn't resist coming over to say hello. You were everybody's heartthrob in high school. Anyway, I feel kind of like family. You wouldn't remember this, but my Grandma was Judge Dawkins' secretary for 40 years. So we always looked up to your family.

"Honestly, I don't know why I run on at the mouth so. Listen, I totally understand why you wouldn't want to come back to Riverton. Honest to God, nothing ever changes. Same old, same old…"

"Good to see you again," he stammered, glad for the excuse to gather his things and get in line at the boarding gate.

The crowded shuttle bus eased away from the terminal toward the parking strip where they would board the small prop jet into Riverton. Everybody stood, hanging perilously onto metal poles or synthetic loops of bright blue fabric. Lee could see the top of Peggy Phillips' silvery blonde head toward the front of the bus, laughing and chatting cheerfully as the bus swerved, pushing her into the crowd nearby.

In the short walk from the terminal, Lee had been struck by a blast of hot air, waves of it radiating up from the pavement, mingling with the exhaust from the bus. Like the terminal, the bus itself was freezing, providing welcome if disorienting relief from the weather outside.

Despite the emotional distance he felt from the people surrounding him on the bus, Lee Addison knew full well that his own DNA carried the markers of Riverton, Arkansas, just as surely as theirs. Home. Founded in the early 1800s by Scots-Irish immigrant farmers, its laws and morals had been shaped by several generations of Lee's ancestors, itinerant circuit riders who practiced both law and ministry and kept the moral compass correctly aligned in that corner of the state. During his youth, Lee's maternal grandfather Corky Dawkins had been an eloquent, highly regarded superior court judge, active in politics and civic affairs, bequeathing to the Addisons a respectable position in the community even after the divorce of Lee's parents.

Coming from the Bay Area where airports were filled with people of diverse origin, speaking languages from all over the globe, the median skin color like a double latte, Lee was struck by the starkly different mix of people on the shuttle. About half the passengers were black and, from what he could tell, a group of them had travelled en masse from LA to a reunion at Dunbar High School. Several were wearing sweatshirts touting the now-defunct black high school's historic football prowess. They laughed and chatted in a tone of voice several decibels higher than anybody else on the bus.

Where Peggy stood, the travelers were white, their faded blue jeans cinched below portly bellies, their speech nasal and flat, sounding to Lee's ear more like East Texas twang than the soft aristocratic accent he remembered from his childhood, a legacy to the South from the Protestant farmers who had emigrated from Northern Ireland in the 1800s.

As they boarded the small aircraft, two seats abreast on the right, one on the left, the entrance was clogged because two passengers near the middle of the plane had been issued identical boarding passes. Ensconced in the disputed seat was a wiry, dark woman of indeterminate age, dressed in her Sunday best and clearly uneasy to be travelling alone by plane. Bright eyes shone from a wrinkled blue-black face topped with a red and silver hat worn at a jaunty angle. The matching floral red-belted dress, though frayed, was immaculately cleaned and pressed. She occupied the window seat on the right and Peggy Phillips had taken the seat next to her on the aisle. A ruddy, heavy-set young man with uncombed hair and faded jeans thinning at the knee was leaning across Peggy to demonstrate to the lady that she was in his assigned seat. Rattled by the encounter, the lady could not locate her ticket, already stowed in the carry-on luggage under the seat. Peggy looked at the proffered ticket and turned to her.

"He's right, ma'am. You're in the wrong seat. You need to go back to the front of the plane and talk to the flight attendant."

Disturbed by the implied accusation, the passenger scrambled to gather her belongings from under the seat and from the overhead bin, slowing the boarding process as she made her way to the front of the plane. By the time she reached the flight attendant, her travel dress was darkening under the arms, and she looked disoriented as she tried to understand what had gone wrong.

Lee had taken his assigned window seat near the front of the plane and was looking forward to identifying familiar landmarks as they approached Riverton. Just before the announcement was made to prepare for departure, the deposed passenger, red hat ajar and luggage dragging, was escorted by the flight attendant to the empty place beside him. The overhead bins were now full so her suitcase was taken off to be gate-checked. Lee helped her stow her personal items.

Her hands were shaking as she tried to fasten the seat belt.

"They always seem to overbook planes these days," Lee said. "Travelling has gotten to be harder and harder."

"Sho is. Mmmmm Hmmmm." She pulled a lace handkerchief out of her purse and mopped her brow.

"Is Riverton home for you?" Lee asked.

"Yes sir. Born and raised. My name's Lovey. I been livin' with my daughter and her children in Dallas, but I got some family problems back home. So I'm comin' back to Riverton for a while. My granddaughter there, she's havin' a hard time. She lost her boy in a drowning accident. Don't seem to have no heart for the other children."

chapter two

As the first sounds of morning penetrated his dreams, Lee rolled over and luxuriated in the softness of his mother's silky sheets. Law school graduation was just a week behind him and he was still dreaming about the elements of a cause of action. Definitely not like waking up in Palo Alto. Too much sun for so early in the morning. He was aware of a dustiness in the air and the familiar smell of old sofa stuffing, Lemon Pledge and the distinctive metallic odor of the air conditioner.

He was home. A place where he belonged in a way he never could at Stanford. And yet, for the first time, he thought of this as his mother's house and of Riverton as a place he would visit.

The stately house had been built by his grandparents in the early part of the Great Depression when money was still flowing. White ionic columns stood at the entrance to the circular driveway announcing to all who approached the three-story brick home that this was a family of means. Lee's grandmother Roberta Dawkins had insisted upon stretching her husband's pocketbook to build the biggest home in Riverton, understanding that the success of his new law practice would depend in large part upon his status as a leading citizen of the community.

Not that Lee cared about social status. He had always been a quiet thoughtful boy, an overachiever, open in his social and political views, a good listener. His self-contained, solitary nature couldn't have been further removed from the social aspirations that drove his mother. Class consciousness had died a century ago, thank God, finally giving way to the more rational culture of meritocracy. He would succeed to the extent of his talent and effort, and Lee Addison was on track to go very far indeed.

Third year had been brutal, with law review and a class load heavy in finance and economics. Lacking the easy confidence of some of the kids from the coasts, he had needed good grades to prove that he belonged. It had been a fine achievement for somebody from the Arkansas outback to wind up in the top ten percent.

Lee's natural reserve had kept him from being spotted as a star by the professors at first. The girls noticed him of course—the natural grace in the way he moved and a quiet intelligence emanating from dark amber eyes. He could fend off a professor's Socratic challenge in a soft confident voice, the trace of a Southern accent serving to soften the edges of any legal argument. As time went on, he earned admiration and respect from both students and faculty.

As he launched his career, he had to admit that the lessons learned after twenty years under Frances Addison's roof were bearing fruit. Without even thinking about it, Lee could disarm a potential critic with good manners and expressions of warmth, skills learned at his mother's knee. *Darling, it pays to treat people with courtesy no matter how you really feel about them. You never know when you're going to want a favor from someone.*

What an enigma she was. His mother didn't really like people. Frances Addison had a sharp tongue, and she saw the foibles of the Riverton social scene with a clear and cynical eye. Even as a child, Lee could hardly miss the instant reversal of his mother's tone of voice the minute a passing friend was out of sight. She would laugh aloud at the pathetic naiveté or the frightful sense of fashion of some friend she had just sent off with heartfelt hugs and kisses.

Had his mother been different before the divorce? He couldn't imagine what it must have been like for her to be left with two kids to raise after their father took off with the minister's daughter, never looking back. Frances was a proud woman and it must have been humiliating. Probably still was.

Lee suspected his mother had been born with a nasty streak, more likely a cause than an effect of Trey Addison's leaving her. Well, maybe she wasn't perfect, but God knows she had pushed with every ounce of strength she had to make sure Lee and M.J. had the same opportunity for success as children from intact families. It could have been difficult in a small town like Riverton to be the child of a single parent. She wouldn't have it for a minute. Wouldn't hide from the remarks people made behind her back. Wouldn't see her children left out of anything. Still reeling from the scandal, Frances would be damned if her daughter was going to miss the Country Club Easter Egg Hunt, and you could bet M.J. would be the best-dressed child there.

Lee was a teenager when his parents split up, well-liked, a star in school, busy with his own life. He was at the age when a kid needed to begin to separate from his family anyway. Sure, it was a different matter when the parent did the separating. But after his father left, Lee regained his composure and worked even harder to be good at everything, to please everybody.

None of it had worked so well for his sister. M.J. needed people. Needed a father *and* a mother in ways Lee never had. She was a cuddler. He remembered the five-year-old rolling out of bed, her hair sticking up in all directions. After trying first to crawl in bed with her mama and being summarily sent on her way, she would leap into big brother's bed, full of plans for the day, chattering away as Lee grumbled about his foreshortened sleep even as he ruffled her hair and let her snuggle under the covers.

Remembering her as a child, Lee felt a paternal wistfulness to realize that M.J. was growing up. His reverie was broken by the sounds of conflict as his mother rousted M.J. out for school.

"Mary Jackson, you have thirty minutes to get out of the house. I won't have you lying around and showing up late for first period again. I do not understand, at your age, why I have to drag you out of bed in the morning."

"Mama, please…"

"Right now, M.J., and I mean it."

"Shit."

"And don't be thrashing around. Lee got in late and is still sleeping."

"Oh, right. God forbid I should disturb anyone."

To the sounds of thumps, groans and slammed doors as his sister got ready for school, Lee thought how little had changed in his years away.

Before he could fall back asleep, his door flung open and sixteen-year-old Mary Jackson burst in.

"Hey, wake up, big brother. Rise and shine."

Even in his state of semi-consciousness, Lee was surprised by how much M.J. had changed. Her sandy blonde hair was three shades lighter and styled to give full accent to multiple ear piercings. Dark green fingernail polish. At least there was nothing hanging from her nose or tongue.

"Hey, Sis, look at you. Come here and give me a hug."

M.J. threw herself onto her brother's bed, dislodging him from his cocoon and squeezing his neck with genuine affection.

"Sorry I couldn't come out there for graduation. How was y'all's last year?"

"Okay. Not so many boring cases to read. People finally kind of quit trying to prove something, I guess."

"It's going to be so cool to hang out with you this summer."

Their conversation was interrupted by the sound of a phone ringing from inside Lee's backpack. He stumbled out of bed to pick it up. "Hey, Michelle. Can I call you right back? I'm just sending my sister off to school."

M.J. was interested in her brother's cell phone, still a rarity in Riverton, and even more interested in the girl who had called.

"Who's Michelle? She your girlfriend?"

"No," he replied. "Just a friend from school."

"Hey, I've got a great idea," M.J. said. "Nathan Jamieson is having a party tomorrow night to celebrate his graduation from U of A. Why don't you come with me? Everybody in town will be there. Maybe even Annie." A sly grin reminded Lee of what a sweet, charming girl his little sister could be.

The door opened without a knock and Frances Addison glared at her youngest offspring.

"M.J., why on earth did you come in here and wake your brother?"

"See you after school," M.J. said to Lee, ignoring her mother. Her big smile said everything about the affection she felt for her brother.

And with that, M.J. pushed past her mother, out the door and could be heard pulling out of the driveway at full throttle.

Frances Addison bore little physical resemblance to her son. Even before makeup was applied, she had the look of a woman trying too hard to hang on to the one asset she could count on. In spite of the fact that no one besides M.J. and Lee ever saw her in a bathrobe, she must have spent a small fortune on what she was wearing. Of course, his mother's philosophy was clear. It didn't matter how little money you had as long as everyone else thought you were loaded.

She of course had sufficient trust fund money to do just fine. Her father had been a successful lawyer. She would never need to work, even without support from Trey. Corky and Roberta Dawkins had not approved her choice of a husband. Even though Trey had come from a good local family, he lacked drive and self-discipline. But the children of World War II veterans were indulged and given freedoms their parents couldn't have imagined. So Frances made her own choices, and she had to live with them.

"Darlin', I'm sorry she woke you. Can you get back to sleep?"

Lee stretched and let out a contented yawn. "I don't think so, Mama. I guess I'm still in exam mode."

Frances sat down on the side of the bed. Lee was the one project in her life that had turned out well.

"It's wonderful to have you home. We are going to have a grand summer. Claude and Susan can't wait to have you over for dinner. They want to hear all about Stanford and your life in California. I wish Daddy could have known what you have accomplished. Oh, and I am hoping you'll come with me to the Club today for lunch. It will give me a chance to show you off to the bridge club before we start at 2:00."

Lee was noncommittal.

"Honestly, honey, Hank Greene was so impressed that you made law review. He says only the top students from the best schools get into law firms like Pickford Martin. You know, Hank and Miriam have separated. It's so unfortunate, especially for the children."

Lee detected an ever-so-slight tone of satisfaction in his mother's voice.

"Maybe Hank would like to spend the next year in the salt mines in my place."

"You will do wonderfully there and they are lucky to have you. I am so proud of you. And so glad you're home for the summer. What can I fix you for breakfast? I'll stir up some pancakes and bacon by the time you get downstairs."

Lee pulled a clean pair of jeans out of the disheveled mass of clothes spilling out of the suitcase. In creased jeans and button-down shirts, loafers worn in just enough not to look new, Lee carried himself with the posture of someone accustomed to being watched.

Fumbling for his cell phone, he dialed a familiar number and waited for Zoe's voice. "Zoe. Did I wake you up? Michelle just tried to call me. Thought she might be with you."

"Jesus, do you know what time it is here?"

"Since I got dragged out of bed at this ungodly hour, I thought you should have to suffer along with me."

"Fuck you, Addison. I've slept less than four hours. But, God, I miss you already. What are you going to do with yourself for a whole summer in Arkansas? Have you lost your mind?"

"You know why I'm doing this. Anyway, while you're buried in the tedium of taking the bar, I'll be in court. Think about it. Real cases that actually go to trial. A judge. A jury. You'll have to ask for my advice when you start your clerkship in the fall. Do you know what Michelle was calling about?"

"It's Jason. He called her yesterday afternoon while I was in bar review class. Really depressed. He got an incomplete in that finance class. It'll probably wind up as an F. It will totally screw up his GPA."

"Well, that is a problem of his own making. I could see it coming. Another self-destructive impulse hits the mark."

"Well, we're having a beer tonight. I want to be there for him."

"Don't sacrifice your body in the service of sympathy, Zoe."

"Thank you for the concern, counselor. I suppose you think I'm adopting summer celibacy as I dream of my favorite study partner stuck in the Arkansas outback. I need a recreational outlet to take the edge off this bar review crap. Can't afford to screw up before my clerkship even starts."

It stung a bit to think about Zoe's clerkship. Lee felt he could have landed one too. Maybe not on the Federal bench. Zoe's record at Stanford had been nothing short of amazing and she deserved this. But he didn't want to wait another year to get started on the big-firm track to partnership. Still, she was always a step ahead of him in terms of intellect, if not ambition. Lee's self-image was bolstered by the fact that his ego was strong enough to handle a female as smart as Zoe.

"I'm going to miss you, Zoe. I mean it."

"Me too. My bed is feeling very big and very empty. Call me tomorrow."

"Bye."

Just thinking about Zoe here in Riverton was disconcerting. He couldn't imagine Zoe and his mother in the same room. Zoe was too outspoken, too smart, too…New York.

Crisp bacon floating in a pool of maple syrup and melted butter from the pancakes, Lee inhaled the sweet carbs, free at last from the West Coast obsession with health.

"I was thinking about a quick run to shake off the jet lag," Lee said as his mother hovered. "But after this breakfast, maybe I'll skip it. Too much humidity anyway."

Frances leaned over and kissed her son on the head. "You wouldn't

marcia kemp sterling

want to jog around here, honey. I don't think it's safe. Poor little Riverton is turning into a slum."

Transformation of the economy from transportation to manufacture and, most recently, to information technology had fallen hard on Middle America. The impact of globalization on blue collar jobs was not yet widely understood, and so Riverton's white community tended to see the town's deterioration as a by-product of racial integration and the failure of its poorest citizens to do what was required to achieve upward mobility.

"Lee, I hope you'll have some quality time with M.J. this summer. I'm worried about her. At her age, reputation is everything. It's as if she does everything possible to give people the impression she's the town tramp."

"Oh, come on, Mama, you know that's just M.J.'s rebelliousness. She knows how to push your buttons."

"Her grades are dreadful. She refuses to come to church with me. And she spends time with the most unsavory characters she can find. I don't know what's going to become of her."

"She'll be okay. These are hard years for everybody."

"Darlin', you don't understand how different it is for girls. And you didn't act out like M.J. does."

He smiled ruefully, shaking his head. "You just didn't know about it, Mama."

chapter three

As she pulled into the parking lot at Riverton High School, M.J.'s stomach tightened. For as long as she could remember, her days had begun with a terrifying entrance into a world of peers who would assess her, judge her and find her wanting. Thank God summer vacation was almost here. She resisted the instinct to check herself in the rearview mirror. The key to survival was to make sure people knew she didn't give a damn. And M.J. was an expert at that.

The ten-minute drive to school was the last safe part of M.J.'s day until the bell would signal her escape at 3:30. She had always preferred her fantasy world to the real one. As a kid, she imagined herself to be funny and popular and generous in spirit. In fact, she was always a little out of step, not cool enough to become anybody's best friend nor perceptive enough to know when she was being shunned. With adolescence had come the cold reality of rejection and the evolution of her fantasy persona as a hard-edged skeptic who didn't need anything or anybody.

As she passed through the school lobby and into the courtyard at the center of the classroom buildings, the chatter of female teens rose like birdsong in the early morning air. Each small circle of girls was closed, access limited by unstated but universally acknowledged membership rules. On the way to the appropriate circle, the girls made eye contact with every person they passed and greeted both friends and strangers with the obligatory "Hi." While the greeting distinguished Southern adolescent girls from their peers in other parts of the country, it implied no invitation and no softening of the invisible lines surrounding the exclusive circles. The boys were similarly circled up, regaling each other with jokes and sports talk.

The racial distribution of students waiting to enter first period was as rigid and predictable as if it had been mandated by law. If you were black, you walked through the lobby and turned left into the shop area, hanging out there with friends until the bell sounded. Whites turned right at the bulletin board into the inner courtyard. In classes and on the sports teams, the kids mixed it up. Lab partners were assigned and project teams formed with intentional racial mixing. But socializing outside class was strictly separated by race just as surely as though Little Rock had never happened thirty-three years earlier.

M.J. kept her eyes on the ground as she passed through the buzzing courtyard. She had timed it perfectly, arriving at the doors just as the bell rang for first period.

M.J. Addison had been a beautiful baby—a perfect baby. Hard to say when she stopped being beautiful. Most kids went through an awkward stage at one time or another, coming out of it when they mastered a new skill and somebody noticed. Or they had a parent or grandparent who could see their unique beauty instead of the flaws. Somebody who loved them so much that even the failures, the clumsiness, the shyness, the spilled milk were charming and funny.

It was not uncommon for a mother to learn to love herself as she came to accept the imperfections of a beloved child—especially a child of her own gender bearing similar physical characteristics, as was the case with Frances and M.J. But during M.J.'s formative years, Frances was so overwhelmed by her own loss that the process worked in the opposite fashion, and she began to transfer her own self-loathing onto her chubby, charming daughter, slowly turning into a tintype of her own young self.

It would be easy to blame Frances for not really seeing the child, for fretting about M.J.'s flaws instead of experiencing the wonder of her cheerful, bumbling exploration of the world. But Frances had been dealt a heavy blow by Trey's rejection and she wasn't well-equipped to handle it.

The daughter of Corky Dawkins, one of southwest Arkansas's best known jurists, Frances Addison could have been, *would* have been, a most successful Riverton matron if the cards had fallen her way. She was smart, attractive, funny in a cynical and understated kind of way, and perceptive. Some of these same qualities worked to her detriment when the public humiliation of Trey's unexpected and shocking infidelity and abandonment pulled her up short.

Whether or not her mother was to blame, M.J. had never been comfortable in her own skin. And yet she had eyes of the clearest pale blue that sparkled, becoming almost transparent in sunlight. And her smile, which lately came all too seldom, lit up her face in a stunning flash of brilliance.

M.J. had just started elementary school when the scandal erupted. It was the loss of her mother, torn from her by grief and rage and humiliation, that left the child without an anchor. Her father had never been around much anyway. Her physical needs were met well enough by the revolving door of colored help who were expected to cook, clean and take care of the children, many of them walking away from the job after unacceptable levels of abuse from Frances, often just as the children had begun to bond with them.

Finding her usual spot in the back row of English 2, M.J. watched as her classmates poured in. The boys were uniformly dressed in rumpled blue jeans and disreputable t-shirts. The girls, thought M.J., must have spent hours preparing for their first-period entrance. Long blonde hair flowed over tanned shoulders highlighted by the spaghetti straps of clingy pastel shirts that just covered their slim waists.

M.J. feigned interest in her nails to avoid eye contact. She didn't have to look to know that their clothes fit their perfect bodies in exactly the right way. Her own blue jeans were appropriately faded but in all the wrong places. They rode up too high when she sat down, exposing poorly selected red socks and expensive shoes that were all wrong for jeans.

As a child, M.J. had been sent to school dressed like a China doll, everything matching, bows in her hair, black patent leather Mary Janes on her feet, every day a new color-coordinated outfit from Mama's last trip to Neiman Marcus in Dallas. When she reached the age of emancipation from her mother's wardrobe authority, M.J. could have been accused of selecting her clothing with the sole purpose of making her mother uncomfortable. In truth, she had no sense of what she looked like and couldn't have put herself together in an appealing way if she had tried, which she had in fact stopped doing long ago.

M.J. didn't like the changes brought by puberty. The classmates she envied had kept their slim androgynous junior high body type and hadn't started to plump up in gross, unexpected ways.

Cookie Stafford found her seat two rows in front of M.J. and immediately started whispering and laughing with a friend across the aisle. Cookie was charming and funny, always maneuvering to be the center of attention. It was hard for M.J. to remember that they had been close in elementary school, sharing rides to slumber parties and swimming lessons at the Country Club.

Cookie turned to the two boys seated behind her, oblivious to M.J.

"If y'all want to come by Jayne Ann's before the party, you need to be there by 6:00."

M.J. had scarcely spoken to Cookie Stafford since their argument in seventh grade when she had called Cookie a racist. M.J. had struck up a close friendship with a black boy in her middle school drama class, and Cookie had tried to convince her to end the relationship with the boy. Within twenty-four hours of the girls' argument, Cookie had single handedly convinced their group of friends to ostracize M.J. With the speed and ruthlessness that only pre-teen girls can muster, M.J. was thereafter excluded, without a word of explanation from anybody.

Tuning out Mrs. Martindale's monotone voice, M.J. thought about her brother. From the time they were children, Lee had looked after her like a parent. Maybe he was the only person in the world who loved her just as she was. She thought about afternoons in the woods at their uncle's farm, Lee's firm grip on her small hand, the sun filtering through the pines in yellow streaks onto the clay-colored earth thick with fallen needles. She would watch him gathering stones and branches, props for a game he had in mind, not saying much, intent on his task. Even as a kid, he already possessed that complete self-sufficiency and quiet confidence that would set him apart. Didn't need a soul. Sometimes she wasn't sure he remembered she was there, so deeply was he engaged in his imaginary games. And when the shadows lengthened and the clearing radiated the still heat of late afternoon, he would take her hand and lead her back to the barn where their cousins would be doing chores.

Her mind was a million miles away from English 2 when Mrs. Martindale asked her for the second time what the protagonist was trying to achieve in *The Old Man and the Sea*. By the time M.J. heard the question, the whole class had turned in her direction. The looks ranged from ridicule to thinly disguised pity. M.J. was so surprised to have the class gawking at her that she couldn't speak.

"Mary, I've asked you a question twice now. Are you with us this morning?"

Snickers and guffaws.

"I'm not sure," she said.

"You're not sure. Have you read the book?"

"Yes, ma'am. Some of it."

"Then you must have a feeling about what the main character is trying to achieve."

M.J. knew she should say something. But by that time, the subtle looks of disdain from her classmates had turned to spurts of laughter and whispers between friends.

"All right, Mary. I want you to come by and see me this afternoon after sixth period."

As students spilled out of the classroom into the corridor, M.J. headed to her locker, head down, moving deliberately.

As she opened her locker, her old friend Lionel Mason tapped her shoulder. He was peering around a stack of library books, his bespectacled black face lit up with affection and good cheer.

"Jesus, Lionel, you're carrying around half the library."

"Hi, M.J.," he said. "I've got to check these in today."

They had become fast friends in seventh grade, both hooked on the Narnia stories and a band called The Grateful Dead that Lionel had discovered in an old *New Yorker* archived at the library. But that was Lionel. Marching to the beat of his own drummer. Eventually, her friends' disapproval and her mother's objections had led M.J. to distance herself from Lionel. Increasingly isolated, by the time she started high school, M.J. had an attitude, and nobody was willing to get close enough to risk her sharp tongue.

"Are you going to the party Friday night?" Lionel asked.

M.J. was surprised. If Lionel knew about the party, it had to be something special. "I don't believe it," she said. "You're actually going to a party? Shut up!"

He laughed at that. "No, I'm not going. Just heard about it. Tell me you're not going with that old dude you've been seeing from the arsenal."

The government munitions plant on the outskirts of Riverton was one of the area's biggest employers and one of the few remaining places in Riverton that offered a reasonably secure blue-collar career path.

"Dude, you're worse than my mother. As it happens, I'm going with my brother. Lee's back for the summer. Anyway, so what if Buddy is a little older? He treats me a lot better than any of the retards in this school."

"By now I should know better than trying to get into your business. All I can tell you is that everybody says he's bad news. Why does he want to hang out with high school kids anyway? Whassup with that? Shouldn't he be doing something with his life—like going to college maybe?"

"Lionel, you know what I wish you and your friends would do? I wish y'all would mind your own business. Buddy treats me like I'm old enough to have some sense, which is more than I can say about anyone else in my life."

"Whatever. I gotta go, M.J. See you."

chapter four

Lee drove toward Meadowview on the eastern edge of town where most of his friends from high school now lived. He remembered Riverton as a lovely and affluent, if somewhat provincial, world of golf and coming-out parties. But the town had changed. His old neighborhood was falling apart as Riverton's poor black families, half the city's population, moved closer to downtown. Mostly invisible to Lee growing up, the black help who worked in and around the Addisons' home lived in a part of town he never entered. So depressing to be back in the South, he thought, staring out at the desolate streets. We will never stop paying for the sins of our fathers.

He turned to his sister, noticing for the first time her skimpy attire, bare midriff, too little skirt exposing too much leg. But after years of watching his mother's futile crusade to dictate M.J.'s wardrobe, he stopped himself before saying anything.

"Looking forward to the party?" he asked.

"Yeah."

"I don't know your friends anymore. Last time I was here, you were hanging out with those heavy-metal kids. The melancholy Goths. That's what happens when you read too much Jane Austen. Looks like you've moved on. No black trench coat."

M.J. laughed. "I still listen to Metallica and Anthrax. Totally. But no, I don't hang with those guys anymore. They're losers. Not any nicer than the so-called popular crowd that dumped me in junior high. If people have to be all negative about everything, I don't want them in my life."

It was a problem at M.J.'s age, Lee thought, not to fit neatly into one of the categories. She was not artsy enough to be a hippie or studious enough to be a brain. Not popular enough or athletic enough or nerdy enough. The worst possible combination of neediness and insecurity.

"What about this guy you're seeing?"

"Mama doesn't like him. She's all freaked out because he's a little older and didn't go to college. But he's cool. Works out at the arsenal. He'll be there tonight. Buddy Parish."

"Sounds old to me."

"Don't worry. There'll be plenty of old people at this party. Betty Jo planned it to celebrate Nathan's college graduation. Their parents are totally cool with it. Everybody is back in town for the summer. I know Adam Jacobsen and Mike Thompson are going to be there."

"How was school this year?"

M.J.'s antennae immediately sensed a lecture. Lee knew she hated school. The feedback from her teachers, principals, coaches, her own mother for chrissake, was always the same. *If you tried harder, you could be just like your brother.*

"Shitty, like it always is."

Lee shot her a glance. In his mind, she would forever be a six-year-old mud-streaked tomboy following him and his friends around, fetching Cokes on demand, cheerful, curious and eager to please. She had grown into a rebellious teen. Still eager to please, which was not at all helpful in navigating the hazards of the middle years. She had inherited none of their father's dark, brooding good looks, but was a fair likeness of their mother at the same age.

"M.J., this will pass. I'm far enough from high school to tell you it's probably the worst time in your entire life. You just have to get through it. Once you get out of here, you'll figure out who you are. Don't let yourself be influenced so much by other people's values."

As they circled onto the loop, the brick monster homes got bigger and farther from the road. Jesus, these people have hidden themselves from contact with the world. Why on earth would anyone want so much space? Lee's sensibilities had been profoundly affected by three years in Palo Alto. He didn't find these places attractive anymore. As they approached the Jamiesons, cars were parked along the road for three blocks in each direction. The rhythmic thud of music echoed through the pines. The evening air hung hot and sticky over the neighborhood.

"I'm not sure how long I want to stay at this thing," Lee said. "I'll let you know when I'm ready to go. You can either come with me or get a ride with someone else."

"Okay. See ya." She was out of the car and off to find friends.

The buzz of early-party energy animated the house. Groups of young people were chattering, everyone straining to be the center of attention. Pockets of laughter erupted as the first drinks were consumed. Makeup was still fresh and too heavy for the lighting which had not yet been dimmed.

The foyer opened into a spacious living room filled with massive pieces of furniture, no doubt placed by a designer and meant to be seen instead of used. There were color-coordinated throws, vases and paintings. To the left of the staircase, a wide corridor led into a huge granite-filled kitchen with stainless appliances and more room than any one family could ever fill. Every empty space was occupied by bands of young people, drinks in hand. Voices were raised to transcend the music, which pounded strains of Bon Jovi throughout the house from the massive speakers in the family room, while the Red Hot Chili Peppers thumped on a different beat from the basement.

Lee stopped to absorb the scene. The pitch was an octave higher than he had grown accustomed to in the academic West Coast enclaves where he had been living for the past three years. Not that parties were that different anywhere. There was the heavy drinking at the outset to take the edge off. People trying too hard. Then as the alcohol kicked in and the volume went up, the party began to fulfill its purpose, dulling the edge of the day's failures and stresses and moving you into the rhythms carried around in the lower registers of your brain. The early-party conversation may have been different at Stanford, but the end game was the same.

"Lee Addison, as I live and breathe."

Betty Jo Jamieson gave Lee a kiss and pulled him toward the kitchen.

"Now that you're a fancy California lawyer, I never expected you to show your face around here again. We have missed you *so* much. Honestly. Come on now and let me get you something to drink."

Lee could sense the eyes on him as they wended their way through the crowd.

"Lee, my man, good to see you."

"Hey, y'all, look who's here!"

As Lee sipped a truly terrible glass of California Merlot, a stream of well-wishers found their way into the kitchen to say hello.

"Well, look what the dog drug in."

Mike Thompson hadn't changed a whit in the past ten years. The artificial redneck accent covered a subtle sense of humor and warmth that had been an everyday part of Lee's life since second grade.

"Hey, Mike, great to see you, man."

"I heard you were going to honor us with your presence this summer. Sounds like we'd better sign up for the Little River cabin right now. Just like the old days. Lots of beer, plenty of bait."

"You're on, buddy. Just give me a date."

"So you're going back out to California in the fall?"

"Yes, I've taken a job at a San Francisco firm."

"That's where the money is, I guess. Tell you what, I can't say I blame you."

"Well, I couldn't come back here. Wouldn't fit in anymore."

"Hell, it wouldn't take long to forget about this podunk town."

"You know that's not what I mean. It's just that this place never changes.

And after you've been away, it's hard to come back."

"It's hard to come back even if you haven't been away."

"Are you really going to take over your dad's business?" Lee asked him.

"Guess so. I worked in Little Rock for a couple of years after college. Liked it over there pretty well, but this is home."

The volume of the music had increased as an ebullient flock of teenage girls crowded into the kitchen, spaghetti straps glistening on golden skin and laughter modulated by soft Southern drawls. As Gloria Estefan beckoned the partygoers to their feet, Mike was pulled away by an invitation to dance. Lee wandered out of the kitchen, through the back sitting room and into the formal gardens, where a number of people had gathered to escape the noise and find some privacy.

The intoxicating warmth of the Southern evening swept over him as he meandered through the garden, lightning bugs and cicadas evoking childhood memories of baseball in the street after dark and beer with teenage friends in the back lanes of Hastings Park. They had tried to grow gardenias outside the apartment in Palo Alto, but the buds fell off before the blossoms could open. There, it was too cold to go outside after dark anyway.

Lee spotted M.J. holding court with three older guys and wondered if one of them was her current boyfriend. He didn't like the fact that she was seeing someone who worked at the arsenal. Likely no college degree. And too old to be with a high school sophomore. She had a beer and was laughing at something one of the guys had said. Trying too hard, as usual.

Not wanting to be his sister's keeper, he returned to the house through the back parlor and almost bumped head-on into Annie Rayburn. She was arm-in-arm with a tall blond guy, the type who would play water polo. Equally surprised, Lee and Annie both stopped dead still in the doorway. She was as beautiful as ever, but no longer a teen. During the six years since he had seen her, Annie had developed into a young woman of exceptional grace and self-possession.

They stared at each other for what was probably five seconds but felt to Lee like an eternity. Annie caught herself and turned to make conversation with her companion, her face expressing none of the rancor or regret she had struggled with for years. She gave Lee no time to say anything at all.

He didn't move and was glad there was no one else in the room who could witness his reaction. From the time he had broken off the relationship, he had experienced recurrent dreams about Annie. Unbidden and unexpected, she would show up in the middle of whatever subconscious battle he was fighting.

He knew it had been the right thing to do. During his undergraduate years at Tulane, he had needed to be free to explore and grow, to get as far away as he could from Riverton, Arkansas. The sophistication of New Orleans was intoxicating to a young Arkansas freshman. Drawn to worldly girls, he had been easily aroused by any female with a sharp tongue and an aggressive intellect. He had spent six months shacked up near the French Quarter with Karla, a tall, striking grad student from Hamburg who opened him up to ideas continents away from anything he had ever known.

Lee had approached his undergraduate education with a drive and intensity no one could have predicted. He knew that success at Tulane was his ticket—his mother had done that much for him—and nothing and nobody would get in the way of his determination to achieve academic success.

The lights had dimmed and the volume of the music increased, so that the house shook with the rhythmic beat of drums and dancing feet. He slipped into the dark of the basement and watched. For most of these people, this would be the best time of life. At the peak of their looks, sexual hormones raging, the social ritual of mating played out symbolically on the dance floor.

M.J. came up behind him with an affectionate squeeze.

"Hey, guys, this is my big brother. He's a California lawyer, so don't try anything with me, or he'll sue you."

M.J.'s voice was already slurring. Her disreputable trio still in tow, she sashayed past her brother, leading a short, muscular male, about Lee's age, onto the dance floor. Without acknowledging Lee, Buddy Parish drew M.J. close, the two of them moving in a bear clutch better suited to slow music than the grinding beat of the song. Parish had a reddish-blond crew cut and a tattoo on his left arm. Unconcerned that M.J.'s older brother was watching, he grabbed M.J.'s bottom and whispered something in her ear that caused them both to laugh out loud.

Turning his attention toward the far end of the room, Lee's eyes followed Annie Rayburn. Auburn hair with shades of gold and copper fell past her shoulders and caught the shimmering light as she moved to the music. Her sensual grace was improbably coupled with a self-contained dignity that made it clear she was off-limits. Wearing jeans and a silky pastel blouse that reflected the diamond glitter of the strobe light, she hadn't put on a pound since high school. Mesmerized, Lee felt a momentary flush moving over him, equal parts guilt and desire.

Quick to regain his composure and eager to escape a setting that held nothing but discomfort for him, he wandered back upstairs.

After another hour of small talk with old friends, Lee was ready to leave. M.J. was no longer on the dance floor. He went outside, hoping to find her in the garden.

Sitting alone on the concrete ledge of the side porch, Annie Rayburn looked up. Neither of them said anything for a long minute.

In the silence he could hear the cicadas singing in unison to the deep thump of the music. The aroma of honeysuckle was so strong he felt a little dizzy.

Lee let his breath out slowly. "Annie, can we talk?"

She didn't respond, just watched him. Taking time, as always, to make sure she was under control.

"I'm here for the summer. I understand completely that you may not want to have anything to do with me, but I'd like to have coffee sometime.

Just to try to explain…why it happened the way it did."

God, what made him say that? What on earth could he say that might explain or excuse how badly he had treated her?

Still she simply watched him. The night was warm, sweet, full of the sounds of cicadas and frogs, full of possibilities.

"There's nothing to talk about." She didn't take her eyes from him, didn't blink. Annie had always been like that, sufficiently self-contained to tolerate silence that would have moved anybody else to say one inane thing or another. Her eyes shone with what could have been tears or anger, but with a determination to hold a composure that would prevent him from ever knowing which. The moonlight painted them in perfect equilibrium.

Then at the same time, both Mike Thompson and Annie's beach boy escort came through the door.

Mike took one look at the two of them and almost backed into the house, but paused when he saw that Annie's date had arrived on the scene as well.

"Hey, gorgeous," Mike said to Annie. "I thought y'all were going to invite me over. I brought Tommy one of the new 'Hook 'em Horns' t-shirts."

"Tommy would love that, Mike. You should come by for Sunday dinner."

Lee felt Annie's eyes burn through him. He had enjoyed a special relationship with Annie's younger brother, a boy with Down Syndrome and a heart as big as the sky. The breakup had been so abrupt and so painful that it kept Lee away from Riverton during most of college and law school. On the rare occasions when he did come back, there was no way he could have shown up at the Rayburns. He had been like family. None of them could have forgiven him.

Mike put his arm affectionately around Lee's shoulder. "The scotch is open in the poolroom, pal. Let's go find something superior to that wine. I want you to tell me all about law school."

Inhaling the rich, burning velvet of Howard Jamieson's 12-year-old

Talisker, sipped to the soft click of pool cues, Lee was glad to be in the company of an old friend.

"I guess it was inevitable that y'all would wind up outside together. I never should have let you out of my sight."

"Oh come on, Mike. I ran into her and felt I should say something."

"I was in Austin when you broke off with Annie. She, of course, was up in Fayetteville. But everyone in town talked about it that whole Christmas holiday. Annie must have hated that. Course, with her, it never shows. But I think it took her a while, you know, to get past it."

Lee focused on the color of his scotch without responding.

"You're not going to occupy yourself with a fling this summer…"

Lee didn't let him finish the thought, but grabbed a cue and headed for the empty table. "Let's see if you remember how to do this."

Time got away from them in the banter of old friendship. Suddenly Lee realized he was exhausted and looked at his watch.

"I've got to get to bed, man. I'll call you next week. Let's think about a fishing trip out to Little River."

"Okay, bud. Great to have you back."

Part of the discipline of preparing for finals was maintaining regular hours for study and sleep. Even with the final push, Lee had rarely stayed up after midnight. But he hadn't fully adjusted to Central Time and was surprised that it was almost 2:00 a.m.

Lee hadn't seen M.J. for several hours. As he slipped into the hallway, he ran into Peggy Phillips.

"I've been looking for you. It was so weird running into you at DFW. After all these years. Twice in a week now, isn't it? Hate to say this, but your sister and your ex-girlfriend are in a row downstairs."

"What?"

The information was too incongruous for him to process. His sister and Annie? But why? He regretted that last scotch and studied Peggy with suspicion.

"M.J. was throwing up in the downstairs bathroom. She had been locked up in the guest bedroom with that guy she's going with and came out to find the bathroom. Annie just happened to walk in on her."

The hard-core dancers were still at it in the basement. Peggy led Lee from a side door into the guest bedroom suite. Several couples had discovered the bedrooms, close enough to the music to transfer its seductiveness to a more intimate setting. A small crowd had gathered in the sitting room outside the bathroom, where M.J. was seated on the floor at the end of a sofa, her head in her hands.

Her boyfriend was trying to pull M.J. to her feet as Annie Rayburn stood over them glowering.

"Come on up, baby. Let's go back into the bedroom."

Annie reached out and put her hand on his arm.

"M.J. is too drunk to go anywhere with you."

"What the fuck has this got to do with you?" Parish was in Annie's face, and he was furious. Annie didn't move. M.J. made a feeble attempt to get up, but slid back to the floor.

Lee pushed past Buddy and squatted in front of M.J. "Come on, sis. Let's get out of here."

M.J. started to cry, mumbling to herself as Lee led her out of the house.

He was quiet as they drove out of Meadowview and onto the loop. M.J.'s sobs subsided into breathy gasps and sniffles as they made their way to the old state highway.

Lee wasn't sure where he was going. He couldn't take her home in this condition. She was too drunk to hear him even if he had known what to say. Good Lord. Made his skin crawl to think of his sister fall-down drunk and locked in a bedroom with that creep. Lee glanced sideways at his sister, who was slouched against the car door, apparently asleep.

He couldn't rationalize the feeling of shame that swept over him. Maybe he had too much of Frances Addison running through his veins. What an irony that his mother, who cared about nothing so much as her own reputation and status, had to endure the humiliation of an out-of-control teenage daughter.

At the far end of the loop, Lee pulled into Denny's, glad it was still open. He went around to M.J.'s side of the car and shook her awake.

"Wake up. We're going into Denny's for coffee."

"Mmmm. I'm too tired and too drunk."

"That's the whole point. Get out."

Lee was too tired to make conversation, but he was able to coerce his sister into a second cup of coffee. "Come on outside. Let's walk."

"Oh, Lee, you're such a good big brother. I'm glad you're home."

chapter five

M.J. wouldn't remember the drive home or how she got into bed. As the effect of the alcohol wore off, she slept restlessly, alternating between sweats and chills as she tossed the quilt onto the floor, then reached for it again, turning her pillow in search of a cool place to rest her aching head. At some point she rose to take an aspirin and tried to mitigate the dryness in her mouth with a full glass of water. By the time she fell into a deep sleep, the dusky pink of sunrise was already filtering into her bedroom.

The setting of the dream was a familiar one, an idyllic valley high in the Ozarks where many of M.J.'s midnight fears and fantasies had first arisen. She had been seven years old, a first-time camper. The physical beauty of Camp Ariadne had left a permanent imprint and in times of anxiety or restlessness, its images drifted through her dreams.

A long string of candlelight twinkled and twisted its way down meandering trails as the girls celebrated the end of camp. Each camper carried a small paper plate with a lighted candle attached by wax drippings. As the line of girls approached the river tributary, each floating candle was launched into the creek to make its way gradually downstream in a symbolic display of camp unity and devotion to the ideals of Ariadne. The curving flotilla of flickering candles looked like strings of miniature Christmas lights draped across a mountainside. Years after she had forgotten about her experiences of Camp Ariadne, M.J. held a visual memory of that mountainside candlelight ceremony.

Frances had missed out on Camp Ariadne herself, in spite of Roberta

Dawkins' obsession with exposing her only child to the best Arkansas had to offer. Frances had been pampered and spoiled in every conceivable way, but her parents never got around to sending her to the elite Ozark camp. Determined not to make that mistake with her own daughter, Frances hoped the elite camping experience with daughters of the state's best families would give M.J. an edge socially. Maybe at Ariadne she would pick up some of the sophistication of the girls from Little Rock and Fayetteville.

But camp had been difficult and traumatic for the youngster. The illusory calm that accompanied the recurring dream of drifting candlelight inevitably jerked her awake with an overwhelming feeling of fear and anxiety. Under normal circumstances, Frances wouldn't have sent her seven-year-old away from home for a month. But it hadn't been an ordinary year. Trey's scandalous affair and his sudden exodus from Riverton had devastated Frances. Lee was old enough to be off with his friends, working afternoons at the Country Club pool and preoccupied with his own life. But M.J. was still underfoot, needier than ever, and Frances didn't have the energy to care for anybody besides herself that summer. Camp Ariadne had been around for fifty years, developing the character and leadership skills of young Arkansas women. It would give M.J. supervision, outdoor activities and a chance to mature and learn critical social skills from her fellow campers and counselors. And it would give Frances time alone, time to stay in bed all day if she needed to, to weep and scream and pull herself together as she faced the prospect of raising two children by herself.

M.J. had been terrified to go. They had driven halfway across the state and up winding mountain roads through the hand-hewn wooden gates of the campground, where a buzz of activity filled the air as girls of all ages talked and laughed, most of them wearing matching Ariadne t-shirts. Many of the campers seemed to know each other from years past, as hugs and greetings were exchanged on the grassy hillock in front of a rustic wood and stone mess hall.

Frances had delivered M.J. to her counselor and quickly said her good-byes, eager to be alone to deal with the trauma of starting over as a divorced mother of two. M.J.'s counselor, Marianna, home from college for the summer and happy to be back at the camp where she had spent the summers of her own childhood, was a smart, outgoing sophomore at Vanderbilt, skilled at outdoor sports, good with kids and in a relationship with one of the lifeguards that had begun the summer before.

"Why don't you go up the hill and look for our cabin, M.J.? I'll catch up with you in a few minutes."

M.J. refused to wander up the hillside trails by herself and stuck close to Marianna. The counselor introduced her to some of the kids who would be in her cabin, but M.J. lowered her eyes, not making it easy for the other girls to get to know her. Several were from the same town and had taken off in a pack to explore the grounds.

The month dragged on endlessly and painfully. Had she been a little older or had she come to camp with a friend, M.J. might have thrived in the beautiful mountain setting. But she was unsettled from the upheaval at home and lacked the confidence to ease into unfamiliar social routines.

The camp subscribed to a traditional set of values, designed to teach leadership skills. The kids were evaluated weekly by their counselors. They were praised and rewarded for prizes in canoeing, archery and drama. But M.J. wasn't good at any of the sports and did nothing to engender team spirit among her cabinmates. So the weekly feedback from Marianna, though delivered kindly and without criticism, made it clear that M.J. had a long way to go to live up to the Ariadne ideals of young womanhood.

Years later, even though M.J.'s familiar dream always started with the magic of the candles floating down the mountainside on a warm Arkansas evening, she inevitably woke from the dream in a sweat, reliving the shame of being a second-grade bed-wetter. She had suffered from the problem long before the chaotic events of the springtime had disrupted life at home. She was always careful not to drink anything before bedtime. At home, she had taught herself to wake in the night and make her way to the bathroom down the hall, thereby avoiding the sulfur stench of wet sheets the next morning and her mother's critical mutterings as she directed the maid to strip M.J.'s bed. But at camp the latrines were down a dark road, not easily maneuvered at night, even with the help of a flashlight. And at camp there was no maid to change the sheets. Marianna had smelled the urine and made M.J. skip chapel to hang the wet sheets across the hawthorn bushes beside the path. The other girls had whispered and giggled when they returned to the cabin, the offending linens rustling in the morning breeze for all to see.

The morning after the Jamiesons' party M.J. jerked awake from a deep sleep and into the harsh sunlight of 11:00 a.m. with a sick and shameful feeling in the pit of her stomach. The embarrassment had nothing to do with the party or with her dream, which she couldn't remember. But, as was so often the case as she transitioned from the shadowy world of sleep to the light of day, she had a vague memory of trails of sparkling light, followed by an inexplicable feeling of shame.

chapter six

The sun was cutting through the shades and directly into his eyes by the time Lee woke up. His mouth felt like cardboard and his head throbbed. The house was quiet.

He crept downstairs in search of coffee and was relieved that his mother was nowhere to be seen. A note up on the board said "Must have been quite a party. I'm off to the Club for tea and will let you two sleep. Love, Mama."

Armed with a large mug of commercial pre-ground coffee, Lee made his way back up the stairs to his bedroom. There was no sign of activity from M.J.'s end of the hall.

When he turned on his cell phone, Lee discovered that he had missed several calls from Zoe. After downing a glass of water and three Tylenol, Lee propped himself up on two pillows, took a long swig of the bitter, flavorless coffee and dialed.

"Hi, beautiful. Are you up?"

Zoe was out of breath. "I'm almost up to the Dish. Michelle and I are squeezing in a quick run before I go back to the deadly serious work of bar preparation."

The Dish, Stanford's satellite dish located at the high point of the golden foothills that rise gently behind the red-tiled roofs of campus, had become a popular running and hiking trail for students and locals, its demanding vertical ascents along a three-and-a-half-mile loop contributing to the California obsession with health and fitness. The year-round mild climate of the Midpeninsula enabled flocks of graying environmentalists in sun-shielded clothing to share the path with young mothers pushing baby carriages up the hill and hard-core runners who pounded the paths without loss of breath.

Zoe was in good shape but Lee could tell she was breathing hard. "I tried to call you last night," she panted. "Where were you?"

A sound from deep in Lee's throat communicated the weight of the hangover, only partly a result of the alcohol. "At a party. Lots of old friends and pieces of my life I'd just as soon leave behind."

"You can't go home again, you know."

"Right. It's just that M.J. is seriously screwed up. I feel like I need to try to do something to help her while I'm here."

"What's her problem?"

"It's a long story. What's up with Jason?"

"More bad news. He checked himself into the hospital for some reason. Seems like he's having some kind of emotional crisis. Let me call you back after the run."

Inspired by the call, Lee downed the last of the coffee, pulled on his running shorts and shoes and headed out across Peach Street for a quick run.

Although it was only 10:30, it was already too hot and humid for serious exercise, particularly in light of his state of post-party dehydration. He headed west toward downtown and tried to ignore the pounding in his head as he ran along the sidewalk.

As he passed church row, there were already cars filling several of the lots. Why would people be at church on a Saturday morning? Then he remembered what it was like growing up in a place where the church was the center of the community's social life. People would come in to tend the memorial gardens, bake for the Africa fund luncheon, attend women's circles or Bible studies.

Beyond the churches, the streets were bleak with boarded-up windows and barred doors. Despite the heat it felt good to run, but also like moving through water. No wonder the area lacked economic growth—too hot and humid to think straight.

As he turned onto Oak, he passed a small, wizened black woman sitting in a rocker beneath a willow tree.

"Where you goin' in such a hurry, boy?" she cackled as Lee pounded past.

He could hear her laughter as he jogged down the block.

The downtown stores were just opening for business and Lee ducked down First Street past the old train station to avoid shoppers. It was a part of town that hadn't changed much since his childhood. The downtown stores formed a sterile row of one- and two-story 1950s vintage shops, most in need of paint and repair. The old Five-and-Dime had a new name, but its inventory didn't appear to have changed much. His grandfather had lived in the Manchester Hotel on Broad during the last years of his life. Lee remembered a thriving business district where prosperous shoppers found the latest in everything. The efforts at downtown historic preservation had generally failed, but they had done enough to keep First Street from falling into disrepair.

By the time he turned back onto Peach, Lee was drenched in sweat, his heart pounding. He heard a voice from under the willow tree. "Here he come. Here he come. They didn't catch him yet. Lord, Lord," she laughed.

Lee looked over to see the same ancient black figure rocking under the large weeping willow near the corner.

"Slow down, boy. Come over here."

"Good morning, ma'am."

"Come over here. Let me get a look at you."

Lee ducked under the willow fringe and greeted his elderly neighbor with a smile. Behind the huge tree was a small unfinished wood-framed house, its porch tilting to one side and a chimney that appeared to be gradually separating itself from the cottage. Still, the porch was swept and dark purple curtains hung regularly from each window. The yard was overrun with crabgrass, waist-high weeds and untrimmed crepe myrtles growing wildly on both sides of the house. The weeping willow covered the entire corner of the yard. Although the temperature was already in the mid-80s, it was dark and cool under the spreading umbrella of the willow.

Lee extended his hand to the small figure. "I'm Lee Addison. We're practically neighbors. I live down about three blocks, just past the Baptist Church."

"You in that big ole brick house with the round driveway?"

"Yes, ma'am. I grew up there and have been away for a few years. I'm just back for the summer."

"That big ole house down there? Wasn't that Judge Dawkins' house?"

"He was my grandfather. My mother and younger sister live there now."

"Oh my goodness. Judge Dawkins' grandson is out here running around the streets like a crazy man." She chuckled to herself as she contemplated the unlikely genetics.

"I'm Etta Jones, your neighbor. You go fetch that chair on the porch and come set with me for a spell."

"Maybe another time, Miss Etta. Today's my first day at a new job and I've got to get cleaned up. Maybe I'll come down here and see you this weekend."

"You better do that, boy. We neighbors." She paused for a minute. "You know, I'm wonderin' if you chasin' after the wind? They's nothin' under the sun to be gained from chasin' after the wind."

Just a few blocks past where the ancient figure rocked, Lee turned into the long oval driveway to his family home. Mama hadn't kept the yard in the pristine state he remembered from childhood, but it was still an imposing estate. Camellias and azaleas lined the driveway and were sprinkled among the tall pines throughout the yard.

As Lee headed up the front steps through the two concrete circular columns, his cell phone rang. He settled on the front steps.

"Hi babe. What's up?"

"Are you in a place where you can talk?"

"Yes, just got back from a run. It's already about 90 degrees and I'm wet from head to toe."

"I wanted to tell you about Jason."

"Have you seen him?"

"No, but it's more complicated than I told you. Jason came to me right after you left. Really was thinking he and I might, you know, get something going while you were gone. I don't know, he said he had been in love with me for three years. Felt it was a betrayal of his friendship with you, but couldn't help it. Honest to God, Lee, it was so bizarre. Not at all like Jason. The next thing I know, he doesn't show up for exams and has checked himself into the hospital. I tried to see him, but they won't let me."

"What can I do?"

"Nothing. Nothing I can do either. Apparently his parents are on their way out here. Jeff knows the parents and they have been in touch with him, so I'm hearing about all this through Michelle."

"I'm sure he's okay. Everybody is pressured at exam time. I'm surprised more people don't go off the deep end."

"I guess. Anyway, I feel terrible about it," she said with a sigh. "What's the thing with your sister?"

"Oh, God, she's just kind of lost her way. Hooked up with a boyfriend five years older, a slimy high school dropout who's part of a crowd that's probably the closest thing Riverton has to a gang. Last night she got so drunk at this party that I had to rescue her from shacking up with this guy in our host's guest bedroom."

"Loosen up, Addison. It's just your family's inherent sexuality. I've noticed the fact that her big brother has trouble keeping his pants on too."

"Very funny."

It took only a minute on the phone with Zoe for Lee's attitude and accent to revert to an entirely different style.

"When do you start the job?" she asked.

"On Monday."

"I miss you, babe."

Wiping drops of sweat from his forehead with the sleeve of his t-shirt, Lee stared past the circular drive to pavement already reflecting radiating currents of rising heat that distorted the lines of the church dome beyond. "Me too," he sighed.

Avoiding the Persian carpets in the formal entry, Lee headed for the kitchen where M.J. was pouring a large glass of orange juice.

"Oh, shit, am I hung over. I have some distant memory of you forcing coffee down my throat at some restaurant. Coffee. That's what I need right now."

"Here, let me put on another pot. Mama doesn't have any decent coffee though."

"Thanks. I'm wasted. And thanks for getting me home. It was a great party, wasn't it?"

Lee eyed his sister narrowly as she stumbled into the sunlit breakfast room and collapsed into the nearest chair. Her platinum hair was a mass of unruly spikes. Flushed and disoriented, she took an occasional swig of juice, staring blankly into the back yard.

Lee poured two cups of coffee and brought them over to the breakfast table, sliding in across from M.J.

"Jenny told me the Jamiesons spent $5,000 on that stereo system," she said, her voice still raspy with sleep.

He sipped his coffee without taking his eyes off her. Clearly she was oblivious to the embarrassing scene at the party. "M.J., we've got to talk about last night."

"What? Don't tell me you've fallen in love with Annie again."

"We're not talking about me. We're talking about you. What in the hell were you thinking of?"

She gazed at her brother obliquely without saying anything. Lee couldn't tell if she was ashamed of herself or simply trying to avoid the conversation.

"What's your problem?" she said. "You had too much to drink plenty of times in high school. Forgotten what it's like to have fun?"

"I'm not talking about the fact that you were drunk. Why did you let yourself get involved with that creep, Buddy Parish?"

"You're like everybody else. Just because he's not all preppy, you think he's a bad person. I like Buddy. He's not phony like the kids at school."

M.J. glared at him with righteous indignation. He couldn't tell whether she really didn't remember a thing about the episode outside the bedroom or whether last night's behavior had become typical. Before he could pursue the cross-examination, Frances Addison pushed through the front door, bags in both arms.

"Here are my two sleepy-heads! Glad to see you didn't stay in bed all day. I ran into Trudy Giles at the Club—she lives across from the Jamiesons— and she says the house is in utter disarray. Martha called in a cleaning squad of hundreds. They apparently didn't get the last of the kids out of there until after 3:00 a.m. Can you imagine? Based on all the thumping around in the middle of the night, you two must have stayed to help clean up."

Lee and M.J. exchanged looks and rolled their eyes.

"Well, you know Nathan really wanted to go to medical school," Frances explained, "but he wasn't accepted anywhere he applied. I think Martha and Howard were trying to do something to cheer him up."

Lee noticed his mother's obvious pleasure in the Jamiesons' disappointment. "Med school is a tough admit everywhere these days," he said.

"I know it is, darling, but none of these local boys could have achieved what you have. I'm not going around town bragging about you, I promise. But I can't help being proud of you."

M.J. studied her coffee. She was used to all the accolades directed to her brother. Mama would be on a high all summer just from having him around.

"I want to hear all about last night. Did you see lots of old friends?"

M.J. grinned. "He saw Annie all right. She looked hot."

Frances shot her son a sideways look.

"Lee, don't you dare get caught up in that again. Annie Rayburn is a lovely girl, but she comes from a family without anything to offer her. It's not surprising that she wound up back here in town teaching. Anyway, I know you've got that smart Wellesley girlfriend waiting for you back in California. When you choose a wife, you have to think about someone who can share the financial burden with you. And who can raise your children to make something of themselves."

Lee slid out of the seat and took one of the bags from the counter. "Let me help you put away these groceries, Mama, before you pick out a wife for me who can get my children into the right prep schools."

Lee gave his mother an affectionate hug and started loading her purchases into the refrigerator.

His mother continued her diatribe. "M.J., it's the same thing I've tried to tell you time and again. Life is hard. The way you're going, you won't be able to attract a husband with any kind of potential. You've practically ruined your reputation here in town by spending time with the wrong people. And you've got to bring up your GPA if you expect to get into the kind of school where you can meet someone with promise."

Without another word, M.J. glared at her mother, refilled her coffee cup and headed upstairs.

"You see how she acts, Lee. I cannot communicate with your sister anymore. She resents everything I say. I only want her to be happy."

"Of course you do, Mama. M.J. will be all right."

Upstairs M.J. flipped on her stereo and slid across her bed onto her stomach. She lay there for a few minutes, eyes closed, fingers extended, letting the thump of Metallica's percussion erase the sting of her mother's words, made all the more bitter because of her brother's presence.

She had heard the same goddamned lecture over and over. She would never NEVER live the kind of self-serving, calculating, money-grubbing life her mother lived. Not ever. Never. Jesus. Same bullshit, all her life.

And why in God's name did Lee just sit there pretending to agree with her? Where was his fucking honesty? Is that what his glorious education had been about? Making money? Being better than everyone else?

She replayed the lecture in her mind, this time saying all the things she couldn't find words for in a real conversation. Articulate, calm, in charge. She could hear herself convincing both of them that she was better than that. She would choose her friends for themselves, not their social class. They might not belong to the Country Club, but at least they wouldn't judge people by how much money they had.

Thank God she had Buddy, someone strong and mature, someone who made up his own mind about things. He wasn't worried about hanging with the "right" people or going to the "right" schools. She thought about the two of them living together, somewhere simple. Just an ordinary life. No need to impress anybody. Maybe a little wood-frame house out in the country, a fence around it with some climbing roses. A dog and cat.

She knew Lee didn't buy into his mother's old-fashioned opinions. He didn't want to upset her so he wouldn't rock the boat. Why should he? He'd be out of here in no time. He and Buddy would get along great if they got to know each other. She didn't know why Lee was so upset after the party. So she and Buddy had a little too much to drink…that's what you did at parties. Lee had forgotten what it was like to be young.

chapter seven

His first day of work in Riverton began like all Lee's mornings. He rolled out of bed, sleepily pulling on gym shorts, an old t-shirt and well-worn tennis shoes, and got in forty-five minutes of hard running before his shower, exchanging greetings with the ancient lady down the street who appeared to occupy the chair under the willow tree at all hours of the day and night.

Lee loped into the driveway, thinking about the day ahead. As he opened the door, he heard his mother's voice raised in fury.

"How dare you speak to me that way!"

M.J. was standing at the foot of the stairs in a short, sleeveless night shift, which had slipped off her shoulder and was hanging precariously by one strap. She was glaring at her mother. "You're a great example of making something of your life," M.J. muttered. "When was the last time you did anything to be proud of?"

The rebuke left Frances speechless. Her face turned a darker shade of red as she considered her child with an expression of anger and dismay, then she turned away before the tears began in earnest.

"Thank God Mama isn't alive to see what has become of you," Frances said softly, a tremor in her voice. "Your behavior is a betrayal of everything this family stands for."

"I don't care what you think," M.J. snapped. "It's my life." She swung around and stamped up the stairs.

Frances watched M.J.'s retreating figure, shocked by the bitterness in her daughter's voice.

Lee put a reassuring hand on his mother's shoulder. "It's just teenage hormones, Mama. Don't be upset."

He glanced at the grandfather clock, not wanting to start work at Townsend by showing up late on the first day, and knew he had to get into the shower. "We'll talk about it this evening. I've got to get out of here."

Frances remained very still, staring blankly at the empty staircase, then looked up at Lee with an effort at a smile. "Go on, darlin'," she said, her voice still tremulous. "I don't want you to be late. I'll put some eggs on right now."

To his surprise, his mother smelled of alcohol. "Don't bother. I'll pick up some coffee on my way in."

Glad to be out of the house, Lee pulled into the law firm parking lot and straightened his tie.

Townsend, Greene and Platte was on the top floor of the First American Bank building, five blocks from the far end of the downtown shopping area. Lee had jogged past this area on his morning run, but hadn't been inside the bank building since childhood. The elevator was ornate, with mirrors and a crystal chandelier and filled to capacity with Riverton bankers and lawyers on their way to offices on the upper floors. Lee pushed the button for the top floor.

Hank Greene emerged from his office and shook Lee's hand.

"Wonderful to have you here for the summer, son. I'm glad you were able to work it out with the San Francisco firm to get some time off for the bar exam during the winter. They must want you pretty bad. We are honored to have Corky Dawkins' grandson at our firm. I hope it will be a useful learning experience for you. I'm working on an interesting case where I can really use your help."

Hank was in his mid-fifties and had retained a handsome ruggedness—tanned, fit, a full head of white hair. His gracious professional demeanor reflected the best traits of the Southern gentleman lawyer.

By late morning Lee had already read several boxes of documents pertaining to the case he would be working on. He pushed back to give himself a break from the tedium of sorting through reports. He was thinking about M.J., wishing he knew what to say to her. She was so busy fighting Mama that she was oblivious to her own problems. He shook his head, remembering the embarrassing confrontation at the Jamiesons' party.

Reaching into the box closest to him, Lee dug out the police report he had been studying and reread the cursory record of events.

At 4:30 p.m. on Tuesday, May 3, 1988, a call was received at the Midtown Precinct from the Marcus Hospital Emergency Room, reporting that an ambulance had been dispatched to the Bend Recreation Area regarding a possible drowning. On arrival at the scene, the officer approached two medical emergency personnel in the vicinity of the swimming reservoir. They reported that they had pulled a body from the northwest corner of the reservoir 20 minutes earlier. The drowning victim had been in a partially submerged position, face down in the water. They attempted resuscitation for some 10 minutes without success. The victim was a black male adolescent approximately 5 foot 6 inches and 120 pounds. The body showed no external contusions or other injuries.

The report went on to record interviews with several people at the scene of the drowning, including three friends of the victim who had accompanied him to the Bend, none of whom had witnessed the drowning. The boys identified the victim as Dewaine Washington of Riverton, said he could swim "some" and claimed that he had left them floating in inner tubes near the beach to go to the bathroom at approximately 2:00 p.m. When he didn't return, they searched for him throughout the Bend. Upon arriving at the swimming hole, they saw a small group of people gathered near the cliff wall where a body had been identified floating in the water. Though the body was face down in the water, the boys recognized the victim as

Washington. They were told that emergency assistance had been called. At that point the boys ran to Mercer's Bait Shop down Aston Road and called their parents before returning to the scene of the drowning.

Lee scratched his head. Maybe the boy decided to stop for a swim on his way back from the bathroom. But if he really was a mediocre swimmer, why would he have stopped there by himself? Particularly unlikely he would have dived off the rock, if that indeed had caused the accident. The diving rock was a place to show off, and you'd want your friends to watch.

Lee's cell phone buzzed and Zoe's number flashed across the screen.

"Hey, what's up?" he said.

"Just checking in on you. Are you at the office?"

"Yes, buried under boxes of documents in a conference room. They've put me on a pretty interesting case, though. We're representing the city against a wrongful death claim. Some kid died in a swimming accident out at a dammed-up section of the river on city property. Family is claiming the city should have put up warnings, that kind of thing. I'm just getting up to speed on the background."

"I hope you saved your notes from Markman's course. What about sovereign immunity?"

"We're looking at that. Turns on insurance coverage. Whether or not it applies, it's still important to create a disincentive for these kinds of lawsuits."

"God, why did I know you'd immediately get sucked in on the side of whoever has the power and the money? You're not even three weeks out of law school and already hard on the path of screwing the little guy."

Lee shook his head in irritation at Zoe's predictable politics.

"Come on, Zoe. This is ridiculous. Kids have been diving off rocks and swinging ropes into that pond for fifty years. That's where I learned to drink. It's just one more example of a society where anybody hit by an unexpected tragedy thinks it's an opportunity to make money. Something bad happened? Somebody's got to pay."

"God forbid taxpayer money should go to someone who really needs it. Lee, have you looked at the data on the gap between this country's richest and poorest citizens? Go pick up yesterday's *Times*. There's a great piece starting on the front page of the business section."

"There is not a place within twenty-five miles of here where I can find a *New York Times*. I know because I went on a search yesterday. Not exactly aligned with Southern political sentiments. By the way, how's Jason?"

"I'm sorry I didn't get back to you on that. Things have been crazy here. From what I know, he's out of the hospital and gone back to Phoenix with his parents. I assume he'll have to finish classes in the fall, but I guess I really don't know."

"Do you have a home phone number for him?"

"No, but I'll try to get one. I miss you."

Lee thought of Jason Levine as a competent, grounded guy, and the concept of his being admitted to a psych ward was difficult for Lee to grasp.

"Hey, Addison," Zoe continued, "here's an idea. An offer you can't refuse. Michelle's brother has invited all of us to spend the July weekend after the bar exam at his Carmel Valley place. Runs on the beach through the morning fog, pasta dinners with pinot from his wine cellar, jazz in Monterey. Why don't you fly out for a few days?"

"You forgot to mention 'no humidity.' That just might have done it. No, I really can't, Zoe. I don't think I could ever make myself come back here if I did that. Anyway, I don't have the time or money to fly back out. It's going to be a pretty short summer, anyway."

"Okay, handsome, I'll talk to you soon."

"Ciao."

Checking in with Zoe was like a breath of fresh air, cutting the thick Arkansas humidity, heavy with legions of ancestors and the guilt-filled history of the South. Even though the air vents in the conference room where Lee was working spewed icy particles of Freon-scented coolness, the place bore a weight he couldn't shake. He had to wonder how long it had been since anybody had tried to open one of these windows.

Hank stuck his head into the conference room. "Hey, Lee, want to come join Vernon and me for a bite of lunch?"

Lee needed a break from sorting through documents and was glad to take the opportunity to get to know his colleagues better.

The dark, upholstered lounge was filled with businessmen from the downtown offices and stores. The bar was smoky and crowded, but they retreated to a table in the corner where Hank kept a standing reservation.

"I know Frances is thrilled to have you home for the summer," he said. "She is awfully proud of you, you know."

"I appreciate the opportunity to get some exposure to courtroom law before I start in San Francisco in the fall. I've started to go through the boxes. Also looking at some of the Arkansas statutes."

"I think you'll find this Washington case interesting. We've gotten most of the city's work for the last couple of years. It's just like every place else, I guess. Everyone is litigation happy. You see how it's changing the way people do business. Protect your ass at all costs. Put warnings all over your store and trucks and products that nobody will ever read or care about. Out there in California, y'all don't have so many poor people, but around here they just hope somethin' bad will happen so they can go find an ambulance-chasing lawyer and make a quick buck."

He turned to Vernon Minor. "We see it all the time, don't we, Vernon?"

"I tell you what, it's not just the blacks neither. Ever'body wants somethin' for nothin' around here," Vernon responded.

"That's right," Hank agreed. "It's got nothin' to do with skin color. But it often is the people who don't work and don't pay taxes who are quickest to put their hands out for the taxpayers' money."

The waitress had come to take their order. "You want your usual, Mr. G?" she asked Hank.

"I was just looking at the sovereign immunity statute," Lee said, after the orders had been taken. "That should give us some protection."

"You're not wasting any time getting your head into this case, son, and that doesn't surprise me a bit, knowing your family as I do. The River Bend Recreational Area is a wonderful asset that belongs to this city and all its people. I'm sure you remember it from growing up here. These days, it's filled every weekend with families picnicking, swimming and hiking the trails. These kinds of plaintiff's lawsuits can cause cities to close down recreational areas. And that would be a great shame."

"After I've done an initial document review, I'll start to pull together some summaries for you. When do you expect to start the depositions?" Lee asked.

"Not for another couple of weeks, but I do want you to go through the interrogatory responses. They just came in. I'll bring you in to brainstorm with me before we start to put together the deposition scripts."

Lee didn't yet know Hank Greene well, but he felt sure he could learn valuable skills from the older lawyer.

"We've got to find time to get in a round of golf out at the Club," Hank said. "I've got a standing foursome on Wednesday, but maybe we could get a tee time Saturday morning."

"I'm pretty rusty. Didn't really have time to play during law school. But I did bring my clubs home. Love to get out there."

As the business lunch crowd milled around the restaurant, Lee felt the familiarity and discomfort of being back among his own people. Nobody would mistake this for a lunch crowd in Silicon Valley. People are more outgoing here. More body contact, cigarette smoke, liquor instead of wine. Everybody was five pounds heavier. Fewer women, no blacks, no Asians. The women more social than the men. Everybody was more social than Northern Californians. Instead of chrome, glass and outdoor light, there were shaded lights and velour padded cushions.

It was appalling to Lee that people of his generation chose to stay in Riverton. Even people who had spent four years in more civilized places often opted for the comfort of home. It had to be based on fear, fear of failure, fear of the unknown. What did they find to say to each other, these people who had been friends since childhood? What did they know or care about the issues shaping the last decade of the twentieth century?

By the end of the afternoon, Lee was eager to get outside despite the heat. He turned into the high school parking lot with the idea of cornering Coach Matthews on his way from the gym. Out of habit, Lee parked in his old spot at the back edge of the lot, between the gym and the path leading out to the track.

Walking toward the back of the parking lot, he heard the squeal of tires behind him as an old Chevrolet jerked abruptly into gear. He glanced up to see the back of his sister's head nestled against the driver. Neither Buddy Parish nor M.J. noticed Lee as they headed toward the parking lot exit.

Instead of turning into the locker room, Lee strolled toward the track, his mind filled with angst about his sister. From the far end of the stadium, a solitary figure entered the field, extending a run with some hard intervals on the track. His first reaction was astonishment at the masochistic decision to run on a June afternoon in Riverton. His second reaction was to admire the grace of her movement and the athleticism of her stride. Only then did he recognize the figure so familiar to his dreams over the past six years.

Annie Rayburn was running flat out in the late afternoon Arkansas sun. Portions of the track were shifting color as the sun dropped slowly behind the far side of the gym, but the heavy humidity hung over the field like a blanket. She wore athletic shorts and a sleeveless t-shirt, her hair pulled back in a pony tail, arms and legs tanned from daily exercise in the early summer sun.

He watched, transfixed. Like everything else she had ever done, Annie was approaching this workout in dead earnest. He expected she would pull up, take a breather, but she pushed on. He was too far away to see her expression, but then he didn't have to see it. It had been six years, but in his mind's eye the slight furrowing of the golden brow, the way her mouth set when she was concentrating, the determination in her eyes when she was trying hard, all were imprinted flawlessly in his mind.

By the time he descended the stairs down to the track, she was starting to slow down. She hadn't seen him yet. Lee settled onto a bleacher and watched.

He knew immediately when she recognized him. A slightly different set to the jaw. Another crease just beyond the brow. After two more circuits, she stopped in front of him.

Sweat was dripping from her face, flushed crimson with heat and exertion, breath still short from the workout. To him, she was fiercely beautiful, her natural grace enhanced by the rosy glow of health. She leaned against the railing and considered him evenly. No words, she just looked, sweat dripping into her walnut brown eyes.

"It's the wrong time of day to run, Annie."

She was still, her breath beginning to slow. He couldn't read her face. He had never known anyone whose emotions showed so little in her face. And yet it was an amazingly expressive face, complex feelings clearly locked in internal conflict.

"I'm not stalking you. I had planned to stop by and see Coach. I...just saw you running. I wanted to thank you for taking care of M.J. at the party. I don't know what I'm going to do with her."

Annie dropped her eyes and looked at the ground for a minute. Then she said, "I'm glad you're spending some time with her this summer."

"Yeah."

An awkward silence set in. Annie Rayburn had greater capacity to stand with someone and not say a word than anybody he had ever known.

"I wanted to talk to you. I've never had a chance to explain...to apologize...for how it happened. Could we meet for coffee or something? I really do want to talk to you."

She studied him with her inscrutable silence. "No. I don't want to do that."

"I didn't mean to go out or anything. I just want to talk to you."

For just a minute, Annie's eyes glistened with what could have been anger or grief. But she stemmed the emotion. "It was a long time ago. There's nothing to say. I have to go."

With that, she loped off in the direction of the field house. Lee took a deep breath. *Jerk, what made you ask? Of course she doesn't want to see you. She probably thinks you're looking for a summer romance.* How could he even begin to explain to her that his life now had nothing to do with people in Riverton? Nothing to do with her or with romance. This summer was about family. A way to touch his roots before his real life began.

But for somebody like Lee Addison, his own bad behavior was something he could not tolerate. For most of his life, he had been respected and admired by the people who knew him. He didn't walk over classmates to serve his own ends. He was ethical and responsible. Not in a prissy way. He could be one of the guys. He didn't hold himself above anyone else, even though he knew his academic record and law review credentials spoke volumes.

Here he stood, face-to-face with the one person who knew him best, at least during his formative years, and he had treated her poorly. He hadn't been modest or thoughtful. And she had trusted him. Her parents and her disabled brother had adored him, had looked up to him. And he had walked away from them all without so much as a backward glance.

Annie could have let him off the hook. It had been six years, after all. What was it that she wanted? They had not been sexually intimate, at least not in the "go all the way" sense. As a teen, he had wanted her deeply, blindly, to the exclusion of all other feeling. Her reluctance, and too much pent-up, unresolved longing, too many evenings stopping short of completion that left them both aching, made him an easy target for the sophisticated girls at Tulane.

For a long while Lee sat alone, the heat of the Arkansas afternoon soaking into his work shirt.

chapter eight

Lee knocked once, then opened the door to his sister's room. M.J. was sprawled on her bed listening to U2. Smells of candle wax, tobacco and sickly sweet room freshener mingled in the air. He wondered whether M.J. had started smoking. Her room was a study in transition from childhood to adolescence. Favorite stuffed animals rested against the wall beneath punk rock posters. Heavy metal magazine covers lay atop the complete set of *Little House on the Prairie* books that she had read three times by fifth grade.

"Come on, Sissy. Come running with me. I'll go slow, I promise." Lee sat down on the edge of M.J.'s bed and poked her good-naturedly.

"Stop. I can't keep up with you. I haven't been running for two years, since I dropped out of track."

"I'll buy you an ice cream cone down at Brooks if you'll keep me company."

She smiled at her brother. In spite of himself, he was a sweet guy. It was so cool, having him in town. The house was a nightmare when she was alone with Mama.

"Okay, but you'd better not push me too hard."

Frances poked her head out of the kitchen as her children came down the stairs and headed out the front door.

"I can't believe you got your sister to go. Oh, darling, you are so good for her. I know how much she looks up to you." Frances leaned over and kissed Lee on the cheek.

They followed Lee's usual route down Peach to the corner shaded by the big willow. M.J. was surprised when Lee left the sidewalk to dart under Etta Jones's tree.

Etta was sitting in her usual position, delighted to see her new friend.

"Miss Etta, this is my baby sister, Mary Jackson Addison. We call her M.J."

Etta looked M.J. up and down before replying. "What kinda name is that for a girl? Does your whole family run around in the heat like this? I never saw such a family. Come over here, girl. Let me get a look at you."

Unaccustomed as she was to taking orders, M.J. looked disdainfully at the dark figure, then did as she was commanded.

"I never seen you come by here before. You live in that big fancy house down there, behind the church? Judge Dawkins' house? Got everything you want. Why you so sad?"

As the recipient of this diatribe from the small, toothless street lady, M.J. was speechless.

"Give me your hand."

After a moment's hesitation, M.J. extended her hand. Miss Etta turned it slowly, studying each side. Finally, she released M.J.'s hand. "I be praying for you, child.

"When you gonna come have tea with me, Mr. Lee?"

"Maybe tomorrow. I'll try to get out early enough to stop by for a few minutes."

Lee took the lead as they headed over toward the post office.

"You are not going to have tea with that crazy lady."

"She's my pal, M.J."

M.J. was working harder than she would have liked to admit, keeping up. She didn't want to look bad.

"You're doing okay for a juvenile delinquent."

"At least I'm not over the hill yet."

They kept up the pace to the far end of Broad. After a high five to congratulate each other on the effort, they settled into a booth at Brooks and ordered two chocolate malts.

"This will offset any possible good you did for yourself by running over here, sis."

"Thank God."

She looked at Lee with a twinkle in her eye. Her brother was the only person in the world for whom she felt any real affection. Lee knew that intuitively and felt reluctant to spoil the mood with a morality lesson.

"Are you excited about working in San Francisco?" she asked.

"It's more about the kind of work I'll be doing—IPOs and venture capital. Helping new high-tech companies get funded."

The allure of being a business lawyer in the fast-paced Bay Area had captured his imagination at the end of his first year at Stanford. Like many others, he had started law school assuming he would become a criminal lawyer, like in the movies. It didn't take long to see that the most ambitious students would chase the money into major law firms with careers in big-time securities litigation, where cases always settled before they got to court, or in corporate law where a lawyer's skill bore on structuring complex business transactions rather than resolving disputes.

"I don't even know what you're talking about," she laughed.

"Well, you'd better figure it out. Otherwise, you'll never keep up with what I'm doing."

"I could never keep up with you anyway."

"IPO means Initial Public Offering. That's how everyone in Silicon Valley gets rich. They work hard when the company is getting started and later, when it goes public, they sell their stock and make a lot of money."

"Why is it so important to you to get rich?"

"That's not what I meant. The lawyers play a big part in helping these companies grow. Technology is changing the way the world works, and it's fun to be part of that."

"Fun? It wouldn't be fun to me to be a lawyer. All y'all do is fight with people."

"That's what I'm trying to say, M.J. In the kind of work I'm going to do, there aren't winners and losers. Everybody is making money, and everybody is happy. What's not to like about that?"

"I wouldn't like it."

Lee looked at his earnest, strong-willed little sister and had to laugh. "You don't have to be a lawyer, M.J. You don't have to be anything you don't want to be. Well, you'll probably have to earn a living somehow or other. Most people do."

"Mama never worked."

"Well, she was born in a different time. And, by the way, she'd probably be a hell of a lot happier if she did work."

"Who would ever give me a job? I can't do anything."

"You'll learn. You're still a kid."

"I'm not a kid."

"M.J., I want to talk to you."

She stopped, put down her spoon and looked at her brother suspiciously. "Oh, God, don't tell me Mama set you up to lecture me."

"Don't be so paranoid. I haven't talked to Mama about this. I wouldn't talk to her about this.

"If there's one reason I'm back here this summer, it's you. Riverton isn't exactly where I want to be right now. Mama has her own agenda. But I'm worried about you too."

"Oh, great. Just what I need. I'm not you, okay? There's other things in life besides being rich."

"I didn't have a chance to get to know the guy you're seeing. What's he like?"

"I'm not exactly seeing him. We're just friends."

"Where did you meet him?"

"We hang out at some of the same places."

"M.J., I'm not cross-examining you. I'm worried. I don't think much of the guy from what I've seen, and I can't understand why you're spending time with him."

"You don't even know him, so how can you judge him? Why are you all freaked out about Buddy?"

Lee sighed. "I've got to talk to you about what happened at the party. I think you were too drunk to remember it."

M.J. glared as she sucked down the last drops of her malt with a loud slurp. "Whatever. Let's get out of here."

On the way out, Lee paid the bill and followed M.J. down the block. She tried to set a pace that would prevent her brother from talking, but he was in better shape. He eyed her as they headed back toward Peach.

"I gather you don't want to talk to me."

"Nope."

Back at the house, M.J. scooted upstairs to the privacy of her room. Why was he being so strange about the party? Granted, her fierce headache had been proof certain that she had over-indulged in Jack Daniels Saturday night. But it was ridiculous for him to act holier-than-thou about getting wasted. What about all his New Orleans partying, after all? Guys could get away with so much.

At least he hadn't brought this up in front of Mama. God knows she would be the last person in the world who could complain about getting drunk. Lee had no idea how many nights she drank herself into oblivion on the couch. And the next morning she literally had no clue whatsoever what she said or did. Not to mention hitting on old men. What was wrong with her anyway, that she couldn't act like other mothers?

M.J.'s imagination moved seamlessly from anxiety about the circumstances of an unsatisfactory life to the fuzzy comfort of her fantasy world. She could see herself responding smartly to Lee's cross examination, lecturing her mother about drinking, crossing the high school courtyard as a figure envied and admired. In her mind's eye, she virtuously rejected the materialism and shallowness of the society she was forced to inhabit without exhibiting any of the characteristics of the insecure outsider.

M.J. picked up the phone and dialed. "Hi Buddy, what are y'all up to?"

"Hello, sweetheart. We're at the Oasis playing snooker. Pissin' away the afternoon. Why don't you come out and play?"

"Mama is downstairs and still sober. Not to mention big brother."

"Well, maybe later. After Mama passes out and uptight big brother goes to sleep."

"Maybe tomorrow. I'm wiped out. Lee made me go for a run with him and I'm completely out of shape."

"A run? Jesus. You'd better get out here and have some beers. I don't want you to lose that beautiful baby fat."

That stung, but she shook it off. "Lee has been lecturing me about misbehaving at the party. It's totally ridiculous. As if he never got drunk."

"What is his fucking problem?" Buddy was distracted by someone talking in the background.

"Hey babe, I gotta go. Tomorrow."

But M.J. couldn't shake the feeling that her brother was disappointed in her. She hated getting older. She hated her body. Lee had loved her like nobody else when she was a kid. Now that she was older, he would wind up finding her disgusting just like everybody else.

chapter nine

When Lee jogged in under the willow tree the next day, Etta beamed with genuine pleasure.

"I've got our tea ready. Come with me."

Lee followed the elderly woman, who leaned heavily on her cane as she hobbled toward the house. The aging clapboard cottage, an anomaly amid the rectangular yellow-brick commercial buildings in the mixed-use neighborhood at the edge of downtown Riverton, was sorely in need of paint. With its sagging porch, rough exterior and corrugated tin roof, the house looked like something from another century.

The dirt path leading up to the porch was overrun with crabgrass and dandelions that had sprung up randomly from the red clay earth. Bees hummed around undisciplined honeysuckle, and crickets chirped from all corners of the yard. As Lee followed Etta through a loosely hung screened door into the cottage, the first thing that captivated his imagination was the smell—a sweet incense-like odor, coupled with the earthy aroma of steeping tea.

A single room served as living room and kitchen, the purple curtains lending a strange glow to the room. The house was dark, with stripes of light where the curtains didn't quite fit the window openings. But it was tidy, wood floors swept clean and kitchen counters arrayed with colorful artifacts.

Sunflowers in a blue glass vase had been carefully placed at the center of the table.

"You sit right there, Mr. Lee." She directed him toward a small wooden chair by the table.

Etta lifted an old-fashioned floral teapot and slowly poured steeped amber liquid into matching cups placed on either side of the table. Then she sat in the chair opposite Lee and raised her cup in his direction.

"When you share the cup with a friend, it mean somethin'," she said. "I thank you for sharing this tea with me this morning. Like Jesus said, a new covenant made from water and spirit." She shook her head and smiled in Lee's direction. "I guess we now blood brother and sister," she added, chuckling at the improbable union.

As the warm fragrance of the liquid rolled around his tongue, Lee wondered what kind of tea it was. It bore an aroma and flavor that were entirely foreign to him. In the Bay Area he had tasted many varieties of imported leaf tea from China and Japan. This one had a heaviness and pungent aroma that he had never experienced. Briefly the thought crossed his mind that he could well be drugged by this strange old lady, about whom he knew nothing.

Although Lee was a natural introvert, he had learned to keep a conversation going and was expert at making people comfortable in his presence. Therefore, it was quite out of character for him to remain silent as he sipped tea with the dark presence across the table. She seemed quite content to share the silence with him.

"I'm worried 'bout your sister, Mary Jackson. She's too angry and sad, a young girl like that."

It was an extremely odd pronouncement from someone he didn't really know and who certainly didn't know his sister. Could her reputation be so tainted that even the black community gossiped about her?

Lee shrugged. "She's going through some difficult years. High school, you know. And she and my mama really don't get along very well."

"I know. But there's a hurting in her, deep down. I want you to bring her here. She needs somethin' to protect her."

Oh boy, here it comes, thought Lee. The witch doctor's remedy for M.J.'s malaise.

"I'll see if I can get her to come by again. Maybe let her have some of this great tea of yours."

"You know, it's okay to be angry, but the Good Book say if the sun goes down on our anger, it make room for the devil."

"I'll ask her to come see you."

"Tell me, Mr. Lee, about you. You don't fit here anymore, do you? But they's somethin' pulling you here, I know that. And it's not that sad sister of yours either."

"I really am here for my sister. And for Mama. She raised both of us alone. I'll be starting a big job in San Francisco in the fall and I'm not sure when I'll get back here again."

"Maybe, but I think you're here for something else. You just don't know what it is yet. Remember what they say about people who wait on the Lord. 'They shall mount up with wings like eagles, and they shall run and not be weary.' I never saw anybody who could run around like you do and not get weary. That's how I know you are here for a reason."

Etta got up and hobbled over to a dusty, waist-high bookcase where she picked up an old picture.

"I understand about taking care of your sister," she said. "Let me show you something."

It was a fuzzy black-and-white framed photograph of three young children, a boy and girl about ten, the girl holding an infant. The children were poor, dressed in ill-fitting but clean clothing and leaning against a bare, open wooden porch. The contours of the small frame home appeared similar to the house where they were sitting. In spite of the apparent poverty, the kids had a twinkle in their eyes and were grinning from ear to ear.

"That's me with my twin brother, Axel, and my sister Lovey."

"My goodness, that's an old photograph."

"Man come by here with a big old camera and axed Mama if he could take our picture, and she let him. And then he sent this picture to her in the mail."

"You grew up in this house?"

"Sho did. Lived here all my life. Lived here during both of the big wars. When we was babies, this house was on the edge of town. This street was a dirt road that led over to Adams, and the colored people lived all along that road. I can remember my shoes was always covered in that red dust from the road. Then the town built up and most of the colored people moved further out. But Mama stayed and later so did I. Both of us, stubborn as a fence post. When we put down roots, they go deep."

"Are your brother and sister still around here?"

"Lovey lives in Dallas with her daughter and her grandchildren. But she's back here in Riverton for a while. Axel, he's dead. Went away to Europe in World War II and fought for his country. But he didn't die 'til he got back here."

"That must be hard, to lose a twin."

"Oh yes. I still think about Axel."

Lee was silent.

"You wanting to run away from here real bad, ain't you? I see you running as fast as you can to get away from here. But what about that girl? What about that beautiful girl?"

Lee looked at the crinkled face, small black eyes dancing. I guess M.J. was right. She's a bit off her rocker. But sweet and surely harmless.

"You're right, there are lots of beautiful girls here in Riverton. But there are beautiful girls in San Francisco too."

"Oh, yessir, they sure is. But you know that's not what I'm talking about. Not just beauty of the face and figure. I'm talkin' about a beauty that goes directly into your heart. A beauty of soul and spirit. You know what I'm talkin' about, honey."

Lee puzzled as to what might be the proper answer to this line of questioning. Again content to let the silence stand, he sipped his tea. The two watched each other, eyes locked. He was starting to feel a flush over his body. That was not so unusual after a hard run. Probably the impact of hot tea at a stage of heartbeat recovery where he usually rehydrated with cold water.

"I saw a beautiful girl yesterday," he offered. "She was running around a track. Over at the high school."

"Yessir. You did. You surely did."

At that moment there was a rapid knock on the door and a young man, somewhat heavy and with a ready smile, entered the front door.

"Hey, Granny, you entertainin' a visitor today?"

He was followed by two children who looked to be eight or ten.

"This is my grandson Calvin."

"I'm just bringing you a basket of fresh tomatoes from our garden and a couple of squash I picked."

Lee took the intrusion as an opportunity to make his exit. "Miss Etta, thank you so much for the tea. I need to be going now."

"You come back soon, promise?"

chapter ten

Axel Jones had been the twin destined for something big. Everybody said it, from the time he was two.

"That child, he gonna do somethin' in this world, gonna *be* somebody."

Etta didn't feel slighted. She knew he was special and she loved him as much as everybody else did.

Having twins, that had taken Tanette and Jingo by surprise. She was big, for sure. Jingo kidded her unmercifully.

"Lawd, woman, that baby gits any bigger, you won't fit through this kitchen do' no mo'."

Jingo always found something to joke about. He was a tall, wiry man, black as pitch, a great storyteller and as unreliable a man as ever lived. But what he lacked in industry and dependability, he made up for with a spontaneous laugh and an ability to find wonder and joy in the moment.

Both Jingo and Tanette were of that second generation of free Southern blacks who bounced around the segregated South as twentieth-century industrialization changed the way people—black and white—lived all over the country. Their parents, born into emancipation and the hope of having a place in a reconstructed South that had been devastated by the Civil War, only slowly came to understand that freedom without opportunity was just another kind of slavery.

Jingo had grown up with limited expectations. He didn't count on much, so when things went his way, it was all upside. Tanette was different. Her grandmother had the gift and burden of tawny skin born of a master's seed somewhere in her family's American journey. And with her light skin came the privilege of class within the enslaved people of the agrarian South, keeping her inside the big house and within earshot of the conversations, ideas and values of the Southern gentry.

And so Tanette, like her mother and grandmother, bore testimony to the matriarchal pillars of church, family and propriety. They and the other women of their community had held fast to those values throughout the new century, protecting the children and holding families together, in spite of generation after generation of fathers rendered impotent by lack of earning power and the self-respect that goes with it. She always said "Aunt" in the way the British said it, never the flat, nasal "Aunt" of poor people.

By the time Etta was old enough to remember, Jingo's marginal role in the family was already crystal clear. The twins couldn't have been more than four. It was the first Christmas Etta remembered from her childhood.

"Jingo, get in your suit. We got to get to the church in fifteen minutes."

Mama had always been the one to get them to the A.M.E. Zion Redeeming Grace Church every Sunday morning and two nights a week, with their Daddy delaying and complaining and sometimes refusing altogether.

But that Christmas Eve she had drug all three of them out the door, her high heels catching on the uneven surface of that clay-colored road as they rushed toward the small white structure on the edge of the meadow just outside their neighborhood.

Etta could still smell the honeysuckle and feel the itch from the wild berries that lined the dirt path leading to the church. For her mother, the church had meant everything—community, respectability and a set of values that provided structure and meaning, something to aspire to and to believe in.

That night Etta's daddy had walked as slowly as he possibly could, lagging ever farther behind the family, his passive resistance the only vehicle for control or autonomy he could muster.

Etta was dressed in her red velvet, one of the best hand-me-downs they had gotten from the white lady Mama kept house for, still serviceable after the hem came down the second year in a row.

Etta and Axel squeezed onto the backless wooden bench beside their mother who had kept open the space to her left for their father. Jingo never showed up.

Etta was too excited to notice or care as she and Axel whispered about the pine branches and beautiful red candles on the table at the front of the church, just beside the manger scene with Miss Addie playing Mary and Lawanda Giles' baby up there in the box supposed to be Baby Jesus, but fussing and carrying on so you couldn't really believe he was. And Brother Jones up there wavin' his arms and talkin' so powerful about how Jesus would redeem us all and bring us to the Holy Land.

Etta remembered the walk back home that night, with Mama pulling the two of them along the dirt road from Redeeming Grace to their house in a tight grip. And Daddy nowhere to be seen. Not that night and not the next morning when Mama cooked their Christmas pudding and let each of them open their Christmas present that had appeared overnight on the hearth in front of the fireplace.

The little wooden doll that Etta got that year remained her favorite toy until Axel and some of his friends stepped on it and broke off its head during a game of football out in the front yard.

But the enduring memory of that Christmas was not the doll or the pudding or the church pageant, but Daddy coming in the front door late Christmas Day, weaving around and talking funny, and Mama quiet and glaring at him, angry voices coming from the bedroom, and then right in front of the kitchen sink, Daddy hitting her, hitting Mama in the face, and her lip bleeding and puffing up and for a few days after that she didn't even look like herself. But what Etta never forgot was Axel. How he rushed into the kitchen and pushed Daddy as hard as he could and yelled at him. "You leave Mama alone."

And Axel was just a little kid. But as strong and determined as if he had been six feet tall. It was so unexpected that Mama and Daddy both stopped fighting and stared at Axel.

Daddy finally started laughing like crazy. "Well, ain't you the tough little man?"

And then he just broke up laughing again. He was always like that. He could see the humor in anything.

chapter eleven

The office was humming with activity as the team of attorneys working on the Washington case gathered in the front conference room. Hank, his junior partner Vernon Minor and their second-year associate Fred Wiggins welcomed Lee to the team.

The first stages of preparation for trial had been completed before Lee's arrival. Hank introduced Lee to the other attorneys and summarized where they were in discovery and trial preparation.

Having worked last summer at Pickford in San Francisco, Lee had participated in several team meetings for civil cases he had been assigned to. He knew the drill. In law firms like Pickford, where legal remedies entailed major financial consequences, the litigation teams were bigger and the boxes of documents were delivered by the truckload.

Lee had read through the background materials and felt he understood the facts of the case. In May 1988 Dewaine Washington, a 14-year-old black male, had skipped school to spend the day out at the River Bend with his younger brother and a couple of their friends for a day of fishing and swimming. The boy left his friends and apparently went for a swim in the reservoir where his body was found face down in the water. Washington was dead by the time an ambulance reached the site. His family had sued the city for wrongful death as a result of their failure to maintain a safe environment at a location known to attract young people.

Five miles north of Riverton, Little River is slowed by a natural dam, where the stream widens before turning south. This section of the river is lined with cottonwoods, the red banks sloping gently into a reservoir long popular among locals for swimming, fishing and family gatherings. Fifty years earlier, the city had purchased this strip of land along the river's bend and installed picnic tables and barbeque pits. The intent had been to improve the property for the creation of a permanent park for the citizens of Riverton. With the advent of the automobile, the River Bend first became the favorite spot for young lovers to park on moonlit nights. By the time Lee was in high school, teens were affluent and fully mobile, and the Bend was the center of illicit social activities from booze and sex to drag races up and down the hilly gravel roads leading to the river.

Recently the park had became racially charged, with rumors of fights between Riverton's young blacks and the rapidly growing contingent of Hispanic youth from families working in the chicken-packing plant near Seminole. In spite of the distaste felt by some about the Bend's new multi-racial and multicultural mix, young people of all races and social classes continued to be drawn to the cool moving water and the area's lovely natural setting.

The Washington case was important because it represented a growing epidemic of personal injury litigation that was threatening the fiscal stability of local municipalities and burdening companies with an untenable added cost of doing business. As the U.S. had become more and more litigious, the concept of the unfortunate accident had given way to a widespread belief that whenever something bad happened, someone was to blame and someone had to pay.

It was unclear the extent to which this increase in attribution of blame coincided with the secularization of American society. Without a god or karma to account for misfortune, it was necessary to find malfeasance and to make sure the guilty party paid recompense to the victim.

The increase in litigation and the costs incurred across society were made manifest particularly in class-action lawsuits. Lawyers all over the country were beginning to understand the economics of contingency litigation, especially where you could find a whole class of people who claimed to have been harmed by a company's product or on the property of a corporation or a governmental entity. The outcome of the Washington case could provide fodder for hungry personal injury lawyers and would effectively dangle a carrot in front of potential Riverton claimants that could cost the city much more than the penalties associated with this single matter. The *Gazette's* initial front page coverage of the accident was sufficiently interesting to attract attention from regional papers as well. There was the race card, the possibility of foul play, the death of an apparently appealing youth who was a leader in his school, and the ubiquitous heartbroken family.

"Good morning, gentlemen." Hank Greene had been typecast for the role of Riverton lawyer, with his full head of white wavy hair, proud bearing and orator's deep resonant voice. He was at his best in front of a crowd. Having assumed the role of humble, sincere country lawyer before juries for the past thirty-five years, Hank Greene's courtroom persona had become who he was. The Deep South accent with its gentleman-farmer diction was a legacy of his mother, but, when he was intent on touching the emotions of a juror, his words flattened and rolled into a cowboy-hillbilly twang reflecting Riverton's proximity to the Texas plains and the Ozark hills, lending a down-home humility to his arguments that appealed to juries and softened his patrician demeanor.

"We've got a tiger by the tail with this Washington case," he began. "It's going to require the best thinking we've got in this firm to get a good outcome for the city. Anything short of that would set a terrible precedent for the future. Vernon, you had a chance to look at the latest document production?"

Vernon Minor had a thin, angular frame, with freckles visible on all exposed parts of his body. The reddish-brown tone of skin reflected weekends exposed to the Arkansas sun as Vernon did chores around his farm or hunted in the woods west of Adams. He would have looked more at home up to his elbows in the shrub brush behind his property than he did in a highly regarded law firm. But the farmer's demeanor concealed an intellect that was shrewd and perceptive. Like lots of farm boys who earned a place in Austin's much sought-after law school in the early seventies, Vernon cared little for the pretensions of law practice. But he had an eye for the truth and a photographic memory that had become invaluable to his senior partner in the courtroom. Vernon could put his hands on any document in the case files during cross-examination, often passing the relevant piece of paper to Hank before Hank even realized he needed it.

"Yeah, I looked at 'em. Seem like nobody saw the boy go into the water. He could have been on the rope and swung too far back into the cliff. Or he could have jumped off the diving rock and hit something. Or maybe he was just a poor swimmer. Truth is, we don't know what happened."

Since Lee had not met Vernon before his arrival at the firm, he wasn't sure how to size him up. Lee's upbringing usually endowed him with immediate information about Riverton natives. The default assumption was that competence was highly correlated to pedigree. Of course, since Lee had attended public school in Riverton, he bore witness to the occasional success story, where a child of simple country people blossomed into someone with a combination of brains, drive and self-confidence, someone who could thrive in college and build a successful career despite the limitations of his upbringing. Annie Rayburn had been like that in a way. But most of those kids wound up failing to realize their potential just because they didn't have a role model or anything to aspire to. Vernon Minor was an unknown, but Lee's first impression was surprise that someone of Vernon's demeanor had been asked to join a firm like Townsend, Greene and Platte.

"We are so pleased to have the assistance of Lee Addison with this case. As y'all know, he's Corky Dawkins' grandson, so he's got law in his blood. Lee, welcome on board. We can use another good mind to understand the circumstances of this accident and formulate an approach to the defense of our client.

"By the way, don't underestimate the smarts of this Washington family.

They been in these parts for generations, and it's a huge family. The mother is a basket case, but she's got lots of support and they know exactly what they are after.

"Lee, I want you to work closely with Vernon, as well as doing your own analysis to help us sort through various approaches to this case. You'll do your share of shepardizing cases and writing memoranda. But first I want you to get your head into the facts of the case. Read all the reports and documents we've got through discovery. Go out to the Bend and see if you can reconstruct what happened. I'll give you access to people who can talk to you about Dewaine Washington's background and the circumstances that led to his death."

chapter twelve

Lee's car pulled off the gravel road into a packed dirt lot and came to a stop in the only shady spot left. The air shimmered as heat rose from the surface of the clearing and the heavy sun ricocheted off metallic car roofs. As he stepped into the thick warmth, Lee was glad he had thought to change out of his work clothes.

Ducking under a low pine branch, he emerged into a partially cleared picnic area that ran along the south bank of Little River. For a minute, it was hard for Lee to reconcile the scenario of buzzing activity with the tranquil park of his childhood. Though it was the middle of a work week, dozens of people were gathered in the river's picnic area. Families clustered around tables of food, each group distinctive in its racial and ethnic character, as children chased one another along paths leading down to the river.

Following a trail toward the east end of the swimming hole, Lee inhaled the familiar smells of this strip of river land. Closer to the water, the heat relented but there was still a heaviness in the air to which he had been oblivious as a youth. Memories of afternoons fishing with friends along the bank, campouts with the Scouts, summer afternoons watching girls with bronzed skin and sun-bleached hair sunning themselves on the beach crowded his senses. He climbed to the lookout point above the swimming hole, found a shady spot under a pine and leaned back to watch the activity.

It had been eight years since he had last visited the overlook. The vista of Little River's graceful curve southward stretched before him, with cottonwood canopies following the sweep of the river. Pine forests spread beyond the river as far as he could see, their deep green foliage contrasting sharply with the rich red clay of the riverbank. On the far side of the river, following the curve of the stream as it headed south, the gradual incline of the riverbank provided a perfect beachfront for swimmers and sunbathers. Just as he remembered, the strip was filled with crowds of teens out of school for the summer, floating in large black inner tubes, kicking and splashing in competition with friends, or stretched out on towels or on huge boulders at the edge of the river, soaking up the hot Arkansas sun.

Lee had always felt a kind of ownership of the Bend because of his grandfather's role in raising funds to support development of the site. His proprietary feeling toward Riverton's public places differed from what he experienced in the Bay Area. As much as he loved the sight of the Golden Gate Bridge emerging from the morning fog or the ash-blond hills rolling one on top of another behind the Stanford campus, none of it felt like a birthright.

The swimming hole itself, with its diving rock and huge branches extending into the water, was on the near side of the river, closest to the lookout. It too was filled with young swimmers, mostly male, some cavorting in the water, a few perched on boulders at the far eastern edge and a couple lined up to hurl themselves into the deepest part of the pond from a large rock below Lee's perch. He was amused to see two boys preparing to leap simultaneously from the rock in spite of a shiny new sign stating in bold red letters "No Diving." He had to wonder if the sign had been placed there as a result of Dewaine Washington's death. There had been similar warnings on the diving rock in years past, none of them there for long and all ineffective at dissuading youth from demonstrating their daring from the rock's natural platform. The only thing missing was the heavy rope that used to hang from the largest cottonwood where kids could swing out over the water and plunge into the pond.

From his vista, Lee could not see the picnic area where Dewaine Washington's friends were apparently gathered the day he died. Based on the number of people at the Bend this day, it was hard to imagine that Washington drowned without anyone seeing him, even given that the accident had occurred on a May afternoon before school was out for the summer.

The sun slipped through the cottonwoods in streaks and patches. The green barrier of mature trees between the sky and the red earth tamped down but could not extinguish the summer heat. Lee tried to imagine what it was like on the day the boy died. That early in May there would have been splashes of pink, fuchsia and white scattered throughout the hillside forest from small volunteer dogwoods and redbuds still in bloom. The sky would have been lit by a softer sun, exposing patches of color in the understory of tall deciduous trees not yet leafed out.

He sighed, promising himself a trip back home during springtime.

As he surveyed the scene, Lee heard the laughter of young voices coming up the path in his direction.

"Come on. Let's shake him. Get over here."

A couple of boys, maybe twelve or thirteen, mounted the hill, sweating and giggling, then slipped behind a rock near the top of the trail.

From farther down the path, another voice could be heard.

"Hey y'all, wait up."

More sniggers from behind the rock as the faster climbers whispered and kept out of sight.

There was considerable huffing and puffing as the latecomer slowly ascended the path.

"Eddie, dude, wait for me."

Lee was sitting at a high point in the outlook clearing where he could see both the kids behind the boulder and the ungainly figure emerging from the path, dripping with sweat and breathing hard.

"Hey, where are you guys?"

He was stockier and several years older than the two boys who had preceded him up the path. The boy's face, red and dripping, reflected concern and puzzlement, yet his full, upturned mouth bore an expression of trust. His entire torso, drenched in sweat, was foreshortened and rounded down symmetrically from a thick neck. The squat figure wore a striped t-shirt that had hiked up, displaying a full belly, which extended over short, stumpy legs, his round face and slanted eyes textbook markers for Down Syndrome.

As the new arrival turned toward the outlook, two figures, giggling uncontrollably, dashed out from behind the boulder and bolted down the path at breakneck speed. The boy looked back toward the path in surprise as the sounds of laughter and rolling pebbles receded down the hill. In spite of the features characteristic of developmental slowness, his face was remarkably expressive, reflecting an unusual mix of resignation and understanding. This wasn't the first time friends had delighted in the sport of losing him. The abandonment triggered neither anger nor hurt. Maybe puzzlement at the predictable pleasure this game seemed to give. His attention turned to the effort that would be necessary to get back down the hill. He turned back with a sigh, sweat still dripping, and started toward the path.

"Tommy," Lee called out, in a voice more choked with emotion than he intended.

As Lee waved to him from the overlook, the boy turned toward him, excitement palpable upon recognition of the familiar voice. Lee hurried down the trail, and as he stepped into the clearing, pure joy flooded the boy's face, which was lit up with an irrepressible smile.

"Lee!"

chapter thirteen

Tommy wove through the picnic tables with Lee's hand in a death grip, a glowing smile still covering his face.

During the years of Lee's high school romance with Annie, when he had spent as many afternoons in the Rayburns' small home as he had in his own, he had formed a close relationship with Annie's little brother. And Tommy Rayburn adored Lee.

In the years before he and Annie were together, Lee had seen the disabled boy around town from time to time, and was put off by his strange appearance and awkward gait. Annie and her parents were not shy about bringing Tommy to football games, potluck suppers or anywhere else families gathered. Lee would have died of embarrassment with a brother like that and couldn't imagine how a girl like Annie Rayburn could hold her head up the way she did. But, from the time he was born, Annie defended her brother with fierce devotion, meeting any attempt to tease him with an icy rebuke.

When Lee started showing up at the Rayburns after football practice, Tommy latched onto him as the brother he'd never had. At first it was an unwelcome and awkward adulation. Over time, the boy's generosity of spirit and cheerful demeanor won Lee's affection. After a while, in Lee's eyes the only thing that made Tommy different was his courageous and cheerful heart. Sure, at first the fishing trips had something to do with wanting to win Annie's affection. Lee's unerring instinct for approval was surely at work as he pursued Riverton High's prize date. But his friendship with Tommy

Rayburn brought its own rewards. Lee was never as relaxed and happy as during those long afternoons sharing a riverside stump with Tommy, the two of them casting for trout or tromping through the brush looking for blackberries.

As Tommy and Lee approached the picnic table, Gerald and Rose Rayburn were busy unloading sandwiches and salads from baskets and grocery bags. They stopped what they were doing when their son announced his prize find. Lee's unexpected reappearance caught both of them by surprise, a moment of awkwardness for everyone. For all the years Gerald Rayburn had toiled to earn a living driving for the bread company, the light of his life had been his daughter. His hostility toward the young man who had caused Annie so much heartache could not be easily disguised. Rose, much harder to read, showed no emotion.

"Well, Lee, nice to see you. How are you, honey?"

Tommy's exuberance softened what could have been an awkward encounter. The boy's face was still flushed with excitement.

"I was up at the outlook and Lee just walked out and he said 'Tommy'."

Lee put his hands on both of the boy's shoulders.

"I've been fine, Mrs. Rayburn. I'm home for the summer, working at one of the Riverton law firms."

"We're so proud of you, Lee. We've heard all about how well you've done at Stanford."

Rose Rayburn couldn't say a bad word about anyone. A warm welcome is what Lee would have expected of her. Whatever anger she may have felt about his breakup with Annie would of course be carefully hidden, both in the interest of courtesy and to protect Tommy's enduring affection for Lee.

"We're goin' fishing this weekend, right, Lee?"

Lee was torn between the urge to excuse himself as quickly as he could and the knowledge that Tommy was overjoyed to have found him. "We'll see, bud."

"Sit down, Lee. We want to hear all about your experiences in

California."

Lee didn't sit, but was physically unable to make a gracious exit as Tommy had wrapped himself around his waist.

"I'm going to be working for a San Francisco firm in the fall. I wanted to have a last summer with Mama and M.J. before I start. So I'm working at Townsend to get some courtroom experience. The work I'll be doing out there is more on the finance side of things. Corporate and securities law."

She poured a glass of lemonade and offered it to Lee.

"Are you still teaching, Mrs. Rayburn?"

"Oh, I retired last year, I'm happy to say. Gerald too. He's had some health problems, so we're enjoying being around the house."

Again, an uncomfortable silence fell over the group as Annie Rayburn emerged from a hillside path, carrying a plastic cooler in one hand and a basket in the other. She stopped short when she saw Lee. The brown eyes that said so much registered Lee's presence, saw her brother clutching his waist, understood the encounter with her parents. In an instant, her eyes flashed with surprise, anger, a rush of memories. And, just as quickly, she regained her composure.

"Can't believe this place is so crowded on a Wednesday afternoon. I could hardly find a place to park," she said.

"Annie, I found Lee."

"I see you did, Tommy."

"We're gonna go fishing on Sunday."

Rose stepped in to extricate Lee from Tommy's embrace. "Come on, Tommy," she said gently, loosening her son's grip. "Let's have some lunch. Lee, why don't you sit down and eat something with us?"

"Thanks, but I really can't stay. I'm out here doing some work for a case we have."

"You don't have to go yet, Lee," Tommy insisted. "Puh…lease. Stay with us for lunch."

Disarmed by Tommy's determination, Annie quickly set aside her misgivings. "Really, Lee," she said. "Sit with us for a bit. You don't need to feel uncomfortable. High school was a long time ago."

The tension dissipated as easy conversation flowed over barbequed chicken and potato salad. Lee knew this family would do anything to give Tommy a few minutes of happiness, including overlooking the sins of an old boyfriend. Mightily uncomfortable himself, he would have loved to find a graceful exit. There being none, he settled into the picnic and tried to avoid eye contact with Annie.

"I saw Mike and Adam at the Jamiesons' party. Mike said he's been out to see you all since he got back."

"Mikey hasn't changed a bit. He's just about the sweetest guy in the world," Annie responded. "He came out to take Tommy fishing."

"We caught a big old pike," Tommy gushed. "I like Mike better than Scooter Nash."

The other three Rayburns studied their plates at the mention of Annie's current boyfriend.

"Scooter's a radiologist at the hospital. Just finished his residency at Baylor," Annie offered.

Rose quickly changed the subject. "Are you enjoying your work at the law firm this summer?"

"They've got me working on a civil case pertaining to a drowning out here a couple of years ago."

Both Rose and Gerald looked up at Annie.

She sighed. "Dewaine Washington was my student. A great kid, full of himself and a little cocky, but really talented and determined to get ahead. He was one of the rare ones who actually had a chance. Came from a big extended family that has been around here forever. The mother had three children from three different fathers, none of whom stuck around to help raise the kids. The other two kids are as troubled as their mother. But Dewaine was different."

She was quiet for a minute.

"For all the psychology we studied in my education program at Arkansas, I never read anything that could explain a kid like that. Couldn't have come from a great genetic pool, and God knows he didn't have anyone at home to encourage him. But he was smart. And determined. It was a tragedy."

After making arrangements to pick up Tommy on Saturday for a fishing expedition at Cowell Creek, Lee excused himself and headed back toward the parking lot.

"Lee, plan to come in and have dinner with us when you bring Tommy home," Rose said.

Once again he felt stupidly tongue-tied in the company of the Rayburns, and "That would be great" was out of his mouth before he knew it.

Following the path toward the lot, Lee was beating himself up for his clumsy management of the encounter. The last thing in the world he wanted was to reopen old wounds with Annie. She and her folks were good, kind people. He had treated her badly. He was in town for three months and the last thing he wanted to do was to kindle a summer romance with a high school girlfriend. Not that she had done or said anything that made him think that was possible. But the uneasiness he had felt in her presence left him reeling, not a feeling he was accustomed to.

As his car pulled out of the lot, he dialed Zoe's number on his cell phone. "Hi, babe. Are you in the office?"

"No, I'm actually on my way down the Peninsula this afternoon. I'm on a moot court panel at the law school. Then meeting Jeff and Michelle for dinner."

"Tell them hello for me."

"How's the drowning case going?"

"I'm on my way back to the office from the site. I know this place like the back of my hand. But being out here again, I don't know how the kid drowned without anyone seeing him. Seems so improbable he would have gone over to the pond by himself while his friends were back at the beach.

And even more unlikely he would have dived off the rock there. It's a pretty long drop. Not the kind of thing you'd do by yourself."

"What does the autopsy say?"

"That's another problem. They didn't do an autopsy. The family didn't want it."

"There must at least be a coroner's report."

"It gives the cause of death as drowning based on examination of lung tissue and airway constriction. The report noted a contusion above the left temple without a break in the skin. It was inconclusive about whether the contusion was from a prior incident or whether it had occurred in connection with the drowning."

"Alternative theories of death?"

"If he was on the rope swing, there's a chance he could have banged his head against something, swinging back too far. Or he may have dived off the rock and hit something underwater. Or maybe just got into trouble swimming out there by himself. Also, apparently there was some kind of altercation between Dewaine Washington and his friends, all black, with some Hispanic kids earlier in the afternoon. But I haven't talked to any witnesses who claim to have seen other people in the vicinity when he died. He was off by himself in a part of the river that's not visible from the picnic area. You can't rule out foul play but there's no evidence of it at this point."

"Addison, wouldn't you know it? You're playing sleuth in a small-town mystery to prepare yourself for doing venture capital and IPOs for the high-tech industries in the Bay Area. Now tell me again why it is you're doing this?"

chapter fourteen

Vernon Minor peered into the door of Lee's office. "Got a second? I've been through your list of questions for the younger Washington boy's deposition. I think you've missed some things."

Lee regarded the older attorney with a wary eye. "Come on in and sit down."

"Here's what I'm thinking. The boy was just twelve when his brother died. Got to have shook him up pretty bad. Course he's had some time to think about it and get his bearings. But he and his mama damn sure have a personal interest in making this look bad for the city. You can bet he'll be well coached in how he's going to paint the city's negligence in maintaining the Bend. That's why we got to lead him down a whole different path.

"You did a nice job of framing the questions about the obvious warnings. But I don't think you pushed hard enough on the fight with the Mexican kids. And I think you're missing one aspect of the case altogether."

Lee had spent the better part of a day drafting the discovery documents and bristled at the advice from someone who didn't strike Lee as all that brilliant. Still, he was here to learn whatever these guys could teach him.

"The papers were full of praise from teachers and preachers and such about what a good kid this Washington boy was," Vernon said. "Well, what I want to know is, if he was such a nice boy, what was he doing out at the Bend on a school day, taking his younger brother with him, getting into fights and maybe drinking and God knows what all? This boy comes from a troubled family and I'm just not buying the story that he was all goodness and light. We are dead in the water in court if we can't show some of his character flaws. And the deposition of his friends is where we've got to start."

"Has Fred come up with anything on the boy's character in his investigation at their schools?" Lee asked.

"Course most of the people over there won't talk to him. But he has come up with some stuff that's going to help with this. Let me get him in here to work with us on this."

Fred Wiggins was only a couple of years older than Lee and much more tentative about asking questions or challenging assumptions. Lee had the outsider's edge, free from the need to protect his job by getting the older lawyers' approval. As a result of his cautiousness, Fred was viewed by Hank and Vernon as someone with limited promise, not likely to have a long-term future at the firm. He was an awkward, gangly young man, his frame not yet sufficient to properly fill the business suits he wore to work. He might have been a boy dressed in his dad's clothing. He had tried to befriend Lee, both as a peer and as somebody wanting to increase his own stature in the firm, but Lee had kept his distance.

Fred followed Vernon into the conference room, balancing a notebook on top of a box of documents he was carrying.

"Fred, why don't you go through your notebook for Lee? Tell him what you've found out about those Washington kids and their buddies."

By the time Fred had finished reading through his exhaustive notes, Lee was surprised and impressed.

It seemed likely that the kids *had* been drinking beer before the drowning occurred. The police found a couple of empty beer bottles on the hill near the swimming hole where the boys had been seen talking to a group of teenage Mexican-Americans. The police lab was working on matching up fingerprints left on the beer bottles. This opened up a great opportunity to put the other boys on the defensive during their depositions.

It also added to the growing impression of Dewaine Washington as a boy with problems—skipping school, bringing along a young brother, drinking beer at age fourteen.

If the firm was to be successful in defending the city from claims of negligence or reckless disregard for public safety, it would be important to paint a picture of the victim that would show him to be the kind of young man who could have contributed to his own accident through careless risk-taking.

Vernon's theory of an altercation with the Hispanic kids, kids who had also skipped school to spend that spring day at the Bend, was a little more problematic, though witnesses had seen the two groups in contact with one another and perhaps even exchanging heated words.

Lee thought it was a stretch. "I'll work on that section of the deposition script," he said. "But it's clear from the reports I've seen that those kids left the Bend an hour or so before the accident. I haven't seen anything to make me think they could have been involved in this."

Vernon leaned back in his chair. "Just a feeling I got. There's nothing in the record that explains the accident in a way that rings true for me. And even if those kids were gone before the drowning occurred, it's good to get the younger Washington boy off his rehearsed track for a bit. We're more likely to get something useful that way."

"Okay. We'd better subpoena the Hispanic kids for deposition as well. Their interrogatories weren't that helpful but maybe we can get a little more out of them in person."

Lee spent the rest of the afternoon expanding the questions and marking up his deposition summary for next week. Conference room claustrophobia was setting in when Hank pushed open the door.

"God, boy, you're up to your elbows in paper. I saw your mama at the Club at noon and talked her into meeting you and me for a drink at the River Inn. Are you getting close to a place where you can wrap it up for the day?"

Hank and Lee had already finished a scotch by the time Frances sashayed through the bar door, shopping bags hanging from both arms. Lee was now up to date on the successes and failures of the Riverton football team for the past ten years, had heard about recruits for the Razorbacks up in Fayetteville and had been regaled with courtroom tales from Hank's early days of practice in Riverton.

"Well, well, here are two of my favorite people," Frances purred as she approached the table and accepted Hank's peck on the cheek. "Aren't I the lucky girl, to be hosted by the two best-looking men in this place?"

Frances was dressed in a bright emerald suit, with pearls around her neck and perfume that transformed the atmosphere at the table. As she made small talk with Hank, Lee watched his mother with interest. In spite of the ravages of age and lifestyle, Frances was someone who continued to make a statement. Like all the women of her age in Riverton, she was much more skilled than any of the men at keeping an entertaining discussion going, sprinkling her conversation with witty insights and giving rapt attention to the person she was speaking to. He wondered how this social energy had developed through the generations of Southern women and why it seemed so specific to one part of the country. Things may have changed here at last for women of his age, but in his mother's day, their social presence was really all they had to sustain themselves.

"Let me order you your Manhattan, Fran," said Hank, signaling the waiter. "This boy of yours is somethin'. Not that that's any surprise to either one of us. Smart as a whip all his life and he's going to be a wonderful attorney, just like his granddaddy."

"Well, thanks for the good words," Lee said, "but it's clear I've got a lot to learn. Vernon tore apart the depo outline I've put together."

"Ole Vernon is smarter than he looks. He's got great intuition and can juggle a lot of detail. You could do worse than having him as a mentor."

"I know that. I really appreciate the time he's spending with me. And you too. It's giving me a perspective on the law that I know I'm not going to get in San Francisco."

"Well, the timing worked out just fine for us. This Washington case is a big one, and it's great to have your head into it."

"You did a good job with this boy, Frances. Rearing him by yourself. I tell you what, that's not easy."

"I think he turned out all right. But I wish y'all could talk him into staying here in Riverton."

After a long day, Lee was hoping this social interlude was going to be short and sweet. But Hank and Frances were settling into their second drinks, clearly enjoying happy hour. Frances had always liked a drink, but this visit was the first time it had occurred to him she might have a problem.

After making his excuses, he left his mother and Hank in the bar and headed for his car. He was enjoying the feel of the warm, moist evening air on his arms and decided to walk down the block through the midtown business district. He had missed his morning run. Cocktail hour had destroyed any incentive for serious exercise, but he decided to walk for a bit instead of heading back to the house. This part of town had grown up after he left. It lacked the charm that the downtown used to have, but provided a modern shopping district for the neighborhoods in the north.

The stickiness of the day hung over the early evening air, with scarcely any relief even though the sun had gone down behind the hills. Nonetheless, he was enjoying the sensation of being supported by the heavy air as he strolled the neighborhood, breathing deeply and letting the sounds and smells of the evening take hold.

As he crossed the street to turn back toward his car, the familiar tones of church music floated through the air, *Immortal, invisible, God only wise…* Of course, it was Wednesday night. People went to church twice a week. Nothing ever changed in Riverton. People were stuck in the past, seeking the comfort of religion to give meaning to their lives.

The church wasn't familiar to him, but the architecture was surprisingly beautiful and traditional, though it was a new part of town. Based on the rich variation of tones that reached the sidewalk, the organ had to be huge. Like the heaviness of the air, the music took him back to a thousand Sundays, to times when life was simple and everything was new. As an altar boy, he had often arrived early at the sanctuary at St. Bede's to check the candles. It wasn't necessarily a religious experience, but the size and richness of the place awed him and filled him with a feeling of mystery and magic.

He remembered asking his mother about religion after his first year at Tulane, questioning the assumptions he held as a child. Most of his college friends had been raised in churches or synagogues, but by the end of that first year away from home, they had reached a common conclusion that religion was the opiate of the masses, established to shield the naïve from the terrible certainty of death.

"Why is it that people reject religion when they are young but then take it up again when they get older?" he had asked his mother.

She thought about it for a minute. "At some point life becomes too hard to navigate all by yourself," was all she had said.

The new church was Methodist. Like the Episcopal Church, the Methodists had their roots in England. But they had done away with the formality of the Anglican Church to minister to the lower classes—the coal miners and other victims of industrialization. The Methodist Church, however, hadn't clung to its humble beginnings, especially in the New World where it spread rapidly among the struggling immigrant population, refining itself along with them as its congregants became people of property and standing in the community.

Finding himself drawn to the door to listen to the music, Lee peered into a large foyer that led to a finely decorated sanctuary that was almost full. He slipped inside and found a quiet place in the corner where he could listen without being noticed.

The Methodists could sing, he'd say that for them. The music continued with magnificent hymns, all familiar and evocative. *Great is thy faithfulness…Be still my soul.*

His soul was anything but still. The summer so far had been nothing but unsettling. Family troubles were bad enough. Then there was Annie. No accounting for the feelings there. God, she was beautiful. He had chosen to end that relationship. He hadn't wanted to be tied to a small-town girlfriend. Hadn't wanted to be tied to anyone. Even with Zoe, there weren't really any ties. They were good for each other. Zoe was her own person. Sex was good. Their minds laced together in such interesting and energizing ways. He wasn't thinking about marriage with Zoe. Not yet anyway. But they were compatible and she would be an amazing mother, he was sure of it. Probably take two weeks off work to deliver each child. Give them the best of nurturing, intellectual stimulation, exposure to all the things that made life interesting. Teach them to engage in the political process. She would take Lee with her on her quest to make the world better. If his career proceeded the way he expected, he would make plenty of money as a partner in a big San Francisco firm. Maybe he'd leave to do investment banking or venture capital, with even more potential for the big bucks. That would give Zoe the freedom to pursue all her heroic change-the-world dreams.

So it was weird and annoying to Lee that for six long years, the person who visited him in his dreams was Annie Rayburn. He'd be drifting in and out of a sweet, satisfying sleep after great sex with Zoe, her head still in the crook of his arm, and there floating through his fantasies was Annie, her yellow-brown eyes gazing straight into his soul. *Surely the presence of the Lord is in this place.*

The music went quiet as the order of worship changed. Then, looking up from his chair in the corner of the foyer, Lee was, again, face to face with Annie Rayburn. This time they both froze.

And he will lift me up on angel wings. Hold me in the breath of God. Make me to shine like the sun.

Quietly, they watched each other, not blinking. Finally he stood up, took her by the arm, and led her outside. They stood on the walk, facing each other, without speaking for what seemed an eternity. Then they folded into each other and kissed for the next eternity.

Annie stepped back, a look in her eyes Lee couldn't read.

"I'm…I'm sorry I kissed you," he stammered.

"You didn't kiss me. I kissed you."

She turned and disappeared back into the church.

chapter fifteen

Lee had been soaked by a morning thunderstorm, the heavy sweet-and-sour smell of sulfur filling his senses as he ran past the old brick railroad station and a once-elegant downtown hotel, now inhabited by drifters down on their luck. After the rain let up, he added an extra two-mile loop to take advantage of the coolness in the air left in the wake of the passing storm.

It had become part of his morning routine to stop at Miss Etta's and so he turned into her yard and ducked under the willow tree, dripping with sweat from the extra-long run.

"Look at you, boy, you a mess," she laughed, eyeing the soggy figure.

"Miss Etta, it's a good thing I like you so much. Only my best friends get to see me like this."

"Come on in," she said, shaking her head at his disreputable appearance, "and let me fix you somethin'."

He wondered again what it was that kept him coming back to this house. With the trial bearing down on them, he needed to shower and get on to the office. Discovery was going well, but there were a thousand things yet to do to prepare the best case possible for their client.

But he followed his new-found friend into the house.

"Just sit back and relax, boy. I'm making you something new today, gonna make you feel better."

Lee took his usual chair across from Etta and felt his cares dissipate as she poured his tea. Something about her movements reminded him of the slowness and precision of a formal Japanese tea service, an almost mystical stillness, the serving ritual more important than the tea itself. She treated him as someone of honor, a guest to whom the gift of hospitality was graciously given.

She sat across the table and they sipped in silence.

"Why you so sad, honey?"

"I'm not sad. It's just a strange summer for me. It's taking me back to see some things I didn't want to see. And making me long for some things I can't have. Shouldn't have."

"Well, that's life, ain't it? Always wanting what we can't have. Don't be so hard on yourself, boy. You used to controlling everything…but the heart…," she laughed at the inevitability of it, "the heart, it can't be controlled."

Lee wondered at the quiet he felt in Etta Jones' presence. Did she have a filter on the front door that shut down the left brain? Was the tea laced with mushrooms?

"You know it don't matter if you're a prophet or talk like an angel, if you don't have love, you have nothing. Loving and longing for someone, them are good things, boy. *Good* things."

Later, as Lee jogged up the circular driveway to his front door, M.J. was pulling out, the low-pitched thump of the radio penetrating the evening air. She stopped the car and rolled down the window.

"Too bad you have to work. I'm off to the Bend for the day to celebrate end of school."

"Sophomore class party?"

"God no. I'm going with Buddy and the guys."

"I thought he worked."

"He got laid off last week. They are such jerks at the arsenal. We'll celebrate that too. See ya."

Feeling helpless, he watched his sister drive away. Instead of heading upstairs to get ready for work, he drifted into the living room and sank into a sofa. The sunlight, sharp and clear after the rain, illuminated millions of tiny dust particles on its golden stream through the leaded glass and onto the velvet sofa. No one ever sat in this room and nothing had been moved since he was a child.

With his parents divorced and the family living off whatever money Mama had inherited, it was this house that gave legitimacy to the proposition that the Addisons were a family of means. He could remember once hearing a fire engine pass his school and imagining with dread and horror that their home could be on fire. In his mind, there would be nothing left for the family if that happened.

Lee could hear his mother's voice coming from the kitchen and moving his way. Frances didn't see her son as she paced through the hallway, intent on the conversation.

"Darlin', of course the children are going to resent it. You mustn't talk to them about your personal life. Children don't even believe their parents *have* a personal life, much less any need for the other sex. Don't let that worry you."

Realizing he was hearing a private conversation, Lee sank more deeply into the sofa.

"Come on, let's just plan on a quick drink together. I promise you'll feel better. You're working too hard, Hank, and you know it."

Frances was leaning against the sitting room wall, the phone in one hand and in the other what looked for all the world like an 8:00 a.m. highball.

"Not even for half an hour? I could drive out to the Pub. Nobody would see us there." She sipped from the glass, listening intently. "Okay, but you call me tomorrow, promise?"

After ending the call, Frances sighed and took a long, deep drink from the tumbler. She stared out the window without seeing, her face expressionless.

Lee felt embarrassed to have overheard a conversation not meant for him. Hank Greene? His mother had been isolated and lonely for as long as he could remember. Bully for her if she could get old Hank interested. Lee would feel less guilty leaving Arkansas for good if she had a man in her life. Still, it was strange to think about his mother and Hank Greene together.

He slipped into the hallway, opened and shut the front door and strode into the kitchen.

"Honey, you are so industrious. I can't believe you went out running in the middle of that downpour."

"It kept me cool, Mama. No problem."

"What can I fix you for breakfast?"

Lee was momentarily distracted by the gallery of old family photographs that covered the walls of the short hallway off the kitchen. Many of the pictures brought back childhood memories, the gallery an embarrassing homage to young Lee Addison the athlete, the scholar, the apple of his mother's eye. There were fewer pictures of M.J. and none at all of their father.

He was studying a picture at the end of the hallway—his mother, holding baby M.J., was standing in front of their old blue Cadillac. Lee, somewhere around nine and dressed for church in suit and tie, was climbing into the back seat as Grandmother and Granddaddy Dawkins held open the car door. Maybe they were on their way to M.J.'s baptism. He wondered where his father was. Taking the photograph, he guessed.

It was a handsome family portrait. People of importance, contented with their lot in life.

He studied his grandfather's expression. Since Lee had been home, his grandfather's name kept coming up. He remembered him of course, but they were the memories of a child and Lee didn't know much about the man himself, his character, what drove him. He had died while Lee was in junior high. Granddaddy Dawkins had been a fixture in the community and in their lives. From a boy's perspective, he had been an imposing figure. Didn't spend much time talking to the kids. He used to pretend to find coins hidden somewhere on Lee's person and turn the change over to the boy. That was about all Lee could remember.

Corky Dawkins was reputed to be a very capable attorney. Lee supposed he got the lawyer genes from him. In the photograph he had the look of a busy man, a man of property, someone accustomed to being observed. The presence of the camera didn't seem to affect his bearing or his focus on what they were doing.

Nearby there was a black-and-white photograph of his grandfather as a younger man. He was wearing an army officer's uniform, and he and Grandmother appeared to be headed out for an evening on the town. If the depression affected their lives at all, you couldn't tell it from Roberta Dawkins' elegant dress and the diamonds sparkling around her neck. She had been a beautiful young woman—tall and lithe with shiny dark hair down to her shoulders and almond-shaped eyes that simmered.

Lee's mother came up behind him.

"They were quite the society figures, weren't they?"

"I was thinking how little I remember them," Lee said.

"Daddy was a pillar of this community. In the newspaper all the time. Active in state politics. Everybody looked up to him. And in her day Mother was considered the most glamorous woman in Riverton."

"Today we have nothing equivalent to the glamour of that era. They were an artifact of the past," Lee said. "The roaring twenties, when people spent money like water."

"Remember though, Lee, they lived through the Great Depression. And Mother didn't come from people of wealth. I don't think she ever forgot that, not for a minute. So she was particularly careful to carry herself in a way that reflected her station and Daddy's."

"She was a snob you mean."

"No, that's not what I mean. In those days they expected the upper classes to dress in a certain way and act in a certain way. Even the poor people wanted that and expected it."

"And what about the black people? Did they want it too?"

"It's so easy for people today to attribute blame for the mistakes of earlier generations. Things change. The way we think about morality changes. Mama and Daddy couldn't have imagined the world the way it is today. They couldn't have pictured black people running big businesses, being elected to high offices, accumulating wealth. Don't you see," she said, touching his arm for emphasis, "if they had been able to imagine it, they would have done something to change things."

chapter sixteen

M.J. Addison pulled into the almost-empty Bend parking lot, grabbed her gym bag and picnic basket, and headed through the picnic tables down toward the river. It was too early for the crowds that would fill the place by 11:00. She was looking forward to being by herself. The scenic river valley was spread out before her in all its glory. The twittering of birds and the rustle of industrious squirrels filtered through the pines as the Bend's natural inhabitants hurried to complete daily chores before the heat set in.

M.J. was wearing cut-offs and a sequined tank top ordered online from one of the designer shops in Dallas. Despite her effort to broadcast indifference to society through unconsidered grooming, she wore expensive clothes purchased with the credit card her mother freely offered. But no matter what she wore, she remained uncomfortable with the changes that had taken place in her body since puberty, and as a result, tried to make herself invisible to obscure her burgeoning curves.

She blamed her mother for her poor sense of fashion. Frances was always willing to spend money on clothes, but the torture of submitting to her antiquated tastes was more than M.J. could bear. Throughout her youth, she had spent endless, painful hours in changing rooms as Frances bemoaned her daughter's appearance, searching for clothes that might correct the errors of nature.

M.J. left the picnic basket on the shore and waded out to a big rock, where she sat looking out at the curve of the river, her feet splashed by the cool, flowing current. She was glad to have arrived first, to have a little time alone. What a relief to be out of the prison of high school. Two more years. Then she could be her own person.

The sun was warm on her back, and the distant squeals of happy swimmers were mingling with birdsong and the gentle swish of water over rock. She was happy to be outside, looking forward to a day with Buddy. What a difference it was, having a boyfriend out of high school. He was crazy about her. Couldn't keep his hands off her. It was new to M.J., this physical attraction between a guy and a girl. For the first time, she sort of understood it. Something nobody could take from you that was all your own.

The way Lee kept pestering her about Buddy, he must have guessed they had done it. Well, so what? She was careful, and so was Buddy. There wouldn't be any risk of pregnancy.

She didn't understand why people made such a big deal about sex. Before it had happened, that first time she and Buddy had sex in the back seat of his Chevy parked in the far corner of the lot behind the Cantina, she had thought it would be a bigger deal. Everybody talked about sex all the time, talked about it like it was the most powerful thing in the world, life-changing, unforgettable. As it was, she thought it was fairly disgusting—sticky, messy, with Buddy grunting and groaning and thrashing around. But it didn't hurt or anything. And the amazing thing was how it had changed the way Buddy treated her. All of a sudden he was calling her "sweetheart" and "baby." "You're my girl, M.J." Always hitting on her, wanting to get her alone. M.J. had never had anybody want her like that. There was a power in it. He made out to be such a tough guy, but she could wrap him around her finger, just by putting out. So easy. She even liked it in a way. Liked feeling like a bad girl. What would they say—her mother, the Sunday school teacher, the cheerleader who sat in front of her in biology? M.J. smiled to herself.

By the time her friends arrived, the beachfront was starting to fill with people and the sun was rising hot in the morning sky. Buddy's ever-present friends had brought dates, people M.J. hadn't met before but obviously quite a bit older than she was. They swam and soaked up the sun's intense rays for much of the morning, then picnicked on Kentucky Fried Chicken.

They had located a private cove upriver from the Bend itself and settled in after lunch to have a few beers. Aron lit up a joint and passed it around. M.J. liked the feeling of getting high on booze, but smoking dope didn't do anything for her. She shook her head when the weed came around and Buddy offered her a Newport instead. She slipped the cigarette from his pack and steadied his hand as he held out the burning match, feeling right away the kick of the nicotine.

As Buddy massaged her neck, M.J. relaxed into the summer afternoon, a pleasant buzz inside her head. It felt good to hang around people who didn't judge her.

Buddy leaned back against a log and inhaled deeply. "I don't think your brother likes me."

"He's just like that, not very friendly when you first meet him. He isn't exactly shy, but he doesn't go out of his way to get to know people. He likes you fine."

"That was a fuckin' great party, wasn't it?"

"Yeah, but, God, was I hung over. And Lee gave me such a hard time about it."

"Well, shit, he drug you out of there, like he was your old man or something. He was pissed off."

"I don't know. Honestly, you'd like Lee if you got to know him."

"No way, baby. Anyway, he'd never approve of me. Not classy enough for his baby sister."

"He's not like that, Buddy."

"Honey, believe me, I know how it feels to be looked down on. Had that shit all my life and it don't make no difference to me. Started with my parents, stuck there in that hole-in-the-road oil town. No way for Daddy to make a living except that filthy work on the rigs. Sweating in the hot sun and drinking up the paycheck. When I came along, it was just another mouth to feed, they made that clear enough."

M.J. leaned over and stroked his cheek. "I'm here for you, Buddy, and I don't look down on you. My mama has always thought I was a loser too."

Buddy pushed her hand away. "You know what, M.J., it's hard to feel too sorry for you, living in that big old house. Money to burn. They wouldn't let me in the front door in a house like that."

"Yes, they would. I can't ever get you to come in."

He grinned and pulled her toward him. "You're a sweet kid. Just a little confused sometimes. You need Buddy to tell you what to do, don't you, baby?" he said. Then he kissed her long and hard.

After an hour, Buddy and Aron went down to the river to take a piss and make plans for the afternoon.

When he returned, he said, "Baby, I need you to drive me and Aron to the store for something. Are you sober enough to drive?"

"Of course, I'm sober."

She didn't know what the guys were up to but didn't mind driving. They stopped at a couple of stores along Highway 9, but didn't find what they were looking for. They were about ten miles past the Bend when they turned into a small grocery store in a deserted strip mall.

"Keep the car running and we'll be right back," Buddy told her.

After a couple of minutes, Buddy and Rusty rushed out of the store and jumped in. "Let's go, M.J. *Now.*"

"After all this driving around, y'all still didn't find what you were looking for? We could get more beer anywhere. What is it you're after?"

"Never mind, baby. Let's just go on back to the Bend."

Buddy twisted around and winked at his pal in the back seat.

"Oh, by the way, Buddy, you're going to be so proud of me," M.J. said. "Look what I've got for you." She tugged a plastic grocery bag out from under the front seat.

Buddy grinned as he pulled out various letters from the bag, studying the recipients' names and the return addresses. He kissed her cheek. "My own sweet M.J., you are such a stud."

He thinks I'm so naïve, she thought to herself. Thinks I have no idea the kind of stuff they do. Probably stole something back at that store. I could care less. He's always up to something he shouldn't be. Mama would croak if she knew. Tough shit. I'm not a kid anymore. Make my own choices. Buddy has guts and it doesn't scare him to take chances. I'm like that too. That's why we get along.

She gazed at him innocently.

"I don't know why on earth y'all want a bunch of my neighbors' bills, but it was a piece of cake, stopping by their mailboxes and pulling out an envelope or two. I can tell you one thing. Everyone on the block gets a Neiman-Marcus bill on the same day."

"Just a little experiment I'm doing, darlin'. Studying the marketing habits of the rich and famous."

chapter seventeen

Tommy Rayburn was waiting on the front steps, his tackle box and fishing pole in hand.

The Rayburns' house was in the older part of Riverton, one of several dozen small brick vintage-1940s homes lining a shady street north of downtown. There was a maple tree in the front yard and a porch with brick facing and a sliding swing where Lee had spent evenings talking with Annie about what they wanted to do with their lives.

Tommy spotted the car before Lee pulled into the driveway and was up on his feet, shouting to his mother, before Lee could get out of the car.

"Mama, we're going now, we're going."

It was the earliest Lee had been up since finals and he was still half asleep. It had been pitch dark when he backed the car out of the garage and edged quietly onto Peach Street, but now the eastern skies showed a narrow strip of light as the new sun made its way toward the edge of the horizon.

Rose Rayburn stepped out on the porch to see them off. "Lee, you are coming back for dinner, aren't you?"

"Yes, he's coming, Mama."

"Sure, I'll be here."

Once ensconced beside their favorite fishing hole out at Cowell Creek, Tommy's excitement subsided and the two old friends settled into an easy rhythm, watching the corks bob in the water, chatting comfortably about the likelihood of a bite given the weather, the month, the ecological shifts in the environment and the appetite of the fish.

The boy had always been good company. Often childlike in expression, he was plenty smart and saw things with a straightforward honesty that Lee found appealing, even as an adolescent.

The early morning air was fresh and all around them nature was taking care of chores—toting sustenance into the ant hole, pecking at insects with the tip of a long beak, sipping dew left from the humid night before the sun could dry it up. It was the best time of day in Arkansas, with no human voices to break up the skittering, twittering business of daybreak.

Lee felt utterly and completely relaxed and happy. He was glad he had endured the misery of the jarring alarm to be in this place before it was spoiled by engines gunning down the highway, heat and humidity, smokestacks and car radios.

His young adult life had been so intense, so purposeful, that there had been little opportunity for quiet. When he was alone, there was always a casebook that should be read, always a *Wall Street Journal* nearby, promising insight into financial trends and analysis of the latest proposed merger. Staying up to speed on current business news had been useful in his third-year classes in corporate finance and antitrust. It would be even more important next year when his business clients would expect him to understand the environment their companies inhabited and the issues that could create risk and add to the cost of doing business.

Tommy re-baited his hook and tossed it into the deep part of the creek near the granite boulder. "I'm helping the coach this year," he told Lee. "Bringing towels to the players, helping Nattie clean out the locker room, stuff like that. Next year, he's going to make me assistant club boy and I'll get to sit on the bench with the team."

"That's super, pal. How's the team look for next year?"

"Well, old Bobby Lee graduated. So we got to get a new quarterback in there. Got a new black boy from out there at Rogan Springs. He can throw that ball."

They watched the dragonflies circle their lines.

"Lee, I'm sure glad you're back. Annie too."

Lee knew better and didn't respond.

"We were sad when you were gone."

"You know I'm just here for the summer, Tommy. I've got to go back to a job."

"No you don't. You've got a job here. Mama told me. You're finding out about when that black boy died."

"Yes, I'm working on that case."

"I was there. When he died."

Lee looked up in surprise. Sometimes Tommy's sense of time and place was imprecise. Doubtful he was actually at the Bend when the death occurred.

"Tommy, were you really there?"

"Really, Lee."

"Did you see the boy? Dewaine Washington? I mean, before he drowned?"

"Before and after."

"Did you see him and his friends fighting with anybody?"

"No. They didn't have a fight. But those big boys were teasing those black boys. Calling them chicken. That's not nice."

"Did you see anything else, Tommy?"

"No. Look at that one, Lee! Did you see that trout jump?"

The sweet silence of the morning was broken as Lee's thoughts turned to the case he was working on. He had made the decision at the beginning of his third year to pursue corporate law instead of litigation. There was too much pressure, too many late nights and too many emotional ups and downs in courtroom law. It wasn't that he didn't think he would be good at it. He had excelled in the mock trial competitions at school. And, after all, his grandfather had been a storied courtroom lawyer. Made the juries cry. But why put yourself through that?

They split up the sandwiches packed by Rose Rayburn and chatted amiably over lunch. It would be easy to misunderstand Tommy's straightforward and simple view of the world as lack of intelligence. For Lee, it had always been a mystery to watch the boy, so like Annie in some of his gestures and a certain look he got behind the eyes when he was thinking about something. She was deep and thoughtful and smart as hell. And for some reason Lee felt the boy was smart too. Just different. And as fine a person to spend a day with as Lee had ever known.

When they returned to the house, it was filled with smells of simmering okra and purple hull peas, pot roast simmering in the oven.

Lee had spent the last part of the drive home from the creek thinking about what he would say to Annie over dinner, how he could keep up a comfortable, light conversation with her and her parents without appearing either overly interested in Annie or overly uptight about being in her presence. So it was a surprise to him when he realized that the table was set for only four.

His disappointment passed quickly enough but not before he recognized the anticipation of seeing Annie for what it was. Don't go there, he thought. It'll be a mistake. It's good that she's not here. He tried to convince himself of that as he slid into the familiar chair across from Tommy.

Rose was bringing dishes from the stove top and adding to the assortment on the table.

"Tommy was talking to me about the Washington boy's death out at the Bend. Was he really there the day Dewaine Washington died?" Lee asked.

Rose glanced at her son. "He was there. What a terrible tragedy. It was pretty upsetting to Tommy, with all the panic, police sirens and such. It was a hard thing to understand, wasn't it, son?"

"Yeah, that boy died."

chapter eighteen

When Lee got to the office on Monday, Vernon was in his office before he could put down his briefcase.

"I knew it. What did I tell you? Those boys were out there drinking and making trouble. I knew it."

"What are you talking about?"

"If you'd been in here on Saturday like I was, you would have seen it. There's a new report from the lab. Fingerprints of all four of those boys on the beer bottles. They were out there drinking, playing hooky, fighting. No wonder somebody got hurt."

Vernon's face was fixed with certainty and determination. Lee hadn't warmed up to him personally but he could see how effective he was at lawyering. He himself tended to see things in shades of gray, but to Vernon there was only one right answer and it was whatever he was arguing for at that moment. No uncertainty. No doubt.

Lee could remember Zoe complaining about the "blame the victim" theory of defense she observed during her externship with the public defender's office. For a moment he wondered whether he was cut out for the profession he had chosen. When you got right down to it, he was more of a thinker than an advocate. Maybe that was why his grandfather had become a judge.

"We see this kind of thing down here all the time," Vernon said. "The TV reporters like to talk about the South as backward and racist and all that, but they don't have to live with this. They say this fourteen-year-old colored boy was the brightest and best their community has to offer and he was cutting school and out there at the Bend drinking and fighting. And those Mexican kids probably come across the border illegally, or at least their parents did, trying to get in on our entitlements and the benefits of a better life that our ancestors built with their sweat and blood. Well, I tell you what, you don't get to a better life until you're willing to study harder and work harder than the next guy. That much even an idiot like me figured out. You don't get there by cutting school and spending the day drinking beer with your friends at age fourteen."

Lee looked down at his notes and tried to resist the impulse to respond.

Hank Greene stuck his head into the office. As he had become aware of the personal relationship between Hank and his mother, Lee felt awkward in his boss's presence.

"I just looked at it, Vernon. You're right. Amazing. Boys, we've got to be careful how we handle this. It's a powerful weapon to use in the depositions but I don't want to show this to the plaintiffs just yet. Vern, what have you reviewed since you saw the lab report?"

"I went back over the depositions of the Mexican kids. If both groups of kids were drinking, that could have set the tone for some kind of conflict. There's a hell of a lot of cross-alibiing going on with the Mexicans. If they jumped that boy as a group, you can bet they're all covering for each other."

"I'm going to call Quincy again," Hank said, "and tell him we're sending another round of interrogatories for his clients. He'll pitch a fit, but I can't tell him what we've found. Not yet."

Hank was pacing, his mind working a mile a minute.

"Lee, I want you to go back through the physical evidence. Also, in light of what we've found, go back out to the Bend. See if you can put together a timeline, based on the coroner's report."

Lee spent the rest of the afternoon locked in the conference room, going over documents to make sure he hadn't missed anything, or on the phone with the lab. It didn't make sense. The Hispanic kids would have had to return later in the day. Not that they couldn't have done so. But nobody saw them at the Bend after 3:00 o'clock.

By 7:00 Lee felt brain-dead and drained of creative ideas. When he shuffled into the house, his mother was in the kitchen, staring at the floor and nursing a martini. She was clearly distraught and had been crying.

"What's the matter, Mama? Have you been fighting with M.J. again?"

"M.J.? No, I haven't seen M.J. all day. It's nothing, really, son. I'm just a little upset about something…personal."

Her words were slurring badly. Lee was tired and dismayed by his mother's drinking. He opened the refrigerator to find something to warm up.

Frances rose from the table, swaying as she headed for the door. "Honey, I'll be out for just a little bit. I hope you don't mind fixing something for yourself," she said, collecting her purse and car keys.

"Whoa, Mama, no you don't. You're in no condition to drive. Whatever it is can wait until morning."

A sob came from deep in her throat. "It can't wait. I have to go see about something."

"Okay, then I'll drive you."

At his mother's direction, Lee drove into the Southgate addition, headed to her still-unidentified destination. After turning into a street unfamiliar to Lee, she asked him to slow down while she peered out her window into a driveway.

Suddenly the tears started flowing again. "Take me home," she said quietly.

Puzzled, Lee glanced back at the driveway his mother had just inspected. Hank Greene's car was parked there.

"The bastard. I knew he didn't care about me. But the Massey girl? My God, she's younger than his daughter."

After they returned to the house, Lee helped his mother into bed. Her room hadn't changed since he was a kid, her dressing table with its threefold ornate wood-framed mirror loaded with cosmetics and jewelry, a strong scent of musty perfume in the air. He closed the bedroom door behind him and shook his head in dismay.

The house felt cold and empty, and Lee turned on the TV for distraction. His mother's drinking problem had been long in development, so it wasn't shocking that it had gone as far as it had. But this business tonight was degrading. The fact that she had been seeing Hank Greene socially, romantically he supposed, didn't bother Lee. Many people older than his mother found relationships later in life, sometimes second or third marriages. It was a good thing, really, for seniors to find partners. Mama was bright and lively after all, and for someone her age, attractive enough, he supposed. She had as much right as anybody to find happiness.

The cable TV anchor continued to regurgitate the news. Even though his thoughts were elsewhere, there was comfort in the genial, modulated voice of the newscaster, and Lee needed company.

His attention was momentarily drawn to the melodrama playing itself out in Iraq. He wondered about the effect on the American democracy of the numbing, mesmerizing flow of twenty-four-hour cable news, making every molehill into a mountain and delivering the same homogenous version of world events to the entire country. Why in God's name are we going into that part of the world anyway? Got to be about the oil, he thought.

The front door slammed as M.J. returned to the house. She was surprised to find Lee in the living room in front of the television.

"Having a lively evening, big brother?"

"Hmmm. Guess so. Shall we make some popcorn?"

They sat in front of the TV, not needing to talk much, sharing some old jokes, into the early hours of the morning. He was of no mind to ask her about their mother's emotional state, and neither did he feel grounded enough to give any morality lectures. For her part, M.J. would have liked to talk to Lee about Buddy and their relationship, but she didn't want to spoil the mood. When they were alone together like this, Lee was reminded of the sweet, eager-to-please sister he had helped raise. Halfway through the movie, M.J. dozed off, her head tumbling onto her brother's shoulder, safe and warm. As she slept, her face reflected the childlike innocence that he remembered. God, let her get through the next few years safely, he thought.

After M.J. had gone upstairs, Lee pulled out his cell phone twice with the intention of calling Zoe. It was still early enough in California. But each time he put the phone back in his pocket without dialing. He wasn't sure what he wanted from Zoe or how to begin to explain how strange it was being back home.

He rummaged through the highboy near the sofa where Frances kept the piles of photographs intended for scrapbooks that had never been completed. Before the divorce, his mother had been a meticulous collector of pictures, clippings and memorabilia. She was proud of her family and proud of her heritage. Perfectly posed photographs of Lee and M.J. in their Sunday attire were treated with the same care as the yellowing newspaper clippings of her parents, all carefully labeled in scrapbooks that filled several shelves. After the divorce, the scrapbook collections ceased. It was as if, having fallen short of the perfect life she imagined for herself, there was no longer any point in keeping a record.

Lee pulled out a handful of snapshots, many of them from family gatherings when his grandparents were still alive. There were pictures from the Bell family reunions in White Rock, where his grandmother's country kin lived, rows of relatives lined up three deep, the faces too small to identify, for the mandatory photograph at each year's gathering.

Lee studied several pictures of his father. Some of the photos of Trey with other family members had escaped Frances' purge. In most of the snapshots, Trey was talking or laughing, usually involved in a game or an animated conversation or horsing around with the kids. He was quite a contrast to the sober and controlled Dawsons.

Lee couldn't for the life of him understand what could prompt a man like his father to walk out on his family. Looking at the pictures caused a tight feeling in Lee's throat that he didn't like. Wouldn't a father want to know how his son was getting along? Would he be proud to know Lee was at Stanford? Could he have made a difference in M.J.'s life if he were still around?

He flipped to a picture taken just outside the Riverton Little League Park. Lee, wearing a brand-new red-and-white tee-ball uniform with long socks and black and white cleats, was walking into the park, one hand holding a well-broken-in baseball glove and the other in his father's hand. His memory flashed to a scene of his father holding up Lee's mattress to place the closed baseball glove underneath so that it would hold the crease. Mama likely would have taken that photograph from the parking lot as the two of them entered the ballpark. Lee stared at the image for a minute before moving on through the pile of pictures.

Maybe Trey Addison was one of those people born without any self-control, who acted on impulse and possessed no ability to delay gratification. There were people like that. M.J.'s rebelliousness followed the same pattern. Well, he may have taken me to Little League games, Lee thought, but he sure the hell was a disappointment over the long run. Now I'm stuck having to act like a father to M.J. and even to my own mother. Thanks for nothing, Dad. Thank God I've got the Dawkins genes.

In the years he'd been away from home, Lee had held an image of Riverton and of his family drawn from his memories as a child. He thought of his mother as smart and capable, the only daughter of a successful Arkansas judge and his beautiful wife. A respected family. A prosperous town. It was a static image, like an old black-and-white photograph, carefully positioned in front of a cardboard backdrop. Trey Addison tended to fade into the background. After all, people had always told Lee that he was nothing like his father. Instead, he had inherited Grandfather Dawkins' brains and self-discipline. It was this family portrait that Lee chose to carry with him.

chapter nineteen

Frances Dawkins and Trey Addison had been the envy of Riverton society throughout the post–World War II economic boom—rich, good-looking, sociable, privileged. Even during the tumultuous sixties, when the rest of the world was turning its back on tradition, Riverton remained in a time warp that harkened back to an earlier era characterized by country club debutante parties and gracious homes maintained by colored maids. But when the reality of a changed world finally reached Riverton—a world of rebellion, counterculture, civil rights and experimental drugs—the Addisons and the world they had inherited, built on the values of a previous century and the spoils of a discredited economic machine that relied on free labor, were out of step. And Frances had just turned forty.

After Corky Dawkins stepped down from the bench, he and Roberta had turned the big house over to Frances and Trey and their two young children, and moved into a fashionable hotel downtown, only to have their retirement years foreshortened by Judge Dawkins' early heart attack and his wife's losing battle with cancer a few years later. Frances had been schooled in her mother's maniacal focus on the importance of social standing, an obsession Roberta had carried since her father's catastrophic losses during the Depression. As a result, Frances spent her days among the other affluent mothers at teas, bridge games and cocktail parties. Trey owned and managed Willards, the town's largest department store, having inherited the store and the position from his father. He played in several standing golf foursomes and was a popular, gregarious figure at the Club. Trey had been blessed with the gift of gab, the key to popularity at social events and essential to taking the edge off competitive golf, thanks to his unending repertoire of clever directives to the ball.

Years later, when Frances would try to recollect how everything came unhinged, it was as baffling to her as it had been at the time. The growing apart had been gradual and subtle. Between her busy social schedule and care of Lee and M.J., she hadn't paid attention to Trey's increasing absence from home. He had been asked to teach a class at the junior college in business management and that first evening class had led to his infatuation with the college, his young students and the new way of looking at the world that he was fast absorbing from them.

He had been invited to join an evening discussion group started by his old friend Bucky Colton, a psychology professor at the junior college, and attended by some of the more open-minded students at the college. Discussion groups led to encounter groups, which led to marijuana and Betty Sue, the young, wild and voluptuous hippie daughter of a fundamentalist country minister with a church in the hills north of Little Rock. For Betty Sue, Riverton Junior College was as good as the Haight-Ashbury if only because it was out of reach of her manipulative, charismatic, controlling father.

After being promoted to dean of students, Bucky Colton had talked Trey into teaching his first class at RJC. Trey and Bucky had grown up together in Riverton, part of the generation born before the war under the influence of adults still shaken by the Depression. But when their fathers came home from Europe, they were also the beneficiaries of the good times that followed the war. To the victors went the spoils. The America of Trey and Bucky's youth was rich in opportunity, the only place on the face of the earth that had not been devastated by the war. Even before the huge population of war babies started collecting the entitlements that were theirs in this brave new world, Bucky and Trey and their friends had learned they could be anything they wanted and have everything they wanted.

Trey was the kind of man who was generally content with life. In many ways, his marriage to Frances Dawkins was satisfactory. She was an attractive woman and brought to the marriage both money and access to the upper echelons of local society he never could have achieved on his own.

By the late 1970s, he was teaching at the college two evenings a week, often stopping by Bucky's house for a drink afterward. Trey's marriage to Frances had gone stale. Now that they had a second child, the household was increasingly focused on the children, even with full-time help in the kitchen. Frances was more interested in the latest Junior League event she was chairing than in her husband. They headed to the bar for cocktails each evening as soon as Trey walked in the door. Before the maid had dinner on the table, they had downed a couple of highballs. By the time Frances got the kids in bed, they would regularly fall asleep in front of the TV, one or the other finally getting up to turn off the television and stumble up to the bedroom.

Having a buzz on made Trey more amorous than he might otherwise have been, given a wife who was not naturally affectionate and a marriage that had lost its spark, but Frances was less and less welcoming of his inept, alcohol-fueled advances.

As the relationship devolved into a marriage of convenience, Trey spent more of his evenings at Bucky's, enjoying the lively discussions and debates among the students and the occasional faculty member drawn to the free-thinking crowd that had begun to spend evenings regularly at Dean Colton's home.

Trey Addison was stimulated by the free, youthful, open-minded society he found among these students. The tone of their gatherings was frank and open and it was an easy step from sharing candid thoughts about personal lives to genuine intimacy. Betty Sue Richards was a passionate and fearless seeker of the truth. No bullshit. No capitulation to outmoded social norms.

She had been the pursuer in the relationship. It had started with a confrontation between the two of them in a group called "Phony

Friendships" that hammered away at the vapid rituals their parents thought of as friendships. She was all over Trey as a "rich spoiled aristocrat wasting his life at country club parties." The encounter had been particularly biting and continued in the small guest bedroom downstairs off Bucky's pool room long after the group ended. The sex was fierce, almost violent, and Betty Sue didn't stop berating him until they lay in each other's arms, exhausted and satisfied.

The affair maintained its passion even as Betty Sue's attack on Trey's social life diminished from a ranging exorcism to a tongue-in-cheek harassment that incorporated both her disapproval and her intense attraction to his maturity and his place in a world she was actively rejecting. By the time Frances discovered what was going on, her husband was utterly and completely under Betty Sue's spell.

Frances was oblivious, perfectly content with her life, in spite of her husband's absences, until the night M.J. was rushed to the hospital with a ruptured appendix. Frances had tried frantically to reach Trey at the numbers she had for him and finally, with M.J. in surgery and a copy of a brochure she'd found on Trey's desk with "Alt U Group Schedule" on the cover, she had driven to an address listed for the class and stumbled into a scene she couldn't have pictured in her most far-fetched conception of her husband's evening activities.

The small house held about a dozen long-haired young men and women who were leaning against cushions on the floor, the girls wearing long skirts and beads, the sweet heavy scent of marijuana carried on the pounding bass and screeching lament of Janis Joplin that blasted through the cottage at full volume. Trey was sitting cross-legged on the other side of the room, his arm around an attractive, laughing young woman with long curly black hair and earrings hanging to her shoulders.

In spite of the incongruity of the scene, Frances understood the situation immediately. The image of him there, slightly stoned, leaning against the girl, stupidly happy, had been seared into her mind, where it would remain.

"Trey, M.J.'s in the hospital," she had said simply, flatly.

He never tried to explain and she never asked. She had known instantly that he was gone. It was just a matter of time.

In the weeks that followed, weeks of silence between them, she panicked, trying to hold him with sex, with the kids. But it was clear that his heart was elsewhere. His position in society no longer mattered and whatever loyalty or affection he felt for the children or for her had been superseded by something more powerful.

So when he left with the girl, it wasn't so much the loss of him, for she had understood that right away, but it was the scandal, the embarrassment, the humiliation of having to play the abandoned divorcee, knowing that all over town titillating whispers were being exchanged about Trey and "the minister's daughter."

In the weeks and months that followed, Frances put one foot in front of the other and tried to keep her head up, in spite of the nightmare that was swirling around her. Thank God Mama and Daddy didn't live to see this, she would say to herself.

chapter twenty

The depositions had gone on for two days. Lee was glad to leave Vernon to finish up with the last of the witnesses as he returned to the storage room where evidence for the Washington case was accumulating. He leaned back in his chair and rolled his head to release the muscle tension accumulating in his neck.

Hank had made a few token appearances during the depositions, but was leaving most of this part of the preparation to Vernon. It was clear to Lee, however, that Hank and Vernon were on the same page with respect to strategy about defending the case. There was enough circumstantial evidence of misbehavior on the part of the victim to complicate his family's claim that the boy's death was due to negligent maintenance of the park by the city.

The kids apparently had been drinking, and there were indications of some kind of altercation with a group of teens—nothing strong enough to threaten criminal action against the older boys, but plenty to muddy up the question about cause of death. Now they had to convince the Washington family's attorney of the viability of their accusations. Quincy Brown was an experienced attorney and would surely talk the family into settling the case if he believed the wrongful death claim wouldn't play well to a jury.

For his part, Lee was now convinced that Dewaine Washington's death had been an accident. Nobody could place the Hispanic kids anywhere near the Bend after they had piled into cars in the middle of the afternoon. Nothing suggested that any other person had a motive to kill Dewaine

Washington. Lee had said as much to Hank and Vernon, who shrugged off his misgivings without explanation, apparently attributing his skepticism to lack of experience.

Lee was frustrated that so much time had been spent pursuing theories that blamed the victim, implying the Washington boy was directly or indirectly responsible for his own death, and so little time on the city's efforts to keep the Bend safe for its citizens. On several occasions he had raised questions about whether or not the "No Diving" sign was in place at the swimming hole at the time of Dewaine Washington's drowning, only to have that line of inquiry dismissed by Hank and Vernon. Apparently such signs were frequently installed by the city and stolen for bedroom decor. Vernon did eventually acknowledge that the city had put up the current sign after the drowning. Lee wanted to investigate further the possibility of a prior sign that might help their defense, but little had been done to follow up.

After the last deposition Lee and Hank drove together from the office to the Country Club, where most of Riverton's socially minded citizens were gathering at a fundraiser put on by the local medical auxiliary for the new children's wing at Marcus Hospital.

"I have to stop by the pro shop," Lee said after Hank parked his Mercedes near the entrance to the club ballroom. "I'll see you inside."

Restored bronze lamps cast a golden glow over the massive turn-of-the-century clubhouse that was the centerpiece of the Riverton Country Club. Dusk was settling in on the well-irrigated and neatly clipped greens and fairways as the last western light lent a rosy elegance to the classic white clubhouse. A portico with white columns, harkening back to a time of Southern affluence, ran along the back of the clubhouse, its facade punctuated by classic dark green shutters and awnings. During Lee's youth the Club had been the site of hours and hours of golf rounds, lifeguard duty, debutante balls and Sunday noon dinners. The crickets were already chirping loudly as the late-round golf carts pulled in front of the pro shop to drop off bags, most of the players heading to the locker room to shower before the benefit.

The clatter of metal cleats on the brick walkway and the warm wet air carrying the heavy fragrance of honeysuckle mingled with the rhythmic chirping of crickets and the high-pitched swell of stringed instruments emanating from the ballroom. Avoiding entrance into the glittering, noisy ballroom as long as possible, Lee wandered toward the eighteenth hole and watched the final foursome launch their balls toward the green. The smell of cut grass, fertilizer and Arkansas clay carried on the heavy air of a summer evening brought back days of adolescence when time seemed infinite, hormones were raging and life was one discovery after another. He strolled toward the edge of the pine grove where one of the golfers had shanked his short iron into the green as the first golf cart pulled up near the ball.

"You didn't finish your follow-through, pal."

Mike Thompson gave a slightly embarrassed grin as he saw his old friend wandering the course.

"Hey, man, where have you been? The summer's getting away from us."

Mike was one of the few golfers Lee knew who could talk nonstop until he started his backswing without destroying the concentration needed to make clean contact.

"Come on, baby, sit. *Sit*." He glanced up at Lee. "Haven't lost the touch yet. She's on the dance floor."

"That was a golf shot right there," Lee said.

One of the players holed a long putt from off the edge of the green.

"Good God almighty," Mike complained. "You're killing me, Cal. There goes my movie money."

Lee waited for the foursome to finish putting and then walked with Mike back to the pro shop. Two of the players were guys Lee knew casually. "You've met Scooter Nash, haven't you?" Mike asked him.

Lee shook hands with the man who had been Annie's date at the Jamiesons' party.

"Scooter's the new radiologist at the clinic. Been here, what, two years, Scooter? Lee Addison, one of my best buddies growing up. Lee's back here for the summer, just out of law school. Going to start work in San Francisco in a couple of months."

"I have a close friend who's finishing a residency at UCSF. We were roommates in med school. Jim Wilkinson."

"I haven't moved up to San Francisco yet. Just finished law school at Stanford, which is down the Peninsula. But I'm looking forward to living in the city next fall."

"Great town. Very European," Scooter intoned, holding up his five iron to signal the shop boy to come clean his clubs. "Good to meet you."

Lee and Mike ordered a couple of beers from the pro shop bar and found some chairs on the west porch overlooking the dimming ninth fairway.

"When are we going to play a round, Lee? I've got this foursome on Wednesdays, but I can get out of work another day if you can play."

"We'll play, man. I'm just up to my eyeballs in this case at work. Say, how serious is your friend Scooter about Annie?"

Mike chuckled as he shot Lee a wry look.

"Kind of gets under your skin, doesn't she? Don't go there, baby. That's over." Mike took a swig of his draft beer. "I don't know, honestly. He's the new eligible guy in town and Annie's always the prize around here. They've been going around together quite a bit. Don't know if they're sleeping together, but I'd guess so. Still, you know, Annie keeps her distance. I don't know if she's in love with him or not, but I think he's pretty much under her spell. I guess you would know about that."

"Guess I would."

Lee sipped his beer, grateful for Mike's company. People in Riverton seemed to feel the need to fill every silence with genial chatter. He loved sitting outside, absorbing the smells and sounds of the warm summer night.

"How's your sister doing? You didn't lose any time jumping in to rescue

M.J. I didn't see y'all leave the party, but everyone was buzzing about it."

Lee didn't want to be reminded of his sister's perilous journey through adolescence. He supposed the whole town thought of her as a troubled teen, which made him feel defensive. M.J. would get her bearings in college, where her need for acceptance would be met by people who would recognize her sweet nature and appreciate her.

"I don't want to butt into family business but you ought to know what I'm hearing. People say she's dealing drugs," Mike said.

"That's ridiculous. M.J. may have experimented with drugs for all I know. But dealing? Mike, she's a kid. She wouldn't know how to get drugs to sell. Believe me, she's not that sophisticated."

"She spends a lot of time with those guys from the arsenal. They aren't teenagers anymore."

As he made his way through the ballroom crowd toward the bar, Lee's frame of mind was considerably darkened by the discussion with Mike. He couldn't take the accusation seriously, but the fact that Mike did gave him pause. Lee was realistic enough to know that some kids got so far off track during high school that they never recovered.

The Country Club ballroom was buzzing with conversation as most of the Riverton establishment had showed up to support the Medical Auxiliary's gala fundraiser. Bars were set up at both ends of the large hall, which extended much of the length of the clubhouse. A string quartet was playing "Eine Kleine Nachtmusik" from the bandstand. Chandeliers sparkled overhead as the clink of glasses punctuated the hum of conversation. Lee had known many of these people all his life and was stopped several times before reaching the bar. Spotting Scooter Nash and Annie Rayburn across the room, he intentionally drifted in the opposite direction.

Frances Addison was as animated as anyone in the room. She was engaged in lively repartee with a group of friends, including Hank Greene, and had her circle thoroughly entertained with whatever she was saying. As Lee watched her out of the corner of his eye, he could see why many people found his mother attractive. She didn't have to work hard at being socially lively. He wondered how much she was drinking and if he had to worry about yet another family member tonight. M.J. wouldn't be here of course. As much as she was like Mama in her need for people, somewhere along the way M.J. had become wary. She hated this kind of event.

Frances noticed Lee leaving the bar and pulled him into her circle. "Darlin', come here and say hello to Sarah and Chuck. Y'all remember my son Lee, don't you?"

Knowing how much it meant to Mama to brag about his accomplishments, Lee gracefully submitted to the exposition, answering questions politely as he chatted with his mother's friends.

"And he's doin' a hell of a job for me at the firm this summer," intoned Hank. "Wouldn't your granddaddy be proud of you? We don't get Stanford lawyers down here every day, you know. Course you better be careful out there, Lee. My daddy always told me when they tipped the country up on its edge, all the fruits and nuts rolled out to California."

A deeply tanned woman with curly blond hair grabbed Lee's hand.

"Hank is right. Judge Dawkins would have been so proud of you. He was a wonderful civic leader in this town. He would be horrified to see what's happened to Riverton, the way the town has gone downhill ever since the Earl Warren Supreme Court shoved integration down our throats."

As the discussion moved from family achievements to politics, Lee extricated himself from the center of the group.

In spite of the narrow-mindedness of local politics, he was relieved to have the conversation shift so he could justifiably migrate to the periphery of the circle. He was starting to experience the familiar and uncomfortable feeling of being physically in the middle of a large group of people but emotionally as isolated as if he had been washed onto a deserted island. Lee knew that his ability to relate to people was inversely related to the size of the crowd and the volume of activity. He was never lonely when he was alone but could feel completely isolated in the middle of a crowd. He couldn't look at his watch and, since he hadn't driven his own car, he was stuck on Hank's schedule. He pulled his mother aside, agreed she would get a ride home and then left the Club in her car.

Glad to have the house to himself, Lee checked the telephone for messages.

"Lee, it's Rose Rayburn. Listen, Tommy is doing the Scripture reading at church on Sunday and as you can imagine, he's very proud of himself. He's so crazy about you, I know it would mean a lot to him if you could show up there to hear him. It's the Methodist church over in the midtown area. Anyway, honey, if you've got other plans, don't even worry about it for a second. I just thought I'd let you know. You don't need to get back to me."

chapter twenty-one

The alarm went off way too early for a Sunday morning. Lee didn't want to miss Tommy's reading. Arriving at the church a few minutes before the service started, he made a point of finding Tommy, already seated near the front of the church. His joy at seeing Lee was manifest.

"I'm going to read the Bible, Lee."

"I know you are, bud. You'll do a great job."

"Yeah, I will," he responded warmly. Tommy had a way of accepting praise that was one of his most endearing qualities.

Rose and Gerald started to scoot down toward Annie to make room for Lee. "Here, sit with us."

"No, thanks, I'm going to sit in the back," Lee said. "Good luck, Tommy." He gave the boy a squeeze on the neck and moved to the back of the church.

It felt strange enough to be in church, but given the powerful experience he had had here with Annie, he felt unsettled. His state of mind hadn't been helped by his most recent stop under Miss Etta's willow. That lady had to be some kind of mystic. Said the damnedest things. That morning, for example, he'd been worried about his sister, worried about the work he was doing. Jesus, it was bad enough to have Zoe lecturing him about blaming the victim. What was it Etta had said? *You're still a young man, but you are morally responsible, before God, for what you do in your work. If you see the truth, you must say the truth.* What was that supposed to mean?

Church services had always provided the perfect backdrop for Lee to do some of his best thinking. The ancient fables taught from the pulpit could be twisted to provide morality lessons for the twentieth century, but the logic wasn't easy to follow. The music was beautiful in its own way but not really his taste. So as he had always done, he tuned out the admonitions from the altar and sorted through his checklist of things to do. The sounds however had a Proustian effect, with images of times past drifting into his thoughts as the organ music swelled and the familiar poetry of ancient Scripture filled the sanctuary.

And what was it Etta had said about Annie? Well, maybe not Annie. She didn't know about Annie. *If you have a need for someone, like that beautiful girl, you have to be honest about that too. Being truthful to yourself is even more important than being truthful to other people.*

When it was Tommy's time to read, Lee found himself tensing up like a parent whose kid is coming into a game as the relief pitcher. Tommy took his time and looked over the congregation before he started. "I am the resurrection and the life," he said, stumbling over "resurrection," but finishing strong. "Those who believe in me, even though they die, will live."

He paused and Lee, the last person likely to be moved by Scripture, was touched by the power of the words, coming from Tommy.

"And everyone who lives and believes in me will never die."

He paused after "never" to emphasize its meaning. Something about the boy's slow delivery made you want to listen.

When the minister again assumed his position in the pulpit, Lee's attention wandered. Nobody would ask for a kid with Down Syndrome, but Tommy Rayburn's earnestness was touching, touching in a way it wouldn't have been if he were like everybody else.

From the front of the church the minister's voice rose and fell as he read words first spoken by illiterate nomads living in tents in Middle Eastern deserts three thousand years ago. It was a stretch to extrapolate their vision to the modern world. *If you think that you are wise in this age, you should become fools so that you may become wise. For the wisdom of this world is foolishness with God.*

Even though he hadn't seen Annie, except for their brief, intense meeting in front of the church, Lee knew that her presence in Riverton this summer was creating a distance between himself and Zoe. He hadn't admitted it to himself until now, but he was picking up the phone less frequently and had less to say when they did talk. Something about the South in the summer—sultry, aimless, scented with memory and longing. It was hard to move at the pace he was accustomed to. His real life was quickly fading. His mind felt sluggish. No wonder they lost the Civil War.

I want you to be wise in what is good and guileless in what is evil.

The problem with basing your ethical values on text written thousands of years ago was that so many of those people's beliefs about the world had been completely discredited. Ministers were careful to pick and choose the sections of text they recited, but portions of those ancient writings were still pretty disturbing to modern sensibilities. Slavery? No problem. Killing everybody who believed differently than you did? That's fine. But God forbid you should eat shellfish or wear mixed fabrics. And think of the wickedness that had been done in the world in the name of religion—from abuse of women to persecution of the Jews to the brutal aggression of the Crusades.

There are better ways to spend a Sunday morning, he thought to himself. In Palo Alto he liked to drive out to one of the trailheads in the hills above campus on a Sunday morning and run through the fog and mist until the sun broke through, bright and hot. In an hour's time he'd go from goose bumps to sweat as the temperature rose twenty degrees in the course of a morning's run. And then a sweet fresh fruit pastry and rich hot coffee at the Woodside Bakery. Now that was a religion he could live with.

Outside the church he waited to congratulate Tommy.

"Come on by the house and have some Sunday dinner, Lee," Rose Rayburn urged. "We want to have more time to visit with you. The summer is getting away from us."

Lee glanced at Annie for approval.

"Come on over," she said. "I can't stay long. I'm getting in shape for a marathon in Dallas next month."

Sunday dinner at the Rayburns consisted of a spread designed to destroy your cholesterol level in a single sitting. The aromas were already wafting out the front door and through the neighborhood. The table overflowed with multiple dishes of meat, greens, peas, cornbread and pudding as it did every Sunday. Friends, relatives and neighbors, made welcome by Rose Rayburn to drop by uninvited and join the feast, were helping their plates and finding an empty chair or stoop where they could sit and visit with other recipients of the Rayburns' bounty.

Lee remembered his first visit to the house. It was a good deal more modest than what he was used to. But he had never felt so much at ease anywhere, except maybe in the privacy of his own bedroom. Rose's warmth and graciousness led her to invite old and new friends to Sunday dinner wherever she met them during the week. She genuinely loved people, so for her to have a house full of friends was a joy. Nobody felt the weekly feast was an imposition because the pleasure Rose found in having people enjoy her food and her hospitality was wonderfully apparent.

Lee filled a plate to overflowing and found a spot by Tommy outside under the hickory tree in the backyard. He didn't know the others who joined them at the table, but they were as friendly and warm as the hostess herself. Rose's son, in spite of the genetic defects that would keep him a child forever, had inherited his mother's happy spirit and love of people. He had become a fixture in Riverton and nobody was troubled by the aspects of Tommy's speech and appearance that made him different. Full of life and energy, it was the disabilities themselves that kept him from changing and that endowed Tommy with an ageless innocence and openness.

Annie had changed into shorts and stopped by the table on her way out.

"You can't run right after eating," Lee cautioned.

"I've had enough of Mama's Sunday dinners to know when to stop.

I've got to take some food to Nana's. Then I'm just going to stretch and do some intervals at the high school before I start my distance run later this afternoon."

"Where do you go?"

"I'm trying to do ten miles on Sundays, on that path around the lakes out toward New Washington."

Lee hoped to make a quick exit himself, but he kept running into people he had known growing up who were eager to hear about his plans. The conversation rarely drifted to matters political or religious, but when it did, he was inevitably surprised at the contrast between local beliefs and the values he had adopted during his years of study in places far from home.

These people were not as backward and stupid as the intellects on the West Coast believed. But they did constitute a single tribe in a way that big urban areas did not, and the frame of reference was remarkably homogeneous and unique to this part of the country. Almost like another language. He could see why TV spots featuring a Southern governor or minister sounded so strange to people who had never lived here. Like most people who had lost a war, Southerners had never quite gotten over the destruction of the agrarian economy of the region. There was a wariness toward outsiders, almost a chip on the shoulder, even a hundred-and-twenty-five years later.

After saying his good-byes to the Rayburns, Lee drove home, pleased to find his mother and sister having a genuinely cordial conversation.

"There's coffee in the pot. Come sit with us," his mother said.

"I was telling Mama about your friend down the street—Miss Etta," M.J. explained.

"That house has been there since I was a child. Probably there before Daddy built this house. I think I've seen her sitting out under that willow. I don't know how old she is. More than eighty, I'd guess."

"You know her then?" Lee asked.

"No, not really. When I grew up, the races didn't mix. They had separate schools. It was better in some ways. For them, I mean. The black people weren't expected to compete in our world."

"I remember Grandmother Dawkins talking like that before she died," said Lee. "How integration was going to lead to the disaster of mixed races because the white girls would have their heads turned by the athletic skills of black football players."

"Oh my God," M.J. laughed. "That's terrible. She was a bigot."

"That's the way people talked in those days, M.J.," Frances explained. "Grandmother grew up in a very different world. She wasn't a bigot, at least not in the way you mean it. She probably never knew a black person besides the ones who worked for her family. For a century white people had thought they were being benevolent to give the blacks something to do and a way to keep themselves fed and clothed. But times change and now we're exposed to real people and we understand what terrible things black people had to live through during those years. If our grandparents had read the books we've read and seen the same movies and TV, they would have understood the world differently."

M.J. went upstairs to listen to music as Frances and Lee sipped coffee at the kitchen table. It was a considerable relief for Lee to see his mother in better spirits.

"I was thinking about that black kid M.J. was so close to in junior high," Lee said to his mother. "Does she still hang around with him?"

"No, not really. I think there's some pressure once they get in high school, you know, to stick to their own kind."

"He was a nicer kid than some of the people she hangs around with now."

"Lord help me, I know that's true," she agreed. "I wish she made better choices. It's fair to criticize me for discouraging that friendship with the Mason boy. People were starting to remark on it. I felt it could hurt her reputation and her chances. I mean, it's fine to have a friend like that, but when you're old enough to start going out, it can become a problem."

Lee restrained himself from reacting to this statement and said no more on the subject. "I've got to go for a run before it gets any later," he told her.

"Honey, it's too hot to be out running. It can't be good for you."

"I'll find some shade."

Lee parked off the New Washington road in a pine grove and followed the trail toward the watershed. Once it flattened into a trail, he jogged eastward toward the ranger's station on the hill. Thanks to a cloud cover, the strength of the sun was muted, but the humidity remained high enough for Lee to quickly break into a sweat as he crested the rolling hillside. He saw Annie running in his direction from the far end of the first lake. As she approached, he slowed his pace.

"Don't think for a minute you can keep up with me, considering the size of your Sunday dinner," she said, passing him without slowing down.

Lee turned and picked up the pace behind her. "You're probably right. Figured you needed company way out here."

The trail cut a narrow winding path through the underbrush just above the first tier of swamp grasses. The path wasn't wide enough for two, so Lee let Annie set the pace ahead of him, both of them concentrating on the trail as they jogged up the gradual incline.

He expected this would be the toughest part of the run. There was no shade on this side of the lake and, though the sun had begun to move toward the horizon, it still carried enough strength to sap his energy. In spite of his morning runs, the Arkansas humidity had diminished his interest in pushing his cardiovascular limits. After the big midday meal, he wasn't yet into a comfortable rhythm. After passing the first ridge, Lee found his rhythm as a runner's high started to settle in. When they began to circle the far end of the cutback, the path widened and Lee moved alongside Annie.

"There's a long stretch of poison ivy just past that scrub pine," Annie warned, "so stay to the right."

"I'm surprised how low the water is this year," he observed.

As they entered a stand of pines, a thick layer of fallen needles muted their footfall, the heat momentarily tamped down by shadow. The pungent sweet smell of pine sap took him back to campfires and fishing trips, with the insistent voices of cicadas echoing through the trees.

At this stage of a run, worry and anxiety began to dissipate. Lee was getting tired, which prevented his busy mind from circling around responsibilities and problems. It was enough to just keep moving.

Sweat dripped from Annie's neck onto her already soaked running shirt and she wiped her forehead with a damp sleeve, then pulled back into the lead as they turned toward the northern reach of the lake. "I want to show you something," she said.

Turning away from the main trail, she followed a narrower path up an exposed hillside. The path curved its way through rocky outcroppings into another pine grove that led to an overlook. Below them the sun slanted into a shaded valley surrounded by low hills, the lengthening shadows imparting a complex depth and color to every shape and texture.

"See where the grove opens up at the western edge of the valley?" Annie asked. "The water comes out just beyond the cottonwood stand."

They stood in silence for a long time, cicadas filling the warm dusk with rhythmic pulses. The creek below was abuzz with activity as a family of diligent beavers created patterns in the water transporting sticks to a partially completed structure.

Lee stood behind Annie and placed his hands on her arms. She didn't move, nor did he, as they stood transfixed.

"It's getting dark," she said finally. "Why don't you come to my house for dinner? Around seven o'clock? I've got some pasta and salad we can throw together."

chapter twenty-two

Annie's house was set back from the street behind a rustic twig fence overrun with old roses. A flagstone path meandered through blossoming hydrangea and lovingly tended crepe myrtle to a modest wood-framed cottage. A pair of floral rubber clogs and garden clippers rested alongside a small potting shed. As Lee rang the bell, he felt like a kid on his first date, scared and excited and heady from the scent of the jasmine bush that climbed the trellis beside the front door.

His normally analytic mind had been racing from the minute he returned to his car for the trip home to shower and change. The fragments of desire that had been drifting through the air every time he and Annie crossed paths had kindled into a flame somewhere deep inside. He suspected that she wanted him as much as he wanted her. Why else would she have invited him to dinner? It was a bad idea for a million reasons. He didn't care. The parts of his brain with roots as deep and old and instinctive as the first man to walk upright on this earth focused his mind, leaving no room for reason or practicality.

"Come on in. I've just started the water."

Lee pulled up a stool and sipped a glass of Sauvignon Blanc as Annie put together dinner. The conversation was light as they caught up on old friends, remembered awkward or amusing episodes from their youth, discussed the joys and pains of running during the Arkansas summer. But the electricity between them was palpable.

Lee was watching her at the stove stirring the spaghetti, testing for the al dente crunch, engrossed in what she was doing. Before he had time to think about it, he had slipped off the stool and was there beside her, encircling her. Annie turned toward him with no restraint and no looking back.

An hour later they were still in bed, the spaghetti cold on the stove, Annie's auburn gold hair flowing over Lee's shoulder, her head resting on his arm. They were quiet, both lost in their own worlds. Lee leaned up on his elbow and reached to touch her, lightly, with reverence, inspecting.

"God, you're beautiful," he said finally.

"Don't even say a word, Lee Addison. Am I crazy or stupid or what?"

"What."

She pushed her hair out of her eyes, looked over at him as if to glean some meaning from this and laughed.

"I could see this coming like a freight train. Knew it was going to happen as surely as day follows night. And I'll be damned if I could do anything to stop it."

He turned toward her. "Any regrets?"

She sighed, considering him, her eyes soft. "God no. That was just about the nicest thing that has happened to me for as long as I can remember."

"Funny," he said. "I've dreamed about this for so long. About you, I mean. I was just about to fall asleep. Snapped out of it because I didn't want to wake up and find it was just another subliminal fantasy."

She was quiet for a minute. "Me too," she said. "How many nights I've tossed and turned with your ghost weaving its way into my dreams. Come to think of it, how can we be sure this isn't a dream?"

"Tell you what," he said. "It's got to be real so long as one of us stays awake. Let's take turns sleeping so that somebody is always awake to make sure it doesn't slip away."

Annie laughed. "Me first," she said. "Wake me up if you get tired."

Another hour passed.

Annie moved first. "Roll over, Beethoven. My arm's asleep and I'm starving to death. I'm going to put on the spaghetti."

Lee drew her in more tightly. "Don't go. We can probably survive here a week without food."

Laughing, she tossed a pillow over his head, and slipped out of the bed and into the shower. By the time Lee was up and dressed, the spaghetti was cooking, the salad was ready and the music was playing. He could tell that Annie had moved on; she was more remote, friendly, but in control of her own space.

They had dinner over quiet conversation and when they had finished the meal, Annie pushed her plate back. "Lee, I want to say something to you that you may not understand. This has been wonderful. It was as inevitable as the tides. I couldn't have stopped it if I wanted to, and clearly I didn't want to. But I've got a life here. And I can't throw everything away. I've got...I've got somebody who cares about me, somebody I love and may decide to build my life with. I feel terrible about this. He wouldn't understand and I'm sure he wouldn't forgive me. And I wouldn't hurt him for anything in the world."

Typical of his gender during times of relationship discussions, Lee didn't know what to say. So he just watched and listened.

"For a while, when you first got here this summer, I was overwhelmed by the flood of feelings that swept over me every time I saw you. I thought it was about our history. You know, I was angry at you for a very long time. She'd enough tears to float the Navy. But it was so long ago, and it *was* just a high school romance after all. I thought I had moved on. But every time I saw you, I felt like my body was inhabited by an alien force. The more I fought it, the more I wanted you. The minute you appeared on the trail, I knew tonight was inevitable."

She wrinkled her brow and looked pensive.

"But truth is, I think we both had a lot of pent-up sexual drive from too many years of coming close and never *doing* it. So, it's not surprising really that we wound up in bed. It was great, really it was. But understand, we can't start going around together this summer. If you care for me at all, Lee, you've got to help me with this."

Lee Addison, the master of words, always in charge and in control, couldn't think of a single thing to say. Suddenly he felt incredibly sad. As if he might burst into tears any minute. "Okay," he said quietly.

"Do you think, Lee, we could be friends? Just friends? My family loves you. You've always been Tommy's hero and as you can see, nothing will ever change that. I do want to know what your life is like. I want you to be happy."

Although he continued to feel like the village idiot, without a rational thing to say, Lee was surprised to hear these words come out of his mouth. "Give me a week, Annie. One evening is not enough. Give me a week and after that, I promise to leave you alone. I can't stand the thought of walking away."

She regarded him with genuine shock and bewilderment.

"What are you talking about?"

"I don't know how I can promise to leave you alone."

She eyed him cynically.

"Okay, Lee, let's talk about you. Are you planning to move back to Riverton? This is where I'm going to grow old, you know. I have a brother to take care of and my family needs me. Do you want to set up a little family law practice here?

"And, I know there's someone in your life out in California. Your mama has been more forthcoming about that than you have, I must say. Were you going to fill me in on her as part of the one-week package?"

She was mad now, the skin just in front of her ears blushed with emotion.

This was enough to wake him from his stupor and evoke a response. "I'm sorry, Annie. I don't want to be dishonest with you. And I wasn't thinking about some kind of life-shaping arrangement. I loved being with you, being close to you. I don't want to go. I don't have any cosmic answer as to why that is. I hardly know what's going on right now, but I can promise you it's not a devious plan to exploit you. I'm sorry. Really. I have been seeing someone for about a year. Her name is Zoe Perinsky. A law school classmate. I'm very close to her. I respect her. We're not living together. But she'll be in San Francisco next year too. I'm not sure where it will go."

"Do you think this is fair to her? Were you thinking about her when you made the one-week proposal?"

"Shit, Annie, no I haven't been thinking about her at all today. I've only been thinking about you. Not about fairness or candor or political stability in Palestine. Clearly, I'm not thinking, period. I'm bargaining for more time with you, that's all. You don't want to give me a week? Fine. I'll take an hour and a half if that's all I can get. Am I bargaining away my soul here? Maybe I would if you'd let me stay. I can't explain it. I'm sorry."

Again they were quiet. Then they reached for each other, hungry, blind to caution or consequence.

chapter twenty-three

For the first time that summer, Lee was in the office before anyone else arrived. The lights were on but he had to make his own coffee. Having missed his morning run, he felt scattered and was grateful to have a few minutes in the document room before having to dive into problem solving. Boxes marked "Washington Case" covered the table top and were stacked along the walls of the conference room. He pushed several boxes aside, slipped into one of the leather chairs, and then let his face drop into his hands.

God she was beautiful. It had to have been the best night of his life. What was he thinking of? Was she still in love with him? Would she come to California? She would hate it there. She wouldn't understand his friends. Wouldn't fit into the single-mindedness of Silicon Valley. Anyway, she had made it clear that she couldn't leave her parents with the responsibility of Tommy.

Lee shook his head to try to focus on the stack of documents cluttering his desk. He opened the package from the legal transcription service and began skimming the latest deposition transcripts. Vernon was clever, he had to say that for the guy. He led these kids along patiently, suiting his own purpose, peppering his conversation with friendly, low-key comments timed perfectly to gain trust and encourage lengthy responses. Puzzled by the line of questioning, Lee wanted to review Vernon's timeline of the alleged attack. Crossing the foyer to see if Vernon's office was unlocked, Lee turned the handle and flipped on the light, opening the white board to reveal the elaborate flow chart. He studied the movements between 2:00

and 4:30 p.m. outlined on the chart and again wondered how Vernon and Hank could believe that the Mexican-American teenagers had jumped Dewaine Washington without being seen or heard.

He was turning to leave when his eye fell on an open spiral notebook bearing Vernon's scratches and doodles. There were cryptic references to the Washington case, some of the witnesses and pieces of evidence the team had been grappling with. Near the bottom of the page, under "Notes to Self," Lee read:

Revise Gonzalez depo para 3/conflict/return to Bend?

Fred: Check civil procedure requirements re lab report

Disposition of sign: RA Sampson/lab

Who was R.A. Sampson? As he tried to decipher the remaining notes written in Vernon's left-handed scrawl, Lee heard the elevator door open. Not stopping to turn out the light, Lee made a quick exit through the secretary's cubicle and met Vernon on his way in.

"I was just studying your timeline for the new set of questions I'm putting together," he admitted. "I want to get that draft to you before noon."

Lee didn't pause to hear Vernon's response and was sweating by the time he reached his own office. He was convinced that Vernon knew perfectly well that the boy's death had nothing to do with those Hispanic kids. It was one thing to mount a creative and aggressive case for your client. But this was starting to give off a bad odor.

He flipped through his Rolodex for the lab's phone number and dialed. "This is Lee Addison from Townsend Greene. Wondering if I could swing by to see you about the Washington case?"

The lab was adjacent to the courthouse annex, located in a portable unit connected to the annex by a covered walkway. After earning a forensics degree somewhere in Oklahoma, Max Kingston had come to Riverton to complete his training. He was working under a respected veteran in Riverton, and was getting up to speed quickly.

Kingston was also the firm's contact for the Washington case and had worked closely with Vernon on analysis of the evidence. He was about Lee's age, a rotund red-cheeked young man with a rural accent, very accommodating and friendly.

"Yes, I confirmed the fingerprint analysis with Vernon. But you should know that black lawyer for the family has been coming over here too, poking around. I always stay in the room if he's going through stuff. I don't trust that guy."

Lee spent half an hour reviewing files and going through boxes of evidence from the scene of the accident. Hank and Vernon had been in and out of the lab regularly over the years and played poker once a month with Gerald Battson, the longtime lab director. Gerald had urged Max to bend over backward to help the team from Townsend Greene, impressing on the young intern the importance of developing a good working relationship with members of the local bar.

Lee had found nothing else new in the forensic files and nothing about a sign or anybody named Sampson.

On his way out, he stopped by the cubicle where Max Kingston was working.

"Thanks for your help with that. By the way, have you guys seen anything relating to a sign or any kind of warning that might have been posted out at the Bend before this accident?"

Max started to say something and then caught himself—or so it seemed to Lee. He was quiet for a few seconds before responding. "No, I don't think so."

Lee thanked him again and just before pushing open the door turned to him once more. "You don't happen to know someone by the name of R.A. Sampson, do you?"

"Oh, sure. Rusty Sampson," Max replied. "Director of the Riverton Parks and Recreation Department."

Lee was on his way back to the car when his cell phone rang. When he realized it was Zoe, he decided not to answer. Couldn't talk to Zoe, not that morning. Think about Zoe later, he told himself, not now. Grateful that it was quiet at last, he was getting into the car when his phone started to ring again.

"Jesus, Zoe, let it go," he said aloud, glaring at the phone. But when he realized it was his mother's number, he picked it up.

"Lee?" whispered a very tentative young voice.

"M.J.? Is that you? Not like you to be up so early."

"Lee, I need to talk to you. Can I see you today?"

"Sis, I'm at the lab and heading back to the office to do some prep for the trial. Can it wait until tonight?"

There was a heavy silence on the other end of the phone.

"Are you okay, M.J.?"

"Not really."

"How about lunch? Can you meet me at Sam's in about an hour?"

When Lee entered the restaurant, she was sitting with her back to the door in one of the green vinyl booths, still as a mouse, studying her multi-ringed fingers. He paused to study her. Something about her stillness in the midst of all the clatter caused his heart to clench. So self-sufficient all his life, he had been unable to provide the guidance that might have made a difference, and he felt an almost parental despair about the aimlessness of M.J.'s existence.

He slid into the booth opposite his sister and offered her a tentative smile. "Sorry to be late. I can't seem to get my head out of that damned case."

Chatting with M.J. was like extracting a molar. They made small talk, Lee doing most of the talking, without any signal from M.J. as to what exactly she wanted to talk about.

"So what's going on, M.J.?"

She sighed. Her eyes welled up but she didn't cry, and she continued to study her bitten nails, as if to control her feelings. He could see that she was a mess but felt helpless in the face of her despair.

She hadn't thought through exactly what she wanted to say to her brother. It had taken courage to call him at all. But now that she had his attention, she was having misgivings.

The truth of it was, she was a little out of her depth with Buddy. She knew that.

Last night things had gotten ugly. It was just that he kept pushing her into all his schemes, and half the time she didn't even know what he was up to. She knew he wouldn't get her involved in anything that could hurt her or cause trouble. But he was into what he was into, and he didn't always stop to think. He didn't think it was a big deal for her to carry the little bags of weed to a couple of kids at school that he knew. She wasn't "dealing" or anything. Just delivering something for him. There was no risk, he claimed. He was the only one taking any risk. But she wasn't stupid. If she got caught, they'd never believe she didn't know what she was carrying.

"Lee," she said, "when you're with a girl and things aren't going so well and y'all, I mean, she has a mind of her own about some things…well, what I mean is, do you ever get pissed off? I mean, how do you work things out if, like, she acts like a bitch and you get pissed off?"

"Who's pissed off, M.J.?"

"I'm just asking, like, how do you work it out if you want one thing and she wants something else?"

"Well, there are always differences. Sometimes, to make a relationship work, you have to compromise. You can't always have things your own way. Both of you have to give up something. You know, to make the other person happy. But, M.J., if you're talking about your relationship with Buddy Parish, sometimes it's just the wrong person. Sometimes it doesn't work out. And shouldn't work out."

Of course, she thought to herself. *He doesn't think Buddy is good enough for me. Wants me to be with a rich college guy.*

All of a sudden she realized that he couldn't fix it. Nobody could, really. She had always thought of her brother as magic, someone who could do anything, take away any hurt, solve any problem. But, just that moment, she couldn't even think of a way to articulate what the problem was.

"Look, M.J., you need to pull yourself out of this funk. Take charge of your life. Figure out what you want and go for it. You don't have to be…"

His chain of thought was interrupted by a wide shadow cast across the table as the cheerful face of Tommy Rayburn appeared, sliding into the booth beside M.J.

"Hi Lee! Whatcha doing?"

M.J. felt some relief at the interruption, having realized the futility of turning to Lee for a fix. Lee, for whom everything was easy, solutions all so obvious, couldn't even see the problem. Would it have helped if he, if anyone, could feel what it was? The anxiety, the unmet longings, the bleakness of getting out of bed every day?

"Want to come with me out to the Bend today, Lee? I'm going to bike all the way."

"Can't do it, Tommy. I've got to work."

"M.J., do you want to go to the Bend with me? We could lie on the rocks and get a suntan."

"I can't." She studied her hands.

"Why don't you take Tommy out there, M.J.?" Lee suggested. "It's too far for him to bike."

She sighed, knowing she was trapped.

"But before you go, Tommy, I want you to tell me about that day out at the Bend when Dewaine Washington died."

They walked outside. The early afternoon heat and humidity had already kicked in and M.J. wished she had found a parking place in the shade. As she started the car to get the air conditioner going, Lee pulled Tommy aside.

"It's important for me to understand what happened that day out at the Bend, the day Dewaine Washington died."

"Okay."

"What were you doing out there anyway? Weren't you still in school?"

"It was a prep day for special ed, so we had the day off. Mama said I could go out there with Eddie and Sam."

"Were they with you when you saw the black kids?"

"No, they were in the tubes. I went over there to go to the bathroom. Then I was watching them."

After fifteen minutes huddled up with Lee in Sam's parking lot, Tommy hopped into the passenger seat beside M.J., who leaned out the car window and gave her brother a peck on the cheek. Then she cranked up her mother's old green Buick, which had been deemed big and clunky enough to keep her safe, and exited the parking lot in the direction of the Bend.

"I haven't been in your car before," Tommy said.

"Well, it's not much to write home about."

"Yeah. Look at that old Ford! That's Mr. McAdams' car. I've seen him working on it almost every day when I bike down Birch Street."

Tommy prattled on nonstop throughout most of the drive, requiring little to no encouragement from M.J.

It was hot at the Bend, too hot to move, too hot to talk, and she was relieved to have a companion who didn't demand any effort on her part to fill the silence.

They settled into a spot along the water where they spread their towels. M.J. lay on her back, hoping the sun would cook all the negative thoughts out of her brain and trying to ignore Tommy's chatter.

Sweat was dripping from her body and an annoying fly kept landing on her right hand. She could shake her fingers and the fly would take off, only to land again seconds later. Cracking open one eyelid, she glared at the offending pest, an ugly creature with beady eyes and blue-green wings.

Shit, she thought to herself. Even the bugs won't leave me in peace.

"Let's go in the water, M.J. I'm hot," Tommy said.

She waded out to a rock just off the bank and kept Tommy company as he splashed at the edge of the water.

"Look at the tadpoles, M.J.! They're biting my toes."

She hadn't wanted to blow off the afternoon, but it was funny how her mood was lifting. How could that boy be so damned cheerful? Going through life with people staring at him wherever he went? She had felt the eyes of strangers follow them as she and Tommy passed along the trail by the picnic tables on their way down to the water. She guessed that he was just oblivious.

Tommy was giving advice to a boy trying to get his toy boat to stay afloat. The boy was too young to notice anything different about Tommy and they were playing companionably at the edge of the water. M.J. was happy to have some time to herself to relax. The boy's mother, however, soon became aware of the odd older boy who was playing with her son and, sensing something troubling about Tommy's demeanor, she removed him to another part of the beach. Tommy either didn't notice or had experienced the same reaction from adults so many times that it didn't faze him. He continued to entertain himself happily, trying to catch a tadpole in a plastic cup.

M.J. stretched out on her stomach over the rock, letting her fingers slip down into the coolness of the rippling water. She maintained this position as long as she could until her back and the tender skin behind her knees felt as if they were emitting as much heat as they were absorbing and she turned to face the sun, rotating slowly like a pig on a spit. Then she spread out her arms as if on the crossbeam of a crucifix, feeling the penetrating, healing power of the sun on her face, stomach, arms and legs, baking every thought out of her mind, letting the dark emptiness flow from her fingertips and the tips of her toes, leaving an empty shell without a care in mind or heart.

Drips of cool water on her pink midsection roused her from the warm darkness and she squinted up to see Buddy Parish hovering over her.

"Wake up, M.J. You're cooked."

"Don't. That's cold."

"I didn't know you were coming out here today."

She pulled herself up and stretched. "God, it's hot."

"Hey, baby, I'm sorry about last night. Honestly. I was totally out of line. I was having a shitty day and I shouldn't have taken it out on you. Come on. Drag yourself up from there, gorgeous. My boys are down at Big Rock with some chicks we met from Richmond."

"Oh, I can't. Got talked into bringing Tommy Rayburn out here and I've got to get him home."

"Come on down, just for a few minutes. I want to make up with you. Got some cold beer."

She splashed over to the bank where Tommy was poking at tadpoles with a stick.

"I'm going downstream with Buddy for a few minutes, Tommy. I'll be back soon."

M.J. and Buddy slipped into the private clearing that had become their clubhouse. The girls were about M.J.'s age, enjoying the attention of the older boys and the grown-up feeling of holding a can of Bud. They were friendly enough and M.J. reached into the cooler for a beer, drinking deeply of the cold bitter brew. She settled in next to Buddy, glad to be in the shade. It felt good to be one of the crowd. Buddy handed her a cigarette. She knew the other girls envied her familiarity with the guys and with this private retreat.

Buddy massaged her sunburned shoulders.

"You forgive me, don't you, sweetheart? I'm such a dick."

She laughed.

"How's it going with your brother?"

"Oh, okay, I guess. We had lunch today. He's so busy with his job that I don't get to see him all that much. Once summer is over, he'll be back to California as fast as he can."

"God…California," Buddy sighed. "That's where I'd like to be. Maybe you and I can take a trip out there sometime to visit him."

"Oh my God. That would be awesome. We'd be all mellow, cruising past the Grand Canyon. Stop in Vegas and L.A. on the way."

He leaned over, still rubbing her neck. "Fuckin' A, baby. Maybe we'd stay out there. Get a little place on the ocean. Learn how to surf. All that California shit."

They laughed at the improbable scenario. Anything to get out of here, she thought. Buddy wasn't such a bad guy. She didn't give a shit what her family said about him. It was her life.

One beer led to another and suddenly she realized with a start that the shadows of the cottonwoods were lengthening. She leapt up. "Tommy. I totally forgot about him. I've got to go."

M.J. ran along the creekside path, muttering to herself about her stupidity. When she got to the beach area along the river where Tommy had been trying to catch tadpoles, he was nowhere to be seen.

Quickly she ducked into several of the spots where he liked to play, but without any luck. Finally she climbed up the northern edge of the levee, out of breath and regretting the beers, and scanned the river in both directions.

With Lee talking about the Washington boy's death practically every day, M.J. was seized with terror that Tommy might have drowned.

On the far bank close to the picnic tables, four or five people were gathered on the riverbank. It looked like they were attending to someone lying on the beach at the edge of the water.

"God damn it," she whispered through clenched teeth as she ran toward the open beach. How could she have been so stupid to put Tommy's life in danger?

After discovering a family building a sandcastle near the shore, with Tommy nowhere in sight, M.J. ran to a public phone and dialed Lee's cell number. How was she going to explain this?

Lee was abrupt on the phone, informing her that Tommy had called his parents after he couldn't find her and they had come and picked him up. He was ticked off, but M.J. sunk to the ground with relief. Thank God Tommy was safe.

chapter twenty-four

Vic's Cafe had the appearance of every other Arkansas breakfast diner in every other strip mall in the state. They served the mandatory eggs and sausage with grits on the side and biscuits with gravy if you really wanted to ruin your figure. The unpublicized but universally known secret of Vic's was their good strong Italian coffee and even a passable cappuccino.

It was out on the interstate, well past the turnoff for Townsend Greene. But on those mornings when Lee was sleep-deprived or anticipating a particularly demanding day at the office, he would take the long way to work and stop by Vic's for coffee.

He had stayed late at the office the night before, trying to finish the review of case law relating to potential liability of city directors in cases where gross negligence had been alleged against Arkansas municipalities. There were a couple of cases on point and he knew Hank would be pleased with the work. But he felt groggy and in need of strong coffee.

It was unusual to order coffee to go at Vic's, but they knew Lee by now and had a Styrofoam cup ready for him. As he stopped at the cash register to pay, Lee brushed past a table where Annie and Scooter Nash were having breakfast. Never one to show emotion in a public place, Lee was so surprised to see the two of them together that he paused at their table. Even though the newly rekindled romance with Annie had no strings attached, it hadn't occurred to him that she might still be seeing Scooter Nash. He had been so obsessed with her, so swept up in the passion of the moment that he hadn't thought about the parameters of their new relationship. Had he been capable of such insight, he would not have been caught short by the unexpected encounter and would have reacted quickly enough to give them a formal nod and keep going.

As it was, he was stupidly frozen in place, the hot coffee starting to penetrate the Styrofoam.

The flood of feelings was powerful, though Lee couldn't have explained why. The possibility that he might not have her, that she might choose someone else, was incongruous. Their relationship had felt so right, so inevitable. And for all of his guilt and regret about walking away from Annie during college, it hadn't occurred to him that she might reject him now. Just the sight of her there with another man seemed profoundly wrong.

Scooter looked up at him with disgust and anger. Annie seemed to be as flummoxed as Lee was, staring at him with dismay.

Scooter turned to her with a mix of surprise and disillusionment. "So this is how you set it up, Annie? Have the new guy show up on cue? I thought you had more integrity than this. Don't know why I wasted my time."

He lurched up from the table, pushed past Lee and strode out the door.

Unaccustomed as she was to being on the receiving end of criticism, Annie was shocked by the outburst and hurt by Scooter's accusations. Her eyes welled up with tears.

"I guess I interrupted something," Lee finally said.

He was still stumbling through the initial shock of finding Annie and Scooter together. The full implication of Scooter's outburst hadn't really registered.

"Oh Lee, for Christ's sake, just sit down. Your timing is lousy."

By the time he was made to understand that he had walked into the middle of Annie's breakup with Scooter, Lee had calmed down, the initial clench of fear that he might lose her having eased.

"I'm sorry to have stumbled in at the wrong time," he said apologetically.

"Oh well, I can't blame Scooter for being pissed off. When you look at it from his perspective, I was just stringing him along and dumped him the instant an old boyfriend showed up in town. He's a fine person and I care about him. For all his achievements, his life hasn't been that easy. And we had just gotten to the point where he could talk to me about that. I feel terrible letting him down."

"I'm sorry, Annie," Lee said, reaching across the table to touch her hand. "This wasn't your fault. You didn't mean for it to happen. And I'm sorry to have walked in here when I did. But I'm so goddamn glad that I'm the one sitting here with you and he's the one stomping out to the car."

They talked quietly, happy to be in each other's company.

Annie looked at her watch.

"I can't believe you're whiling away the morning at Vic's. Things must have slowed down on the Washington case."

"Not at all, unfortunately. The case is heating up. I was going to call you this morning anyway, especially after the fiasco with M.J. and Tommy."

"Oh, don't worry about it. That kind of thing happens to Tommy all the time. He gets himself somewhere and can't find whoever he's supposed to be with. Luckily people in town know Tommy so well that there's always somebody who comes along and takes care of him."

"Well, I am so disappointed in M.J. It's one thing to be irresponsible about her own life, but to go off and leave Tommy alone like that…I guess I'm particularly dismayed about it because it was my own fault. I encouraged her to take him out there. Thought it might do her some good to worry about someone besides herself."

"He's okay, Lee, really. But is she?"

"I don't think so. But I'm no help to her. I think I'm part of the problem."

"Well, that may be. But I suspect you're part of the solution too. M.J.'s a sweet girl. Pretty and smart too. But for some reason she doesn't believe in herself."

"I just hope she learns to believe in something before she screws up her life in a way that can't be fixed."

"Me too," Annie said, reaching across the table to entwine her fingers in his. "I woke up this morning thinking about you. It's funny. I'm usually such a cautious person. But for some reason, I'm able to accept this—finding you again, I mean—as one of the little miracles that life brings you sometimes, along with all the crap."

"Can we just have a quiet evening at your house tonight? You don't have to be at the church, do you?"

"No. Want to come for dinner?"

"I should probably be home for dinner and spend a few minutes with Mama and M.J. But I'll come over after that. Hopefully I can get out of the office at a reasonable time."

"You're having to work too hard. I thought this was supposed to be a low-key summer job."

"Probably would be if I didn't feel so conflicted about this case. I'm not comfortable with the position the firm is taking, and yet it's not my place to drive the strategy. I'm not even a member of the Arkansas bar. I know these guys are good lawyers. But it's interesting to see how you get sucked up into doing what's good for your client, even when that isn't necessarily the right answer."

"I'm sure they respect your views. You should let them know what you think is right."

"I don't want to come across as the know-it-all kid with idealistic views. I'm just learning, you know."

The waitress came by to clear the table as Annie shuffled through her purse for her car keys.

"By the way, Lee, put July 23rd on your calendar. Mama and Daddy are going to have a big party for Tommy's birthday. Two weeks from now."

"The 23rd. I'm going to have to be away that weekend. That's one of the things I wanted to talk to you about today. A close friend of mine from law school, Jason Levine, is having some emotional problems. A group of our friends is getting together in Carmel that weekend. I wasn't planning to go.

Can't really afford it. But Jason asked me to come, and I feel an obligation to him. I've already discussed it with Hank and he's okay for me to go. I'll just be gone three days, but I'll have to miss Tommy's party."

"Oh, he'll understand. Sounds like it's important to go."

"I don't want to be away from you right now. For a million reasons the timing is all wrong. But Jason called me—I think he's really having serious problems—and I feel like I need to be there.

chapter twenty-five

At the end of a muggy morning run, Lee turned into Etta Jones' yard and jogged over to the small porch at the entrance to her cottage where she was sweeping up.

"You're up and about early today."

"Well, Mr. Lee. How you doin' this morning?"

"It's too humid for running in this God-forsaken town," he said.

She laughed and pushed one of the porch chairs in his direction.

"Come sit with me just a minute and tell me how you are."

"I'm doing just fine. Busy. And I've got to travel out to California next week to see some friends, so I'm under the gun to get my work done before I go."

"How's that sister of yours doin'?"

"The same, I guess. Depressed, aimless, fighting with my mother."

"Honey, you got to lift up that girl. That's what family is for. She need to know you going to be there for her."

"I'm trying. But I'm not so good at it. I'm not used to getting in the middle of someone else's business, even if she is my sister. Anyway, as her older brother, I'm afraid I may be hurting rather than helping the situation."

"You may or may not be, honey. But Jesus has saved many a young soul on the path to heartache. You can't feel angry or alone if you've been washed in the blood of the lamb."

"I don't know what I'm going to do without you when I go back to California in the fall. I've gotten used to a little homespun religion every time I go for a run."

Etta chuckled. "I'm gonna miss you too. My children and grandchildren all live out in the country now. Closer to the farm where Mama come from, near Newton. It's a nice community out there, and it's better for the children. Oh, they get into town and come by to see me every week, but it's not the same as having them nearby."

"Why haven't you moved out there, closer to your family?"

"Guess I'm too independent and ornery by now. I'm used to taking care of myself. And I've been in this little house a long time. I was born here."

"I met your grandson that time he came by when we were having tea."

"Oh, yes, that's Calvin. Got four of my great-grandchildren and there's twelve more. And all of Lovey's brood that still lives around here. Course Ruby lost the one boy. Out there in the river. She hasn't gotten over it neither."

"You showed me a picture of your family. Your sister was quite a bit younger, wasn't she? Younger than you and your brother?"

"Oh, yes. Much younger. She was still just a kid when Axel died."

"You said he fought in World War II. So did my grandfather. It's sad that he survived that awful war and died after coming home. Grandfather Dawkins was shot in the leg over there and was lucky to survive. He had a limp for the rest of his life."

"It was scary, sending your loved ones way across the ocean to that war. But Axel, he wanted to get out of this town *so* bad."

Lee needed to get cleaned up for work, but he had grown fond of his elderly neighbor, the way she listened, and her own stories.

"Grandfather Dawkins had started his law practice here in Riverton during the Depression years," Lee told her. "He used to tell me stories about that time. The world was a different place then. Life was a lot simpler."

"Well, maybe simpler for your family. Not so simple for mine."

"Were you old enough to remember the Depression?"

"Oh goodness yes. Those was *hard* times. Didn't have two pennies to rub together."

It didn't take much to get Etta talking about the old days and about the brother she had loved so much.

By the time Hitler was consolidating his grip on Germany and starting to march across Europe, Etta and her twin brother were out of school and earning a little money doing odd jobs around the neighborhood. The country had settled into a deep economic depression, and there weren't even jobs for white people, so time hung heavy on the hands of young people in the poor black neighborhoods of Riverton. Etta had responsibility for taking care of her little sister Lovey while her mama cleaned house for a couple of white ladies across town. But there was not much for Axel to do.

The twins had worked hard in school, thanks to their mama's discipline and encouragement, and they had been among Dunbar High's best students. The school, drafty in winter and steamy in summer, had been built by the neighborhood back in 1910. The textbooks were passed along from the white high school on the other side of town whenever they got new books. But the Depression had cut into the white schools' funding too, so the textbooks at Dunbar were falling apart, and there were too few of them at that.

Axel was good at sports and had lots of friends. His father had left home when Axel was just six, and the boy took on the mantle as "man of the house," a job he felt perfectly capable of doing. The church was their authority figure, disciplinarian and patriarchal head of the family, as it was for so many of the families in that neighborhood. That church and the preachers who led it filled the shoes of many a wandering father. Within the congregation, there was accountability, enabling mothers to raise their children without the isolation that would later plague single mothers in the big cities. Axel, Etta and Lovey might be able to get away with falling behind on their chores or even their homework, but they *would* be in church three times a week, healthy or sick, rain or shine.

When Axel reached his teens, he began to push back against his mother's regimen. Although he and his friends stuck to their own neighborhood most of the time, they had begun to venture farther afield as they grew older, sometimes crossing the tracks to explore downtown Riverton.

One evening when he was sixteen, Axel and two of his friends from the football team hiked several miles across town, enjoying the first warm spring evening, laughing and horsing around as they went.

"LaRon, I see you watchin' that saucy ass Meribell in English every time she walk to the board," cracked Axel.

They began to evaluate the anatomy of all the most appealing girls in their class at Dunbar, each description leading to peals of half-embarrassed, half-delighted laughter.

Henry Clay was a light-skinned Negro with fine European features, a natural-born comedian who could lay down hysterical one-liners with a straight face, causing Axel and LaRon to laugh so hard there were tears streaming down their faces. The chatter got sillier and sillier as each boy's laughter infected the others.

That probably accounted for their failure to see the two cars with white boys sitting on fenders and leaning against the brick walls in the alley behind Max's Soda Shop.

"Hey, nigger, that better not be a white girl you talkin' about."

The flat nasal voice was high pitched and shrill. A square-faced teen with a short reddish-blond crew cut and pimply face stepped forward from the alley as he spoke.

The boys hadn't been watching where they were going and were nearly even with the alley by the time the taunting voice stopped them in their tracks. The ensuing melee broke out so fast that none of the boys could later recount exactly how it happened.

The white teens had come at them furiously, without forethought or warning. Enraged at the violation of their territory and driven by a tribal instinct to destroy the alien invader, they hurled racial epithets, profanity and fists, chasing the boys down alleyways and into corners. The dark night was punctuated with the clatter of running feet and the pounding of fist against flesh.

When the sirens finally came, Axel, Henry and LaRon were thrown into separate squad cars, each boy too terrified to feel physical pain, just a dull throbbing from head to toe, a warm wet metallic taste and a terrible shaking from somewhere deep inside.

It was not so much the attack itself that changed the way the boys saw the world as the long night in jail and the racist taunts and threats from the cops, no less strident or bitter than those of the white boys.

Etta would never forget that night, Mama's worry turning into fear, too scared to go looking. Etta stayed home with Lovey, and Mama went over to the church to ask the deacon what to do. People searched for the boys around the neighborhood, and some even ventured into the white parts of Riverton. But nobody was brave enough to go to the police station.

Etta fell asleep on the couch while Mama was still out and didn't hear her come in.

"Etta, baby, come on to bed now."

"Is Axel home?"

Tanette sank into the couch next to her sleepy daughter and put her head into her hands.

"No. He was with Henry and LaRon. None of them come home."

Etta couldn't remember her mother ever crying before, even back when Daddy left. It scared Etta.

She was already up the next morning when Mrs. Clay knocked on the door.

"They got the boys down to the police station. Says they was causin' trouble with some white boys. We got to get some money to get them out. I'm goin' over to Aunt Maude's but then we need to go down to the church and talk to Brother Marvin."

Etta would never forget the way Axel looked when he walked in the door with Mama that afternoon. Seemed like he had shrunk six inches. The swollen face and red gashes made him look horrible, nothing at all like Axel, and the slow way he walked, limping and stumbling along. It was like the brother she knew had disappeared and some evil spirit had been left in his place, ugly and small and scared.

What she remembered most was Mama coming at him again and again, not holding him and loving on him like she usually did. "Why in God's name would you mess with white boys? What was you thinkin' of? Don't you never, *never* mess with white boys. You don't look at them. You don't talk back to them. Not *ever.*"

And Axel's pitiful rejoinder. "Mama, I didn't. I didn't say nothin' to them. We was jus' foolin' around. Walkin' down the street and cuttin' up and laughin'. Didn't bother no one."

Mama's shaking voice had a sharp, mean edge to it that Etta had never before heard. Even though she was trembling from head to toe and her voice lost its pitch and was quivering, it was still mean. "Don't you *never* laugh in front of white boys. They hate that more than anything. You don't look at them. You looks down. And you don't never, *never* laugh around them."

Axel wouldn't ever tell Etta anything about what happened. It was like it was a boy thing—black boys, white boys—and she wouldn't get it. In fact, he quit talking to her about everything after that. He quit talking to Mama too.

chapter twenty-six

Lee had just slipped on his jacket and double-checked the knot in his tie when his phone began to ring.

"Hey, Zoe. You survived! Tell me what I've got to look forward to."

"God, what an ordeal. We had to take the exam down in San Jose in this huge exhibition hall with two hundred other people. Drove down there the day before, just to time ourselves, figure out parking and all that. On the first morning of the exam, Jeff insisted we still get up an hour early to build in time for a flat tire. About ten minutes into the first essay question, everybody started typing like crazy. Out of the corner of my eye, I could see the guy next to me just sitting there, hadn't even started. I swear to God, he sat there all morning, glassy-eyed, staring into space. Freaked me out. I started to wonder if he had a gun. The guy never came back after lunch."

"Do you feel like you did okay?" he asked.

"Who knows? It's over."

"At least you and Michelle and Jeff had each other. I'll be the only person from Stanford taking the February exam."

"Wish I could think of something positive to tell you about taking the bar exam, but nothing comes to mind. So what's up with your case?"

"I'll tell you about it when I get there. We've been up to our eyeballs the last few days, trying to get the plaintiffs to settle, which is the reasonable thing for them to do. But reasonable isn't in their vocabulary, so we're assuming this thing will go to trial."

"Well, just wanted to check on your arrival time," Zoe said. "Were you able to change the flight and come into San Jose?"

"No, I'm still on the original one. SFO, noon tomorrow. Don't bother to come into the airport. Just pick me up on the upper level. I'm not checking bags."

"Okay, we'll head straight down to Carmel, unless you need to stop in Palo Alto for any reason."

"Not unless we're picking up Jason."

"He'll already be down in Carmel Valley. You and I will be the last to arrive. It's going to be an awesome weekend. So beautiful on the Monterey Peninsula. And I've missed you so much."

Lee would have preferred to rent a car and drive down 101 by himself. His relationship with Zoe, with all that had changed during the summer, was not on his agenda for the trip. The weekend was about Jason. But Lee couldn't have broken it off with Zoe by phone. That wouldn't have been fair to her. They would have a chance to talk during the two-hour car trip, but Lee didn't want their personal relationship to become the focus of the weekend and overshadow their concern about Jason, which was the reason Lee had come.

He hung up the phone, worried about how he'd manage this visit, the relationship with Annie being so new and so important to him. He would focus on Jason and keep that at the center of the weekend.

Jason had been one of Lee's closest friends from first-year law school. Lee had not been sure about Stanford at first. He had arrived well before fall classes started and was put off by the chilly fog and the reserved culture of Northern California. He had scanned the administration bulletin board for housing ideas when he spotted Jason's notice for a male to share his apartment.

They bonded right away. Jason was outgoing, funny, adventuresome. Having grown up in the Sonoma farmlands north of San Francisco, he knew the Bay Area well and loved getting up to the city and exploring offbeat music and poetry.

Lee had watched Jason's enthusiasm broken by the tedium of law school, the competition for grades and jobs at the best firms, the randomness of fair outcomes in the courts, and all the rest. Early on, it was clear that the law was not where Jason should be, but he stayed the course and forced himself to endure three years of reading case law. By the end, he had lost his confidence and any sense of what lay ahead. But Lee hadn't seen Jason's ambivalence about school as a precursor to emotional problems. It was hard to take seriously Zoe's alarm about Jason's condition. At least Lee would have a chance to see for himself.

Glancing at the wall clock, Lee gathered the papers he had been working on and dropped them into his briefcase.

This is not a good age for the poets among us, he thought, considering Jason's dilemma. Perhaps the most materialistic era in the history of the world. With the stock market soaring, there was money to be made everywhere. All you had to do was grab the golden ring. So much for the idealistic notion that the purpose of education was to make your life richer or to become a better citizen.

Lee grabbed his jacket and headed for the door. The Washington case was in full pre-trial mode, and he wanted to make sure his files were organized before leaving for the long weekend.

There was a knock on his bedroom door and Frances called in to him.

"Good morning, glory! Do you have time for breakfast with me?"

"Just a quick bite, Mama. I've got to get to the office. I want to leave things in reasonable order in case Hank or Vernon needs to access my files over the weekend."

Bright morning sunlight warmed the breakfast room as mother and son chatted over eggs and bacon.

"Honey, I'm sorry that so much of your time at home has been spoiled by our problems here. You didn't need this. I guess I'm at one of those transition places in my life and not doing so well with it. I've never known what to do with M.J., how to help her. She thinks I don't love her, but you know nothing could be further from the truth. I want so much to protect her, but everything I say feels like a criticism. Maybe I dropped the ball somewhere along the way with her. But honestly, all I've ever wanted was her happiness."

chapter twenty-seven

The Washington case team was already in the conference room when Lee arrived. He pushed open the glass door and stuck his head in. "Sorry to be late. Let me get my files and I'll be right in."

Hank was reviewing the list of cases that would be used in court to support the firm's defense of the City of Riverton. He turned to Lee for the statutory law he would weave into his opening and closing arguments. It was frustrating to Lee that Hank never asked his opinion on the theory of their case, just the mechanics. He had tried on several occasions, always unsuccessfully, to convince Hank and Vernon that their theory of foul play as a defense to the city's liability in the Washington death was not supported by the evidence.

"The interjection of uncertainty about cause of the death is important to defeat any claim of gross negligence or intentionality that might negate the sovereign immunity defense," was all Hank would say.

Lee had spent most of the prior afternoon marking up jury instructions, a mechanical task but one that could work to his client's advantage by limiting the matters left open to the jury. Also, if the jury wound up rendering a verdict that exceeded the authority of the judge's instructions, it was easy grounds for reversal on appeal.

He was meeting Annie for lunch. He wouldn't see her again until after the California trip and he knew she was wondering what the trip would do to their relationship. She hadn't asked whether he planned to say anything to Zoe. And Lee was too busy to think about it.

This close to trial Lee's focus had to be on getting the data organized in a way that it would be readily available to Hank during examination of witnesses. Lee's job was to support the senior attorneys.

Vernon's notes continued to trouble Lee. They made reference to a sign and to the guy who was head of the Parks and Recreation Department, but Lee didn't have time to follow up before his trip. He had stayed in the office late the entire week before to make sure he left Townsend's litigation team with solid records covering the part of the trial prep that was his responsibility.

Lunch was likely to be all too short and he dashed out the door to meet Annie. She was already waiting for him at a table, her smile warming the room.

Kissing her on the cheek, he slipped into the chair across from her.

"I can tell this case is turning out to be more intense than you expected. Funny. I never thought of you as someone who got stressed out."

"I don't think I've changed. But I see the layers of moral complexity in a way I couldn't as a younger person. I don't like the way this case is being handled. I understand the need to fight for what's the best outcome for your client. That's how the adversarial system works. Two capable attorneys seeing the world entirely through their own client's perspective, using every skill, every wile to win. Somehow or other, the court system is supposed to take those two, one-sided, self-interested views of the world and come up with a just result."

"I guess it works most of the time."

"I'm not so sure about that. In the first place, the representation is never equal. So a big advantage goes to the client with the best lawyers and with the most money. The other thing that's bothering me right now is that it circumvents the kind of rational thinking and ethical analysis we learned in school. You have to be passionate about getting the best deal for your client. You think about the other side's arguments of course. You have to do that to be ready for the trial. But it's more like a football game than the pursuit of justice.

"I don't think I'd be a very good lawyer."

He looked at her with amusement. "Well, you'd be a pain in the ass to some of the people calling the shots, that's for sure."

She laughed and dropped her eyes.

"The thing is, Annie, I don't care enough about the people involved here to really stick my neck out. I think if I were a permanent associate in the firm, I would fight Hank on his approach to some of this. But, as it is, I'm a short-timer. All I can do is to create animosity if I push Hank and Vernon to abandon their scorched-earth approach. They aren't going to do this my way no matter what I say."

"You may not care about these people, but I do. Remember, Dewaine Washington was my student. A great kid. And the mother is trying. She's part of that Jones-Mathis clan that lives on the outskirts of town near Newton. You know, the matriarch is that friend of yours down the street, your shaman."

"Miss Etta?"

"Yes, Etta Jones. She would have been Dewaine's…I don't know, maybe great-aunt."

"I've met some of her family coming and going at the house. She's a wise lady, by the way. M.J. thinks she's nuts, but that's not at all true. Anyway, much as I love my elderly neighbor, I'm not going to the mat during a summer job to try to change the minds of lawyers who have been doing this kind of thing for forty years. What do I know? Anyway, I'm out of there in a month and a half."

"All the more reason to speak your mind. Who cares what they think? You've already got a job in San Francisco."

"Speaking of San Francisco, my flights are firmed up."

Annie's eyes looked straight into his soul and for a minute Lee felt utterly exposed.

"I don't want to go. It's disruptive in terms of the case, not to mention my state of mind more generally." He reached across the table and squeezed her hand. "I feel like I've just found you again."

"I don't want you to go," she said with an effort at a resigned smile.

The moment was interrupted by the waiter's appearance. Just as he started the recitation of the day's specials, Lee and Annie looked up to see Scooter Nash with a young woman being escorted to a table behind them.

"I guess your friend has moved on. Managed to mess that up for you, didn't I?" He gave her a sheepish grin, realizing how perfectly pleased with himself he felt.

"Oh, it wasn't just about you," she said. "I feel bad about how it happened is all. I don't like to treat people that way."

Lee wondered if her last statement was a reference to his own more equivocal moral principles. "Do you want to leave?" he asked her.

"No, of course not," she said. "Anyway, you're the one who's leaving."

"Annie, I'm just going back for a weekend."

"Back to your real life. To your friends who will be part of your new life in San Francisco in the fall. It won't be the same when you get back."

"Of course it'll be the same." Lee knew she was talking about Zoe. "There's a friend in trouble who needs me. Surely you wouldn't want me to refuse to be there for him."

Annie didn't answer. Because she *did* want him to refuse to be there. She hated those people, that place. They would own him soon enough. She hadn't asked him about Zoe, whether he had told Zoe about them. She wouldn't ask.

"Annie, I love you, do you know that? I'm like a fifteen-year-old, can't sleep at night, think about your beautiful face in the middle of depositions, crazy in love with you. Can we go to your place right now and spend the rest of the day in bed? I'll convince you that you don't need to worry about one weekend in California."

She laughed at Lee's charming way of reducing all the complexities of the world to what felt good right now. "No, you've got an early flight. And lots to do before you go. I'm taking Tommy out to my aunt's for dinner and TV. But I'll miss you."

When she woke the next morning, her heart was heavy.

He would be gone by now.

God, if I could hold him, I would. I'd make him give up his ambitions and his dreams. Just to see him every day. Hear the sound of the door opening when he comes home from work. Raise his children. He's so damned controlled. I know he loves me but that won't be enough to hold him. His heart will never affect his decisions. And it isn't just about Tommy and my responsibility to take care of him here in Riverton. I know that. Lee wants a pedigree. Damn that Frances Addison. Somewhere in his core, he carries her values. But my love would change that if we had the time. God, grant me the serenity…If it is meant to be, he will come back to me.

chapter twenty-eight

Back in the Dallas airport, Lee could scarcely believe it had been only six weeks since he had passed through on his way home. A lifetime ago.

Thank God, he thought to himself, no Christian proselytizing this time. The accent no longer grated on his nerves. Maybe he'd even miss that feeling of acceptance in the tone of voice, the slight uplift at the end of a sentence that told you the other person wasn't completely sure about what they had just said. In the Bay Area, everybody was certain they were right about everything. No question marks at the ends of sentences there. When he got off the plane in San Francisco, he would be surrounded by a sea of strangers speaking in foreign accents and avoiding eye contact. Anonymous. Everybody chasing the almighty buck.

He guessed it was a good thing he was taking a break from Riverton. There was something about the South that tugged at you. You could stick up your nose at the prejudice, and the obsession with religion, and the idiotic need to make nice with everybody who walked by. But it grabbed you just the same.

Once the 727 had passed over the craggy Sierra fortress that isolates California from the rest of the country, Lee took a deep breath and began to look forward instead of back. He knew that the two parts of his life didn't line up in the right way. But he was happily anticipating the clear, crisp air of the West, hoping that his direction in life would follow suit.

As much as his left brain directed him westward toward the future, something much more intuitive in the lower registers of his mind's circuitry pulled his heart back home. Although he was excited to be meeting up with his school friends, the cabin in the airliner felt cold and sterile, and he was already homesick for the sounds and smells of the soft, warm familiarity of Arkansas.

His disorientation wasn't so much about the familiar cocoon of home and kin as it was about being in love, maybe for the first time in his life. As a teen, he had been crazy about Annie, but it had been a self-centered, lust-driven need to possess her. Still lust-driven, he guessed, but quieter and deeper, something *sacred* about it. God, that was a word she would use. Every time his thoughts drifted to what it meant for the future, he would reject the urge to think about it, not wanting the rational engine that had always charted his path to interfere with something finer.

But even as his heart yearned back to home, Half Dome rose majestically outside his window, and he was awestruck, as he had been on his first trip to Northern California, by the power of this land of mountains and deserts. People had struggled to get here from insect-ravaged farms on the prairie and the dry dust of Oklahoma and Arkansas, leaving everything behind except the desperate hope of finding gold or arable land, the rawness of the West only modestly tempered by the Spanish missionaries from Mexico who had faced down hostile natives to civilize this beautiful promised land.

The plane banked right to circle into Santa Clara Valley and up toward the bay. Lee watched the squat single-story buildings, home to myriad technology startups, emerge amid the brown hills of mid-summer, hills that had still borne the green cloak left by winter rains when he left just six weeks earlier. He had never quite bought into the California myth of golden hills, these seasonal grasses that browned up a month after the last spring rain. They looked like weeds to Lee, more brown than golden. But the contrast with the Ozarks was striking, and his heart leapt in anticipation of California's unique beauty and the way a hot, dry summer afternoon would succumb to the chill of evening fog.

As he slipped into the passenger seat beside Zoe, Lee was relieved that Jeff and Michelle were in the backseat, riding down to the Monterey Peninsula with them. He and Zoe exchanged a warm hug, then he leaned over the seat to shake hands with Jeff and Michelle. Their small section had bonded so tightly during that intense first year that their study group had become lifelong friends. As a clan, they had faced the terror of Socratic argument from Stanford's best faculty, overprepared for the first exams, practiced their moot-court arguments, fallen in and out of love with each other, dressed for their first job interviews and studied for the bar. Lee had good friends at home and in college, but nowhere else had he bonded with a group of people so much like himself.

"Tell me about the bar," Lee asked as he turned to greet his friends. "Was it a nightmare?"

Michelle groaned.

Michelle Chen had made close friends with Zoe from the first week of class three years ago and they had run the Dish together twice a week throughout law school, braving the chill of early morning fog, faithfully setting aside for one hour the endless grind of cases, briefs and review required to be ready for questions in class and exams. Where Zoe was quick, assertive, funny and opinionated, Michelle had spent her entire life in fear of making a mistake and, as a result, rarely did so.

Jeff Wong had not been in their small section but was a friend of Jason's from undergraduate days at Princeton and had been included in the small circle of friends who studied together, played together and ultimately lived together in a rented house in Palo Alto's College Terrace.

Jeff and Michelle had kept their romantic relationship confidential until the middle of the third year. Zoe had been increasingly absent from the suite she shared with Michelle, often choosing to stay the night in Lee's single room at the end of a one-on-one late-night debate. All four of them felt empathy for Jason, left as odd man out, especially because of the poorly disguised passion he had held for Zoe since orientation.

"It's over, man, that's all I can say," Jeff said. "We're leaving on Thursday for two weeks in Paris."

"That's tough, Jeff. As I head back to Arkansas. The temperature has been above 100 most of the summer since I've been home, and it's always humid. You sweat through your shirt by the time you walk ten yards from your air-conditioned car to a freezing cold building."

"No amount of hot, humid weather can match the pure torture of the bar," Jeff replied. "Just wait, my friend."

"After the exam," Michelle said, "we dropped Zoe at the house. Jeff said he wanted to show me something. He parked on the Oval, took my hand and led me into the chapel. I thought he had gotten religion or something from anxiety over the bar. Then he gave me this."

Michelle extended her left hand over the front seat, the diamond flashing in the afternoon sun, the smiles from the backseat equally brilliant.

"Oh, man, congratulations, you two. That's wonderful news."

Lee was glad Zoe was driving. He didn't want to look her in the eye just then. Having heard the news the week before, Zoe acknowledged the announcement with a crinkle at the corner of her eyes and a slight smile.

The conversation turned to the bar, new jobs, Silicon Valley startups and gossip about classmates. The fact that she was driving didn't isolate Zoe from the center of the conversation, and Lee was swept off his feet, as he had been so many times before, by her intelligence and wit, by the depth of her understanding of ideas. His attraction to her had been grounded in a deep respect. He felt again the power of her mind, awed by her commitment to make the world a better place.

As the Honda slipped past the golden Peninsula hills and down through San Jose, the impact of summer heat on the landscape became more visible. The remaining orchards in the valley required elaborate hydration systems, and the untilled landscape was dusty and dry. As they followed the twists and turns from Gilroy toward the coast, the landscape changed again. Long before the Pacific came into view, the reds, oranges and pinks of ice plant and multihued succulents clinging to the dunes lent the air a pastel tint.

The cypress stands of the Monterey Peninsula could have been conjured up in the mind of an artist to frame the reds and greens sprouting from the dunes against the black rocks and the blue Pacific.

After skirting the ocean along the peninsula, they turned inland toward Carmel Valley, where Michelle's brother Tony had built an 8,000-square-foot mansion for his family, based on proceeds from Ionica's IPO.

Tony and Michelle Chen had been raised like so many children of Asian immigrant families, families that had been on the move since the Communist revolution ran them off mainland China onto Taiwan. Opportunity drove them east to California in order to give the children a better life. They had lived modestly in Cupertino, both parents working long hours at chip-manufacturing companies, where technical expertise was needed, but a solid grasp of the English language was not, saving every penny for the kids' education.

Becoming not just rich but very rich as he jumped from one high-tech startup to the next, Tony had bought his parents a lovely home in Los Gatos and married a beautiful Southern Californian.

Zoe's Honda turned left into a gated community of multi-acre lots, all set far enough apart to see little other habitation, the vistas sheltered by the rolling hills that extended toward Pebble Beach, 17-Mile Drive and the village of Carmel. Here the hills really were golden, or at least a light blond hay tone that felt fresh and sunny, just far enough off the beach to elude the fog line.

As they ascended the driveway, Megan was in the front yard and hurried over to greet them. "The lawyer bus has arrived!" She hugged Michelle and offered a friendly wave to her compatriots. "Tony is in town for a meeting, but he'll be back soon. Wish we had more time with you guys, but we're almost packed to head out of here. Let me help you get your bags inside and show you around."

The house was strikingly modern, built into the hills to blend seamlessly with the native environment. From every room large plate glass windows looked out over the hills. The house was filled with art and artifacts crafted in Native American patterns that Megan had gathered on trips to Santa Fe and Los Angeles.

"Oh, by the way," Megan said, "your friend Jason called to say he had problems with a flight delay and wouldn't get in until tomorrow morning."

chapter twenty-nine

"God, I'm bummed that Jason isn't getting in tonight. We have such a short time together as it is." Zoe threw her shoulder bag onto the sofa and approached the window to take in the spectacular view. "This place is amazing."

Lee was kicking himself for not foreseeing the awkward inevitability of room assignments. Based on input from Michelle, Megan had assumed that Zoe and Lee would share a bedroom, and he could hardly have broken the news of his new relationship in front of everybody. So now here they were, roomies, while he faced the unwinnable choice of making a public breakup with Zoe the focus of a weekend meant for Jason, or staying put in what would plainly be a betrayal of two women he adored.

The bedroom was twice the size of Lee's Palo Alto apartment, with a rock-lined walk-in shower and spa open to the hills. Sliding glass doors provided access to a huge side patio with fountain art and the sound of water trickling through the Zen-like rock formations. He was keenly aware of the sounds—water and birds and the occasional sea breeze filtering through live oaks. They walked out onto the patio and breathed deeply. Fragrances of rosemary, eucalyptus and rose petals danced in the breeze. Although it was mid-afternoon, the warmest part of the day, the air felt light and dry.

"Let's go out and explore while we can," Zoe suggested. "Why don't we follow the trailhead behind the shed?"

They hadn't touched, except for the cursory greeting in the car. Typical of Zoe, she seemed to intuit that the time wasn't right. In addition to all else, they were close friends, and both of them were looking forward to talking about ideas, doing what they could to support Jason, being in the moment in one of the world's most beautiful places.

Michelle and Jeff joined them on the outing and, after a full afternoon hiking the hills and watching the sunset from the Carmel Beach, they returned to the house where Megan had carefully set aside dinner ingredients for them to prepare. They had cooked many meals together, though never in a kitchen so magnificent, and they shared duties comfortably, sipping a light Viognier and exchanging stories about the summer and expectations for the fall in San Francisco.

Lee's internal clock was still on Central Daylight Time, so he begged off at midnight, leaving the others deep in conversation.

The next morning Jason greeted his classmates with warm handshakes and hugs all around. He had a Midwestern build, not heavy but solid, dark blond curls, a ruddy complexion and a ready smile. "How you surviving Arkansas, man?"

"Is this place amazing or what?" Jeff chimed in.

"How was the bar exam?" Jason asked.

The affection was heartfelt and mutual. Jason's arrival instantly changed the dynamic of the group. No longer two couples, they were just friends again, with the easy rapport that makes conversation light and meaningful without having to say much.

After giving Jason the grand tour of the Carmel Valley house, they settled in on the patio around the burning fire pit, opened some ales from a local brewery and pushed back, soaking up the sun and the cool breeze that blew off the Pacific and crept up into Carmel Valley.

Zoe pulled Jason onto the rattan sofa beside her. "I am so glad you're here. I've been seriously worried about you." She ruffled his hair and leaned onto his shoulder. "Tell me you're okay."

No one but Zoe could have broached the awkward subject of Jason's emotional problems, but she was not one to avoid delicate issues.

He smiled and shrugged. "Don't know. Guess so. It's been a kind of weird time. The parents kind of freaked out, I think. I'm staying at this hospital for another month or so. Out on weekend leave."

Everybody seemed to be waiting in case he wanted to say more.

"Man, don't feel like you have to talk about this if you don't want to," Jeff said finally.

"Oh, I can talk about it. They seem to think I'm a bit paranoid. Wanting to give me some serious drugs. But I need to finish up in the fall, and once you're taking those psychotropic drugs, you get real zombie-like. Better to fight off the demons for now."

They dressed for the evening, looking forward to dinner at one of Monterey Peninsula's best restaurants, with jazz into the evening. By the time they rolled back into the Carmel Valley estate, lightly buzzed from the drinks and music, it was well after 1:00 in the morning. Lee and Zoe passed through their room and out onto the gently lit patio, listening to the rustle of the breeze and the sounds of wildlife foraging in the hills. His warmth encased her against the chill of the evening, and they didn't speak further before falling into bed with a hunger for each other that had been building all day.

chapter thirty

Lee woke with a sinking feeling of dishonesty and regret. Zoe was still asleep, and he watched her with a mix of curiosity and guilt. What in God's name did he want? He shouldn't have slept with her. How can he love them both?

Zoe opened one eye and reached for him sleepily.

"Zoe, wait."

His head hurt and his mouth was dry. And he really didn't want to have this conversation. But he said, "We've got to talk."

She watched him with a gimlet eye as he stumbled through the explanation—the summer romance, the disorientation of being at home again, too much to drink last night. He still loved her, but there was someone else. His mumblings and justifications became more disjointed as he tried to parse some logic from his dilemma.

"You son of a bitch." She threw a pillow at him, then stomped out of the bedroom without even hunting for her robe, leaving him in abject silence.

When he finally emerged from the bedroom, Jeff and Michelle were having coffee in the kitchen. They acknowledged his entrance, studying him with dismay.

"Zoe and Jason are out walking," Jeff said. "Do you want to go into town for a pastry?"

"I need coffee," Lee mumbled, reaching for a cup.

By the time they got back from Carmel, Zoe's things had been cleared from his room. The rest of the weekend was tense, Zoe non-communicative and glued to Jason.

Lee was on his way down the driveway to dump a load of bottles in the recycling bin when Jason came up behind him. "You're an asshole, Addison," he said, swinging around in front of Lee. "She's too good for you."

"Man, you don't know anything about what's going on. Don't get in the middle of this," Lee muttered, dodging past him toward the bottom of the hill.

"Fuck you," Jason called after him.

With flights booked out of SFO early on Monday, they had planned a quiet afternoon and evening around the house on Sunday. The Chens returned from their trip before noon. Tony was planning to grill fresh salmon for their last dinner, but no sooner had he walked in the door than he got a call about an emergency at the company. He offered a tour to anyone who wanted to go along for the ride to San Jose.

The group had planned to hike in Point Lobos, which under ordinary circumstances Lee wouldn't have missed. But he was happy for an excuse to avoid further conflict with Zoe and Jason, so he accepted the invitation.

Ionica had grown rapidly since going public, but to Lee's eye it was indistinguishable from the endless string of hardware and software companies strung out between Mountain View and San Jose. He was surprised to see so many cars in the parking lot on a Sunday afternoon.

"This is Silicon Valley, man," Tony laughed. "Nowhere else on the planet do people have so much opportunity to reap the rewards of innovation and hard work."

Inside Ionica, people were bustling about, typing frenetically into computers and sitting around tables in glass-encased conference rooms, just as if it had been a workday. Most of the desks were spread across a vast open space, with separate offices delineated by low dividers or no dividers at all, the space designed to encourage collaboration.

The people who worked in high tech were no longer surprised by a stock market that seemed to know only one direction—up. The Valley's preoccupation with semiconductor chips had given way to software, then software to the new darling of venture capitalism, something known as the worldwide web.

"The genius of Silicon Valley is the use of stock options to give employees a stake in the company. They don't mind being here on weekends if it increases their chance to make some money when the company succeeds."

It was a young employee base, multi-ethnic, dressed in jeans and t-shirts and seriously engaged in their work. Lee expected that his law practice would regularly take him to companies like this. It was heady work, with tens of millions of dollars at stake and access to the Bay Area's smartest and most successful business leaders.

By the time Lee and Tony got back to Carmel, the sun was hanging low over the Pacific, the wine was open beside the outdoor fire pit and the salmon was ready to put on the grill.

Zoe was holding court with her feet up by the crackling fire, sipping a Pinot Grigio, with Jason, Jeff and Michelle enjoying her stories of court intrigue. Tony and Lee joined the circle. Jason didn't acknowledge Lee's presence in any direct way, but he did seem his old self—upbeat, funny and hanging on Zoe's every word.

Dinner was served on the patio overlooking the rolling, oak-studded valleys that descend gently toward the coast. Carmel itself would be buzzing by now, the air scented with delicious aromas of free-range meats, fresh fish and local produce. From dozens of small, chic restaurants crowded with well-heeled foodies, the fragrance of dishes prepared by elite chefs would be drifting all the way down to the beach where they would mingle with scents of seaweed and salt amid the stately Cypress trees twisted into strange and beautiful contortions by the powerful winds that blew off the Pacific.

The vista from the Chens' slate deck drew the eye down to the Cypress and Monterey Pine groves that led out past Pebble Beach to 17 Mile Drive, where a bagpiper's lamentations from the terraces of Spanish Bay was lifted on banks of fog along the shore.

As the young lawyers soaked up the views and enjoyed Tony and Megan's grilled salmon with Super Tuscan wines, everybody relaxed, the tensions of the weekend set aside.

After dinner Zoe and Michelle hiked up to the ridge. Jeff had talked his way into a tour of Tony's wine cellar, interested in his latest purchases from Sonoma.

Jason picked up a couple of Tony's Cuban cigars from the silver container open on the outdoor bar and brought them back to the fire pit where Lee was still sitting with his feet up, mesmerized by the movement of the flames in the breeze. He handed a cigar to Lee and offered a light from the end of a balsa stick he pulled from the edge of the open fire.

Neither of them spoke for a few minutes. The heavy musk-sweet odor of the tobacco filled the air and left both of them with a feeling of rich light-headedness.

"I'm sorry, man," Jason began. "It wasn't my place to get in the middle of your thing with Zoe."

The two were deep in conversation when their friends returned. The others went into the living room for dessert and music, but Lee and Jason stayed out on the deck well after the evening chill had set in.

Jason didn't blame his emotional crisis on parents or school or circumstances of life. Nor did he quite acknowledge that he was having problems he couldn't handle himself, problems that were getting worse rather than better. But he hadn't lost his sense of humor despite missteps that could cost him his career.

"They used to call it a nervous breakdown," he said. "I'm not nervous except when carloads of FBI agents start tailing me." He laughed to demonstrate that he still had sense enough to recognize bizarre behavior, even in himself.

"The shrinks keep trying to delve into my childhood to find the roots of my nonexistent impulse control. But I'll tell you, when you're in a psych ward, everything becomes so weird that you really do feel like there's a conspiracy."

They had a candid discussion about Zoe and their common respect and affection for her. Lee didn't try to excuse or defend his behavior, and neither did he choose to pick up on Jason's curiosity about Annie.

Zoe and Lee kept their distance during the rest of the California visit. Zoe drove Lee, Jeff and Michelle to the airport the next morning, and he was never able to get her alone to explain or apologize.

chapter thirty-one

Back in Riverton at the Townsend office by late Monday afternoon, Lee picked through the documents he had set aside for the week's depositions.

He shouldn't have gone to California. He should have told Zoe ahead of time. He sure the hell shouldn't have slept with her.

Jason's interference had not helped. It was out of character for Zoe to let her own issues get in the way of a plan to help somebody else. But she was hanging onto Jason just as surely as he was hanging on her. Christ, that can't help him, Lee thought.

The weekend had made one thing clear. He loved being back in California. No second-guessing that choice, whatever happened with Zoe. The visit to Tony Chen's company had confirmed what he already knew about working in Silicon Valley.

It was a fabulous new age, and he would be in the middle of it. The stock market was flying high—for good reason. The gifted young people running the high-tech companies that had lifted the Nasdaq into the stratosphere were spending their Sundays at work. Not on a golf course like his father. Not sitting in a pew like his grandfather. No, they were at work writing algorithms on a computer screen that would connect the world in a way nobody in the history of mankind had ever imagined.

He had assumed Zoe would be by his side in the new life he was starting in September. Well, maybe not. And that was okay. He would be working with plenty of smart, self-reliant women. The idea of being completely unattached next year was not without its appeal.

What Lee couldn't tolerate, however, was the loss of Zoe's respect. Her friendship was important to him. He picked up his phone and dialed her number. No answer.

"Zoe, it's me. I know you don't want to talk to me. But we have to. About Jason if nothing else. Please call me."

Vernon Minor leaned into Lee's office. "I need a half hour with you sometime before the depositions."

Lee shook himself, determined to stop reconstructing the weekend, and turned to the pretrial responsibilities on his plate. It was scary and it was exciting. "Let me pull together my notes. I'll be in your office in fifteen minutes," he said.

He wanted to read through the complaint again to make sure they were addressing each of the plaintiff's allegations. The Washington family was claiming that the City of Riverton had been grossly negligent in its maintenance and supervision of the Bend Recreational Area. They blamed Dewaine Washington's death on inadequate lifeguard coverage at a facility intended for swimming. In particular, they complained of the welcoming but dangerously positioned rope swing and the hazardous diving rock known to be a magnet for young people, but lacking appropriate warnings of its danger.

Again he wondered about the meaning of Vernon's notations regarding the sign, and scribbled a note to himself to make an appointment to see the Director of Parks and Recreation, R. A. Sampson. He didn't want to distract Hank or Vernon with what was probably a wild goose chase. And he couldn't alert Vernon to the fact that he had read his private notes. But he wanted to make sure he had done everything possible to tie down issues that might be raised by the opposing side during trial.

Lee reviewed the outline he had finished on the flight, as well as his notes on recent case law, then went into Vernon's office.

"Okay, Vernon," he said, his mind intent on what they would need to do to win the case, "let's talk about today's depos. I think we can structure the questioning so that the possibility of an attack by the gang of teenagers will feel like it was their own idea. They of course know we're going to push on the issue of the kids having that six-pack of beer. The witnesses will be prepared to talk about that. We should not make a big deal of it during the depos. If we can get them talking, maybe something will materialize that would be useful during trial."

The attorneys representing the Washington family were full of pomp and bravado, making it hard for their clients to follow the standard protocol of keeping answers short during depositions. It never felt good to a witness to respond with a simple yes or no answer, given the natural human inclination to explain and justify. That reluctance to look bad during private depositions opened the door beautifully to extract lengthy, rambling statements, often susceptible to excerpting to contradict testimony on the stand.

Quincy Brown approached the reception desk with a retinue of five colleagues and settled into the conference room with coffee and pastries. He was a big man, over six feet tall and portly, his mass of curly graying hair offsetting a round mulatto face patterned with expressive wrinkles. Quincy laughed easily, but he was equally quick to sense a slight, his manner turning imperious at any hint of racism or dismissiveness.

Lee had observed Quincy's approach when they had deposed the city's witnesses, and he had been underwhelmed. Admired for his rhetorical prowess but known to overreach in his claims and underperform on the follow-through, Quincy was nearing seventy and increasingly dependent on his younger associates for the attention to detail that he had lost.

Lee was particularly keyed up to get started on the day's depositions. Hank had petitioned the court, seeking approval from plaintiffs' counsel as well, to permit Lee Addison, in his role as law clerk not admitted to practice before the Arkansas bar, to play a larger role in pretrial discovery and in the trial itself than normally would have been permitted. Hank's letter to the judge recited Lee's stellar academic record, including Order of the

Coif at Stanford, as well as his roots in Riverton as Judge Corky Dawkins' grandson. The judge had agreed to his limited participation, and Quincy Brown, sensing an opportunity for advantage, was more than willing to let the inexperienced young attorney take depositions and question witnesses at trial.

Lee had slept fitfully all night, going over the facts of the case and trying out different ways to ask questions of the witnesses. They would be kids, scared to death probably and likely to say as little as possible. He would need to make them comfortable and bring them along slowly in a way that wasn't threatening.

Once the court reporter swore in the witnesses and the formal questioning began, Lee's self-confidence increased. He was a quick study, emulating Vernon's ingratiating style of friendly chatter with the younger Washington boy and his friends, flattery of the mother, and deference to opposing counsel.

Playing off the natural rivalries with the Mexican kids who were at the Bend that day, he elicited anti-immigrant statements that would play well in court. They didn't have to prove that Dewaine Washington was attacked. It was enough to plant a seed of doubt that could give a jury the excuse they wanted to find insufficient evidence of the city's negligence.

After the depositions, Lee worked through dinner and well into the evening to catch up on trial preparation that he hadn't attended to during the long weekend out of town.

It was after 9:00 when the phone rang. He hoped it would be Zoe.

"Hello. Oh hi, Sis."

"Are you ever coming home? I wanted to hear about your trip."

"Just trying to catch up. Are you home? I'll be there soon."

When he arrived, M.J.'s hair was still wet from a shower, and she looked young, scrubbed fresh and lovely.

"Let's load up on snacks and have a party out in the secret garden," he said.

They didn't need lights to follow the gravel path past the greenhouse to what they had always called the secret garden in the most remote part of the Addisons' backyard. The full moon sat just beyond the crook in the big pine, fat and golden in the summer sky, lighting all the hidden corners of the yard. The ivy had grown up and over the wooden trellis that Grandmother Dawkins had installed during the war, forming an impenetrable wall around the small brick patio where a bench and two matching chairs, once painted white but now rarely used and grimy, were positioned inside a circle of multicolored sweet-smelling roses. Long ago Roberta Dawkins had lovingly selected each plant, more for its aroma than the quality of its blossoms.

As children, they had spent many happy hours together creating worlds of imagination inside the rose garden, which easily took on the character of whatever castle or fort was required for the day's fantasy.

Lee juggled a couple of sodas and M.J. brought along a bowl of chips and guacamole. The night was pleasantly warm, the sweet scent of antique roses encircling them. M.J. jumped at the skittering of small animals disturbed from their normal rounds by the rare night visitors, and they both laughed.

Lee told her about the beauty of the Monterey Peninsula, the affluent lifestyle of the dot-com generation spawned by a soaring stock market and the limitless opportunities open to him and his friends launching careers in the midst of the high-tech boom.

"This house was about three times the size of ours, tucked into rolling hills of open space, everything new and modern and artsy. And these guys are maybe thirty-eight. They already have everything. You can sit outside, even in the middle of a July afternoon and enjoy a cool sea breeze, looking out over this amazing countryside as far as the eye can see.

"Michelle's brother took me with him to the company where he's CEO. Wildly successful. Everybody's young and hip and driven. The employees practically live there. Totally into their jobs."

What he didn't talk about, of course, was Zoe or Jason or his failure to deal with the conflicts in his personal life.

"Tony and his family took off for most of the weekend and left us in charge of their Carmel Valley estate, stocked with food and wine. Hot tubs overlooking the hills. Fountains and fire pits. Everything new and beautiful."

"Some day I'm going to move to California too," she said quietly.

"There were trails that ran through the hills," he continued, "weaving through stands of oak and cypress. Wildlife all over the place. And though Carmel is not Silicon Valley—lacks the energy of business entrepreneurs on every corner—it's the most beautiful natural setting you'll ever see."

"Must have been hard to come back here."

"Not hard really. I won't get back here for a while. This is home. It's just that this is a time of so much change in the world. And out there, you're in the middle of it. Surrounded by the smartest people in the world. People our age who are creating technologies that are changing the way we communicate. Nothing is ever going to be the same."

M.J. liked to listen to him talk, the sound of his voice, the way he was so *into* that place and the work he would be doing.

"I might move out there after I graduate. Come out with friends. Get a job."

"You need to finish college first. Too easy to lose the discipline you need to finish your education. There's plenty of time to make money."

"I'm no good at school."

"M.J., you can't make a decent living without a college education. And, by the way, college is fun. Much better than high school. You'll see."

He wasn't listening, but she didn't care. She inhaled the intoxicating sweetness of blood red rose petals, as happy as she had been for a long time, here in the secret garden in the middle of the night, with her beloved older brother all to herself.

The moon rose higher in the sky, not so big and bold but still shining brightly, as a canopy of twinkling stars came alive above them. They took turns telling stories from childhood and laughing together deep into the night.

chapter thirty-two

Lee scanned the schedule posted outside Courtroom B. The Washington case was last on the docket. The team from Townsend Greene had already gathered, prepared to go in case the judge dismissed the early cases quickly. The judge would naturally want to wrap up the easy procedural matters before starting a jury trial that could last several weeks.

Jury selection was critical. Hank and Vernon were looking to Lee to take the lead on voir dire with recommendations on the tough decisions about which jurors to dismiss under one of their limited peremptory challenges.

He settled into one of the polished oak benches located in the hall outside the courtroom and flipped through copies of the questionnaires filled out by the panel called to jury duty. He had already identified several problematic jurors. He hoped the judge would ask the right questions to excuse at least some of them himself so that Lee's team could preserve their challenges for the candidates most likely to go against them. They would of course want to release jurors likely to have a bias sympathetic to the plaintiffs. He would have to be careful not to appear to be targeting black jurors, even though he knew they would inherently have more sympathy for the Washington family, not to mention more likely to regard the city as a deep pocket.

They had been in the office late last night, as Hank made a final attempt to reach a settlement with Quincy Brown before the trial started. Hank and Quincy had been back and forth on the phone all day, Lee and Vernon beside Hank in his office, handing him notes and documents as he argued with Quincy about how the case was likely to turn out in court. It was a delicate negotiation, each side revealing just enough detail about the strength of his arguments to push the other toward a favorable settlement without disclosing the key elements of what he would argue in court.

"Quincy, that's not going to fly with the jury. You know damn well we have plenty of evidence to the contrary.... Well, why not? I tell you what, it makes a hell of a lot more sense than the argument you're trying to make.... Don't poke the tiger, is what I say.... Think about it. If you followed that line of reasoning, the boy would have had to be retarded.... Jesus Christ, Quincy, you can't possibly say that with a straight face."

Hearing one end of many telephone conversations over the course of the day, Lee had learned a lot about the way lawyers practiced their craft. There was no hostility between the two men; in fact, there was a good deal of laughter and friendly banter. After all, they were colleagues and would see one another again in court.

Hank was convinced Quincy had a dollar amount in mind and would settle if he could. He went back and forth with the insurance company throughout the day, testing the waters for how high they would go. In the end, Quincy rejected every offer they made. Hank concluded that Quincy had already decided to take the case to trial, irrespective of its merits, in order to show solidarity with his own community.

When the Townsend Greene legal team, representing the City of Riverton, was called to the defense table, Lee felt a rush of adrenaline as he followed Hank and Vernon to the front of the courtroom. Polished oak paneling on the desks and partitions imparted a veneer of 1920s formality to the courtroom, the very smells of the place evocative of decorum, power and decades of deference to the rule of law.

As potential jurors were questioned by the judge and by both teams of lawyers, Lee passed notes and recommendations to Hank and Vernon. This juror was in the wrong age group or socioeconomic class to be sympathetic to the position taken by the city. That one had a history with the black community that wouldn't surface in a direct examination, but might sway a vote behind closed doors. The next one had job experience too close to city park maintenance and might have inordinate influence over the others and a perspective that was difficult to measure.

The minute Hank Greene stepped up to the podium to make his opening arguments, the courtroom belonged to him. At once affable, humorous and ponderous, he held the jury's rapt attention as he led them through the facts of the case. Deeply sympathetic to the loss suffered by the young man's family, he painted a picture of the series of events that led to Dewaine Washington's untimely death. Throughout the exposition, he showed the heartfelt commitment of the City of Riverton to its citizens and their recreational needs, and the care given to safety and upkeep of the facility. His full head of wavy white hair swayed with feeling as he recounted the tragic sequence of events. His clear blue eyes welled with tears as he spoke of the unfortunate outing. The corners of his well-lined mouth crinkled with subdued mirth when he made a point too delicate to speak aloud but well understood by his fellow citizens on the jury panel.

"We feel the heartache of this family, a young man wrenched away from them before he reached the prime of life. A fine young man, full of hope and promise.

"And yet, as we all know, young people today don't always stop and think about the consequences of their behavior. When you're young, it seems like nothing bad can ever happen to you. The sun is shining and it's a beautiful spring day and you just want to be outside. Catch a few trout. Enjoy the nice weather. Being shut up inside a school room can feel like a prison when you're fourteen years old and the trout are biting and the dogwoods are blooming.

"So maybe you talk a few friends into sneaking off for the day, even bringing along your younger brother. If you didn't bring him in on it, he might tell your mama and then you'd be in hot water, sure.

"You make a plan to meet out behind the tracks and get a lift out to the Bend. It was a day to look forward to. And that six-pack of beer swiped from an older brother's pickup, well, that was just one more thing that would make it a great day. Getting away with something, something your mama would not have allowed.

"You see, this young man didn't think he was doing anything wrong. He just wanted to have some fun. But he didn't have the judgment or the self-discipline to follow the rules. To understand that young people need to be in school. That kids shouldn't drink alcohol.

"Now, that didn't make this boy a bad person. But it does tell you something about his maturity. It does say something about his ability to control his impulses and to foresee the consequences of his actions. These same character traits sometimes cause a person to make bad decisions, to take unnecessary risks.

"And it's only natural that his family wants some retribution for their deeply felt loss. That's so often the way of the world these days, isn't it? Something terrible has happened and someone has to pay. Sure, money won't bring him back, but maybe it will provide some small solace to his grieving family. But here's the problem. If money has to change hands whenever something bad happens, where is it supposed to come from? I'll tell you where. It comes out of someone else's pocket. Every dollar the city pays to make one family feel better takes away a dollar from someone else who needs a desk in school for their child or a library or a free meal. This is your money, the hard-earned tax contributions of Riverton's citizens. Bad things happen to good people all the time. Of course, if there's wrongdoing, somebody should be punished. But where a small city government has been careful and diligent and has provided a lovely playground for its people, does it really make sense to give a big chunk of its resources to one family, just because they suffered an untimely loss? What about other families who have endured losses of their own? And what about their grandchildren? Where will they go for recreation if it becomes too costly to maintain the Bend?"

Hank's opening arguments touched subtly on the possibility of other factors in the Washington boy's death. There were no direct claims of foul play, but enough was said to leave an impression in a juror's mind that the Washington boy was engaged in behaviors that were risky and that the exact cause of his death was unknown.

Lee watched with interest as Hank maintained eye contact with each juror long enough to establish a personal connection. He was careful to avoid any impression of insensitivity to Dewaine Washington's family. The art of storytelling was alive and still held the power to shape the way people saw the world. It was an impressive opening and Lee, like many in the courtroom, was mesmerized by the performance.

chapter thirty-three

After the judge adjourned for the day, with strict instructions to the jury not to discuss what they had heard, the legal team from Townsend Greene agreed to meet at Oakley's Bar across the street from the courthouse for a drink before returning to the office to complete preparation for the next day.

Lee's car was parked around back of the courthouse and as he approached it, there was considerable activity on the grassy knoll beside his parking place. Several young black children were taking turns jumping off the fender of his car in an effort to land on one of the other kids, accompanied by much laughter, shouting and general rowdiness. As he approached, a figure moved toward the kids from another part of the parking lot, admonishing them to get off the car and to be more careful. And there, to his surprise, was his neighbor, Etta Jones, establishing herself as supervisor of the unruly clan.

"Donald Albert, climb down from that car this minute. You got no business jumping on somebody else's property. Don't knock into him like that. You gonna hurt somebody."

Several other adults joined Etta in rounding up the children. A portly lady in formal dress, hat to match, spoke to Etta.

"I'll get them in the car, Grandma. Go on over with Shauna."

"I got to go tend to Ruby. She's pretty tore up."

"Go on, Aunt Etta. Anthony will pick you up over here in a few minutes. I'll look after Ruby. Let's get out of here. These people don't care what happened to Dewaine anyway. I can tell you that right now."

Etta glanced up and saw Lee approaching the driver's side door.

"Oh my goodness. Is this your car these children are destroying?"

"It is, Etta. No harm done. It's a surprise to see you here. Looks like you're taking care of half the kids in town here."

"Oh, they family mainly. Can't keep out of mischief. I hope they didn't scrape up your car or nothin'. You cut a fine figure today in that courthouse."

"You were there?"

"We was watching the proceedings. That boy was my sister Lovey's grandson."

Lee wondered whether she had known all along of his role in the case. He couldn't remember whether he had mentioned to her the name of the firm where he was working. "You know, I can't talk about the case with you. The ethical rules don't let us talk about things that might affect the case."

"Oh, no, Lord no, I wouldn't want you to do that. I didn't mean to intrude on you. I'll be goin' on my way now." Etta turned toward the courthouse, wobbly on her feet but moving with determination. She didn't look back at him.

Lee was so accustomed to Etta's perpetual sunny disposition that he felt stung by her abrupt tone. He caught up with her in the lot. "You're okay, aren't you?" he asked as he grabbed her arm. "Let me help you get into the shade."

"I don't need no help from you. You folks tellin' everybody that Dewaine was out there drinkin' and fightin'. What do you know about that boy? You got no cause to trash him like that. Break his mother's heart. He was a good boy. Didn't drink no beer."

Lee just shook his head. He had nothing to say that would make Etta feel any better about the case or his role in it. Upset and shaky on her feet, he didn't want to leave her in the middle of the parking lot in 97-degree heat.

"Come over here and get out of the sun for a minute."

He took her by the arm and led her over to a bench in the shade of the courthouse.

"Here, sit down. It's too hot to wait out in that parking lot."

Etta was quiet, angry with herself for exposing her feelings. Sure, she grieved the loss of the boy and resented the heartache his mother and grandmother were having to endure. But she liked Lee Addison. Admired him quite a bit. Of course he had a job to do. But why was it always the same? White people implying that if your skin is black, you can't control yourself and God knows what kind of foolish, dangerous trouble you likely to get into. Dewaine wasn't like that, not like that white lawyer said. Sure, he was a child, doing foolish things. He shouldn't have played hookey. Does he think no white boy never skipped school to go out to that Bend? Does that mean he had to die?

Etta took a deep breath. Like so many times in her life, she had to bite her tongue.

Lee eyed Etta with concern. "You're not going to faint on me, are you? You don't look real good," he said.

She made an effort to smile. "I'm doin' better now."

"I'm sorry about your family's loss," he said. "I wish there didn't have to be a trial like this. Sometimes it's the only way you can resolve differences. There's nothing personal meant by it."

"You're right, of course," Etta replied. "I'm sorry to take it out on you. I think I got a little crazy from the heat and looking after those children."

"Well, you should wait here in the shade for your ride."

"Mmmm hmmm. *Sho* is hot. I'm fine now. Thank you so much."

"Can I bring you some water? I can get something in the courthouse."

"No, honey. I'm just fine. Thank you kindly."

"I didn't realize you'd be coming to the trial, even though I think you told me the Washington boy was family."

"Well, I just wanted to be here to support Lovey. You know I helped Mama raise her, she was so much younger. It was so hard on Ruby to lose the boy and I can tell it's worrying Lovey quite a bit. Don't know why Ruby is getting herself so torn apart about this trial."

"I'm sure it has been terrible for the boy's mother. And being here in court doesn't help," Lee said.

She shook her head, exhaling as she studied the stately 100-year-old courthouse.

"Well, it can't bring back Dewaine, that's for sure. But for me, the painful memories…they not so much about Dewaine. We of course miss the boy somethin' terrible. But this is the second time in my life I've been in this courthouse. And my bad memories of this place go back a long time. A *long* time."

"This place was part of my childhood too," Lee said. "My grandfather used to hear cases in this courthouse."

Etta seemed to be lost in thought, silently twisting the handkerchief in her lap. "There was a trial here when Axel died. Same kind of thing. Mama thinkin' she could bring him back by seeking justice. But that was 1945, and there wasn't no justice for blacks back then." Etta looked at Lee, someone she truly considered a friend, and opened up to him about her youth in Riverton and the twin brother she had lost.

When the country went to war, the army made it clear that they needed black men as well as whites to help fight the Germans and the Japanese. Axel and his friends couldn't wait to enlist. They had been listening to the radio too and swelled up at the thought that they could help defend the country—their country—from the evil foreigners.

Like so many boys who left home to fight for their country, the war changed Axel, changed him back to the strong, confident person he had been before all the shocks and disappointments of his teen years had knocked the spirit out of him.

Each time he came home on leave, Etta and her friends would follow him around the neighborhood like a young god. He was so handsome in his uniform, walking tall and straight, with a smile that melted the girls' hearts.

"Man, this here neighborhood changin' so fast," he would say. "White people comin' in here, pushin' all the coloreds further down the road out of town. Folks need to stand their ground, get some backbone."

Axel was always complaining like that, wishing the colored people would stand up for themselves.

The little tin-roofed house that Jingo and Tanette had bought on credit from the bank had once looked out over open fields along a dirt road at the outer edge of town. But in the boom years following the war, Riverton's population grew, downtown expanded and the road was paved over, connecting the town's bustling commercial center with the wealthy neighborhood in the oldest part of town. Wood shanties were torn down and the land bought up for new development. Eventually, even the A.M.E. Zion Redeeming Grace Church sold out and moved further out of town. The Jones house was one of the few structures from the old neighborhood that had survived.

When Axel's unit shipped out for Europe, Tanette was both proud and terrified. The young soldiers were thrilled to be escaping the abject poverty left in the wake of the Depression that had hit the hardscrabble black communities of the Deep South with particular devastation. As Axel's train pulled out of the station, Tanette's heart tightened, but for the first time in her life, she felt that it was her country too and she was sacrificing to defend it. Etta and Lovey stood on either side of her, and all three of them waved until their arms were limp, long after the train had slipped behind Miner Hill and out of sight, taking Axel off to Virginia and to the war in Europe.

Back in Riverton after the war, Axel was a man. Many of the boys who had shipped out with him fell in battle as the black units were sent again and again to the front lines. As friend after friend was left behind in the cold rocky earth of Italy and France, Axel began to feel he was leading a charmed life, impervious to the fire and explosion and chaos that had ripped so many of his friends apart.

He had been part of the liberating force that marched into Paris, where flowers and kisses from beautiful French girls made him feel like a hero. For the first time since childhood, his blackness didn't feel like a curse. In fact, the tall handsome soldier with the quick smile had an exotic appeal for a number of war-weary French women. He learned the delights of sexuality from worldly Europeans for whom the mixing of the races didn't carry the stigma or the threat to social order that it did at home.

Like so many of the black soldiers who came home from the war, Axel found it difficult to return to a world that hadn't changed, even though he had. Once the uniform was off, he was just another Riverton Negro, without a job or money and unwelcome in most parts of town. But he didn't shuffle any more. He couldn't. He carried the erect pride of that conquering hero marching into Paris for the rest of his life.

Etta smiled, remembering her tall handsome brother home from the war, his medals prominently displayed in a folding case on his dresser.

"Oh, you shoulda seen him back here in Riverton after the war. He was all grown up. Sometimes he would get kinda quiet when he talked about the war. But he talked like a man, not a boy. And the girls was after him all the time. He was breakin' hearts right and left. He was a looker, Axel."

"You showed me a picture of him as a kid," said Lee. "I'd like to see what he looked like when he came back."

"Next time you come down to the house, I'll show you the picture of him in his uniform. Lord, he was a fine-looking boy."

"What happened to him? After he got back, I mean. And what was the trial about?"

Etta's dark eyes filled with tears.

"Someday I'll tell you about it. We need a big cup of tea for that story. And here comes Anthony to pick me up. Thank you so much for sitting here and watching after me. I'm feeling much better."

chapter thirty-four

Oakley's Bar, across the street from the county courthouse, had been a watering hole for lawyers coming out of court for more than fifty years. The decor hadn't changed much over the decades. Neon signs over the bar cut through the darkness, the proprietor happy to hang whatever his suppliers sent. Lawyers in three-piece suits and young staffers dressed for court were scattered among the blue jean–clad regulars, some perched on stools in front of the bar and others gathered in small groups sharing courtroom anecdotes. The green-yellow glare of the jukebox, with its vast collection of country rock classics, illuminated the west end of the bar.

Hank Greene and his litigation team were seated at a round table in a dark corner, the only light flickering from two votive candles encased in smoky red glass. Vernon pulled over an extra chair for Lee. The energy from the team was palpable. Hank was holding court, ruminating about the day's events, interpreting the body language of jurors, assessing opposing counsel.

"Could you believe the judge's line of questions to Juror 25? Holy shit. Got up on the wrong side of the bed, I guess," laughed one of the case assistants.

"She totally walked into Hank's scenario, didn't she?" Vernon added. "Bought it hook, line and sinker."

"That young black gal Quincy's got with him, can't be out of law school more than a year or two," said Hank. "But I gotta say, she's sharp. Still, I can't believe he's letting her play such a big role."

"Did you see the look on that guy's face on the far left, front row?" one of them asked. "He is with us all the way, baby. You can take that one to the bank."

"Quincy's opening statement was pretty good on the standard of care issues," Vernon said. "But I expected him to pound on the Hollingsworth case."

"He may be saving that for the close."

"The only thing I wonder," Fred offered, flushed like the rest of them from the excitement, "is why he kept bringing up the issue of warning signs. We can easily show that the city tried on innumerable occasions to put up signs and kids kept swiping 'em."

Lee was thinking of Vernon's note referring to the City Parks and Recreation Director he had intended to see. Maybe I'll get by there on Friday if the judge recesses early, he thought to himself.

Hank took a long sip of his draft beer and winked at Fred. "I know old Quincy," he said. "He'll try to make something out of that."

"Nothin' he *can* make of that," Vernon said. "You set up the Mexican kids perfectly. Enough to lay the groundwork. But you didn't give Quincy a road map. He'll be surprised when we open up that issue next week."

Hank turned to Lee. "By the way, I know you want to keep the Rayburn boy off the stand. But I think we need him to establish the drinking and the altercation with the Mexican kids. I want to give the judge and Quincy notice today that we may bring him to the stand next week. Would you let his family know?"

Lee reluctantly agreed to talk to the Rayburns and to arrange a preparation schedule for an additional witness. He had eventually gotten the full story out of Tommy. On the day Dewaine Washington died, Tommy had seen the Washington brothers and their two friends drinking beer in a protected clearing near the diving rock that overlooked the swimming hole.

Tommy had a way of watching people from secret spots, a habit he had taken up as a defense to so often being gawked at by other people. He saw the boys drinking and cutting up and was still in his hiding place when some older teens, described by Tommy as Mexicans, came upon them and asked the boys to let them have a beer.

According to Tommy, the older boys didn't threaten the black kids and there was not a fight, but they teased the youngsters and goaded them into a bet, offering five bucks if the kids would put up a beer to the first person to dive head-first off the rock into the reservoir. They bickered and bargained, but at the end of the day, none of the younger boys could screw up the courage to go off the rock, even though Dewaine Washington had stood up there a long time.

The teens called them chicken and wound up taking two beers off them before Tommy slipped away.

Lee didn't like the idea of putting Tommy on the stand. He knew Annie and her parents would not be happy. But it looked like it was going to be necessary.

The team of lawyers and legal assistants from Townsend Greene laughed and reminisced, enjoying the camaraderie of a successful day in court. Lee never imagined it could be this much fun—the euphoria that came from working hard toward a goal and knowing it made a real difference for your client. Of course, they were still a long way from victory, but it was a good start. He could imagine himself in Hank's position, making an argument that touched the hearts and minds of the jurors, a profound demonstration of the power of words.

Hank broke up the party early, sending his team home for a good night's sleep and ordering everybody in the office by 7:30 in the morning to go over plans for the day one last time.

Lee tried to call Annie, but she didn't pick up. He was too wired to go home, so he decided to stop by her house anyway. They had scarcely seen each other since his trip to California. The emotional ups and downs of the trial and the pressure of performance under fire had surprised him, leaving little energy to think about what had happened in Carmel or what it meant for his relationship with Annie.

He found her up to her knees in mud working on a broken sprinkler head. It was still hot, but the sun had receded behind the pine-studded hills, leaving in its wake a pink-grey glow over the still air.

A streak of dirt from Annie's nose to her left ear ended in brown rivulets trickling down the side of her neck and into a white t-shirt bearing a faded Riverton Panther logo. When she saw Lee's car pull into the driveway, a smile lit up her grimy, but charming, face.

"Good Lord, woman, you're a mess."

She laughed, pulled herself to her feet and held out her arms. He moved in her direction before realizing that he was wearing his best suit, and stopped in his tracks.

They both laughed.

"Go find yourself a beer," she said. "Give me five minutes to finish, then I'll be in to clean up."

As the warm shower relaxed her sore shoulder muscles and washed the dirt from the afternoon's yard work down the drain, Annie was kicking herself. Why did she get light-headed and giddy every time he strolled in the door?

Minutes before he had driven up, Annie had been thinking about Lee, frustrated at the distance she detected since his return from California. He hadn't talked about the weekend much and in particular had said nothing about Zoe. Had they picked up where they left off last spring? Was Annie just a summer fling, filling empty evenings as he planned for his life with Zoe in California? The only thing he seemed to be thinking about right now was the damned trial.

It wasn't like her to be on the needy end of a relationship. What in the hell was wrong with her, to let this man walk in and out of her life at will, leaving wreckage and emotional chaos in his wake?

But before she could work up a full head of steam, he was in the shower with her, lathered up, soap bubbles everywhere, their bodies slipping over each other, joy and laughter and desire overwhelming them.

Afterward, as she lay in his arms, their bodies still wet and slippery, she was pensive. When the summer was over, she would have to let him go. But, even so, she thought, I wouldn't change places with anyone in the world.

chapter thirty-five

The trial was in session for the rest of the week. Lee was engrossed in the minutiae of the case, taking notes during testimony and handing documents to Hank or Vernon from his briefcase file. There was constant activity at the defense table in the front of the courtroom, where he sat with the rest of the Townsend Greene lawyers. The case was progressing as planned, and the defense team felt optimistic about its chances.

At noon on Friday, the judge declared a recess until Monday morning at 9:00. Lee begged off on lunch with the team, claiming he had to take care of some business and promising to meet them back at the firm mid-afternoon.

Because of the courthouse's proximity to the city administrative offices, he arrived at R.A. Sampson's offices during lunch hour when his secretary was out. Finding Sampson alone having a sandwich at his desk, Lee leaned in and introduced himself. "Sorry to bother you at lunch. I grew up here in Riverton, just back home for the summer, and I'm helping out on a court case."

Sampson stood up and extended his hand. "Rusty Sampson."

"I'm Lee Addison. Do you have a second?"

Rusty Sampson was a nervous, slight man in his fifties. He had a receding hairline, a mild tremor in his voice and a high-pitched laugh that ended almost every sentence. Though he appeared to be unsettled by the unexpected visitor, he was not quick enough on his feet or practiced enough in deception to deflect Lee's request.

"I'm working with Hank Greene on a case and was just curious about how the department keeps an eye on those warning signs out at the Bend."

Sampson was not prepared for the question, stammering as he considered his response. "Well, you know, the kids are forever messing with the signs. We try to chain them down when we can. Whenever they get thrown in the swimming hole, we fish them out before someone gets hurt."

"Do you know when the new sign out there was put up?"

"Couldn't tell you offhand."

The more specific Lee's questions, the more evasive Sampson became. Lee left with a definite feeling that the guy was hiding something. The concept of a sign actually having been tossed into the swimming hole hadn't occurred to him. If there was an obstacle like that at the bottom of the reservoir, that would surely create a hazard for divers.

Lee had to wonder whether Vernon had talked to Rusty Sampson during the early phases of discovery. That might explain the cryptic notes in Vernon's notebook.

Since he was already parked at the municipal building, Lee decided to stop by the forensics lab and have another chat with Max Kingston.

Kingston was again alone in the lab, so Lee had his full attention.

"Hey, I was just over in the municipal building talking to Rusty Sampson. He said something about warning signs sometimes getting pushed into that swimming hole out at the Bend."

"Oh yeah, sometimes they roll them over to the shop with the concrete foundation still attached. Hell of a job to get 'em cleaned up," Max replied.

"You don't have anything like that in the evidence stored for the Washington case, do you?"

Abruptly wary, Max studied Lee for a minute. "Look, I don't know anything about that. If something was pulled out of that pond after the black kid died, it never made its way here and I don't know nothin' about it."

It was late Saturday afternoon at the end of a long day of trial preparation when Vernon asked Lee to come into Hank's office. Lee was exhausted and hoping to get away to Annie's for a quiet evening before facing another long weekend day in the office.

Hank looked up from his work as Vernon shut the door behind them. Both men were grim-faced.

"I got a call last night from Rusty Sampson over at the city saying you had been by there asking him questions about the Bend," Hank said.

Lee reddened, thinking about how he had first read Sampson's name in Vernon's private notebook.

"The way Quincy kept referring to warning signs," Lee stammered, "I wanted to be sure we could respond if we needed to. We didn't interview the Director of Parks and Recreation."

"Look, son," said Hank, "you've got to trust that this firm did its homework on the case in the early part of discovery, before you joined us. I can't have you running off on your own in the middle of the trial trying to create new evidence that we haven't seen before."

On the defensive, Lee chafed at being lectured by the older man. "But if a sign had been rolled into the water before that accident happened," he argued, "that could explain the contusion and possibly the drowning. I didn't want us to be surprised next week."

"Son, you don't run around trying to create the other side's case. That's their job. That's how the system works. Now, I can promise you that if we had evidence of any such thing, I would have long since delivered it to the judge. You are not an experienced enough lawyer to be going out on your own, trying to run down some far-fetched idea you've got in your head about a city conspiracy. That's just your inexperience showing. I know you young people are idealistic and all that, and you want to make sure you're doing the right thing. I respect that. That's how I was at your age. That will help you become a better lawyer. But the way our legal system works in this country is that you are working for the City of Riverton and looking out for their interests. The dead boy's family has a whole bunch of lawyers over there looking out for their interests. I can't have you running off and upsetting our clients with a lot of questions that are not useful to our defense. We're being paid to defend the city against these charges, not solve a mystery."

Lee was pissed off. He understood Hank's point about his obligation to the client, but the lack of moral clarity left a bad taste in his mouth.

He decided to cancel plans for the evening with Annie and work at home, finishing up a summary of cases he had started in the office. There was probably nothing to the feeling he had, that the people at the city knew more than they were saying. Hank was right about his responsibility to the client. But wasn't there some responsibility as an officer of the court as well? He slept fitfully and woke tired, knowing it was going to be another long day.

chapter thirty-six

The following week was a frenzy of activity at the Townsend Greene firm. Whatever unsettled feelings Lee Addison had about the circumstances of Dewaine Washington's death were completely subsumed by the stress and relentless demands of the trial. There were deadlines to meet, new challenges that came up in court, a million details to tie down and data to get into the hands of the lead attorneys.

Tommy Rayburn was a perfect witness, confirming in a simple, straightforward way that young Dewaine Washington and his friends were cutting school, in conflict with older kids from the tough Mexican-American community and engaging in underage drinking. Any of those reckless behaviors could have contributed to the boy's untimely drowning death, minimizing the city's responsibility for the unfortunate accident.

This, like so much else in Lee Addison's life, was coming down to a competition, and it was a contest he very much wanted to win. The other side was out to transfer public wealth out of the city's coffers and into the hands of the family of the dead boy. The Townsend team knew this would put a burden on the city and its taxpayers. Well, he thought to himself, may the best team win.

The pieces of the plan formulated during late-night sessions at Townsend Greene were falling into place. Lee had sole responsibility for cross-examination of two of Quincy's witnesses, winning much praise for the strategy behind his line of questioning and for his demeanor before the court. Examination of witnesses for the plaintiffs was due to wrap up tomorrow and the city could start to present its side of the case. After closing arguments, the case would go to the jury, probably by the end of the week. Everybody expected a verdict in favor of the city.

During Tuesday's mid-day recess, the Townsend team ducked into Oakley's for a quick lunch. Before they could put in their orders, the bartender brought a telephone over to the table, handing it to Hank.

"Call for you, Mr. Greene."

Hank's brow furrowed as he listened without comment for a time.

"Kind of late in the game for that, isn't it, Quincy?"

The lawyers at the table watched Hank's face for clues to what he was hearing.

"You know damn well we have the right to prepare our cross-examination. I don't know if we should allow this witness at all."

"Okay, I want to hear everything you know about him. Right now."

Hank signaled to Fred to hand him a pad of paper, and then started taking notes.

"You know, Quincy, we'll see what the judge says about that. I've got a good mind to object. I can tell you it's not going to happen today."

After he hung up, Hank put the phone on the floor beside his chair and studied his notes.

"Quincy wants to bring in another witness. Employee of the Parks and Recreation Department. Fred, call Marilyn. I want you to spend the afternoon with her getting what you can on this guy. Eldridge Anthony. Maintenance guy."

Vernon shook his head. "Where does Quincy think he's going with this?"

"Hard to say. Says he's a guy who can speak to the safety issues at the reservoir. Hell, he's been through all that," Hank muttered. "Just delaying the inevitable."

By the time Eldridge Anthony took the stand on Thursday afternoon, Hank and Vernon knew all about his employment history, the DUI charge in 1982 and his spotty credit report. What they didn't know was why

Quincy Brown had gone to the trouble to bring him in as a last-minute witness for the Washington family.

Quincy's examination developed slowly and innocuously. Anthony's upbringing and his history of employment with the City of Riverton Parks and Recreation Department. An Employee of the Month Award.

"Mr. Anthony, could you recount for the jury the substance of a telephone call you received at the Maintenance Building on July 15, 1988?"

"Oh, sure. Mr. Sampson, he call me up to run out to the Bend to check about a sign down at the bottom of the swimming hole."

"And could you identify this Mr. Sampson for the court?"

"Oh, that's Mr. Rusty Sampson, my boss. He's head of Parks and Recreation. I been working for him many, many years now."

"And did Mr. Sampson say why he thought there might be something at the bottom of that reservoir?"

"He said the daddy of some boy swimming out there had called him up, said his boy dived off the rock and run into a big ole sign at the bottom of the swimming hole. Thought the city should know about it."

The tension at the defendant's table was palpable as Lee's memory flashed back to his meeting with Rusty Sampson, as well as Hank's lecture about poking around in evidence that they had already covered. Jesus, thought Lee, the guy was lying through his teeth. Why would Hank have ignored something so basic as the possibility of a submerged sign? And how much did Vernon know anyway?

Quincy continued his examination of the witness.

"After Mr. Sampson's telephone call, did you go out to the Bend to check out his concern?"

"Oh, yes sir, I went out there that very day. I got a young man in the building who does our underwater cleanup, and he come out there with me in his swimming suit and went down to the bottom to check it out."

"And what did he discover at the bottom of the reservoir?"

"Sure enough, there was one of our No Diving signs down there. Still had concrete around the bottom. Somebody had just pulled it up and rolled it into the swimming hole, and it had sunk right to the bottom."

"I see," said Quincy. "Did you pull the sign out of the water at that time?"

"Oh, no sir. That take a truck and chain. That thing is heavy with all the concrete on it."

"Did you inform Mr. Sampson of what you had found at the Bend?"

"Yes sir. I called him just as soon as we got back to Maintenance."

"And what did Mr. Sampson instruct you to do?"

"He told me to pull it out of there as soon as I could. Told me I should get out there early in the morning, before the Bend was open, so I wouldn't disturb the folks out there for a swim."

"And did you in fact remove the sign from the swimming reservoir?"

"Yes sir. Did it the very next morning. Charlie come back out there with me to help me get the chain around the sign. Just after the sun come up. We backed up the truck to the pond and pulled it out."

"And where did you put the sign after you retrieved it?"

"Oh, Mr. Sampson said to just drop it off at the dump, and that's what we did."

In spite of a vigorous cross-examination of Eldridge Anthony designed to impugn his credibility, the stark implication of intentional destruction of evidence had thrown the defense strategy into disarray. Rusty Sampson was called in as a rebuttal witness, denying vigorously that the removal of the sign had anything to do with the Washington case. But the impact on the jury had been significant.

When Quincy Brown rose to present the closing argument for the plaintiffs, he was somewhat understated in his recital of the events that led to Dewaine Washington's death. He mentioned the No Diving sign several times, stopping short of alleging intentional destruction of evidence by the city, but hammering on the tragedy that might have been avoided with proper signage on the rock, clearly implying that the boy's head contusion was caused by the sign at the bottom of the reservoir. When he talked about Dewaine Washington, he didn't try to describe him as a perfect boy, but his voice would swell when he spoke of the boy's potential and the chance he never had to grow up and become the kind of person who could contribute to the world in a positive way.

The case went to the jury on Friday afternoon, leaving both sides on pins and needles over the weekend. At 10:00 on Monday morning, the court clerk called Hank Greene to let him know that the jury had notified the judge they were about to deliver the verdict. The lawyers threw on their jackets and headed to the courthouse.

Quincy Brown and his associates were already seated at the plaintiff's table when the lawyers from Townsend Greene arrived in the courtroom. The judge sent his clerk to call the jury room. After they filed into the jury box, the foreman stood and informed the court that the jury had found the City of Riverton negligent in its maintenance of the Bend swimming area and awarded the family of Dewaine Washington $500,000 in damages for his death.

The local newspaper headlined the outcome of the trial with a front-page picture of a tearful Ruby Washington embracing her lawyer Quincy Brown, the elderly barrister beaming from ear to ear. On the *Gazette*'s editorial page, the size of the award was criticized as a threat to the viability of municipal facilities like the Bend, and unjustified litigation was declared to be the ruination of the country.

chapter thirty-seven

M.J. was bored. Although she wasn't looking forward to the new school year, summer was dragging and she needed a change of routine.

At her mother's prodding, she agreed to spend two mornings a week at the hospital doing volunteer work as a Candy Striper, helping the nursing staff with routine patient check-in procedures. But they never had enough work to keep her busy, and she was uncomfortable hanging around with nothing to do.

At least it got her out of the house. M.J. knew she had built a wall that her mother couldn't penetrate, and she didn't feel altogether proud of it. But she was finding it increasingly painful to be under the same roof with her relentlessly demanding mother.

The most recent battle had left Frances once again in tears.

"I know I've failed you. But, M.J., if you don't care about yourself, nobody else will. Believe me, I know about that."

She didn't want to torture her mother. Not really. It was just that she couldn't stand the weakness. Why would anyone look forward to becoming an adult? Always unhappy and bitter, scheming to promote herself at someone else's expense. It was shitty being a teenager, but better that than growing up.

She had believed it would make all the difference to have Lee home for the summer. But it hadn't really changed anything. I don't know why I never saw it before, she thought to herself. It's so obvious. My brother has a big ego.

When the clock finally inched past 12:00 noon, M.J. bolted for the door. Buddy had promised an afternoon movie, just the two of them, and she was to pick him up at Max's after she left the hospital.

"I know we were going to the movies, but Gary Fox has invited a bunch of people out to his house for a swim party. His parents are gone for the week, so should be fun."

"I promised my brother I'd be there for dinner tonight."

"We don't have to stay long. Do you have your swimsuit in the car?"

Buddy slipped into the front seat beside her, and she didn't even try to argue about it. What she wanted never mattered to anybody.

Buddy was in a good mood, probably already high, she thought to herself. He leaned over to give her a kiss, but she ignored his attempt at affection and stepped on the gas.

Turning up the volume on the radio, Buddy started singing along with Cyndi Lauper in full falsetto.

M.J. glared at him.

He ignored her foul humor, singing along at the top of his lungs, the window rolled down and other drivers staring. Finally M.J. reached over and turned off the music. Buddy removed her hand, turned the volume even louder and once again joined in the song, this time in a shrill, off-key pitch. When she reached again for the radio, Buddy slapped at her hand.

"Fuck you, M.J. You can do your 'rich bitch' number on somebody else. Drop me off at the party and just keep fucking going. I've got friends there. I don't need your little spoiled ass with me to have a good time."

Instantly, she pulled to the curb and dropped her head in her hands. "I'm just so tired of nobody ever listening to me. I don't feel like partying. It sucks to be around people I don't know," she said, her eyes filling with tears.

"Hey, hey, it's not that big a deal. I'm sorry, baby. What's the matter?"

She pushed his hand away. "Nobody cares about what *I* want. Not you. Not my mother. It's like I don't even exist."

Accustomed to compliance from M.J., Buddy was surprised at the outburst. He had been attracted to the younger girl for lots of reasons, but especially her deference. So rarely in control of anything in his own life, Buddy loved the fact that M.J. looked to him for direction and didn't mind being told what to do.

As she dissolved into tears, he softened his tone and reached over to massage her neck. "We don't have to go. Don't cry, honey. I'm sorry. I'm just messin' with you. We'll go to the movies."

She pulled herself together, surprised as he was at the outburst and embarrassed about being a poor sport.

In her first real relationship, M.J. sometimes felt like she was trying out roles she had seen on TV or in the movies. How did the popular girls at school hang onto their boyfriends? Putting out must be part of it. But they also knew when to keep their mouths shut. Boys didn't like pushy girls. She had to learn to be soft and sexy and helpless.

Drying her eyes with the back of her hand, she said, "Oh, I'm okay. I don't know what's wrong with me. We can go to the party."

The festivities had started by the time they arrived at the Fox's house. M.J. still didn't feel like partying, but she felt bad about being a bitch to Buddy. After a while, she loosened up. A couple of beers made it easier to hang out with strangers.

chapter thirty-eight

With the trial over, Lee got out of the office early enough to complete a three-mile run before dinner. Sticky and hot though it was, it gave him a chance to clear his head before dinner with his mother and M.J.

Accustomed to succeeding at whatever he took on, he was not happy to be on the receiving end of condolences after the trial's unfavorable outcome. He kicked himself for not pursuing the Sampson lead sooner and with more determination. The mood at Townsend Greene had been grim in the days after the verdict, but Lee felt he had learned a lesson he wouldn't soon forget about trusting his own instincts.

He had finally succeeded in getting through to Zoe the day after the trial ended. His cryptic message about losing the case had been enough to motivate her to call him back. Fascinated by the twists and turns of litigation, she wanted to hear every detail about the arguments and how Quincy Brown had staged the disclosure of the submerged sign through his final witness.

"God, that's great lawyering," she had gushed in admiration.

They had agreed to be friends. No talk about Annie or commitment or what had happened in Carmel Valley. Lee understood better than anyone Zoe's ability to keep her own counsel, especially on matters close to her heart, so he didn't know if she had moved on or not. In any event, he was glad to have her friendship.

But after Friday night's rift, he wasn't sure he still had Annie's. The Washington case debacle was still too raw, and he resented Annie's satisfaction with the outcome. She had dragged him out to one of her school fundraisers, a chicken spaghetti dinner in the high-school cafeteria to raise money for the pep squad so that it could travel with the football team in the fall.

No sooner had he slipped into the bench beside her than people started dropping by with commentary about the case.

"Everybody wants something for nothing these days."

"That boy had been out there skipping school and drinking. It was his own fault."

"I hope y'all are going to appeal."

Annie had finally had enough. It was Herman McAdams' overtly racial characterization of Dewaine Washington's behavior that finally sent her storming out of the cafeteria She had gone to her classroom and was tacking up a map for the new school year when Lee finally found her. She didn't look up when he came in.

"This isn't about the case, is it?" he said.

She didn't look at him, just continued to work on her project.

Lee had left his cell phone in Annie's car, and after letting it ring a few times, she thought maybe he was calling to track down his phone. So she pushed the "Talk" button. Before she could say a word, a woman's voice broke in.

"Hey, babe. Why don't you ever answer your phone? I forgot to ask you something. Do you want me to pick up the apartment lease for you?"

The voice was clipped, a New York accent, so familiar to Lee that she didn't need to announce herself.

Annie was shocked and embarrassed, not knowing whether to hang up or say something. To her it was a harsh voice, aggressive and sophisticated, tied to Lee in some way she couldn't understand.

It so surprised Annie that there was a long hesitation, and she could neither speak nor hang up. Finally she said, "I'm sorry. Lee... I...Lee left his phone in my car, and I was just picking it up for him. Can I give him a message?"

The voice on the other end hesitated as well. "Just tell him Zoe Perinsky called." Then she hung up.

Annie's classroom was infused with streaks of pink, illuminating floating particles of dust as the sun disappeared below the western horizon.

"I'm sorry you had to meet Zoe that way," he said.

She turned to him, her eyes bright with hurt and anger. "So Zoe told you I answered your phone. Just so you know, I also looked at the phone calls you've been making. How many times a day do you call her?"

Lee sighed. "Annie, I had been trying to reach Zoe since Carmel. I told her about you during the trip, and she was pissed off. We've been close friends for three years. I wanted to talk to her about the Washington case. That's all."

"I don't believe you."

Lee crossed the classroom in three long strides and turned her toward him. "I'm in love with you, not Zoe."

At that, her tears started, but she wouldn't let him hold her. "It has always been so easy for you. So easy to come into my life and then walk away again. Well, fuck you, Lee Addison. I don't need you. I can be happy without you. I can have the life that I want without you."

Annie's brave attempt to distance herself hadn't been lost on Lee, and as he jogged across Third Street, he felt a pang of raw emotion, knowing her affection for him left her vulnerable. He was running hard to complete the downtown loop before the sun disappeared into the western horizon, his regret about the trial now overshadowed by a different set of emotions—the confusion and affection he felt toward both of the strong, beautiful women in his life.

Remembering the look on Annie's face that night, Lee sighed as he jogged past the boarded-up gas station surrounded by a chain link fence on the edge of town. Maybe it was for the best. Summer was almost over. What was he going to do about Annie anyway?

Still, he felt heartsick. The thick afternoon humidity clung to him, but he pushed harder to keep up his pace. He felt that he deserved the punishment, that if he sweated hard enough, he might purge his sins. He would probably lose both of them—that would be justice after all.

To make matters worse, as he turned onto Peach, there was Etta Jones, sitting under her willow tree, waiting for him. He almost ran right past her, figuring he had been beaten up enough for one day, but then circled back to say hello.

"I wondered when you was going to come running by here again."

"Now that the lawsuit is over, I need to get back in shape."

"I'm glad it's over," she said.

"I hope your sister and her daughter are feeling better, the way everything worked out," Lee replied.

"Well, nothing changes the fact that they have lost a child. But I suppose there is some satisfaction in feeling like you were treated fairly. Hasn't always been the case in that courthouse. Maybe hard for you to understand. You've never been black or poor or fighting against a system that always seem to come out better for the other guy."

Just then two children, a boy and a girl ten or eleven years old, burst out of Etta's house and took off into her side yard.

"The grandchildren are over here today helping me make a cake for their mama's birthday. Lord, those children wear me out."

"I bet they love coming over here to bake at Granny's house."

She laughed. "I been talking to them about their studies. Jenee, she works hard in school, and she's a good student, but her brother isn't much interested.

"Come over here, kids. I want you to meet a friend of mine."

Etta proceeded to give the children a lecture about the importance of good grades and how hard Mr. Addison had worked in school to become a lawyer. How you need a college education to get a good job and have enough money to live on.

The children were shy and studied the ground during their Granny's lecture.

"My brother Axel—he would have been your great-uncle—was going to go to college. Smart as a whip. But he never had the chance."

At the first opportunity, the kids took off again.

"I always encouraged my children to get a college education," she said. "But these days, kids are so impatient to get some money in their pocket, get married and all that, none of them wants to wait and do the work. Well, Mabel started at the junior college and so did Calvin, but they didn't ever finish. More interested in having a good time than planning for their future."

"I know what you mean. We have the same problem with M.J. Just can't make her realize how important college is. It's not so much about earning a living either. But it does mean a better life, more interesting, more fun. I wish she could see that."

Etta thought about what he'd said. "Well, maybe I'll try that with the kids next time. I like the idea. You know, 'He came that we might have life and that we might have it more abundantly.'

"It comes more natural to you to preach about education than about Jesus, doesn't it?" she asked, chuckling to herself. "But it's the same thing really."

"You're always one step ahead of me, Etta," he said, giving her an affectionate nudge as he turned to go. "I've got to get back to the house."

"Okay. Thank you for stopping by. But tell me, is everything right with you? You know what I mean. You and your sister too. How is it really?"

Like so many of her questions, this one stopped him for a minute. "Oh Lord, it's the wrong day to ask me about that."

Darkness was starting to set in, and he walked the rest of the way home. A visit with Etta always left him pondering the big questions.

chapter thirty-nine

It was dusk when M.J. left the party. She had finally relaxed, in spite of the company of strangers, enjoying the music and feeling fine. But she had promised Lee and her mother that she would be home for dinner. Buddy wasn't ready to go, so he walked her to the car, gave her a kiss on the cheek and went back to the party. By the time she got home, M.J. wasn't feeling great, so she begged off dinner and went up to bed.

Lee didn't mind. It had been a draining day, and he wasn't much in the mood for talk. His mother seemed to sense that. Instead of the usual haranguing about M.J.'s bad habits, she was content to have a quiet dinner with her son. There had been all too little of that and the summer was rapidly drawing to an end. They sat on the screened back porch under the fan, talking of nothing in particular.

Lee slept fitfully and was in the deepest part of a dream cycle when his mother roused him. He had been standing in the back of a small plane, directing people with parachutes strapped to their backs to jump out of the plane. What he remembered as he awakened was Annie. She had just jumped, and he was leaning out the door, trying to assure himself that the parachute had opened.

"Lee, wake up…please."

As he transitioned from the dream to an awareness of his mother's silhouette in the doorway, backlit by the hallway light that sharply outlined her long ruffled nightdress, the anxiety in Lee's mind transferred from

Annie's freefall to the sudden awakening by his mother in the middle of the night.

"Are you all right, Mama?"

"Lee, there are some police officers downstairs. I need you to get up."

And so, the nightmare began in earnest…. Permission sought to inspect the Buick parked in the driveway. The directive to wake M.J. The offer of a voluntary DUI test. And the unforgettable scene of M.J., disoriented, rumpled and terrified into sobriety, being driven away in the back of a police car. He had stood outside the front door and watched as the red rear lights receded into the blackest of nights.

Think, he told himself. *What do I do now? Legal counsel. Who the hell is the best criminal lawyer in Riverton? Call Hank. Make sure she doesn't talk to the police without counsel present. Got to get down to the station. Call Hank first.*

He brushed past his mother who was standing stock still in the living room. No tears, no questions. Just stunned.

"I need Hank's home phone number. Do you have it nearby?"

Frances handed him a slip of paper.

His phone rang for a long time.

"Hank, I'm sorry to wake you like this. It's Lee. Lee Addison. I've got a problem here at home, and I need to find local criminal counsel."

Frances steadied herself and shuffled back into the living room, lights still blazing even though the police officers had left with M.J. half an hour earlier. She was shaking from somewhere near her diaphragm, her breathing rapid and shallow, and she couldn't put a cohesive thought together to save her life. Lee was running around the house, making calls, throwing on clothes, muttering to himself. For her, there was only a cold quiet stillness settling to the pit of her stomach, not quite fear, not yet, but a kind of icy shock that left her mute.

The shade on the Tiffany lamp across from where she sat was ajar, perhaps knocked aside by the man who had sat in the armchair. He had cold eyes and looked ill at ease. *I should think so*, Frances thought, *invading someone's home in the middle of the night.* The light was shining into her eyes, but she couldn't muster the energy to move, nor did she get up to fix herself a drink, greatly needed at this point. She stared at the lamp and decided it no longer fit the decor of the room.

She kept replaying what the officers had said, trying to make sense of the words.

"A hit-and-run accident near Sanford Park…girls on their bikes coming home from soccer practice…a dark green Buick turning off Mitchell, swerving close to the group…sideswiped…not expected to survive."

Lee's mind was racing, though his thoughts weren't much more cohesive than his mother's. He tried to remember the procedural steps required in this kind of case. How did bail get posted? Who decided whether she could be released? Would they even let him talk to her? Why in hell couldn't he remember the way the law worked on involuntary alcohol and drug testing? Seemed like in California you could refuse it, but then that was admissible testimony. He couldn't leave the house until Hank tracked down the criminal defense attorney he was going to call. But he couldn't sit still either.

M.J. had looked so young, so vulnerable—and utterly terrified. She didn't seem to understand what in God's name they were talking about. Could they have been mistaken about the car? Had he told her not to answer any questions until she had an attorney with her? As they led her out the door, she had looked back at her brother with panic. He felt completely helpless.

When the phone rang, both Lee and Frances jumped.

"Yes, this is Lee. Thank you for calling."

Jim Barnett's voice was comforting. Hank Greene had called him. He was a criminal defense attorney. He would meet Lee at the station. He walked through the series of events that could be expected in the next twenty-four hours. Lee felt enormously grateful to be in the hands of someone with experience, someone who sounded strong and thoughtful and not panicked.

"Mama, go back to bed. I'm going to meet an attorney Hank recommended at the station. Hopefully I'll be able to bring M.J. home."

"I'm coming with you."

"You can't. I'll be back in a few hours. Try to sleep. We'll talk in the morning."

chapter forty

M.J. studied her fingernails. The room smelled of disinfectant. It was cold and she shivered, wishing she had brought a sweater. At least she was alone. Not in one of those holding cells filled with prostitutes and homeless women like the ones she'd seen on TV.

Only now was she starting to wake up. The events at the house had been so confusing. It was like coming out of a dream, but then something else happens and you never quite leave the dream. You just enter an even weirder place.

She was groggy but at the same time stone cold sober. She hadn't been that high driving back from the party. It wasn't possible that she had hit someone. And yet, when the guy in the suit described what had happened, she knew. She remembered passing some kids on bikes, and there was a thump against the car. But she had been going slow and had just assumed it was some kid, fooling around, whacking the car to bug her. You can't kill somebody at that speed. Good God. Why didn't she stop? She might go to jail for hit-and-run. She couldn't let anyone know that she had heard that sound. Nobody would believe her. But if she really had hit someone, the other kids would identify the car. Their word against hers. What if the car was dented or something? Anyway, there were labs that could match up evidence. They would know it was her.

She had no idea what time it was. The room had no windows. The brown leatherette sofa where she was sitting was worn and cold. The flooring was old linoleum, a plaid pattern of faded greens and blues. There was a desk in the opposite corner of the room with a green shaded reading lamp on it and a couple of folding chairs nearby. Otherwise, the room was empty.

The tape of the day's events kept replaying in her mind. She had arrived at the Foxes' house at about 2:00. It wasn't a particularly wild party. She didn't get high. Just a couple of beers. In fact, she had thought about having to drive home. Lee and Mama were expecting her for dinner. If she hadn't been so goddamned responsible about getting home, this never would have happened. One minute earlier or later, and it wouldn't have happened. Her life was ruined just because of incredibly bad timing.

It seemed as though she had been sitting in the room for hours and hours. Only one person had come in—a dikey-looking female officer who had talked to her about providing an attorney. Lee had told her not to talk to anyone until he got an attorney there for her, so she hadn't. The lady hadn't pushed her at all. Said they would wait to ask her questions after her attorney arrived.

There were sounds outside the door. Footsteps coming and going. Voices of all kinds, some loud and belligerent, some authoritative. Occasionally people would walk by laughing or talking quietly to each other, all going about their business as if everything were normal.

She didn't remember falling asleep but suddenly realized she had been dreaming. She was in a church or a temple of some kind, colorful and filled with lights strung all over the place, like in the movie from India she had watched with Lee. A guy was sitting up on the altar playing exotic music from an instrument that looked a little like a guitar. Most of the people milling around had light-brown skin like the people in the movie. But the guy playing the music was pitch black, ancient, skinny as a rail, with deep-set eyes that bore into her like a laser. M.J. thought she belonged there; maybe she was brown-skinned too. But suddenly the guy stopped playing and pointed to her, glaring and accusatory. Then everything got very confusing. She had done something wrong but she didn't know what it was. She found a hiding place in a little cove behind the altar. She could hear people's voices searching the building for her. From where she was hiding, the colorful sanctuary looked like a circus with strings of twinkling lights extending from the elaborate carved ceiling toward all corners of the building.

The officer who had talked to her before came back, unlocked a drawer in the desk and removed some papers. She didn't look at M.J. or say anything, and when she left, she shut the door tightly.

M.J. felt like a bug, invisible on the cold brown sofa. She had no idea what would happen next. Nobody had explained anything to her. She had a deep longing, a panicky feeling she had not experienced for many years, of wanting her mother.

Lee was getting a lawyer. What should she say to the lawyer? The whole thing was so confusing. The officer had said "hit-and-run," but surely she would have known it if she had hit someone. Had she really heard something or was she just imagining it? Even if she did hear something, she'd better not tell anybody, not even Lee. The music was on in the car. Was there even a CD in the player? God, how could she not remember that? She was pretty sure a Michael Jackson CD was playing before she picked up Buddy. Was it still playing on the way home from the Foxes'? Why couldn't she remember that? What had she been thinking about on the way home? It was all a blank.

She felt oddly emotionless. Not sad or depressed or anything. Just cold, wide awake and astonished.

chapter forty-one

Frances Addison watched the outlines of the crepe myrtles outside the living room gradually emerge from the dark of the night, first as grey lace framing the eastern windows, then slowly transitioning to a bright pink as the sun approached the horizon. She hadn't gone back up to her bedroom but had found a warmer robe after the chill of the air conditioner had begun to make her shiver.

She had lost track of time but could see that morning was near. Lee had been gone about three hours and was not answering his phone. It was too early to call Hank. She thought about her daughter and wondered when it was she had started to fail as a parent. Had she been so broken up by Trey's infidelity that she had forgotten to be a mother? Or had she butted in too much, trying to force M.J. into a mold she couldn't fit? And what was her daughter feeling right now, locked away in a jail cell, her life ruined? Everything was changed, and changed forever. In the blink of an eye, all the haranguing and arguing were for nothing, and all Frances wanted was to hold her daughter in her arms and cry together until there wasn't a tear left.

When the front door opened, she jumped and was on her feet. Lee sat down with her and recounted the events of the night. The attorney, Jim Barnett, was still at the precinct with M.J. He appeared to be a smart, experienced lawyer and was working on the terms of bail. She would probably be released later in the day. It would be some months before the trial actually started. The inescapable truth was that a nine-year-old girl was dead, having been sideswiped by a car that passed a group of fourth-grade girls biking home after soccer practice. According to the girls, a dark green sedan driven by a teenage girl had veered close to the curb and struck the rear wheel of Susan Barker's bike, causing it to swerve into a ditch. The girl was thrown from the bike and landed on her neck, snapping the spinal cord, which led to instant paralysis and death shortly after reaching the hospital. The driver had not looked back and the car had not stopped.

Frances' mouth was dry and she was shaking. "Can I go down there and see her?"

"No, she's going to be kept busy with a bunch of procedural things. Barnett hopes we can bring her home this afternoon."

"How is she?"

"She's in shock right now, like all of us. I honestly don't think she knew she had hit anyone."

"Oh, God, her life is over, isn't it?"

"Try not to panic, Mama. You need to be strong for M.J. Right now I don't know enough about the law to have any idea what it's going to mean. But she will get through this. We all will."

The next twenty-four hours were chaotic. Lee's work for the firm came to a premature conclusion. He devoted his office time to researching Arkansas criminal law. Hank hadn't talked to anyone else at the office about M.J's accident. The youngster's death had not yet hit the newspaper. Lee spoke to Jim Barnett several times during the day, as well as working with his mother's financial adviser to determine access to bail funds. He was in action mode, tense, worried and pensive, fending off despair by converting anxiety into action. He hadn't slowed down long enough to feel anything nor had he wasted time wondering what his sister was feeling.

Mid-morning Hank Greene came into Lee's office and closed the door.

"How are you doing? Does Barnett have M.J. out on bail yet?"

"Not yet. They're still at the police station. He's going to call me when they have bail posted."

"Son, don't worry about the projects you've got on your desk. Family comes first. M.J. and Frances are going to need you. Is your mother okay?"

"We're all in shock. Jim Barnett has been a godsend. Knows the system and can tell us what's going to happen next. Thank you so much for calling him."

"He's the best criminal lawyer in the county. M.J. is in good hands."

When Barnett called to say that the court had released M.J. on bail and that he would be bringing her home, Lee packed up his notes from the day's research and left the office. M.J. was met at the door by her family, Frances squeezing her tight as tears flowed and Lee holding his young sister for a long time.

Jim Barnett at first declined Frances' offer to come in, knowing that M.J. above all needed some time alone. But sensing the anxiety of all three Addisons, he agreed to sit with them for a few minutes. Barnett was the kind of person who dominated a room. He was a big man, tall and athletic, in his late fifties. His face was worn beyond his years, with bags under his eyes that at first made him look tired and overworked. But his energy belied that first impression, and the man's passion for his work transformed his lined face into one of compassion and commitment.

He had been a Marine in Vietnam and had been introduced to the law as a JAG staff assistant. The Marines paid for law school at University of Arkansas. He had overcome a tough childhood to get where he was and so possessed a natural empathy for people in difficult situations. Even when it became apparent that a client was guilty, he never lost sight of what circumstances beyond their control might have led them there. Above all, he was not prepared to have his clients screwed over by the system.

Even Lee, for the first time in twenty-four hours sensing that someone else was in charge, took a deep breath and waited for Barnett to give them some direction.

"Look, I know you are all in a state of shock right now. You've got to put one foot in front of the other and get through these next couple of weeks. We live under a rule of law in this country and M.J. will be treated fairly. In the meantime, I don't want any of you to speak publicly about what happened. This will get into the news, and I'm afraid it's going to be a fairly big deal in this town."

Frances gasped. Of all the thoughts that had careened through her mind during the day, this one hadn't even occurred to her. Of course, everyone in town would know about it. A child had died. What about the girl's family? People would say terrible things about M.J. Some people would hate her. Some people would hate all of them.

"I work with a gal in Little Rock who is an expert in media management. I'm going to call her when I get back to the office and she will help us work out a strategy. In the meantime, do not speak to anybody except close friends who can be trusted not to repeat what you say. I have already gone through this with M.J., but all of you must remember that what you say to a friend or neighbor could get repeated in the newspaper or worse, found to be admissible in court. Lee, you especially, you're going to want to get in the middle of this thing. You can't do it. I'm happy to talk to you lawyer to lawyer and to consider your ideas and answer your questions. But you are too close to this to be making any decisions. So don't try to manage your sister or be a lawyer to her. She's already got a lawyer. All she needs from you right now is to be her big brother."

chapter forty-two

When the shrill repetition of rings began to feel like a jackhammer, Lee finally disconnected the telephone and the answering machine. The newspaper account had been stunning. Front-page headlines, an unnamed high-school driver suspected in a hit-and-run, pictures of a smiling blonde nine-year-old in her soccer uniform, praise of the much-loved youngster from her teachers and her pastor. It hadn't taken long for word-of-mouth around Riverton to identify the unnamed teenager. People in the neighborhood had seen the police cars at the Addison home and watched through half-closed blinds as M.J.'s green Buick was towed away.

Lee had picked up the first couple of calls. When reporters from across the state began calling, he quit answering the phone. The doorbell was next. Jim Barnett had to arrange for a security firm to keep intruders off the property.

The three Addisons were like prisoners in their home. At Jim Barnett's instruction, M.J. couldn't leave town. She also couldn't leave the house because of the reporters. The family doctor dropped off some pills to help M.J. and Frances sleep, and a few friends had left dishes of prepared food with the security guard out front, as if in anticipation of a funeral.

The television was kept on in the den at all times, and they circulated through the room in ones and twos. It felt too oppressive for all three of them to sit together, whether in front of the TV or in the formal living room, so they chatted in passing and tried to calm their depression and anxiety with the distraction of daytime soaps and evening sitcoms.

Lee wanted desperately to get out of the house and into the office where he could occupy himself with busywork. But it wasn't possible in the beginning, so he did what work he could from his bedroom and tried to keep a positive face for M.J. and Frances. It would have been a great comfort to have Annie there, but things had been tense with Annie since the inadvertent telephone introduction to Zoe. He had let Annie down one time too many and didn't want to lean on her now just because he was under siege. So he didn't call her. Likely hers was among the many unanswered phone calls.

He leaned back in the Queen Anne desk chair, poorly designed for balancing on its back legs, and closed his eyes. Just thinking about Annie calmed him, even though he didn't want to see her. He felt dirty. Not that he believed the sins of his sister reflected on him directly. But the ugliness of this accident, the gossip, the horror of a child's death would forever shape the image of his family in this town. Of course she was at fault. How had he failed to talk to her after that party about drinking and driving? How could he separate himself from the sin of his own flesh and blood?

He hadn't called Zoe either, though her counsel would have eased his anxiety. For all her sharp edges, Zoe could have provided some toughness and grounding during this crisis. But, he kept telling himself, this wasn't about him. His mind had not settled down enough to deal with the shadow of fear and shame that kept encroaching on his thoughts. It was M.J. he had to think about, and somehow it seemed critical to keep sorting through possible solutions, approaches to the case, information that might be helpful to Jim Barnett.

He was sorry his mother had seen the newspaper. Reading the emotional and scandalous headlines made the disaster so much more real. At the same time, it was like reading the script of a play that had nothing to do with you. How many times had he skimmed over somebody else's scandal, some anonymous tragedy, without giving it a second thought? It was either interesting or not, quickly read and tossed aside between sips of coffee. Things were so different when you were in the middle of it. Lee and Frances agreed to stop delivery of the paper and to keep the news articles about the accident out of M.J.'s hands.

Surprisingly, it was Frances and not Lee who was best able to comfort M.J.

She knocked softly on her daughter's door. "Can I come in for a minute?"

M.J. was sitting at her desk, staring at a blank sheet of paper. Frances came over to her and patted her awkwardly on the shoulder. They had not been a family that engaged in touching, and Frances wasn't sure how to reach out to her daughter. But she squared her shoulders and came around to face M.J.

"It is going to be all right, you know," she said.

M.J. stared at her mother without revealing any particular emotion.

"M.J., I can't even imagine what you're feeling. But it must be scary and unreal. I'm scared too. You know, we move mindlessly through life as if everything will just keep on being the way it has been and then something happens. And suddenly everything changes. That's how it was for me when your father left."

M.J. looked at her mother in surprise. In all the years since he left, Frances had rarely talked to her about her marriage or her father's disappearance.

Frances eased herself onto the edge of the bed.

"I guess I've been a terrible mother to you. Always critical and pushy. But, don't you see, I was scared for you. Being a woman is the most helpless thing. Men can do what they like. They sashay through life and take what pleases them and toss off whatever gets in their way. I wanted you to be strong so you couldn't get hurt. I didn't want you to ever go through what I did."

It was immensely quiet in the house.

"I hardly even remember Daddy. Do you know where he went? I mean,

I know he ran off with that girl."

"I heard they moved to California. Don't know if that's true or not. He stayed in touch for a year or two. Even sent money a couple of times. Birthday cards to you kids. Signed the divorce papers and agreed to pay alimony. But it was only a few months after he signed the papers that the checks stopped coming—and the birthday cards. I guess I could have hired somebody to try to locate him, but it didn't seem worth the trouble. He didn't have a real job, as far as I could tell. His aunt said they were living on a communal farm somewhere in Northern California. He could have had more children for all I know. I don't even know if he's dead or alive."

"I wonder if he ever thought about us. Me and Lee, I mean. What we were like as we grew up."

"I don't know."

"Was it always…I mean, did you fight a lot when you were married to him?"

"Oddly, no. Hardly at all. We were like everybody else. I was busy with you kids. He was busy working. We had friends and parties. I had no idea he was having an affair. No clue whatsoever. I felt so stupid."

M.J. tried to imagine what her mother would have been like as a young wife.

"Oh, I'm sure I could have been a better wife. Maybe I'm too difficult for anybody to live with. God knows, my mother never thought I did enough. But, M.J., my point is this. Sometimes life is just goddam hard. And it's not fair. Oh sure, some people seem to sail through with no problems. But I've always had the feeling that even those people in the end have to face hardship of one kind or another.

"Come downstairs. Let's have some tea."

The side doorbell was ringing but Frances let Lee get it. She poured peppermint herb tea into antique cups for herself and M.J. and watched the steam rise upward toward the kitchen ceiling.

The security guard rang the side doorbell occasionally to deliver a casserole that had been dropped off or to notify the family of a message that had been left with him. It was after 4:00 in the afternoon when Lee answered the bell. He was surprised at the intensity of the heat that hit him when he opened the door. However miserable it was outside, however, he would have gladly faced the heat and humidity to avoid another hour locked inside.

"There's a lady out front who would like to speak to you. A black lady, kind of old. Says her name is Etta Jones."

There weren't many people Lee would have let in the door, but for some reason this was a visitor he was glad to see.

"I brought you some of the purple hull peas from my garden, cooked all afternoon in bacon fat. I thought y'all might need something to eat."

Lee brought her into the kitchen where Frances and Mary Jane were sitting over cups of tea.

"Mama, this is a neighbor of ours and someone I've gotten to know out on my runs. Miss Etta, this is my mother, Frances Addison."

Both M.J. and Frances were surprised to see the visitor.

Frances rose to put the pot back on the stove. "Please, sit down. Would you like some tea?"

Lee pulled a chair over for Etta who joined the Addisons around the kitchen table.

"Child, I'm so sorry to hear about your accident."

She reached across to M.J. and placed her hand over M.J.'s.

They had of course discussed the case with Jim Barnett and had talked a little among themselves, but this was the family's first conversation with an outsider about the hit-and-run accident. All three of them found themselves without words, and they let Etta Jones have her say.

"When something bad happens, like this accident, you feel so bad. I know how that feel. And you wish you could go back and undo it. You'd give anything to do over those few minutes and have it come out different. But, honey, you can't do that. Life just keeps running at you, and you got to take what it brings. I know that's hard to understand when you so young. But it's like that for all of us really. You try to do the best you can with what gets thrown at you. And it's how you take it that matters, not what gets thrown. You got to keep your chin up and try to be the best person you can. That's all anybody can expect of you and it's all you can expect of yourself."

After Etta left, Frances warmed up a casserole that had been dropped off that afternoon. M.J. was quiet and Lee tried to keep the conversation going by talking about Etta Jones, how they had struck up a friendship during his runs and her relationship to the Washington boy whose case had occupied Lee's summer.

"M.J., she's right, you know," said Frances. "Darling, why don't you come to church with me in the morning? We need the church to steady ourselves during this time."

"Mother, I haven't been to church for six months. Don't you think it's a little hypocritical for me to show up asking forgiveness all of a sudden just because I ran over a kid?"

chapter forty-three

A week later Lee was sorting through case files in his office at Townsend Greene when the phone rang.

"Lee, this is Jason. I'm sure this is coming from left field, but I'm in Dallas and coming through there tomorrow. I'm driving cross-country. Anything to get as far away from law school as I can for a few more weeks. I hadn't planned to come this way or I would have called you sooner. I'll be passing through Riverton mid-afternoon tomorrow. I'm just wondering if we could have coffee or something."

Lee urged him to plan on staying the night. His mother and sister would enjoy meeting him.

Things had started to get back to normal, to the extent anything in Riverton would ever again be normal for Lee or his family. M.J. was spending most of her time with the attorneys. She had good days and bad days. More than anything, she seemed to be sleepwalking through the crisis. Lee was preoccupied with doing what he could to provide input and assistance to Jim Barnett, though it wasn't clear that Jim wanted his help. Now that the Washington trial was over and the end of summer approaching, there wasn't a lot of work for him at Townsend Greene. But it gave him a place to go and something to keep him busy, for which he was grateful. The people in the office were trying hard to be friendly and cheerful in his presence. But there was now a distance, even with Hank, who had been avoiding Frances since the scandal erupted.

Annie had kept him afloat in his anguish over M.J.'s troubles. She showed up at the house with food, hugs for M.J. and a determinedly upbeat perspective. And then she forced Lee to leave with her and kept him overnight, her touch like salve on an open wound. The next morning they had coffee in bed and talked about everything. All his fears for his sister. His ambition for himself. Where he expected his life to be in ten years. His mother. Zoe. Money and power and anxiety. He told her everything. And she told him about her dreams and her hopes for the future.

For twenty-four hours, he felt like himself again, but it was impossible to sustain any sense of optimism at home. His mother had kept herself together during the initial shock of the catastrophe. As time went on she became more anxious and less able to reach out to M.J. It didn't help that Hank Greene was keeping his distance. Her friends, though sympathetic over the phone, rarely stopped by or invited Frances out. She was gradually coming to understand that for the second time in her adult life, she was going to be a pariah in her own hometown, ostracized by respectable society.

M.J. wasn't talking to anybody either. Buddy Parish and his crowd of rough friends were nowhere to be seen. No phone calls either. She was at that age when bad vibes seemed contagious. M.J. had already cut herself off from people who might have lent support and so she was utterly alone except for her new best friend, Jim Barnett, who spoke to her daily.

Etta Jones had become a regular visitor. She and Annie hit it off right away. Annie had taught several of Miss Etta's great-grandchildren in school, as well as the Washington boys, and they enjoyed sharing stories about the kids' exploits.

The two women, both deeply religious, shared a common conviction that tragedies like the one M.J. was living through are a part of the human condition, to be borne with serenity and, thanks be to God, all things would work for the good in the long run. Lee was sometimes irritated and sometimes amused at their common message, but welcomed the relief they brought from the depression that enshrouded the family.

When Jason Levine showed up on his doorstep, Lee had mixed feelings. He could scarcely have refused the request to stop by, but he didn't relish bringing another outsider into his family's crisis. Jason's outburst in Carmel Valley had been completely out of character. What was more, since his sister's accident, Lee felt vulnerable, and he wasn't sure he trusted his friend.

"Jason, great to see you. Way down here in Arkansas? I can't believe it."

The distraction was good for M.J. and Frances. Lee too was glad to see a face that reminded him of his connection to another life, free of danger and guilt. They spent the afternoon regaling Frances and M.J. with stories from first-year torts, get-rich schemes from Silicon Valley, and commentary about Bay Area politics and economics.

Jason's sense of humor and charm had returned, and his solicitous interest in M.J. and Frances convinced Lee that Zoe had likely told him about the family crisis. They whiled away the afternoon on the back porch as the ceiling fan hummed and Frances plied them with iced tea and shortbread. There was nothing in Jason's manner to suggest he was having problems. Moreover, M.J.'s despondency seemed to have lifted and she was clearly enjoying their guest.

Having been cut off from the outside world since the accident, Lee and M.J. were desperate for an evening out of the house and decided to introduce Jason to some local nightlife. With all the negative publicity in the paper and the gossip about M.J. in Riverton, he made sure they would be far enough out of town to avoid people who knew them.

Jimmy Ray's Honky Tonk Bar and Grill was east of town toward Hot Springs at a bend in the road past the freeway cutoff. Although the sun had not yet settled below the western horizon, the huge triangular parking lot was already filling, and a parade of locals wearing blue jeans and bolo ties drifted into the modest, single-story log building, its entrance framed by two totem poles and a porch on three sides. The interior opened out into multiple smoke-filled rooms, a bar and jukebox up front, a dance floor with automated bronco saddle and bandstand in the largest room to the west, and multiple dining rooms on the other side.

Souvenir signs, black-and-white photographs and farm paraphernalia covered the walls, evoking the old days of farmers, cowboys and wide-open country. The hall led to a large backyard orchard framed by live oaks and filled with picnic tables where crowds gathered every weekend to feast on the area's best hamburgers, fries and local beer on tap.

The lyrics of Waylon Jennings and Merle Haggard wafted through the bar, drowning out the preseason NFL games on the television screens. Busy waitresses in short cowgirl skirts and vests, complete with cap pistols in their holsters and knee-high white boots, maneuvered skillfully through the crowds with trays stacked high. Loud speakers transmitted the music outside, and people were filling up the picnic tables as the afternoon heat began to ease.

Lee, Jason and M.J. found a table under a willow at the far end of the yard. While Lee was trying to reach Annie by phone, Jason went in for a pitcher of beer. M.J. took a deep breath and felt absolutely glorious to be out of the house, looking forward to a fun evening with her brother's totally cool, smart, funny law-school buddy.

By the time Lee was off the phone, Jason was back with the pitcher and three mugs and had started to pour cold draft beers.

"Not for M.J.," Lee said, pulling back one mug. "We've got enough trouble with alcohol."

He looked at her apologetically. "I'll get you a coke."

Lee took the empty beer mug and headed for the back door of the restaurant. Jason and M.J. looked at each other.

"Shit," she said and smiled.

"Here, you can have a sip of mine before he gets back," Jason offered, winking at her. "I had two big brothers. Pain in the ass, aren't they?"

She took a long deep swallow and felt every muscle in her body let go of the tension that had been knotting up her shoulders and neck.

Jason, never one to hold back in a new setting, rubbed her neck. "You look like a girl in serious need of a night out on the town," he said. "Me too. Maybe we'll do some 'lahn' dancin'."

After Lee returned with a coke for M.J., he took turns with Jason telling M.J. stories about the joys and terrors of their first year in law school. He was glad to see his sister having fun for the first time in weeks.

By the time Annie arrived, they had already started on their second pitcher, and the sun had gone down for good. The white lights strung across the trees were twinkling, and though it was still warm outside, the cozy comfort of the southern evening embraced them in an end-of-summer feeling—everything drifting slowly toward a happy ending.

Jason was having a great time in the authentic Arkansas setting, picking up the subtleties of the accent without any problem. Lee wasn't sure whether he was laughing with or at the good ole boys, but he was clearly enjoying himself.

Annie and Jason hit it off right away. She was captivated by his quick wit. For Lee, who had spent so much time in close company with Jason and Zoe, it felt a little strange, but he was happy to see that friends from different parts of his life and far ends of the country could find enjoyment in each other's company.

Once the live music started, they moved indoors. Lee took a deep breath and sighed, realizing how much he had needed this. M.J.'s legal problems had cut into his time with Annie. It was wonderful to have her in his arms and to move together into the music.

And for M.J. it was heaven to be with a guy who could carry the weight of the conversation. He didn't seem to mind holding forth like a stand-up comedian all evening, and all she had to do was laugh occasionally to keep him going. Every time Lee was out of sight, she and Jason smiled conspiratorially as she took a sip of his drink. It was easy enough to feel that she was just like anyone else, entitled to a good time, her whole life ahead of her. Any time thoughts of the accident crept into her mind, a long, slow sip of Jason's drink warmed her belly all the way down, erasing every trace of fear and shame.

It was also obvious to M.J. that Jason found her attractive. He was actually flirting with her, seemingly oblivious to his friend, her brother, just across the dance floor. She would have worried about her words beginning to slur but for the fact that Jason was stumbling a bit himself and didn't seem to care.

When Lee and Annie stopped by the table to tell them that Annie needed to leave, Jason was quick to suggest that Lee should drive Annie to her place and he would see M.J. safely home.

"Don't keep my little sister out too late," Lee admonished his friend as he and Annie left.

Once they were gone, Jason opened up to M.J. about some of the problems he had been having.

"I know about your accident and I'm sure it's been hell for you. I've had a pretty shitty time of it myself this year."

He told her about his troubles at school and the psychiatric treatments his family was insisting on. In turn she told him about how her mother and Lee and everybody else they knew thought she was screwed up, had a drinking problem, messed with the wrong kind of guys, and all that. They commiserated about Lee, how everybody thought he was perfect, how he always thought he knew what was right for everybody else.

As the discussion evolved, Jason's resentment of Lee became more pointed. M.J. was a little taken aback by his characterization of her brother as self-serving and holier-than-thou. She had felt keenly the weight of her brother's superiority all her life, but she also adored him, looked up to him. Jason's comments left her wondering if Lee really did love her, or whether his attentiveness was just one more way to assert his superiority.

"Come on, let's dance," she said, nudging Jason playfully and tugging his arm.

She felt safe in the company of someone older and more mature, and yet Jason knew how to have a good time. He was a fast talker and so funny.

She had enough of a buzz on to keep her in the moment, a blissful escape from all she had been through.

The ladies' restroom picked up Jimmy Ray's country and western theme with miniature wagon wheels on the walls and calico adorning the mirrored wash basins. M.J. was positioned a bit askew on the toilet, her head whirling with thoughts of music and romance. She could hear a gaggle of girls coming in together, full of chatter and laughter.

"Did you see her over by the fireplace, dancing with that guy?"

"She was probably that drunk when she killed the little girl."

"I can't believe she's out here partying in front of everyone."

"She should be in jail."

M.J. froze. She was careful not to move and hoped the girls wouldn't notice her shoes under the toilet door. She scarcely breathed until they had left the bathroom. Sweat was trickling down her chest between her breasts, and she felt nauseated.

Back at the table, Jason had picked up another scotch and M.J. took a quick sip. He wanted to keep dancing but she urged him to leave with her as quickly as possible. "Please, let's just get out of here. We can go somewhere else."

Jason turned onto the road behind the bar and drove about a mile along the edge of the state park until he found a place to pull over.

"What's the matter, M.J.? Are you okay?"

The alcohol had hit her by this time and she was dozing off, her head slumped against the passenger side door. Jason helped her out of the car and they staggered back and forth along the road.

"Honey, you need to sober up some before I take you home to your mother," he said as they walked, though Jason had to admit that he had had too much to drink himself.

M.J. awoke the next morning in a panic, the aura of candlelight spilling down a mountainside leaving her vulnerable and ashamed. Instinctively she touched the sheets beneath her without knowing why. Her mouth felt cottony and tasted like rancid garlic fries. She didn't remember much about the evening at Jimmy Ray's—not the close dancing with Jason Levine or the ugly gossip overheard in the restroom or any clue as to how she got home. She did remember Jason flirting with her. Had it gone beyond that? She smiled to herself, both embarrassed and a little pleased. Jesus, Lee would flip out if he knew. One of his fancy California lawyers hitting on his little sister. Jason must have been turned on by her. Guys were like that. Just like Buddy, always wanting to get her alone. Maybe Jason would want her to move out to California. She could live with Lee while she found a job. Jason would have an apartment in San Francisco looking out over the Golden Gate Bridge. Oh sure, Lee would be uptight about their relationship at first. But he would get over it, happy to know she had found somebody who was responsible and stable. She could finish her high-school degree out there and maybe someday she'd even go to college. But she'd like to work for a while and see if she could make it on her own.

She drifted in and out of sleep, enjoying the vision of life on the West Coast, away from Riverton and the people she knew in high school. But then her eyes opened with a start and she remembered. There would be a trial. She might go to jail. A girl was dead.

The house was quiet when she went downstairs, her mother doing paperwork at her desk and no sign of Lee or Jason. She wandered over to Frances.

"What time is it?"

"M.J., it's almost noon. What time did you get home?"

"Too late. Where's Lee?"

"He had to go in to the office. And Jason had to take off early to get into Little Rock by 1:00. He said to thank you and Lee for everything."

chapter forty-four

Annie had been stuffing envelopes for two hours and was glad when Lee walked in. The small storefront operation out in Warford housed the local office of the teachers' union and she had agreed to meet her annual commitment by giving up a Saturday afternoon.

"Figured you could use some help," he said, a bell announcing his entrance as he came in through the swinging glass door.

Annie rose and kissed him. "I'm so glad you're here. Are you okay?"

Annie was coming to realize how deeply troubled Lee was by the calamity that had befallen his family. The way he kept his feelings buttoned up, it wasn't always there on the surface to see. But he loved M.J. and Annie knew he was terrified of what lay ahead for her. Lee was not accustomed to problems he couldn't fix. Being around his family now left him feeling frustrated and powerless. He was happy to help, but mainly relieved to be out of the house.

Tommy was working at the back table, focused intently on getting stamps aligned correctly on the envelopes. Lee greeted Tommy and leaned over the table to inspect his work, his hand resting congenially on Tommy's shoulder. The boy was happy to see Lee but completely absorbed in the task at hand, squinting at each finished product and, as usual, pleased to be useful.

The one-room office was strewn with papers and boxes. Political posters and notices covered the walls. The pungent greasy scent of pizza filtered through the walls from next door. A single overhead light was inadequate to the work, and in spite of several table lamps contributed by the members, the cloudy day rendered the office gray and melancholy.

Lee carried a folding chair over to the table where Annie was working. "You are up to your elbows in paper," he said, touching her lightly. "Last night was fun. M.J. and I both needed a break from the perpetual doom of home."

"I felt bad about leaving the two of them the way we did. Did Jason take off?"

"He was out of there by the time I got up. God knows how he did it. He and M.J. must have been out at Jimmy Ray's pretty late. She slept in half the morning. It was good for her to get out and have a little fun. Jason's an odd guy. I was close to him once. Not so much anymore."

"He's got a good sense of humor. I think M.J. had fun."

Margaret Harris, the local union rep who managed the office, emerged from the back storage room. She was wearing jeans and a sweatshirt promoting a disco band from two decades earlier, her thinning gray-black hair pulled back in a rubber band. A jowled face hung behind reading glasses, bearing a look of disapproval. Margaret, dour and cynical by nature, had been on the losing end of political causes in Arkansas for so long that every new acquaintance was deemed an enemy until proven otherwise.

"He's here to help me, Margaret."

"Well, we can use all the help we can get," she said.

Lee stood and extended his hand to Margaret Harris. "Lee Addison."

"Sure, Lee, I remember you. Frances Addison's son. I know your Mama from out at St. Bede's. You're in law school."

"Just finished."

"Good to see Riverton High graduates come back home. Too many of our young people move away."

Annie looked down as Lee tried to maneuver the conversation to another topic. "Sounds like the union was pretty active in the last election around here."

"Somebody's got to advocate for the kids," Margaret said. "It's one thing for every living soul with white skin in this state to turn Republican. Now all of a sudden they're trying to make us teach out of books based on medieval science. When we try to get involved, the unions are tarred as left-wing enemies of the republic."

The bell sounded again as a stocky, middle-aged black woman with curly graying hair trimmed close to her head pushed through the door. She was wearing beige capris with Birkenstocks and a short blue-gray sweater that she had knit herself.

"I hope you're almost finished," she said to Margaret. "The rally starts at three o'clock so we need to head out pretty soon."

Margaret didn't look up from the computer where she had begun a calculation.

The new arrival flashed a smile at Annie and Lee, then wandered back to the table where Tommy was still engrossed in his project. "What are you working on, Tommy?"

Mattie Wilkinson had been a young algebra teacher at the all-black Dunbar High School when legally mandated integration and busing changed the landscape. As more articulate and better-trained white teachers came into her school, Mattie held on. She learned from them, struggling to keep kids of all colors on track, kids with wildly disparate backgrounds and resources. As the years passed, Mattie found a way to reach out to the fearful and resentful white teachers who were being dragged into a multi-colored world against their will, succeeding as one of the first black teachers at mostly white Riverton High. By the time she became principal at Dunbar, where she had gone to school herself as a teen and had seen more change than she could have dreamed of in her young life, Mattie was something of a local hero, much loved by kids, parents and teachers alike.

None of that, however, prepared Mattie Wilkinson for the initially confrontational and later intimate relationship she would develop with Margaret Harris, liaison from the superintendent's office. Margaret was disliked by most of the teachers, prickly and critical in her supervision of the school's curriculum, quick to anger and slow to praise. But, in spite of the stern exterior, Mattie came to respect her commitment to the kids and their future, and her colorblind expectation of excellence from every student and every teacher.

Margaret pulled her purse out of the drawer and came over to Mattie who was deep in conversation with Tommy about how to fix the stapler.

"Annie, I'm going to leave for a couple of hours. If you finish up, just make sure the door is locked," Margaret said.

Lee watched them as they hurried out the door and toward the car, heads together, smiling amiably as they shared the day's events. "Old teachers never die," he said. "They just morph into political junkies for any cause that favors the underdog."

"Those two aren't just political junkies," she said. "They have done more to fight for the education of poor kids in this county than an army of civil-rights workers. They've lived together for years. They were both great teachers in their day."

"Lesbians?"

"Lee," she fumed, "why is everything about sex with you? They are two old-maid schoolteachers who work hard to help poor kids around here, kids who will never escape from the dead-end poverty of their upbringing without an education. They're a fixture around town, popular and respected by everybody. What a terrible thing to say."

"Doesn't seem terrible to me," he snapped.

Lee would have found it hard to say why he felt irritated by Annie's conventional views. Sometimes her assumptions about the world were incredibly naïve. The two of them had become so close, and his need for her so great, that Lee sometimes found himself fantasizing about a future together. But the more he needed her, the more cautious he was about their differences. If he was judging her by false standards, it could be blamed on his fear of losing control. All his life so rational, he was scared that his blinding need for Annie would strip away every precaution and leave him defenseless.

He turned away from her and stood in front of the streaked plate-glass window looking out onto the street, rolling his neck to release tension.

"What's the matter?" she asked.

"I don't really want to talk about it. Just tired I guess."

But while he didn't want to discuss the depression that hung over him as a result of anxiety for M.J., he found ways to pick at everything Annie said and make himself as disagreeable as possible.

"I would steer clear of these teachers' unions if I were you. In California they've become a political machine. The teachers are funding liberal causes of every kind, most of them completely unrelated to the schools."

He had clung to her the night before, long after their passion had subsided, and Annie knew he needed her. She knew he loved her, for that matter. But God, he could be a prick.

"Lee, come to the evening meeting with me at church tonight."

"Annie, Christ, will you leave me alone about church? Please."

Because their relationship was expected to end upon Lee's return to San Francisco, they had reveled in the moment, unwilling to break the magic with the minutiae of daily life or the divisive rhetoric of politics and religion. But, in point of fact, Lee was an atheistic, libertarian, social progressive, and Annie was his opposite in every way. She loved tradition and family values and individual people. He loved innovation and ideals and ideas. She wasn't troubled by the intersection of science and religion and clung to the belief that mystery and wonder made life richer and joy more profound. He believed in the power of the mind and the ability of an individual to change the world.

Embarrassed by his surly mood, he rose and went over to where she sat. "Come here. I'm sorry. Let's go back to your place."

Pulling her up, he tried to kiss her, but Annie pushed back.

"No, I'm busy. If you're upset, go home. Try to make someone else feel better for a change."

chapter forty-five

Jim Barnett had summoned the whole family to his office. He had been a regular visitor to the Addison home during the first week after the accident, but later shifted his meetings with M.J. to his office. Today he called Lee and asked all three of them to come in.

Barnett's solo practice was a smaller operation than Townsend Greene and the reception area less formal. Its location near the county courthouse was a reminder of a criminal defense lawyer's need for access to the courts, the bail bond offices and the jail. And yet his office communicated power in its own way just as surely as did Hank Greene's. An impressive array of photographs with dignitaries dotted the walls. The heavy mahogany and leather furniture spoke to the gravitas of meetings held here.

Barnett had represented some of the region's most notorious defendants, including the serial killer who had terrified Riverton in the early eighties. He had been at the forefront of the defense bar's insistence on racially balanced juries to ensure an even hand for the great majority of his clients who were black, many of whom faced an uphill battle to prove their innocence to jurors who equated skin color with a predisposition to steal and kill.

Jim welcomed them into his office. His demeanor was all business. Lee felt a chill as he settled into the oversized leather chair.

"I've finally got the blood test results from the DA's office and I wanted all of you here to discuss strategy. The BAC was .08—well over the legal limits for driving. Arkansas has some very specific sentencing guidelines pertaining to driving under the influence, especially for minors, and this is going to leave us with some difficult choices. Almost certainly there will be jail time."

M.J. didn't hear anything else. At those words, she flushed in a way that might have been a teenage girl's response to a fresh remark from a boy. She felt oddly embarrassed, as if saying such a thing in front of her mother and brother was somehow in bad taste. She liked Mr. Barnett. She thought the two of them had a nice relationship, talking together like adults, working through the details and deciding on a strategy. Jail. She remembered that first night. The photograph and the fingerprints. The coldness of the room. But since then she had somehow felt it would be okay. He would figure out a way. Of course she might have to leave town. Finish school out in California maybe. She knew she couldn't stay in Riverton. She felt strangers' eyes raking over her body every time she went out in public. She knew she could never return to Riverton High. But jail....

She tried to follow what Jim Barnett was saying, but his voice was sounding like a buzzing insect, and she couldn't focus. Lee kept interrupting him to ask questions and she wondered why. Her mother had gone white as a sheet. M.J. was more interested in them than in what Mr. Barnett was saying. Why are they so upset? This isn't about them. She knew she should be distressed but she didn't feel anything. It seemed so unreal, so crazy really. Like a movie. She caught herself about to smile at the absurdity of it but was careful to keep her face blank. Her mind wouldn't—couldn't— follow the trajectory of what this would mean over the years.

On the way to the car, her mother tried to put her arm around her, but M.J. turned away.

"It's going to be all right, M.J. We are not going to let this happen to you. Lee, I think we ought to look for another lawyer."

Annie was waiting at the house when they got back. She urged Lee and M.J. to join her for a hike in the country, get out of the house, get some exercise. Lee had to get in touch with Pickford Martin in San Francisco and work out something to delay his start date. But he encouraged M.J. to go.

Annie would know what to say.

They didn't talk much during the drive out to the national forest. Just inside the park's entrance, Annie pulled the car off the road onto a shoulder near a trailhead.

Annie led the way down a path through the pine forest. The needles were so deep you couldn't see the path, and the sound of their steps was muted by the cushioned surface of the trail. Annie didn't try to make casual conversation. She walked ahead of M.J. in silence. Except for the rhythmic chirping of cicadas, the afternoon was still as they proceeded along a path that climbed gradually up a slope on the eastern side of a hill. The path was well groomed but little used and they saw no other hikers on the way up. Annie pointed out some wild strawberries in an open meadow and warned M.J. against the poison ivy.

Although the pine forest provided shelter from the afternoon heat, M.J. was starting to sweat. She didn't feel well and couldn't keep pace with Annie. The lawyer's words kept tumbling through her mind. Jail. It wasn't that it hadn't occurred to her. But for all of Lee's running around to get information on the case, he hadn't talked to her about the fact that she might go to jail. She had an idea what it was like from TV. In some ways it didn't seem so horrible. At least the women wouldn't beat you up or rape you like the men did. Crummy food and an uncomfortable mattress she guessed. Lots of time to kill. You wouldn't have to go to school.

She couldn't get her mind around how it would be when she got out. She would be an ex-con. Maybe couldn't even get a job. Who would ever marry her? She couldn't stay in this town, that was for sure. Which was fine. But no matter where she went, people would eventually find out. She might meet a guy and he might fall in love with her, but when he found out what she had done, that would be that.

She had found the newspapers in her mother's desk the night before. Mama had saved everything they wrote about M.J.'s accident. Was she going to make a scrapbook? Funny, M.J. hadn't even noticed that the morning paper had stopped. It seemed odd that they never put her name in the paper. Of course everyone knew. That's why they were avoiding her. Even Buddy. After making excuse after excuse, he finally told her yesterday. He was afraid of getting in trouble himself because he had been with her at the party. Afraid they would blame something on him. He had been in too many scrapes with the law. She could understand that. It wouldn't be fair to blame this on him but that wouldn't stop them.

She had been mesmerized by the photographs of the girl. Susan. With all that had happened, she hadn't been able to think of the girl as a real person. M.J. had been angry that the girl hadn't been more careful. She must have jerked her bike into the car's path. Wasn't paying attention. Now M.J.'s life was screwed up forever.

It was a smiling young face, blue eyes sparkling under Dutch-cut straight bangs. She was wearing a Brownie uniform in the picture, her sash covered with badges she had earned by finishing projects. M.J. remembered how her troop leader had nagged them to finish those badges. She had always thought it kind of silly, jumping through all those hoops to get a little round badge. Had M.J. looked like the little girl at that age? Same hair color. The girl wouldn't ever go to high school. Wouldn't get married and have kids.

Quietly M.J. had returned the clippings and closed the drawer, her hands shaking, her stomach queasy.

Annie had stopped ahead on the trail to wait for her to catch up.

"We're almost there. Just about 100 yards up this path. Can you make it?"

They bent under a dogwood branch that had extended over the path near the summit, emerging into a clearing where a park bench overlooked the valley.

"We've made it to the mountaintop," Annie announced. "They must have put this bench in here years ago, the way it's overgrown. I think I'm the only one who knows about it anymore."

M.J. settled on the bench beside Annie and drew her knees up to her chin. The deciduous trees had not started to turn yet, so the vista rippled in shades of green and gray with dappled sunlight brightening the color wherever it broke through.

"This is my thinking place. I come up here to be alone. Sometimes to pray. You're the only person I've ever brought up here besides your brother. For me there's something about getting up high. Helps me clear my head. If the world's this big and this beautiful, it doesn't seem to matter so much when I'm having a shitty time of it."

Annie had always been kind to her but because M.J. knew it was because of her brother, it had never meant much. Still, it felt good to be in the older girl's company.

"I used to come up here and cry, after Lee broke it off. Did that for years. God, we can be stupid when it comes to guys."

Annie laughed a clear, melodic laugh. Not a bitter one. It was genuinely funny to her.

"Are you two going to get married?" it occurred to M.J. to ask.

"Oh God, I have no idea. I doubt that Lee does either. He's got a life out in California that's really important to him and I'm not sure I fit into it. And there's a girl out there. I'll probably be visiting this bench quite a bit after he leaves. He does love me, I know that. But that doesn't mean it's going to work out. Sometimes life just doesn't."

"Do you love him?"

"I do. But it's funny. I don't need him the way I used to. In a way, you can't really love someone until you quit needing them. That's probably hard for you to understand. You're still so young."

"I don't feel young."

"Well, you are. And you're living through a nightmare."

M.J. didn't respond.

"When things get hard for me, I pray. I know church isn't your thing right now. It's the age. Or whatever. But I couldn't have survived this long without my faith."

M.J. didn't want to be rude but she would not pretend to believe in God just because she was in trouble.

"Maybe it came naturally to me," Annie added, "because of my family. You know, with Tommy and all his problems. It changes your perspective to watch someone grow up without the choices the rest of us have. You have to think a little more about what matters."

Annie patted her knee and smiled. "Sorry. I'm getting preachy. Just ignore me. Someday it may make sense to you. This religious stuff, I mean."

After a minute of silence, she continued.

"The way I think about it, it isn't so much about what I understand God to be. Honestly, I have no idea. It's beyond me. But I know I can't make it alone. So I choose to believe. And it comforts me. The concept that there is a force more powerful than I am who cares about me."

"And you don't think that's just making yourself feel better?" M.J. asked.

"M.J., trust me, there's nothing wrong with feeling better. Anyway, for me it has more to do with humility. Lee, for example, is much more certain there's not a God than I am that there is one. But having faith is a humble kind of thing. There's no proof, but you choose to believe. And, for me at least, it has something to do with the fact that our lives are too beautiful and horrible and magical and...*sacred*...to treat them like an accidental evolutionary blip. So I choose to believe in the power of something I can't understand."

chapter forty-six

When Lee called to delay his start date at Pickford Martin, the hiring partner was sympathetic to his need to remain with the family for a few more weeks. He hadn't had to explain the details of the crisis. There was enough cushion in a firm of its size to move first-year associates around from group to group. The firm would give him as much time as he needed to deal with the family emergency.

After he got off the phone, Lee was both relieved and depressed. He couldn't possibly go now, but on some level he would have loved to escape to a busy law practice in San Francisco.

He lifted the phone back off the receiver and dialed Zoe. Especially now, he appreciated their friendship and the comfort he drew from her wisdom and toughness. The distance shielded her from being hurt or tainted by his family's disgrace. She answered right away.

"That's not good news. From all you've said, I was afraid the blood tests would come out that way. If Arkansas is anything like California, there are probably mandatory sentencing laws. How is the choice of counsel working out?"

"The guy is experienced and has a good reputation. I'm pretty impressed so far. I think he wishes I'd get off his back."

"No doubt. On the other hand, those guys are used to dealing with distressed families."

"I guess," he replied. "He told me the other day this wasn't the kind of case he liked to take. I think he's having trouble getting through to M.J."

"He probably sees a lot of families living on the edge," Zoe said, speaking from experience. "Young men who never had a chance, getting shunted into the criminal justice system. It's pretty frustrating to live with that every day. I wouldn't take it personally."

"He's started to interview the kids at the party but he hasn't told me what he's hearing. M.J. has isolated herself from a lot of people during the last couple of years. She has a bad reputation and not a lot of close friends at school. I suspect we're not going to get great character witnesses who will attest to her sobriety at the party."

"Poor baby. She must be a basket case."

"More withdrawn and subdued than anything. She won't open up to me and certainly not to my mother. The thing that pisses me off more than anything is that nobody is coming around to support her. I can't believe she has no friends. She's rebellious but she's a nice enough kid. Even her creepy boyfriend has dropped off the face of the earth."

"Bastard," she muttered, quiet for a minute as she contemplated the depravity of some members of the human race. "Jason said he stopped by to see you in Riverton. Went on and on about your gorgeous house and your night out at a country and western bar. He had some pretty funny stories about Arkansas."

"How is he really?" asked Lee. "I couldn't read him at all. On one level, he seemed like his old self. Seemed to have wiped the Carmel Valley encounter out of his mind. But then we had a late night at that bar and he was out of here early the next morning without even saying good-bye."

"I don't know. I actually don't think he's okay. He's working with the administration at the law school and it looks like they're going to let him finish first quarter. So he's around here a lot. You know I love the guy but not the way he wants. So it's a little weird. I'm just trying to be a friend to him. It's not anything he does or says overtly. I just have a sense that something's not right. Anyway, he seems fine with you and said he enjoyed his short time there. When do you think you'll come out?"

"Probably in another month. The trial won't be until later in the year, but I need to stay here until M.J. and my mother are settled enough to be alone. Then I'll probably come back to be with M.J. before the trial starts."

"Hang in there."

Lee had spent half the morning calling in chits from family friends to fill out a dinner party guest list that Frances was determined to host on Saturday evening. She was being treated like a pariah by her friends at the Club. M.J. was spending every day locked in her room. The phone never rang, and M.J. made no effort to reach out. With her driver's license suspended, she couldn't even frequent her old haunts like the Bend without a willing friend to pick her up. Frances would be damned if she was going to let her daughter wither away in isolation while the hypocrites in this town shunned them.

Lee wanted no part of it. He didn't like to ask for favors, and the few people he still cared about in Riverton—Annie and her family, Mike Thompson, Etta Jones—were already showing up at the house. But the scene last night had been frightful. Frances cried and, to the shock of the son who had known only adoration from his mother, lashed out at him in anger.

"What would you know? When have you ever had to fight for anything? I have scraped and clawed my fingers to the bone to keep this family above water. I will not have my daughter thrown to the wolves. You *will* help me, Lee. I'll be god-damned if they can treat us like lepers."

She had wept and cursed the heavens, and he held her and comforted her as if she were a child. They would have the dinner. He would invite the guests.

He shuddered as he thought about his meeting with Hank earlier in the morning. Nothing could have been more distasteful to Lee than pleading with his boss to come to a dinner he wanted no part of. Whatever the sordid details of Hank's personal life and his relationship with Frances, it was clear he was intentionally avoiding her and determined to end whatever had begun. If that had not been crystal clear before M.J.'s accident and the family's disgrace, it was painfully apparent now. And Lee knew, frankly, that had there been a graceful way to get Lee out of his law firm, Hank would have done so. But Hank Greene couldn't tarnish the benevolent, church-going, pillar-of-the-community image that he held of himself. So when Lee begged him for this small favor, for the sake of his family, Hank could hardly refuse. Lee knew it would give his mother some comfort, even with the certainty that Hank Greene would never again come courting.

chapter forty-seven

Frances worked for two days preparing for the dinner party. She had not used help in the kitchen since Lee left home for college, but called Hattie Davis, her maid for five years, to see if she could come help out. Hattie couldn't work anymore because of her arthritis, but she sent two of her nieces. The girls had been stirring, sifting and baking since early morning. Frances' best silver was polished and sparkling on a dining room table bedecked with a red and gold runner and a centerpiece Frances had made herself of red rosebuds from her garden and filler from the farmers' market. The flowers nicely complemented the sterling silver candelabras supporting three tall red tapers at each end of the table.

Lee and M.J. stayed out of her hair the afternoon of the dinner party, Lee catching up on a memorandum he had to finish at the law firm and M.J. listening to music in her room. As Frances moved chairs to a tighter circle around the fireplace, M.J. turned up Slayer to drown out the clatter of pots and dishes downstairs, trying to distract herself from the dread she felt about the evening that lay ahead. The beat and rasp of the discordant punk sound soothed her in some funny way. She leaned back into the floor pillow, strumming her fingers to the sound of the music. Then she shut her eyes and took a deep breath. *I can do this*. She fished a small key from the outside pocket of her purse and opened the bottom drawer of her desk. The smoky scent of the Johnnie Walker and the smooth surface of the bottle calmed her jitters. She could get away with drinking in her room, but her mother was instantly alert to the smell of tobacco. Pouring a shot into the small glass, she closed the bottle and locked it safely back in the desk drawer.

Downstairs Frances was confident that the girls had everything under control in the kitchen. She checked the guest bathroom, making sure there were matches available to light the candle at the last minute, and surveyed the dining room for anything out of place. She had butterflies, as she always did before entertaining. But she would be glad afterward. She knew how important it was to stay the course. She could do this. It was the right thing for her and the right thing for her family.

Both of her children had tried to dissuade her from the compulsion to entertain, now of all times, but she would not be moved. Frances had lived through enough to know that you had to stare down your demons and hold your head high. M.J. had balked at first, threatening to lock herself in her room, carrying on about her shame and humiliation. *Damn her anyway, that child. The stupidity, the rashness of what she had done.* But M.J. was going to have to face things Frances couldn't even imagine, so she had better toughen up, and fast. Lee had finally convinced M.J. to cooperate. He had sat in her room for hours as she cried and swore. *Thank God he's here*, thought Frances.

It took every bit of guts and grit she possessed to make this happen. She had called, what, six people before she got an acceptance. Even her closest friends, the girls in the bridge club she had known all her life, had stammered and mumbled apologies. There were conflicts they couldn't get out of. The mewling sweetness of their regrets made her sick. She had framed the invitation in a way that would be hard to refuse. Lee would be home only a few more weeks. Who knew when he'd be back in Riverton? *He would so much enjoy an evening with you and Clifford.*

The acceptance from Mitzi Evans had surprised her. She wasn't that close to Mitzi, who came from a long line of prominent Riverton socialites and cared less than most about whether people approved of her or not. Probably accepted because she was curious. Mitzi had brought her cardiologist husband back to Riverton after he finished his residency. He was from somewhere out west and Frances hardly knew him. He didn't seem to care much for society, but he gave Mitzi the money and status she needed to go right on doing what she had always done—drinking, socializing and playing tennis and bridge in the comfort and familiarity of the Riverton Country Club.

The real coup had been Eleanor Marcus. The widow—Mrs. Marcus, never Eleanor to everyone in town—had been married to Riverton's richest citizen, the man for whom the Marcus Hospital was named. She was in her mid-eighties by now. Wasn't seen out socially that much. She was invited to every wedding in town, sending opulent gifts to the assembly line of brides whom she would not have recognized on the street. She rarely showed up at a wedding, or any other event for that matter. Frances wasn't even sure Mrs. Marcus would know about the accident since M.J.'s name had never appeared in the paper.

Frances had continued to save all the newspaper accounts about M.J.'s accident and the girl who had been killed, filing away each story in her desk drawer. She couldn't have said why she kept them but it seemed important. She would pick up each morning's newspaper in front of the supermarket and read it in the car, scanning quickly for any account of the accident, with no interest in anything else. Tearing out the article or editorial, she would shove it into her purse and discard the rest of the paper in a trash receptacle.

Eleanor Marcus would no doubt have read about the hit-and-run accident, but possibly had not heard that Frances' daughter had been the driver. Of course, Eleanor knew everyone of importance in town, but Frances suspected she had few confidants. Maybe she wouldn't have heard the gossip. In any event, Frances had used her best diplomatic skills on the phone—Lee's success at Stanford…his last summer in town…how he had admired Mr. Marcus…her husband's friendship with Judge Dawkins.

Frances had seated Lee at the far end of the table with Mrs. Marcus to his right and D.B. Evans to his left. Frances sat at the end closest to the kitchen, flanked by Hank Greene and Mike Thompson. Mitzi and M.J. took the middle seats. Mitzi set the tone with her wit and charm, holding forth in an animated conversation with Hank about the changing membership standards and poor taste of the Club's new manager. Lee skillfully entertained both Mrs. Marcus and D.B. Evans with topics of benign general interest.

"Good Lord, Hank," Mitzi laughed, shaking her head in mock horror, "have you seen what he did with the green room? Must have thought the golfers would be taking up that space for drinking beer after a round. It's supposed to be set aside for bridal shower luncheons."

"I never get invited to those luncheons, so I couldn't say," Hank responded. "But I'll tell you what. He has hired a fabulous chef for the grill. Just started last week. He knows the way to *my* heart."

"Honest to Pete, Hank, you men have such predictable priorities!" Mitzi managed to flirt with both men and women, having been born with her mother's gift for chatter and just the right proportion of softness and sauciness in her delivery. She did like to drink, however, and was on her second glass of Burgundy before the entree was brought in.

Frances had put a wine glass filled with iced tea at M.J.'s place. As the evening wore on, she noticed that M.J. had finished the tea and had taken advantage of a passing wine bottle to refill her glass. She shot a look of disapproval at her daughter, which M.J. chose not to notice. Well, Frances couldn't blame her, poor girl. She wasn't socially adept anyway and, after everything that had happened, she would naturally feel ill-at-ease around people. A little wine might help her relax, get her through the evening.

Frances could overhear Lee telling D.B. Evans about his upcoming job in San Francisco. "People think of Silicon Valley in terms of computer chips and software, but a ton of venture capital money has gone into startups in the biotech and pharmaceutical fields. If they come up with a viable product, these small medical research companies get bought out by the big multi-nationals about the time they submit the product to the FDA."

Frances was so proud of him. What would a small-town doctor like D.B. know of venture capital and IPOs and leveraged buyouts? Lee could talk circles around any of them. Mrs. Marcus was clearly impressed. She was sophisticated enough to know the power and prestige of the San Francisco financial infrastructure.

Frances reached for the Burgundy and poured another glass for Mike before refilling her own glass.

"I was just telling M.J. about my youngest sister's first summer up at Camp Ariadne in the Ozarks," Mike said to Frances. "I had forgotten that M.J. went up there as a kid herself."

Mike Thompson was the perfect guy to nudge M.J. into the conversation. Smart and self-effacing, he would have done anything for Lee.

"Susie went to Ariadne for about three years I guess. I think it gave her a lot of confidence. She made some good friends up there."

M.J. leaned over Mike toward her mother. "I hated it there."

Frances was surprised by her daughter's tone, which came out louder and harsher than M.J. had intended. But before she had time to worry about M.J., one of the maids came into the dining room and whispered to her. "You have a guest at the door, ma'am."

At the front door stood Etta Jones, holding a steaming pot of black-eyed peas between two large potholders. A frequent visitor during M.J.'s crisis, Etta has eventually earned Frances' respect, but her timing was poor. "I wish I could ask you in, but we're in the middle of a dinner party," Frances said.

"Don't you want to keep these peas for lunch tomorrow? I've got more than I can eat in a week."

Etta came into the kitchen to hand the pot to the girls helping with the party. As Frances thanked Etta and saw her to the door, Eleanor Marcus entered the kitchen.

"I just need another sip of water to take my pill."

"Oh, here, Eleanor. I'm being a negligent hostess. Let me do that."

Mrs. Marcus watched Etta leave, then she turned to Frances. "Was that Etta Jones?"

Frances was already embarrassed that Mrs. Marcus had felt it necessary to come into the kitchen, and absolutely chagrined that she had seen Etta at the door.

"That's a kindly little woman that lives down the street. But you must be right. I think her last name is Jones."

"Good Lord, I didn't know she was still around here. One of her grandchildren used to mow our lawn years ago and she would drop him off. I've always been curious about her. I remember seeing her as a young woman, about my own age, at the Axel Jones trial in the 1940s. Her twin brother. Well, you must remember about that. Your daddy was the judge."

In fact, Frances had no idea what she was talking about.

"She has struck up a friendship with the children," Frances said, embarrassed.

"Her brother was involved in stirring up the Negroes in Riverton after the war. Shot by the police trying to break into a building. After he died, a bunch of colored people from that church that used to be over on Second Street, they made such a fuss about the police killing him that there was a big trial here in Riverton. They accused the police of killing him just because he was black. Reporters came here from all over the place, writing in their papers that our police officers were racist. You know, it was after the war and things were starting to change. President Truman wanted to make sure the Negroes were treated fairly. Your daddy could have told you some interesting stories about that time."

"Here Joleen, get Mrs. Marcus some ice water."

Frances' embarrassment at the untimely visit from Etta Jones was matched by her surprise that Eleanor Marcus seemed to know all about the Jones family. Frances wondered whether her parents had intentionally shielded her from what was going on around them or whether she just hadn't been paying attention.

The disparity between Etta Jones' lifelong awareness of the white community in Riverton and Frances Addison's obliviousness to the black people living in their midst was striking. The two women had lived their entire lives just blocks apart, walking the same streets, following the same seasons. Resilient women, both had faced down disaster and social disapproval with stony resolve. Getting out of town would have been the easy thing to do, but both women had stayed put, right where they were born, their feet firmly planted in the red Arkansas clay.

From the time she was a child, Frances had been taught to treat the colored people who worked and played at the margins of her world with benevolence. Neither of her parents would have tolerated demeaning epithets. They were generous with holiday gifts to the help and always remembered to ask after the families of the men and women who cooked their meals and tended the garden. Frances would not have thought of herself as a person with racial prejudices. She knew people like that in Riverton, crude people who used hateful words, and she looked down on them.

But the truth was that people like Etta Jones were essentially invisible to Frances. She didn't know what to make of the fact that her children seemed to feel some personal affection for this woman. She thought that Lee and M.J. were being kind to Etta in the same way she herself was kind to the nice lady who did her ironing on Thursday afternoons.

After dinner Frances invited her guests into the parlor for liqueurs and coffee. Mike begged off because of an early-morning commitment and Mrs. Marcus explained that she was being picked up shortly and had to decline.

M.J. had been quiet throughout much of the evening, saying not a word during dessert. As people adjourned to the parlor or to say their good-byes at the door, M.J. stumbled up from the table. D.B. Evans extended a hand.

"Oh shit, I'm sorry," M.J. muttered, her words slurring. She had to grab the sideboard to steady herself. Her mother and brother watched her with alarm, and Lee quickly moved to give her a hand as Frances bustled the other guests out of the dining room. Lee held M.J. firmly in his grasp until the last of the dinner guests had left the room, then he turned her toward the kitchen. "Let's get you upstairs."

"I don't want to go upstairs. I want a brandy."

Gripping her firmly by the elbow, he steered her up the back stairs, M.J. muttering to herself, Lee silent and grim.

chapter forty-eight

Jim Barnett was in a meeting when Lee arrived. His secretary suggested that Lee wait. The meeting would be over in the next half hour and she was sure Mr. Barnett could make some time for him. She offered to bring him a cup of coffee and he gratefully accepted. The small waiting room was overly air conditioned and Lee was chilled. The night before, Annie had finally convinced him that he had to do something.

They had been sitting up in her bed, working the Sunday crossword puzzle. Annie was quicker at finding the words, a rare opportunity to outsmart him, and she was rubbing it in unmercifully.

Whatever it was he had said set her off, Annie laughing so hard tears were streaming from her eyes, and it was impossible, even in Lee's state of despondency, not to get caught up in it. Soon enough they abandoned the crossword puzzle, but even in the ardor of lovemaking, one or the other would bring up the joke again and they would relapse into laughter.

He pulled her close and kissed her gently.

Each of them, for separate reasons, had let go of the struggle to keep their summer love affair casual. Annie didn't bring up Zoe's name again. Lee didn't talk about his new job. The effort to pull away in order to dull the anticipated pain of parting at summer's end was making them both miserable. They agreed on a truce. They would relish the rest of their time together and let the future take care of itself.

He was determined to stay the night, tired of forcing himself up and back home so as to avoid another lecture from his mother about the perils of getting too closely entangled with Annie. Because there was nothing he wanted more than to be entangled with Annie—entangled physically and emotionally, and so completely that it would carry him away from all the trouble and stress of the world, safe in the cocoon of her sweet grounded sensibility and loveliness.

He worried about whether it was fair to her, both of them knowing he would leave soon and she would be bereft. Things were so painful and stressful at home that his need for her had become profound. They both understood that. But he did love her. He had always loved her. And it wasn't just physical either. Being in her presence touched something in Lee that he rarely acknowledged. Something spiritual, quiet, deeply moving.

When they woke the next morning, neither of them jumped out of bed. They were content to wake up slowly, murmuring to one another, turning over for a few more minutes of sleep, waking up again, bound together in a groggy embrace.

Annie had finally forced herself up to turn on the coffee, and again they sat in bed talking quietly, sipping hot coffee as the mid-morning sun warmed the room. In spite of living her whole life in Riverton, Annie would not sleep under an air conditioner. Good cross-ventilation and lots of shade trees had been essential in her choice of a home, and the air conditioner was always shut down between sunset and when she left the house in the morning. Sometimes it was too muggy for Lee's taste, but he could hear the songbirds and the rustling sounds of morning outside the window and was glad to be where he was.

"I've been thinking about something you said last night," Annie said. "About the dinner party." It was a sore subject for Annie.

Even though Frances Addison knew Lee and Annie had been together for much of the summer, she hadn't invited Annie to the dinner party. She was friendly and welcoming whenever Annie showed up at the house, but Frances would not go out of her way to encourage the rekindled romance. Annie had brought in dinners, spent time with M.J. and done what she could to support all of them. Frances expressed her appreciation, especially for the time Annie spent with M.J., but it was crystal clear that she didn't see her son's future with Annie and that she feared the young woman's influence.

"You said M.J. managed to get herself drunk at the dinner party, and yet she claimed the next morning not to remember anything about it. I don't know why this is so hard for you to see, but I think M.J. is alcoholic."

Annie had raised this issue before and to Lee's mind it just didn't fit. M.J. was a troubled teen but after all, she was just a kid. Alcoholics were old guys who wandered the streets and hung out at AA meetings, smoking cigarettes and acting sanctimonious because they went another day without a drink.

"Annie, most teenagers drink too much. Maybe you didn't, but I sure the hell did. I'm not excusing her. She's a messed-up kid. And it's not surprising that she'd want to drink too much right now, with what she did and all she's facing."

"Here's the thing," Annie said. "Once you start using alcohol to escape, it can change you. Some people are more vulnerable to it than others. I know about this because of my aunt. Over time it changes your brain."

"She's just a kid. Her brain is still developing."

"Or not. People who start drinking too much at her age get stuck in adolescence forever. And this business of not remembering things the next morning, that's one of the signs."

"Annie, she's got bigger problems than this. She may turn eighteen in jail. Not much chance of drinking too much in there."

"Lee, it's an illness. And it's one that doesn't get cured by itself. Why are you so resistant to helping her deal with this?"

"Look, even if I felt she had a drinking problem, this is the wrong time to get into it. It would hurt her case. Kind of like admitting she had a history of drunk driving and should have known better than to get into the car that day."

In the end, he had agreed to talk to Barnett about M.J.'s drinking and whether the issue of alcohol dependency would be a factor in the case.

Barnett's client meeting lasted longer than expected and Lee was almost out the door when he finally emerged.

"I'm sorry to keep you waiting, Lee. Come on in."

Lee asked Barnett about the impact of M.J.'s blood-alcohol test.

"It's too soon to know. Most likely we'll try to plea bargain. But I'm in the midst of extensive interviews with potential witnesses. And I'll tell you that there have been a number of episodes that are pretty widely known where your sister drank too much. That won't help us when we get to court. I don't yet know who the D.A. will tap for witnesses, but I've heard enough to think there will be people in town who will paint a picture of her as a troubled teen and maybe one with a drinking problem."

"If we thought she had a problem with alcohol—and I'm not sure that's the case, I'm just asking—would it make sense to try to get some help for her now?"

"Not now. I don't want to prove their case for them. Almost certainly, no matter what happens, she's probably going to have to do some alcohol-abuse program. But now's not a good time."

Annie's concern that M.J. might have a problem with alcohol continued to bother Lee. He was determined to talk to M.J. sometime during the weekend. But when he got home, his mother reminded him that they would be out of town for a long day on Saturday, visiting their country relatives in White Rock.

chapter forty-nine

Once they turned off the state highway into the Ouachita Mountains, Lee left the talking to his mother and concentrated on driving. He had made the trip to White Rock many times during his childhood but had rarely driven the poorly surfaced twisting roads himself. He had hazy memories of being jammed into the back seat between his parents as Granddaddy Dawkins navigated the twisting path through the mountains. Or his father at the wheel, urging Lee to start a game of I'm Thinking of Something to take his little sister's mind off the tedium of the drive.

It was too early for the fall color that would soon paint the rolling hills in shades of red, yellow and purple, but the forested canopies over sun-filtered roads and glimpses of vistas over green hillsides showed off the stunning natural beauty of Arkansas. He could well imagine the riverboats unloading young families from Protestant Northern Ireland in the early 1800s, dirt-poor immigrants without a chance at prosperity in the established farmlands of the East, hoping to get their start with cheap land and the promise of opportunity in the underpopulated frontier state.

Grandmother Dawkins had kept touch with her people in the hills west of Hot Springs and joined them for family gatherings at least once a year. After she died, the trips were less frequent as Mama gradually drifted away from her mother's White Rock clan. He didn't remember any of the Bell relatives ever coming to Riverton, even though it wasn't really that long a drive and he had to wonder whose choice that had been.

Today's outing was his mother's latest effort to get M.J. out of the house and away from the isolation forced on them by the scandal. Lee didn't know whether Frances had called her cousin Edna to organize the family picnic or whether the invitation had come from the Bells. And did they know about the accident?

He pulled into an empty gravel spot just beyond the carport of a single-story brick house separated from the road by a big untended lawn. The summer rains had kept the yard green, thanks to the resilience of dandelions, chickweed and crabgrass ensconced in the red clay dirt. Like the other homes in the neighborhood, the small house was unpretentious, not run down exactly but with little care given to appearance.

There were five or six older cars and a couple of pickup trucks, both with gun racks, parked alongside the carport and in other shady spots. One of the pickups sported a "Jesus Junkie" bumper sticker. A yellow Lab approached the car, barking as Lee shut off the engine. From the backyard, smoke billowed out of a grill and Willie Nelson blared from a boombox. It wasn't the Fourth of July but there was an American flag hanging from a flagpole angled out from the house.

A red-faced woman, large-boned and heavy, with a beaming smile, came around from the side yard as the Addisons climbed out of their car.

"Frances, it's wonderful to see you. Oh, my gosh, M.J., you're all grown up, honey. Bless your heart."

Lee got out of the car and was quickly wrapped in Edna Bell's hearty embrace.

"Look at you, Lee! You are a sight for sore eyes, darlin'. We haven't seen you for so long. We are so proud of you. But *why* do you want to stay out there in California? It's too far from home. You belong right here in *Arkansas*."

Lee wasn't sure whether that last statement was meant to be a question or an entreaty, the way Aunt Edna's voice ended up in a high-pitched whine, but he took it the way he was sure it was meant.

Edna Bell was married to J.C. Jr., one of Frances' White Rock cousins.

Junior's father had been the oldest brother of Roberta Dawkins. Lee remembered how devoted to him Grandmother Dawkins had been. Junior and Edna had taken over "head of the family" duties after his mother's death. Their home was the weekly gathering place for Sunday dinner, the midday meal after church, and they also hosted the now-rare family reunions when the Riverton relatives and other Bell relations living in Hot Springs and Little Rock came out to see the family.

Even as a child, Frances was embarrassed by the White Rock relatives, too rough around the edges for her taste and comfort. Still, she tried to honor her mother's commitment to family ties. Roberta Dawkins owed her place in the Riverton community to her husband's heritage and his social position, but she didn't forget where she came from either.

Of course, both the Bells and the Dawkins were part of the great Irish diaspora of the late eighteenth and early nineteenth centuries. Protestant farmers from Northern Ireland often encouraged their younger sons to emigrate to the New World for economic opportunity. Shaping the American character with the appetite for risk typical of younger siblings, they came to America with intact communities of Presbyterians or Methodists, often passing a generation or two in Virginia or Tennessee before looking west for cheaper land and better opportunity.

These Scots-Irish immigrants filled the hills of Appalachia and the farms of Virginia and North Carolina. Some of them became slave owners and many of them sacrificed sons to the cause of slavery during the Civil War. Those who trekked west into Arkansas and Texas worked both with and against the local Indian tribes, and later with and against the local blacks, to carve out their piece of the American dream. Those who made it to the upper echelons of society like the Dawkins, and those who didn't, like the Bells, inherited their ancestors' legacies—dislike of interlopers from the north, justification of the economic institution of slavery as having something to do with "states' rights" and reliance upon the church as the social and moral center of the community.

Edna hooked her arm through Frances' and leaned into her, chatting away and leading the three new arrivals around the corner of the house into a backyard scattered with pines descending down to a creek. A potluck table with a red-and-white checked cloth was laden with plates and dishes offering local fare—turnip greens, okra, simmered peas, squash, casseroles, stuffed potatoes, gelatin salads, deviled eggs, cornbread, grits and biscuits with gravy. Junior was working the grill where barbequed brisket was smoking slowly over coals.

"Good God almighty," he said. "Look who's here."

Junior welcomed them with big bear hugs. He had inherited the Bell looks from his father, the same sense of self and grace that had enabled Roberta Bell to capture the heart of a well-educated young Riverton lawyer, genes that were still playing themselves out in the looks and demeanor of Frances' older child.

"Damn, it's been too long since we've seen y'all. Frances, your kids is almost grown up."

He went over to M.J. and took her by the shoulders.

"Darlin', I'm so sorry about the accident and everything. It must have been terrible for you."

M.J. looked up at her mother, surprised that she had talked to Junior and Edna about the accident. Her face turned red and she dropped her eyes.

"Take it to the Lord, honey. That's all you can do when somethin' like that happens. Too heavy to carry all by yourself."

Frances had hoped that Edna and Junior wouldn't bring up the accident in front of M.J., but it didn't surprise her either. They were that kind of people and it wouldn't have done any good to ask them not to talk about it. She could not have said why it was important for her to come to White Rock, to have the kids with her and to let the relatives in White Rock know about the accident. But their life hadn't been so easy, not for them or their parents before them. They had been through their share of divorces and unemployment. A couple of the Bell kids had even been in trouble with the law. Nothing terrible. The family stuck with them. They had each scraped out a living as best they could, and when somebody ran into trouble, there was always a place to come. It made her feel better to be around people who didn't pretend to be perfect.

Lee was busy greeting long-forgotten cousins, aunts and uncles. He spotted his great Aunt Coot holding court from a rocking chair under the trellis. Coot, the youngest of Grandmother Dawkins' siblings, was the only one of the Bells of that generation still alive. He made his way over to the house to say hello.

"Hello, Aunt Coot. Don't know if you remember me. I'm Roberta's grandson Lee."

"Well, bless your heart. Lee! It's wonderful to see you again, honey. Your grandmama was mighty proud of you. You was such a fine boy. Come on over here and sit with me, pumpkin."

Aunt Coot was skinny as a rail and wrinkled all over her sun-browned face. But her eyes still had a mischievous twinkle. She was the only one of Roberta's siblings never to marry. Lee wasn't sure how well Aunt Coot actually remembered him.

"I'm living out in California now, just finished law school."

"I know you are, honey. You are such a smart boy, just like Roberta always said. Your mama did such a good job of raising you, all by herself like that. Your daddy was a no-account fella, never did right by you kids. But you come up just fine anyway."

Despite nearly a century of hard living, Aunt Coot was still mentally sharp and possessed of a wicked sense of humor. She was never left alone for a minute during the gathering as a parade of relatives made their way over to the trellis to spend a few minutes chatting with her. She always had a story to tell, and despite the fact that many of them were repeated again and again, she was a lively and entertaining companion. Eager to hear the latest news about absent family members, she was especially interested in gossip about the neighbors. "Well, kiss my rusty old toe!" she would exclaim after hearing something juicy, well aware of the entertainment value her intentionally colorful language provided.

M.J. had found her way to two of Junior's teenage daughters, and the three girls were sitting together under a tree, listening to the music. The Bell girls hadn't avoided the vicissitudes of adolescence any more than M.J. had. Halley had run wild in ninth and tenth grade and gotten into her fair share of trouble. Drugs had found their way into the hill country of Arkansas and plenty of kids burned out during their teen years, knowing there wasn't a lot to look forward to after high school. After her junior year, Halley had finally settled down and had a regular boyfriend she was planning to marry in the spring. Like Riverton, White Rock had its share of drinking and sex and driving too fast in cars—just in a smaller setting where more people took a personal interest and things moved more slowly.

Lee didn't have much in common with the Bell cousins his own age, but he listened with polite interest as they talked hunting, football and local politics. He had been too busy at school to pay much attention to politics of any kind, so it didn't particularly register with him that they were referring to the young governor of Arkansas with joking references to "Slick Willy."

"They say he wants to get the Vice Presidential nomination."

"Well, wantin' ain't gettin'."

"He'd get the colored vote."

"That's th'only vote he'd get."

"They say he's part black."

"Wouldn't surprise me none."

"His people never amounted to anything. Can't see as how he'd make it on the big stage."

"He's smart though."

"No, he just kisses up to the right people. Can't trust him."

"You just say that because he favors the blacks."

"Look, I wouldn't vote Democratic if Jesus hisself was runnin'. All they want to do is to take our money and give it to the people too lazy to get a job."

Sarah Jenkins had joined the circle of teenage girls and was asking M.J. about the accident. Jesse and Amanda's daughter, Sarah had known M.J. since they were children. M.J. had never spent a lot of time in White Rock, but Sarah had been her closest buddy during family gatherings.

"Will you have to go to jail?"

"I don't know."

"God, I'd be so scared."

"Nothing I can do about it. I don't really want to talk about it."

"Okay, I'm sorry. I wouldn't either."

Sarah's mother came over to where the girls were sitting on a blanket. "Sarah," she said, "you're going to have to leave pretty soon. You promised Brother Matthew that you'd take up the collection at this afternoon's meeting."

"Mama, do I have to go? I'm talking to M.J. I haven't seen her for so long."

"You can't go back on your word when you take on a responsibility like that, Sarah. Maybe M.J.'ll go with you. It shouldn't take but an hour."

So the girls took Elvin's truck and headed west toward the edge of the national forest, M.J. glad for the excuse to get away from the crowd and eager to accept the cigarette Sarah offered her.

"It's what Elvin gets for leaving these smokes sittin' around in the truck," Sarah laughed.

M.J. liked being with Sarah. She wasn't all freaked out about M.J.'s legal problems. Lots of kids up here in White Rock had dealt with drugs and jail and pregnancies.

Sarah took a long drag on her cigarette and turned to M.J., exhaling. "It's really messed up, isn't it? Shit, M.J., I hope you don't have to go to jail. Donnie Ray's best friend just got out and now nobody in town will hang out with him. Are your friends helpin' you get through this?"

"Not really," M.J. said. "I'm poison to everyone in Riverton. And if they can't support me now, I don't want them in my life."

Sarah tossed her cigarette butt out the window. "I tell you what, I wouldn't either. Who needs friends like that?"

The girls pulled up into a big cleared space at the edge of a wooded area, which was rapidly filling with cars and trucks. People of all ages wearing blue jeans, t-shirts and leather boots filed into a tent.

"What is this exactly?" M.J. asked.

"A revival. Haven't you ever been to a revival?"

"No."

"Just wait. They always get a kick-ass preacher. People get all worked up. You'll like it. The holy spirit will get your blood pumpin' and your heart will open up to the Lord."

M.J. stared at Sarah to see whether or not she was kidding.

"Two years ago at this same tent meeting, I gave my life to Jesus. Seriously. I was into it. Came down front and turned my life over to Jesus. It was the best feelin' I ever had. Course I drifted back into my wicked ways. Maybe Jesus will reach out and take a hold of me again today." She laughed.

M.J. didn't think it was the kind of thing you ought to laugh about, but it was a relief to see that Sarah didn't take it too seriously.

"Or," M.J. suggested, "we could skip the meeting and go find a beer someplace."

"Great idea," Sarah said. "but I did promise the preacher I'd be there to take the collection. And I don't know where I'd find us a beer."

The girls found a couple of empty chairs near the back of the tent.

"Wait here, M.J. I've got to tell Miz Pritchard I'm here."

M.J. watched the people filing into the tent. She was surprised that there were black people, as well as white. Nobody was dressed for church. There was a stage at the front of the tent with a band playing amplified music, a small pulpit and big TV screens on either side of the platform.

The program started with a lead singer, a woman dressed in Sunday clothes but carrying a rhinestone-studded guitar. She led the congregation in several country/religious songs, the words posted on big screens, with sing-along follow-the-dots guiding the crowd through the music.

M.J. leaned over to Sarah.

"I thought this was a church meeting, not a concert."

"It's a revival. We get some good music with our religion out here. Just wait until the real entertainment starts."

The girls whispered and giggled throughout the rest of the music.

The audience was warmed up by a young woman who spoke of her life of sin, how she used to get drunk and not look after the children. But she had been saved by Jesus, washed in the blood of the lamb and redeemed.

"Oh, right," M.J. said to her cousin. "She's probably sinning every night with the preacher."

"She says she's been saved and I believe her," Sarah responded.

Brother Jeremiah was the lead act. The religious revival meeting wasn't too far removed from what M.J. had seen on TV. The guy had an emotional voice that carried across the tent, the congregation responding with shouts of "Amen" and "Praise the Lord" whenever he made a particularly strong point.

M.J. was starting to get silly, whispering off-color remarks into Sarah's ear. Sarah blushed and giggled, but she was starting to be embarrassed by M.J.'s behavior. At one point a lady behind them reprimanded the girls.

"If y'all aren't interested in what's being said, maybe you should go outside."

Sarah turned and apologized, then ignored M.J. as much as she could.

The preacher's message struck M.J. as a self-serving attempt to raise money by appealing to people's emotions. When the sermon reached its climax and people were coming forward to commit their lives to Jesus, M.J. just shook her head. "These people are unbelievably gullible," she said.

Sarah stared at her in disbelief. "After all you've been through, I can't believe *you* don't take it seriously. Jesus can make a difference in your life. You may not like this kind of preaching. I'm not so crazy about it myself. But I do accept Jesus as my Lord and savior. I *do*, M.J."

By the time the girls returned, Frances and Lee were ready for the drive back to Riverton. The Addisons said their good-byes, with hugs all around, and headed home.

M.J. was quiet on the drive.

"What was their church meeting like?" Lee asked.

"It was a revival. In a big tent on the outskirts of town. Loud music and loud preaching and lots of people getting saved."

"Well," her mother said, "keep in mind this is small-town America. It's what they do. It seems strange to us but that's just the way they express their faith here."

"Having known Grandmother Dawkins," said Lee, "I'm always surprised around her family. She was nothing like them. I mean, they're very nice people. But she was a classy lady. Wonder where she got it?"

"Maybe she learned it from Daddy or from his family. It was always important to her to be seen as socially sophisticated. I expect she was trying very hard to hide those small-town roots. Daddy's family was old money and they had lots of education, even going back to the early days of Arkansas. Lots of lawyers and ministers and all. High achievement was very important to Daddy. That's why I wish so much he could have known about your success in school, Stanford and all that. He would have been so proud."

"I've never understood that," he said. "Why should anyone care whether their grandchildren or great-grandchildren succeed after they are dead? For one thing, the genetic pool gets more and more mixed up with each subsequent generation. I'm as much Bell as I am Dawkins. And, God help me, twice as much Addison."

chapter fifty

It was Friday afternoon and Frances was in a slow simmer as she drove home from bridge club. She wasn't particularly surprised that none of her lifelong friends had rallied to her side after M.J.'s accident. The few telephone calls she received were cursory expressions of condolence as if an elderly parent had died. And for all the kind words—I'll be thinking of you and praying for M.J., let me know if there's anything I can do—the fact was that most of them hadn't called back. In public places, she was shunned. The bridge group wouldn't of course ask her to leave, but she knew damn well they wished she wouldn't show up. The same people who had demonstrated their compassion by offering up prayers for her daughter would also walk one hundred and eighty degrees away from where they were heading to avoid having to talk to her. She was of course assigned a bridge partner for each round, but she might have been a complete stranger.

She had felt pretty good about the dinner party. Sure, M.J. had dipped into the wine and embarrassed herself at the end of the evening. But the poor thing was stressed beyond belief, living under the shadow of scandal and criminal charges, all because of one terrible afternoon, one lapse in judgment. For all its disastrous consequence—to her, to the girl, to them all—it was a mistake. It was not as though she intended to kill somebody. She was a teenager, after all. She went to a party and drank too much. There but for the grace of God went any one of them.

Miriam Greene's snide remark had come at the end of the rubber when Frances, after doubling four spades, had gone on to set Miriam's team by three tricks and was enjoying it far too much. Frances was a good card player who loved the competition. Nothing serious of course—two small gift bags nicely wrapped and awarded to the winning team. It was a pleasant way to pass an afternoon and particularly pleasant if you played well and won. Of course some of the girls weren't very good at cards and many of them cared more about socializing than they did about bridge.

Miriam had borne a grudge against Frances for a long time. Hank and Frances had been friends since high school. Their parents were founding members of the Country Club and good friends. Miriam would have heard about Hank and Frances seeing each other after the separation. But it was not as if Frances had anything to do with the breakup of their marriage. Hank needed his friends and needed to start a life of his own. What did Miriam expect?

Miriam had made a point of leaving the Club just as Frances did, and in the parking lot she turned to Frances. "I had tea with Mitzi yesterday. She told me M.J. is going through a pretty bad time."

"Doing as well as could be expected," Frances replied.

"But do you really serve her wine at home? She's just in high school, Frances."

Frances was stung by Miriam's criticism and angry that Mitzi had gossiped about M.J.'s drunkenness. *Well, let them talk.* Miriam Greene was a bitch. Hank was lucky to be rid of her. M.J. only had a glass of wine, after all. Who did these women think they were anyway, implying that she was a bad mother because M.J. had a glass of wine at a dinner party?

By the time she got home, Frances was in a thoroughly foul mood. After being on the receiving end of a few sharp remarks, M.J. knew she had to get out of the house. She couldn't drive and it was too hot to run. But at the first opportunity she slipped out the kitchen door and around the side path to the circular driveway.

She was not dressed for the hot afternoon sun, but nonetheless headed west on Peach, seeking shade along the way. She strode quickly, oblivious to her surroundings, glad to be out. She hated her mother. First she insisted on M.J.'s participation in her stupid dinner party. Then she got hysterical because she drank some wine. Jesus Christ, what was her problem?

Ever since the accident, everybody assumed she was a drunk. Even Lee. She wasn't drunk that day. She was going slow. She had seen a bunch of kids on bikes before she turned into the street. But she didn't see anyone close to the car. Just that sound. Like someone had reached out and hit the car on purpose. Didn't have anything to do with being drunk.

She had even called Buddy and asked him.

"No, honey, of course you weren't. The cops are always looking for someone to blame. They want to look good. Look like they're doing their job. Don't let 'em mess with your mind, M.J."

"Buddy, let's go out and have some fun. I'm going crazy, locked up in this house."

"Can't do it. They would love nothing more than to somehow blame me for all this. I've had too many scrapes, babe."

She understood. Probably understood him better than ever, now that she was a scapegoat too. They didn't care about catching people who really did bad shit. Just find somebody to blame for accidents. Or somebody like Buddy who didn't fit in.

She would have given anything for a drink. It was too hot to be out but she didn't want to go home. There was a sinking feeling in the pit of her stomach and she felt nervous. The same kind of sickening heaviness she felt when she thought about the girl. The dead girl. She had never seen a dead body. Mama hadn't let her go see Grandma Dawkins at the funeral parlor. Said she was too young. And the casket was closed at the funeral. But she had seen them on TV. Kind of waxy looking.

She tried to envision what it would be like. Being dead. Didn't seem so horrible. Just like a long sleep. Kind of peaceful.

chapter fifty-one

Lee was enjoying a rare moment of privacy while his mother and sister were out shopping. His feet were propped on the wicker coffee table at the center of the screened-in porch, the sofa piled with green and navy paisley pillows. He was witnessing the splendid drama of a summer thunderstorm. The smell was acrid and heavy. He watched the pink-black skies, darkening minute by minute as the storm boiled in, lit up brightly by occasional bursts of lightning and then—one thousand one, one thousand two, one thousand three—the rumbling clap of thunder. When the rain finally began, it pounded the earth with a clattering barrage of water, the racket so pervasive that his ears quickly adjusted and he could have sworn that it was quiet outside.

He had lived for three years in a climate so moderate and unchanging that he made plans without considering the weather as a variable, no matter what the time of year. In the productivity-centric Bay Area where nature was predictable and almost always cooperative, there were no excuses from the daily grind. Here, Mother Nature would not be dismissed so cursorily. You had to stop and pay attention. Lee was glad to be distracted and somehow comforted by the idea of a natural world powerful enough to dictate weekend activities.

He was ready to go back, start his law career and leave behind this place with all its wrenching, goddamned Southern angst. But there were things he would miss, and not just Annie. Annie…. She couldn't leave here, he couldn't stay. They weren't meant to be together in the future he had chosen for himself. She would forget him. And he would forget her.

The lush overgrown beds in the Addisons' backyard were absorbing the pounding water deep into the earth and emitting pungent, sulfur-sweet odors. The rain was coming down so hard on the tiled roof of the porch that Lee didn't hear the doorbell at first.

The rector of St. Bede's was hunched under a black umbrella, streams of water pouring from its rim. Lee didn't recognize him at first but the collar jogged his memory.

"Father Desmond. Come in. You arrived in the middle of a deluge."

The tall, angular figure ducked into the porch and let the water run off the edge of the umbrella. Although only in his sixties, the Episcopal priest could have been seventy or more, with a rugged, lined face and receding hairline. Once shed of his rain gear, he carried himself with the dignity and self-possession that Lee remembered from childhood. Desmond Nelson had been rector of St. Bede's since Lee was in Sunday school and wore the mantle of that well-heeled congregation with the bearing one would expect of a community leader.

As a teenager Lee had encountered him frequently on the golf course, amused that the priest had maintained a weekly game with one of the Club's loudest and most profanity-laced foursomes. Born and raised in Riverton, from one of the city's oldest families, Desmond Nelson would have had a prominent place in town even without the status of rector of the town's most prosperous congregation.

These days most of Riverton's mainline Protestant churches were in decline as their congregations aged. On the outskirts of town, new mega-churches were growing by leaps and bounds, pulling in a more youthful population from the town and the surrounding countryside with their casual, community-oriented activities, fiery fundamentalist preachers and country-pop music. They were housed in gymnasium-style buildings with massive parking lots, marketing billboards out front and congregations longing for a sense of community and meaning that they no longer found at home or at work, an energy level that seemed to be missing in the older, more traditional churches.

But St. Bede's had held onto its elite milieu of doctors and bankers who wanted to dress up on Sunday morning, sit in a beautiful sanctuary and listen to traditional Anglican music and the poetry of King James.

Father Desmond was a frequent dinner visitor in the homes of his flock, many of whom had been personal friends since childhood. He was a good conversationalist, appreciated fine wine and was always a welcome addition to a dinner party.

"I apologize for not calling ahead of time. Frances has been after me to get over here and I had to pick something up this afternoon at Norman's. I hope you don't mind my stopping by unannounced."

"Of course not. Let me hang up your raincoat. Come on in. Mama and M.J. are out shopping but should be back any time now. Can I fix you something hot? Tea? Or would you prefer a brandy to take off the chill?"

"A hot toddy would be lovely."

The rector's carefully modulated speech rolled off his tongue with elegance, an Arkansas version of Anglican.

By the time Frances and M.J. returned, the rain had let up. Frances joined the two men on the porch, sipping their warm toddies and talking in low tones.

"At her age she of course keeps to herself, so I don't really know what she's thinking. I think she's doing as well as could be expected under the circumstances."

"Frances, I know this must be a dreadful time for all of you. Particularly for M.J. This is an age when teens need to separate themselves from their parents. That would have been true even had the accident never happened. But this is a frightful experience to go through alone. Have you thought about counseling for her?"

"She's rejected the idea out of hand."

"I'm not sure it's a good idea to give her the option to reject it. I know that a psychotherapist will insist upon the patient's assent to therapy, but a little coercion may be in order whether M.J. likes it or not."

"At least a psychotherapist is obliged to keep disclosures confidential," Lee offered. "That's a better option than sending her off to Alcoholics Anonymous."

"Do you think she has a drinking problem?"

Frances answered a little too quickly. "No, I don't think so. Like any teenager, she acts out sometimes. We had a dinner party last week and she was helping herself to the wine every time my back was turned."

"Because of the circumstances of the accident, the question of alcohol abuse is going to come up," Father Desmond said. "Teenagers do that, you know. As I recall, our generation wasn't exempt."

"Everybody in town is calling her a drunk," Frances complained bitterly, reaching out to freshen his cup with warm water from the teapot. "She's no different from any other teenager. Maybe you can get her to talk to you about it."

"Like doctors and lawyers, we clergy are protected from having to disclose private communications to the court. I do want to talk to her alone if that's possible."

M.J. protested the forced meeting with the Episcopal rector but eventually yielded to her brother's pleading. Sullenly she followed him downstairs and into her mother's study. The room where Frances paid bills and kept up with correspondence was dark and formal, lined with books never opened. M.J. positioned herself on the sofa as far as possible from the rector, and then Lee left them alone together.

Her mood was dark and defensive. She didn't want to talk to Father Desmond. She had grown up at St. Bede's, having been given no choice about attending church until she was in middle school. But she was shy at choir practice and in Sunday school, and the other kids hadn't been friendly. By the time she was able to fight to stay home, her mother was tired of pushing and appreciated the extra time for coffee in bed on a Sunday morning.

Father Desmond extended his hand. "I hope you'll talk to me for a few minutes—as your pastor as well as a friend of your family."

Frances brought in a silver tray with iced tea and cookies, closing the door on her way out. Father Desmond didn't seem to be in a hurry to start talking about anything serious. He was reminding her of childhood experiences at St. Bede's, chatting amiably, recounting amusing stories.

"Sometimes people wonder why parents go to so much effort to get their children to church. Especially since most concepts of theology are beyond their understanding. I think it's because parents want so much to protect their children from the inevitable pain and hardship that comes with being alive," he said. "Giving their children access to the idea of God is often the best they can do to provide a place of safety for later on. We all need redemption in our lives. Even if children don't quite understand what it's about."

M.J.'s mind wandered as the rector's words washed over her. She didn't want these church people trying to help her. She studied her hands as Father Desmond talked of things beyond her experience. Like everything else that had shoved its way into her life during the past month, this scenario— sitting in her mother's study with the rector—possessed an air of unreality. It was a scene that could have been projected on a movie screen, except that it was playing in slow motion, the rector's voice droning on endlessly, the girl trapped in a drama that had nothing to do with her. How could she make him stop? She closed her eyes tightly, wishing herself out of her mother's study and back upstairs to her own room, with her music playing and her mind free to drift and imagine.

The sound of Father Desmond's voice had stopped, and he was watching her, his eyes soft with concern.

"M.J., I can't fix the problems that are causing you so much pain. But the church can help you bear them. You're awfully young to have to deal with such frightening and tragic events. But whether you're ready or not, this isn't going away and you're going to have to deal with it. You'll have to grow up faster than most kids. There's no choice."

He seemed to expect a response but M.J. averted her eyes.

"One of our parishioners at St. Bede's runs a support group for teens with drug and alcohol programs." He held up a hand to ward off the anticipated objection.

"I'm not saying you have a problem. I have no idea. But I trust this person. She's wise and she cares about teens. A retired schoolteacher. Margaret Harris. I wish you would at least talk to her."

And then he was gone. M.J. breathed a sigh of relief, back in the sanctuary of her room, where the rhythmic thump of percussion and bass drowned out the strangling anxiety. The angry heavy-metal message, spewing from hoarse voices, reflected her own feelings about the chaos and bitterness of the world. She thought about the rector's visit...so odd. What would give him the idea that he had the right to come here and tell her what she should do? Well, fuck him. She hadn't committed any sin. She was driving home and the stupid kid had turned into her car. Busy talking to her friends, paying no attention to where she was going. And redemption. What the hell did that mean?

She cracked open her window and lit a cigarette, taking a sip of the whiskey from her stash in the drawer. Leaning back on her floor cushion, she let the slow warmth of the alcohol flow down from her throat into her belly. It had been a stressful day. Shopping with her mother was always stressful, but running into girls from school had been horrible. Then to come home to a lecture from the rector.

Sheila and Trish had acted as if they had seen a ghost when M.J. hurried past them, as they evaluated their new fall purchases before the full-length mirror in the changing rooms. Was that the way it was going to be from now on? She was used to being snubbed by the girls at school. But to have them stare at her like she was a freak? It was so totally messed up.

"Didn't expect to see you here, shopping for school clothes."

What had Sheila meant? That she'd be in jail instead of school? If it was up to M.J., she would take the year off. But Mama and Lee insisted it wouldn't be good for her to sit around the house. She couldn't stand the idea of people staring at her wherever she went. School would be impossible.

It had become a secret pleasure, drinking in her room by herself. No embarrassing scenes. No worries like she sometimes had after a party when she couldn't remember what had happened. There was a feeling of control in knowing that she could make herself feel better right under her family's nose without anybody having a clue.

The house was quiet. Mama was surely asleep by now and Lee would be at Annie's. As she had done for the past several nights, M.J. quietly crept down the stairs, stopping at the liquor cabinet to freshen her drink before slipping into her mother's study. She settled on the Persian carpet, took a mouthful of whiskey and read through the accounts of the hit-and-run accident.

The clippings held a fascination for her. It was like watching a film about somebody else's life. Some nights when she read the stories, she pretended the driver was someone else. Sometimes she wept for the young girl. *Susan Barker*. She imagined how it must have felt, the impact of the car. She thought about the empty place at the Barkers' kitchen table. No matter how hard she thought about it, though, she couldn't undo it. She couldn't bring back the girl or comfort her mother or miraculously let her finish her life.

It would not be accurate to say that M.J. faced up to her responsibility during those late-night marathons. The feeling wasn't exactly guilt and she didn't buy into the notion of sin. But she struggled with the cosmic force that had caused the improbable crossing of paths—hers and the girl's. She knew that it would have been within her power not to be in that place at that time. She had heard plenty of aphorisms from the small circle of people who stood with her. But she was too young to understand what they were trying to say. More than anything else, it was M.J.'s inability to find a framework to explain what had happened, where she might lay down the weight of the girl's death, that caused her despair.

chapter fifty-two

Annie shuffled through the boxes in her study, searching for the posters she would need to prepare her room for the opening of school next week. Getting ready for a new school year was generally a time of anticipation and excitement for her. This year her heart ached at the thought of saying good-bye to Lee. She eased herself to the floor amid stacks of paper and sighed.

She could feel him separating from her, getting ready to go. His desire felt urgent, and he was up and out of her bed quickly. Of course she had expected it. That was their understanding. Knowing it was how he would want it, Annie had played the part perfectly. No strings, no pressure. Just a summer romance. Of course they loved each other, always would, but it couldn't work. Enjoy the moment. Don't think about the future.

Annie knew that she was deceiving herself with all the brave talk of living in the moment. In truth she couldn't bear it. Off to California to his fancy job and his fancy friends—and to Zoe. He would put this place out of mind so fast. It had been a nightmare with M.J.'s accident, a nightmare that would follow the girl for the rest of her life. Lee didn't deal so well with this kind of crisis. He was accustomed to doing everything right, pleasing everybody, laid-back and flexible. But there was no way to schmooze his way out of this one—a sister very likely to be convicted of a felony and put in jail before she was out of high school. Oh sure, they said it would go easier on her because she was a juvenile, but nothing about it would be easy for her. She was at the most vulnerable time of her life, still so needy, caring too much about what people thought, no matter how she tried to hide it.

No, Lee wouldn't be back in Riverton anytime soon.

Annie couldn't find the outline she was looking for, and in frustration dumped a container out on the floor, not caring that pencils were rolling all over the room. She regarded the mess with disdain, pulled herself to her feet and slumped into the desk chair.

"The hell with this," she muttered, grieving for a future that could never be.

By the time Lee arrived for dinner, she had cleaned up, washed her face and put on the cheerful mask that would establish some distance between them, a space intended to shield her fragile heart. If she knew him at all, she knew that her aching need for him would scare him off even faster than his future was pulling him away. She had already started dinner when he came into the kitchen, no longer bothering to knock. He gathered her in his arms and for the next hour they were able to forget the grief each of them felt as the end of summer approached.

They were in bed, Annie's head cradled on Lee's shoulder and each of them lost thought when the phone rang.

Annie's face went ashen.

"Mrs. Addison, are you okay? Where did they take her? We'll meet you there."

Annie was halfway out of bed and heading for the closet before she hung up the phone.

"M.J. took some pills," she said. "Your mother found her on the floor. There was an empty prescription bottle in the bathroom."

They were quiet in the car, each of them trying to understand the despair that would compel a teenager to choose death over life. Lee was filled with self-reproach about escaping the constant anxiety that hung over their family into Annie's arms instead of being at home with his sister.

The emergency room attendant assured them that M.J. was out of immediate danger. With directions to her room, Lee and Annie hurried toward the nurses' station in Wing E of Marcus Hospital, the sound of their steps echoing through the empty hospital corridors. The hall reeked of Pine-Sol and old flowers, neither of which masked the underlying scent of human misery.

The door to Room 462 was propped open just a couple of inches. Lee was relieved to see that M.J. was in a private room. Frances' chair was pulled up close to the bed, but M.J. was facing the wall. She didn't turn as he and Annie entered the room, in spite of the clatter of the door bumping into a movable dinner cart.

Annie hung back near the door as Lee went around to the other side of the bed. Gently he touched M.J.'s hair. "I don't know what I'd do without you, M.J. You're the only sister I've got," he began.

Her eyes glistened, though she didn't reach out to touch him.

Frances had been quiet since Lee and Annie arrived. She sat stiffly on the harsh plastic of the side chair, tears welling up, but could find no words to comfort or assure her daughter.

The details of what had happened became clear after meeting with the medical team and the police who were investigating M.J.'s suicide attempt. Since the accident both M.J. and Frances had been struggling with anxiety and were on prescription drugs. Sensitive to the inevitable risk of depression in a young person with M.J.'s problems, the Addisons' family doctor had ordered the prescription in Frances' name with verbal instructions to give half a tablet to M.J. as needed, cautioning Frances to take control of the pills herself. She had done as instructed, careful to order only small quantities of the anti-anxiety drug. But the pills were not locked up, and in the medicine cabinet where they were kept was also an old bottle of sleeping pills, which Frances had used for years on rare occasions when she couldn't sleep. The cabinet held small quantities of each kind of pill, thanks to which M.J. didn't die. But the combination of the pills and whiskey very nearly cost M.J. her life.

They sat with her the rest of the night, nobody sleeping, few words exchanged. They were in the same position the next morning when the attending doctor came in and introduced himself.

"In circumstances where suicide has been attempted, we keep the patients under observation for at least three days. The psychiatrist who's on call this morning will come in at about ten o'clock. M.J., you'll be talking to her for about an hour. The family will need to be out of here for that. M.J., this is not necessarily someone you'll be seeing long term. But she'll want to meet with you several times over the next few days to make an evaluation. One of the things you'll talk about with her is what to do about longer-term therapy."

The term suicide seemed odd to M.J. She hadn't thought of it that way. She had identified the pills in her mother's medicine cabinet weeks before and had made a small mental note. It seemed important at the time to know there was a path she could take if it got too hard, another option.

She didn't necessarily want to die. But didn't necessarily want to live either. Mr. Barnett had mentioned the possibility of jail several times. Oddly, it didn't seem any worse than anything else. The thing she couldn't get her mind around was what the rest of her life could be. One thing for sure, it wouldn't be what she had always expected or what her mother wanted.

Of course, M.J. didn't have a vision of the future anyway. That was part of the problem. Everything she had tried felt empty and flat. Well, some things felt good for the moment, or at least made her feel less bad—booze, drugs, sex, movies, TV, food. But afterward she felt worse than ever. Was that all there was? You studied hard, went to a good college, married a rich guy, all for the purpose of having more of those things. But why?

Taking the pills hadn't so much been about ending her life. It was fucked up, she knew that. Just an idea that crossed her mind and she wanted to see if the pills were really there where they used to be. Wanted to hold them in her hand, just to see if it felt scary.

For the next twenty-four hours, M.J. was poked, prodded and watched by the suicide-prevention staff, a hovering brother and an anxious mother.

The events of the summer had left Lee and Frances shellshocked. In the wake of M.J.'s attempt to end her life, both of them were wary and subdued. The psychiatry resident who was on call asked M.J.'s family to join him in his office for a meeting with the hospital suicide team, including a psychiatric social worker and a family counselor, as well as the emergency room intern who had admitted M.J.

The office was cold and cluttered and smelled of rubbing alcohol.

"Teenagers find it easy to show their anger and rebelliousness, but it's often harder for a parent to spot the fear and confusion and self-doubt that many of these kids feel. It's obvious that they are hell-bent on self-destruction and doing what they damn well please. But for some reason, young people have a hard time showing how worried and scared they are much of the time," the young doctor told them, shuffling through the reports stacked on his desk. The other professionals, seated in a circle of folding chairs along with the family, nodded in agreement.

"You couple those pressures with alcohol abuse, and of course in your daughter's case with the trauma of the hit-and-run accident and all its legal and emotional implications...well this kind of reaction isn't surprising. Suicide is one of the leading causes of death among young people between fifteen and twenty-four."

They talked about patterns of suicide attempts and how one episode can lead to another, and then the family counselor gave Frances and Lee handfuls of brochures to read.

"When there is a teenage suicide attempt," the social worker told them, "parents often blame themselves. But the teenage brain isn't fully developed. They tend to act impulsively. These kids don't yet have the ability to put their problems in the larger context of time."

While Frances and Lee were meeting with the suicide team, M. J. had her first session with the staff psychiatrist assigned to her case. She wasn't as dreadful as M.J. had feared. A middle-aged Jewish doctor wearing a white lab coat over her dark clothing and practical walking shoes, she peered benignly at M.J. over the top of reading glasses. She was neither harsh nor overly sympathetic, her demeanor suggesting that teenage girls did this kind of thing all the time, not to worry. She asked a lot of questions and didn't give M.J. a clue as to what she thought or what would happen next.

M.J. wondered whether trying to kill yourself was always considered a sign of mental illness, and whether she was in fact crazy. How would she know? She also wondered if it was really a mortal sin to attempt suicide. She thought about some of the TV shows where people attempted suicide just for attention.

She was glad to have a little time to herself. Lee and her mother had gone downstairs for lunch. She closed her eyes, not knowing whether or not she slept. She might still be feeling the effect of the pills. Nothing felt real.

The door opened and Etta Jones was at her bedside.

"Oh, child, what was you thinking of? Once your life is gone, nothing can ever get better."

M.J. opened one eye, not surprised that Etta had come. But she felt so tired she just couldn't muster the energy to talk to anyone, not even Etta.

The old woman sat down beside her and patted her shoulder. "I think about my brother that way. You know, Axel, that I told you about. He didn't live to see integration come to Little Rock. He didn't know about Martin Luther King. Or the Civil Rights Act. Sometimes I think about all that. How surprised he would be, I mean, if he came back today."

There was a tap on the door and Lee pushed it open. He came around to the far side of the bed and extended his hand warmly to Etta. "Good of you to come by."

He then turned to his sister, rubbing her lightly on the lower arm. "I talked to the admitting doctor and they may be able to release you tomorrow if you think you're up to it."

"God, yes. I need to get out of here so I can get some sleep."

"But they say you're going to have to commit to psychotherapy for a while. With the lady you talked to earlier today, Dr. Feinberg. You liked her all right, didn't you?"

"I guess so."

After Etta left, Lee and M.J. were quiet. She was still groggy and Lee was thinking hard about all that had happened. She would mumble to him between naps but he didn't try to get her to talk.

When the nurse brought in dinner, he pestered her to eat the bland offering of pork chop, mashed potatoes and applesauce. After the remains of dinner were removed, she started to settle back under the covers, but her brother stopped her before she could lie down. It was unusual for Lee to speak to her harshly but he was clearly angry.

"God damn it, M.J., you're not old enough to begin to understand what it means to die. For everything to just be…over. Or that life goes from good to bad and bad to good all the time. For Christ's sake, did you think this would solve the problem? Did you think your life was of so little importance? Were you just trying to get attention and sympathy? Jesus…."

She had to marvel at him—still busy fixing things.

At the end of the day, she was relieved to be alone. They had all come, hovered over her like she might break, and left. The psychiatrist, Father Desmond, the lawyer, her family. Nobody seemed to know what to say. Etta maybe. Annie at least could sit with her without lecturing. Tommy. He was the best. With Tommy, no hidden agendas. Everything right out there.

She didn't understand. For her entire life, people had been trying to fix her, haranguing her to do things differently, to excel at something, to be a leader, to watch her weight and curl her hair and do her homework. All of a sudden, just because she took a bottle of pills, you would have thought this fucking screwed-up failure of a life of hers was the most valuable thing in the world.

And what in Christ's name was the big deal about dying? Everybody was going to die. Why did it matter if you were here sixteen years or forty-five years or eighty years? She could see the problem if somebody needed you, like if you had kids and there was nobody else to take care of them and they'd be sad and scared. Then it totally made sense.

Anyway, it wasn't so much that she wanted to die. At the time, it just seemed simpler than dealing with everything that was going on. If she went to jail, it would be weird. At least there would be no expectations of her. It wouldn't disappoint her mother if no one asked her to the prom or if she didn't get into a good college. She wouldn't be letting anyone down. She'd just wake up in the morning, have a crappy breakfast in a big ugly cafeteria, go off and make license plates or whatever you did for a job. Go out in the exercise yard in the afternoon and then read a book. The inmates couldn't be any worse than the girls in high school.

The shrink seemed to think she had an "alcohol problem." No shit. Guess there wouldn't be any place for a little stash of whiskey in jail. That was a downside.

chapter fifty-three

In the first few days after M.J. was released from the hospital, Frances and Lee hovered around her with quiet deference. M.J. felt like a specimen under glass and retreated to her room to avoid their watchful concern. She wanted to tell them that she was okay, that she wouldn't do anything like that again, but it was a difficult subject and none of the Addisons was practiced at discussing anything so personal.

She felt continuing anxiety about the trial, what with the possibility of jail. But that prospect still held an air of unreality for her. It was the very real fear and dread of school, with the anticipated rejection, pity, hatred and ridicule by her peers, that left her in a cold sweat. It was the shrink who saved her.

The psychiatrist set up a meeting with Frances and Lee, an office visit to which M.J. was not invited. She had assured the girl of the confidentiality of their sessions together. Her mother would never know what they discussed and neither would her brother, her lawyer, the police or the judge. So M.J. didn't argue when Dr. Feinberg told her she would be meeting alone with her mother and brother.

Dr. Feinberg opened the meeting without fanfare or emotion.

"I don't think M.J. should return to Riverton High for her junior year," she said, looking both of them squarely in the eye.

"The trial will pull her out of school anyway at some point during the year. And after that, who knows? She hates school and is terrified of the whispers and blame she will have to face. Granted, she can't leave town to enroll elsewhere, but there are courses she could take by mail or on the computer that will move her in the direction of high school graduation, as well as keep her busy."

Their first reaction was concern about what it would mean for college admission, how it might look on her transcript and the like. Dr. Feinberg listened quietly as Frances and Lee debated whether her academic future would be jeopardized as a high-school dropout. Before stating the obvious, she let them finish.

"M.J. is looking at a future that is completely uncertain. She's scared. Going back to Riverton High is more terrifying to her than jail." Dr. Feinberg regarded them with gravitas.

Frances and Lee exhaled at the same time, understanding the truth in the psychotherapist's observation. Lee glanced at his mother and saw in her face an instant flash of despair: the reality of a changed universe had finally sunk in. It didn't take any more convincing for them to agree to let M.J. drop out of school, at least for a semester.

The judge in charge of the case had also instructed Jim Barnett to get M.J. into an alcohol-abuse program without waiting for the trial. Lee suggested they follow up with Margaret Harris, the retired school administrator he had met through Annie, who led a drug and alcohol abuse program for teens at St. Bede's Episcopal Church.

As the summer wound down, Lee continued to work with Jim Barnett on the details of M.J.'s case, which was likely to go to trial in the spring unless a plea bargain was struck in the meantime. Barnett suggested that Lee not delay his return to California, since the legal process would take time to play out.

"You're dealing with this the same way I would in your place," Barnett had told him. "The best way to keep from worrying yourself to death is to stay busy."

Lee had talked the older lawyer into joining him for a beer at Oakley's late on a Friday afternoon, and Barnett was recounting tales of crime and punishment in Riverton.

As the jukebox pounded out stories of love and loss, whiskey and loose women, and lives on the brink of disaster, Barnett opened up about his work.

"I'm not a shrink, but I've been doing criminal defense work long enough to see what happens to the family. It's terrifying when someone you love faces the criminal justice system, with all its implications of danger, jail and wrecked lives."

Lee was quiet, studying his beer as he swirled the glass. "I feel so damned helpless," Lee muttered. "She's just a kid. It isn't fair."

"Well, no, it's not. But I'll tell you what. At least M.J. has a family that can stand beside her, a family with resources to support her and help her get through this and rebuild her life. Most of the families I deal with are the powerless mothers and grandparents of young black men, accused criminals facing bleak futures without security or hope, families who sit in my office with their heads down and their hands clasped, knowing there's not a damn thing they can do to protect their child."

Barnett had let go of his resentment at the neophyte lawyer's need to understand every aspect of Arkansas criminal law and his constant questions and advice on how to pursue the case. Out of compassion, he had kept his door open to Lee, helping him understand the options and listening to his ideas.

While Lee's head was fully occupied with criminal procedure, his heart clung to Annie Rayburn. The crisis had diminished the importance of the obstacles to building a life together and had brought them closer. Annie knew how much he needed her but she was unwilling to use the leverage of M.J.'s crisis to push Lee toward a commitment. When he began to talk about the future and something more permanent, Annie deflected the topic. Better to think about that later. Not now.

If there was one thing Annie Rayburn had taken away from her life-long exposure to organized religion, it was patience. Not doctrine or dogma.

Not the good works to stamp out malaria in Africa. Not the righteous pride of being on the safe side of an unknowable universe. But there was a quiet strength in her that let her accept the joys that came into her life and at the same time enabled her to give them up.

Lee would have set aside every dwindling hour of summer to be with Annie, had he not been acutely aware of how little time he had left with his sister. There were no more signals from M.J. that she was thinking about suicide. Dr. Feinberg had her on antidepressants and had assured the family that she was no longer at active risk of trying to end her life. But leaving her now, with so much uncertainty about the future, felt like leaving town before a funeral. There were a number of variables in the case that might impact how long she would be locked up, but he felt deadly certain she would spend some time in jail, and maybe more than a little. As a person who had worked so hard to suspend safety nets beneath his own life, he couldn't work his mind around the horror of being locked away with criminals, or the daunting prospect of trying to rebuild a decent life once it was over.

Lee's initial optimism about M.J. being tried as a juvenile rather than an adult had faded. The lobby against drunk driving had pushed state legislatures in the direction of a zero-tolerance policy, especially toward minors, the group most likely to disregard the warnings against drinking and driving. With a child dead and a hit-and-run charge, the likelihood of avoiding a felony conviction was remote.

Barnett was gentle with M.J. but he hadn't pulled any punches with Lee.

"Look, son, I know you'd move mountains if you could to soften the blow for your sister. But involuntary manslaughter is a serious felony, and when it occurs under the influence of alcohol, there aren't a lot of degrees of freedom. If we can plea bargain for three or four years, with a chance of parole after two, that's a deal we shouldn't walk away from."

Lee could feel his blood pressure rising every time Barnett started talking about a plea. He knew he was pushing the boundaries with Barnett but couldn't conceive of those critical years of his sister's young life being taken from her.

"Why the hell can't we challenge the blood test? It was more than two hours after the accident. Who's to say she didn't have something to drink after she got home?"

"Think about it. Lee, how is that going to play to a jury? A sixteen-year-old high-school junior drinks beer at a party, hits a kid on a bike without even noticing it, gets home and then goes up to her room to start drinking alone?"

Lee sighed in frustration. "Whatever happened to the burden of proof being on the state? There's a hell of a lot of uncertainty in a two-hour window. A juror would have to ask himself whether he could be sure of the facts beyond a reasonable doubt with two hours unaccounted for."

"Look, Lee, if we get to trial, of course I will play that card. But I tell you what, I don't want to be standing in front of a jury trying to paint a picture that nobody in their right mind would believe."

"M.J. claims she only had two beers," Lee muttered.

"Not saying I don't believe her, but remember, the D.A. is giving us a break by agreeing to the alcohol level they recorded after the arrest. Once we go down this path of the two-hour lapse, it could wind up cutting the other way. And, I have to tell you, M.J. has never said a thing to me about drinking any alcohol after she got home."

chapter fifty-four

M.J. was starting to settle into a fall routine, even though the new normal bore little resemblance to her life before the accident. Getting a bye out of junior year at Riverton High was the big game changer. Lee had worked with her to set up registration for a computer-based high-school equivalency course leading to a GED certificate upon completion of the course. He insisted that she would likely finish high school back at Riverton or, if M.J. had her way, at a boarding school out of town. But she knew that wouldn't happen. When her classmates graduated from RHS, she would be in prison. Still, it was a huge relief not to have to face people. The computer lessons would be easy enough and she was glad to be left alone to study, without Mama or Lee nervously hovering over her.

The other activities that shaped her new routine were her weekly therapy sessions with Dr. Feinberg and participation in a teen drug and alcohol abuse support group, which the judge had ordered. At Father Desmond's recommendation, she was sent to a group led by Margaret Harris, a retired school administrator and long-time member of the Episcopal Church where M. J. had been confirmed.

The support group met on Tuesday and Thursday nights in the basement of St. Bede's. In spite of her familiarity with the church, she was anxious about the group and dreaded the first meeting. Lee had dropped her off in front of the church. Her stomach was in knots as she found her way down a dark corridor to Fellowship Hall. She had attended Vacation Bible School and youth groups in some of these basement rooms, but at night the corridor had a sinister feeling.

Fellowship Hall was brightly lit up for the evening meeting. As she entered the room, she counted about a dozen teens, a couple of whom looked familiar, milling around the refreshment table, filling small paper plates with chips and grabbing soft drinks to take back to their seats, which were arranged in a circle. A tall thin older woman, her hair pulled back in a graying bun, was in deep private conversation with a dark-haired girl about M.J.'s age. The girl, a striking teen with Mediterranean features and a curvaceous figure, was wearing a short skirt and a long full blouse. She was in a serious-looking discussion with the older woman, whose hand rested on the girl's arm as she listened intently to what the teen was saying.

M.J. selected a soft drink from the table, mostly to give herself something to hold onto, and avoided looking at anyone else in the room.

"Let's get started," said the group leader, her private conversation with the girl concluded. "Y'all come on over and grab a chair. For the new people, and I think there are a couple of you, I'll talk about how this works in a minute. I'm Margaret Harris. First thing, we start every meeting with the serenity prayer. We do that not because we're meeting here in a church, but because we get our structure from Alcoholics Anonymous. What they say in AA meetings is that you may or may not believe in a god but this prayer is meant to address whatever or whoever you think of as a higher power in your life."

M.J. watched with interest and skepticism as all the other kids recited the familiar prayer along with the group leader.

God, grant me the serenity
To accept the things I cannot change
Courage to change the things I can
And wisdom to know the difference.

"I want to welcome our newcomers. This is Sean here to my left and over there M.J. Some of you are here because you are working on something and choose to be here. Some of you are here because your parents or a counselor or a judge insisted on it. Whatever your reason, you have to agree on a few simple rules or you can't stay in the group.

"First, please don't come here if you've taken drugs or alcohol before the meeting. I'm not doing drug tests and I may or may not be right about it, but if I think you're on something, I'm going to ask you to leave, and you can't come back.

"Next. What we say in this room stays in this room. You may run into each other at school or at a party or at the movies, but unless you are sure the other person is in agreement, you may not talk to each other, and certainly not to anybody else, about the fact that you are both in this group. What we discuss here is confidential, and it is a betrayal of everybody in this room if you repeat to someone else what you heard here.

"You don't have to talk if you don't want to. But give the other people here the respect to listen to what they have to say.

"You're here because you or somebody in your life thinks you have an addiction problem. They may or may not be right. Doesn't matter. You can still learn something here. Nobody else can tell you for sure if you are or are not an alcoholic or addicted to drugs. So don't waste our time trying to convince everybody you don't belong here. Just take it for what it's worth."

She looked around the circle, as the kids shifted in their chairs. "Okay, anybody have something you want to talk about?"

Silence. At last a compact boy with dancing brown eyes spoke.

"You know," he said, sliding the two words into one so that it sounded more like 'yo,' "I was at a party on Saturday night and tried what y'all were talking about last week. It didn't work. Everybody was on my case about why I wasn't partying, like it was a pain in the ass even being around me."

One of the girls spoke up. She was gaunt, with a long angular face and traces of acne, an unfriendly harshness to her voice. "Maybe it's because they're used to seeing you dead-ass stoned all the time and they just haven't gotten used to the change."

"I just tell people like I'm sick or something," said the pretty brunette who had been talking to Margaret Harris when M.J. came in. "There's no problem in telling a little white lie, is there, Margaret?"

M.J. didn't speak at all during the meeting but when they took a break, the dark-haired girl came over to her.

"I'm Abby," she said with a warm smile. "I know this seems weird at first, but it's not so bad after a while. Margaret is okay. Really."

At the end of the meeting, Margaret Harris asked M.J. to stay for a few minutes.

"Glad to have you with us, M.J. I met your older brother over at the teachers' union office a few weeks ago. And of course the rector here at St. Bede's talked to me about your situation. It must be a terrible time for you."

M.J. didn't answer, just nodded her head.

"Well, if you ever want to talk—outside our group I mean—here's my card. You can call me anytime."

M.J. remained a reticent group participant. But after a while, she got used to the meetings and didn't mind going. Margaret Harris struck her as fair and honest. She wasn't phony. If someone was bullshitting, she'd call them on it. Some of those kids were pretty messed up but that didn't seem to freak Margaret out.

M.J. and Abby were drawn to each other right away, and their friendship extended beyond the support group meetings. Since the accident M.J. had kept her distance from kids she knew at school, not that anyone had tried very hard to approach her. But Abby lived in a small town outside Riverton and they didn't know any of the same people. Her father drove her to the evening meetings at St. Bede's and, after he got to know Lee, he occasionally let Abby stay overnight at the Addisons.

Abby was pregnant. Drugs and alcohol had left her vulnerable to sexual exploitation and, from the age of thirteen, she had lived free and wild right under her parents' noses. She wasn't even sure who the father was. Abby was raised in a Christian fundamentalist tradition, so abortion was out of the question.

It was Abby who pushed M.J. into finally talking about the accident at a meeting. A couple of the kids knew what had happened, but Margaret espoused a philosophy of voluntary participation and she was willing to let kids sit and listen as long as they wanted. When an unwilling or uncommunicative group member was called out, it was inevitably by one of the other young people.

They had been talking about alcohol and marijuana, how they were the same and different in the social lives of these kids and their friends. Many of the teens in the group had started drinking or smoking dope early, even before junior high. Surprisingly, most of them admitted openly that they had a problem. It was almost a badge of honor.

"What about you, M.J.?" Abby asked, turning to her new friend. "Are you alcoholic?"

M.J. was caught off guard and she didn't like being called out. "No," she said, glaring at Abby. "I'm here because the court ordered it."

The first thing these kids had learned about addiction was the characteristic red flag of denial.

"Bullshit," said one of the boys sitting to M.J.'s left. "That's just denial."

Margaret wanted to keep M.J. talking and discouraged the piling on likely to occur among kids with similar histories.

"One of the things you learn," Margaret said, "is that no one else can really say that about another person. And at the end of the day, does it matter what label you put on it? If your use of alcohol is messing up your life, it's a problem.

"M.J.," she continued, "you don't need to talk about the accident. But you've heard a lot of stories in this room. It's not easy for anybody to talk about personal things in front of strangers. But trusting the process is a way of showing respect to the other people here. We want to know you."

M.J.'s eyes started to tear up, the double whammy of kindness and intrusion shaking her guarded demeanor, if only for a minute. "My life is fucked up anyway," she said, keeping her eyes on the ground. "It doesn't matter whether I'm a drunk or not. I'm going to jail."

"Actually it does matter," said David, one of the gentler boys in the group. "No matter how screwed up things are, you can't get off ground zero if you're not honest with yourself."

The kids then rallied around her, truly empathetic, aware that the accident that had unhinged M.J.'s life could have happened to any one of them.

Having pulled M.J. into the discussion, Abby then took the pressure off by talking about the challenges she was facing as a pregnant teen.

A week later, it was Abby Stockton's first overnight at the Addisons and the first night she had slept away from home since she had told her parents about the baby.

Lee unlocked the front door for the girls and introduced Abby to their mother. Frances had heard enough about Abby's situation from Lee to have misgivings about M.J.'s new friend, but she knew how badly M.J. needed someone her own age to talk to.

Once the girls were in the privacy of M.J.'s bedroom, Abby's natural ebullience took over. "Holy shit, this place is amazing. You live in a mansion."

"No I don't," M.J. said defensively.

Abby threw herself onto the fluffy double bed with its pastel quilt and throw pillows and the aging panda M.J. had slept with since childhood.

"You are so lucky. I can't imagine living in a place like this."

M.J. was incredulous. "Lucky?"

Abby pulled M.J. down beside her on the bed. "Look, I'm sorry," she said. "I know you didn't want to talk at the meeting. It's just that you've got to put yourself out there if you're going to get anything out of it."

"There's nothing those meetings can do to help me," M.J. insisted, slipping an old Eagles CD into the player and propping herself up on a stack of pillows next to Abby.

"I think David likes you," Abby said, turning toward M.J. "He almost never says anything. But he was all over it when you started getting down on yourself. I've never seen him do that."

"Most of the kids in that group are losers," M.J. suggested, interested in Abby's observation. "But he seems different."

"Y'all could be perfect together. But, sorry to tell you, David will be out of here next week. His parents are making him go to a boarding school for problem kids. All he did was try marijuana a few times. I think his parents freaked out because he flunked a couple of classes."

"Do your parents make you come to the group?" M.J. asked.

"Well, yes, I guess so. Basically my whole church is making me come. They think I'm the whore of Babylon and if I'd just stop drinking, maybe I could keep my pants on," Abby laughed.

"I don't get it," M.J. said.

"I guess I don't either."

M.J. couldn't begin to comprehend the path that had led Abby to teen pregnancy. The reckless sexual behavior Abby described was apparently triggered by alcohol and, in M.J.'s mind, wholly inconsistent with the self-contained, thoughtful girl who had befriended her. Her parents were deeply involved in a small, charismatic religious sect. Abby had been sheltered from the temptations of secular society by rigorous church discipline, home schooling and evenings in front of the fireplace taking turns reading the Bible. All her childhood friends came from the small group of families in the church. But once puberty arrived, Abby discovered alcohol and sex, freely indulging in both in the fields outside tent revivals and on youth missions.

"I know I'm not ready to be a mother," she sighed. "Mama says she'll raise this baby and treat it like her own child. Great. That's all we need. Another me."

"If you don't want to have an abortion, why don't you give up the baby for adoption?"

"They won't let me."

That much of it M.J. *did* understand. Old enough to get into plenty of trouble but no say in how to deal with it.

chapter fifty-five

The harmony that had kept the Addisons steady since M.J.'s suicide attempt began to unravel as summer drew to a close.

It was a Saturday morning in early September, and Jim Barnett had asked Lee and Frances to come to his office without M.J. The parents of the girl killed had requested a meeting with M.J.

According to their attorney, they were people of deep religious faith who felt they needed to talk personally with M.J. in order to take the next step toward healing and closure. Barnett was dubious, both because of potential implications for the case and out of concern for M.J.'s fragile emotional state. At the same time he was worried about the perception that might be created in the public's mind if word got out that the girl's parents had sought a meeting and had been refused.

M.J.'s mother gasped audibly when Barnett told them about the request. "She couldn't. Absolutely not," Frances insisted.

Lee was quiet, his mind racing, considering the implications.

"I'm not saying she should," Barnett insisted, "but it's a sensitive development in the case. I don't want to trouble M.J. about it until we've thought it through."

Over the days that followed, Lee's position was formulated and hardened. From a lawyer's perspective, it was critical to be able to show M.J. as a young person with deep remorse and with compassion for the parents. Pragmatic above all, Lee concluded that this opportunity could be pivotal in M.J.'s defense.

In the end, it took M.J.'s hysteria, their mother's adamant opposition and ultimately an alliance between Dr. Feinberg and Margaret Harris to convince Lee that such a meeting was more than M.J. could handle.

Lee was frustrated and complained to Barnett.

"We're letting an opportunity get away here. She can handle this, I promise you, she can. It could mean the difference between probation or a short sentence in the county jail, and a prison term for the rest of her adolescence that might ruin her life." He was almost in tears himself, so convinced that he was right about this.

"Since you're so adamant about this, Lee, I've got a proposal for you," Barnett said.

And so it was agreed. They would respond to the Barkers' attorney that M.J. was too emotionally distraught to see them but her older brother would appreciate the chance to meet with them on behalf of his sister and their family.

It was one of those sweltering hot September mornings, the dog days of summer hanging on well after Labor Day to torment the school kids and raise concerns about dehydration at football practice. The lovely fall weather that would color the Arkansas hills and turn the air crisp and fresh could scarcely be imagined as summer refused to loosen its grip.

Lee pulled up in front of a modest single-story home, its smoky blue siding accented by well-tended white trim and shutters, a seasonal wreath with woodcut fall shapes hanging on the front door. The grass was thick and lush, recently cut and edged, a scooter and a baseball glove lying on the lawn near the front steps.

As he climbed the steps to the front porch and rang the doorbell, he could feel himself sweating under his suit and wished he had dressed differently. He hadn't slept well and regretted his immediate acceptance of Jim Barnett's proposal.

Leon Barker, in a polo shirt and pressed Levis, answered the door, as two boys about seven years old pushed past Lee and out into the front yard.

"I told Mrs. Jacobs to send you home right after lunch," he said to one of the boys as he extended his hand to Lee and invited him in.

"I'm Leon Barker."

A woman of about forty-five, her soft brown eyes wary and alert, dark blonde hair curling around a gentle face, stood in the background.

"Come on in. This is my wife Sharlene."

The small, tidy living room contained a sofa and two chairs carefully arranged around a walnut coffee table. The table tops and shelves were filled with cheerful stationery-store knick-knacks and souvenirs from family outings, but especially photographs, including several black-and-white portraits of somber ancestors. Most of the pictures, however, featured their two attractive blond children, the girl a few years older than her brother—school photos, soccer pictures, family trips, birthday parties.

The girl in the photographs was a lively, exuberant child, here with her two front teeth missing, there hamming it up by using one small hand to form rabbit ears behind her father's head. On the piano a toddler dressed for church in purple velvet and lace gazed out from within a gold frame with big blue eyes. On the mantle a Halloween princess, adorned in pink from head to toe, licked a round red lollipop with great satisfaction, her pumpkin-shaped candy container tucked securely under her arm.

Lee looked at the child's face and the pink ruffles, and he saw M.J. at that age, too excited to wait until dark to start trick-or-treating. A profound sense of loss settled over his heart.

"Thank you all for letting me come. I know it's my sister you wanted to see, but she is not emotionally able to do this. I'm sorry."

"Here, come sit on the couch," said Barker.

"Thank you."

"Can I fix you some iced tea?" his wife asked.

"No, thank you."

All three were tense, excessively polite, avoiding both silence and personal contact. Lee waited for Leon Barker to begin the conversation.

"We've been praying about this," Barker said. "You know, trying to just…"

His voice trailed off and he couldn't finish the thought.

"We know some day the time will come when we will wake up in the morning without so much pain, without thinking about Susie the first thing." He was quiet again for a minute, composing himself.

"Sometimes, in the morning when you're still half asleep, you forget she's gone. Just for a minute. And you think she'll come bounding in, chattering away, like she used to. All excited about what she was going to do that day."

Sharlene Barker's eyes were moist.

Barker reached for a scrapbook and flipped it open.

"She was turning into a pretty good little athlete. Loved her soccer. You know, that's where she had been the day…the day of the accident."

Lee had come to the Barkers' house with some specific goals in mind. He knew it would be hard, but he was hoping he could make the parents understand that M.J. and her family were not bad people and that they were deeply remorseful about what had happened. Lee knew the power of impressions on a jury, and forgiving parents in the courtroom or quoted in the media had the potential to impact public opinion in a way that could help his sister. But at this moment he was so overcome by sadness that he found himself without words.

Leon Barker looked at Lee and then at his wife. "I wonder if you would be willing to pray with us?" he asked.

Lee nodded and closed his eyes.

"Lord, you know the suffering we've had in this house," Leon Barker began, "and, Lord, only you can lift us up and give us the courage to go on. And now, Jesus, this young man Lee Addison has come to be with us today, Lord, and he and his family are also in pain. We ask you to lift them up, Lord, and especially to hold his sister Mary Addison in the palm of your hand, Lord, and comfort her, as you comfort us all. We know, Jesus, that our journey through this world is short and we have our loved ones for just a second in the eternity of time. Teach us to treasure that brief moment, Jesus, and to care for our own the way you care for us. We pray especially, Jesus, for our Susie who is there with you in eternal glory right now, her bright smile lighting up the heavens. Hold her gently, Lord. She's not used to sleeping without her old pink and grey blanket. Give us the strength, Lord, to go on without her, for we are weak, Jesus, and we're still stumbling along through the valley of the shadow of death, wanting so much to hang onto our child. Grant us your peace, heavenly Father. Help us to forgive. Comfort the Addison family, Lord. We pray in your holy name. Amen."

When Lee left the Barkers' house, he drove for a long time without any idea of where he was going, an ache in his chest so sharp he could scarcely breathe. He couldn't have said how long he drove around, but he found himself in the parking lot of St. Bede's. Instead of entering the administration building, where he occasionally stopped to see Father Desmond or to talk to Margaret Harris about M.J.'s participation in the teen support group, he found his way to the cool, dark sanctuary. Someone was up front rehearsing on the organ but, otherwise, the church was empty. He slipped into the back pew, dropped his head into his hands, and wept.

chapter fifty-six

M.J. was on the phone with Abby Stockton, inviting her to stay overnight on Thursday. Abby's parents liked the Addisons and, in spite of all M.J.'s problems, felt she was a better influence than some of Abby's friends at home. But they kept her on a short leash and M.J. had to settle for telephone time this week. Still, it made a huge difference to have someone her own age to talk to.

"You should have gone, M.J. Your brother isn't the one who should be apologizing to them. He didn't do anything."

"I couldn't," M.J. replied, a tremor in her voice. "Anyway, there's nothing I could say to them that would make any difference."

"Maybe you're right. But it's you I'm talking about, not them. You know what Margaret's always preaching: 'The first step out of the mess you're in is to look around and admit that there's a mess.'"

M.J. had finally started to open up in the support group, thanks mainly to Abby's prodding. Last night the other kids in the support group had been critical of her refusal to meet with the girl's family.

"Y'all made that point last night. I don't want to keep talking about it."

"Okay. I'm sorry," Abby said, backing off. "I just want you to feel better. You weren't trying to hurt anyone. You didn't mean for the little girl to die."

M.J. was grateful for Abby's friendship. Abby could talk to her about the accident without embarrassment, something no one else did, with the exception of Dr. Feinberg and her lawyer.

But M.J. was tense and anxious. She had spent most of yesterday afternoon in Jim Barnett's office. Discussing the case depressed her.

Barnett had started to call the girl Susan. Of course that was her name, but M.J. preferred to refer to her as "the girl." It made it too real to call her Susan.

Dr. Feinberg had insisted she stop reading the newspaper clippings hidden in her mother's desk. She knew it was bad for her and she had stood by her promise to the therapist to stay out of there. But the truth was she had started to think about the girl all the time. She hadn't asked Lee about his meeting with her parents and he hadn't volunteered anything. But in her mind she had a picture of the girl's face, the one that had been in the paper, and she couldn't shake it.

M.J. had to get out of the house. Head down, she jogged to the far end of Broad Street, hoping she wouldn't be recognized by anyone in a passing car. On the way home, she turned the corner onto Oak.

Etta Jones was surprised to see her at the door. "Why, come in, sugar. I'm *so* glad you came down to see me."

M.J. couldn't have said why she came or even how she got there.

"Lord, it's hot out there. Child, have you been running through the streets like your brother in this heat? Let me fix you some iced tea."

The small living room was dark, as Etta had all the curtains pulled to keep out the heat.

"Come in here and sit down, M.J."

Etta pulled out a teapot, chatting and fussing around in the kitchen.

"You don't need to fix me anything," M.J. protested.

"Oh yes I do. A young thing like you? Of course you need somethin' to eat. I want you to try my cornbread. Here, now taste this. I promise you're goin' to like it."

M.J. turned away, feeling unwell at prospect of eating, and lowered herself onto Etta's small sofa.

Etta sat down beside her and took her hand. "Honey, how are you doin'?"

M.J. started to say "I'm doing fine," but then the tears came from out of nowhere. She didn't cry often and never in front of people. Once she started, though, she couldn't stop, and the tears turned into deep rasping groans that came from somewhere deep in her chest. Etta didn't try to stop her, and for a long time she just shut her eyes and let the girl cry.

When the groans began to subside and give way to gasps and shudders, Etta leaned over, just barely, and took the girl's head, putting it on her shoulder. That started the torrent again and M.J. grabbed the little woman, holding on for dear life, and sobbed, loud and long, Etta rocking her like a baby, making soothing noises and rubbing her back. "It's okay, baby. It's okay to cry. Everything gonna be all right."

Etta was still moving her gently back and forth when the last of her shivers subsided. M.J. felt overcome with sleepiness and as empty as a drum. She let Etta lay her down on the sofa and cover her with a throw. She slept for an hour. When she woke, Etta was in the kitchen stirring something on the stove.

M.J. pulled herself up. "I need to get home."

"Come here, honey. I want you to read somethin'."

The old woman pulled out a chair for M.J. at the kitchen table and pushed an old cigar box toward her, filled with letters.

M.J. opened the letter on top.

Dear Mama, Etta and Lovey,

Today been the scariest day of the war so far. They sent us behind the lines to flush out the enemy troops and lots of our boys was killed. They bodies just lying around everywhere. I had to help bury them, even my best friend over here, Sam Johnson, the boy I told you about from Tennessee. He was shot in his head real bad and he died right away. I feel sick tonight from being afraid and from thinking about Sammy. But we did it for our country and the sarge says we was brave and we heroes. When we come back from this war, everything is going to be different for the Negro in the South. This is our chance to prove we love our country. So I don't mind the smell and the bullets, but I do mind it that Sammy is gone.

I love you,
Axel

"This was from your brother?"

"My twin brother. Daddy left us when we was still young, so Axel had to be the man of the house. I was crazy about him. Kind of like you are about your brother. He always looked out for me."

"Was he killed in the war?"

"Wasn't even injured," was Etta's quiet reply. "The trouble come later."

The boys from Riverton's black neighborhood were justly proud of their service to the country in World War II. But they were too young to understand the transformation of the South brought about by an earlier war, a war that was still personal to many Southerners whose grandfathers and great-grandfathers had died eighty years before in a civil war to preserve their way of life and the livelihood that supported their families.

Throughout the century leading up to the Civil War, the population of slaves in the South had increased year after year as small farms consolidated into massive plantations reliant on free labor to sustain this first iteration of big agrobusiness. So not only had that war destroyed the agricultural economy of the South, it left an imbalance in the racial composition of the region. The white population was afraid, not only of poverty and stagnation, but for their very lives.

By the beginning of the twentieth century, Jim Crow laws separated the races, and the Ku Klux Klan, with roots going back to reconstruction, incited racial hatred, vigilante justice and lynchings all across the country.

"I couldn't begin to tell you what it was like around here before the war," Etta said. "A lot of people didn't want the blacks to go off to Europe and fight the Germans alongside white boys. Guess they knew once we started, we wouldn't ever quit," she laughed.

But thanks to threats of political action by A. Philip Randolph, Roosevelt had finally signed an executive order prohibiting job discrimination in the military and defense industries, which had opened up opportunities for young black men to serve in the war. They were generally kept in their own "colored" units, but they fought and died along with the rest of America's youth. Those who survived had gained courage, self-respect and knowledge of the world. And they came home with high expectations.

"Child, you can't imagine how hard it was for Axel to come back to a town that was still set on keeping him in his place. His heart had swelled up with pride during that war."

M.J. had been mesmerized by the sound of Etta's voice, so firm and settled somehow, even with all the trouble her people had been through.

"I know what you mean," M.J. said. "Not about the black people. But having a brother, you know, that you really looked up to. And then they go away and when they come back home somehow everything looks different to them. Lee seems so far away sometimes. Like this isn't his home anymore."

"It was kind of like that for Axel too. Except he didn't have no place else to go. But I don't think he wanted to be in Riverton anymore. Not a bit.

"He was so smart. People say blacks aren't smart, but Axel was. He could talk on and on about Europe and its history, who was king of this country or that one. He had always been a talker, but, mercy, when he come back from that war, he could talk your ear off."

A look of understanding crossed M.J.'s face as she sipped her tea. "I know all about having a smart brother, if that's what you mean. But what happened to Axel?"

"He was shot by the police. Just for tryin' to get into the office where he had been helpin' out the black war veterans. He had forgotten his key, so he was tryin' to jimmy the lock when the police car came by. They yelled at him to stop, but it made him so mad the way they didn't show any respect. He said somethin' nasty to them I guess. But they didn't even ask him for identification or nothin'. Just shot him in the leg, then beat him to death like a dog. It just about killed Mama."

The night Axel Jones died was one of those perfect May evenings in Arkansas when the days linger ever longer, and the summer heat hasn't yet laid its sticky fingers over the red clay hills and valleys. Although Axel was frustrated that he hadn't found a job, he had hopes of going to college on the GI Bill and had sent his application to Tuskegee where some of the boys in the 92nd Infantry had trained. To fill his time Axel was doing volunteer work down at the office shared by the NAACP and the local VA Support Center to help black veterans who had come back from the war.

"Mama didn't want him goin' down to that office. Thought he might get hisself in trouble with the rabble-rousers down at the NAACP." Etta laughed, thinking about how backward her mama had been. "But you know, even though Mama was right about the danger, Axel was right too. The country had begun to change."

The newsreels shown week after week in the movie houses exposed Hitler's deadly racism and filled American sensibilities with images of the devastation wreaked on Europe's Jews in the Nazi death camps. Even in the South, the Germans had given racism a bad name. And, because of the heroism of the all-black division that became known as the Buffalo Soldiers, many of the white boys, even some from the South, came home with a changed view of their colored neighbors.

But with the world changing around them, in every Southern town and city there were men and women who feared the change and, as a result, hated the blacks in their midst, young men standing tall for the first time in their lives. The KKK had found natural allies in local police departments who felt the threat keenly, since the correlation between crime and poverty followed its usual patterns. And, for some of them, the changes wrought by the world wars—the talk of equality and fairness for the black race—just added to the threat. The world was changing too fast. There was talk of integrated schools and swimming pools. For people in the South, where the black population was large enough to have the potential to change the small-town way of life white folks had grown up with, the prospect of such social change made them afraid. There were too many blacks, and they were too poor. And the fear turned to hatred.

"I was thrilled to have Axel back home. He was a little quieter, but still quick-witted and funny. He teased me about boys and how much time I spent fixin' my hair. But he was never mean about it. Just his way of sayin' he knew I had grown up.

"One night I had stayed out with Charles Morris until after midnight, dancing and drinking at the Town House out at Manderville. When I came home, I was happy as a lark and just a little tipsy. Charles walked me up to the porch and we sat on the step, talkin' about everything and lookin' up at the stars."

He had even kissed her, and when she went inside, Etta was brimming with hopes and dreams. Mama and Lovey had gone to bed but Axel was still up.

"Looks like you had a fine time tonight."

She laughed. "They had a blues singer out at the Town House tonight. Sound just like Billie Holiday. And her backup band played the best jazz you ever heard."

He took her hand and pulled her beside him on the couch. "You got to be careful about whiskey. It feels good while you're drinking it, but men will take advantage of a woman filled with drink."

"Don't be ridiculous, Axel. If Charles Morris tried to take advantage of me, I'd put him in his place quick enough."

"I'm just sayin'…"

She looked at him and smiled. "Since when did you become so fussy?"

"I'm not. I like to have a good time. And I had some great times at the end of the war in Paris. We could go into any bar or restaurant. Whites and blacks together. Nobody cared nothin' about it. You could go dancin' with a white girl and it didn't bother nobody."

"Dancing with a white girl?" Etta was horrified.

"Did that more than once. Had me a white girlfriend in Paris. Couldn't talk to each other much, but she was a good dancer. And she didn't mind I was black. She'd go anywhere with me. Right down the middle of a busy street. Restaurant. Dance club. Whatever."

"What did the white boys do?"

"Nothin'. Well, wasn't a lot of white boys left over there. So many killed in the war. Only time it ever come up was once when some boys from an Indiana Marine unit was at this dance club where we used to go. Outside the restroom one of them pulled me aside. We all used the same restroom. Pushed me into the wall. Calling me 'dirty nigger' and everything. But his friends drug him away and they got out of there. It's just different over there. I can't even explain it."

"You a fool, Axel. You coulda been killed. Good thing Mama don't know about that white girlfriend. Don't try nothin' like that here."

"Even here things are changing. We fought as hard as the white boys. And just as many of us died. This is our country too."

"Axel, don't go gettin' mixed up with those NAACP people. They always talkin' about Negro rights. Mixin' with whites. Get yourself killed."

"And that's exactly what he did," Etta said, finishing the story. "Got himself killed. Not from agitating for civil rights. Just went back to the office one night because he had left his wallet. He thought someone was going to be working that night, so he went by but the place was dark and locked tight."

The police car had come up just as he was trying the door. They kept an eye on those offices. Nigger troublemakers, they would say to one another. Always hoped to catch one of them doing something they shouldn't.

So, it had just been bad luck and bad timing. Nobody was sure exactly what happened. The policeman said he ran into the alley behind the building and that he had threatened them with a piece of wood. The gunshot didn't kill him.

"I could have killed him," one of them said in court, "probably should have. Just winged him in the leg, enough to slow him down," he said.

But then they beat him and kicked him until his whole body was bruised and broken. He died in a cell at the police station later that night.

"They didn't come tell us until the next afternoon," Etta said, a dark look in her eyes. "Said they had trouble identifying him. No wallet.

"Mama had been frantic all morning. Me and Lovey, we were worried too. It wasn't like Axel. There was that time in high school when he had come home all beaten up. This time it was a policeman rattling the screen door. Very polite and all. Told us Axel was dead."

M.J. studied a picture of the young soldier in his pressed army uniform.

"Mama tried to get satisfaction from the law. But in those days they was no way a black woman could get any satisfaction from the white police. They would have strung her up first. But she tried. She was feisty, Mama was."

Etta folded the letter carefully and replaced it in the cigar box.

"Do you see, M.J., why I'm showin' you this? Things happen in this world. Ain't no right or wrong to it usually. Just happen. You got to be brave. And you got to trust in the Lord's goodness. But sufferin'—that's just part of bein' alive. You havin' to learn that a little earlier than some people do. But most of us learn it sooner or later. Us black people, we learned it young too. No point in asking why. Just how it is."

chapter fifty-seven

Having been mired in gloom in an air conditioned house all summer, Frances took advantage of the first cool fall morning to get out into her garden. She found a broad-brimmed hat and a pair of gardening gloves and hauled a plastic trash can into the backyard. The formal plantings in front—the azaleas, camellias and boxwood shrubs—were kept up by the gardeners. Anyway, she wouldn't be caught dead pulling weeds in the front yard. But the annuals she had put in last spring in the backyard had finished blooming, and her big hydrangeas and the morning glories on the trellis needed to be cut back.

She hadn't taken to gardening until after Lee left for college. Her own mother had disdained physical labor, her hardscrabble upbringing having placed Roberta Dawkins as close she would ever want to get to field work. During Lee's high school years, Frances was preoccupied with his sports and other school activities. But M.J. wasn't a joiner, and Frances found herself with time on her hands after Lee left home.

The sun was already high in the eastern sky, but the air was crisp and it felt good to be out of the house. She deadheaded the spent daisies and sweet pea blossoms and went to work on the hydrangeas, stepping back from time to time to admire her handiwork. She was completely preoccupied with the task at hand and for a few precious minutes Frances hadn't thought about M.J., the terrible accident and the hardship her daughter faced. The ringing of the telephone startled her out of a pleasant reverie. Irritated by the intrusion, she pulled off her gloves and hurried through the back kitchen door to catch the phone.

"Yes, Abby, how are you, honey?"

"No, she's gone out with Lee for a little while. Can I have her call you back?"

"Of course you can. We'd be happy to have you overnight. I'll tell Lee to bring both of you back after the meeting."

Frances resumed her pruning, her thoughts turning to her daughter, as they so often were these days. She shook her head, bemused at how perspectives could change. She was grateful beyond belief that M.J. had found a friend. Six months ago, if M.J. had asked for an overnight with a poor pregnant teen from the country, Frances would have been appalled. Now she was just grateful that her daughter had somebody to talk to.

It had been the same with the black boy. Lionel Minor had stopped by the house unexpectedly the day before, dropping off some books for M.J. Frances regretted her interference with their friendship, especially now that she saw the boy with fresh eyes. He was courteous, bookish, almost a nerd really, and infinitely preferable to the older boys M.J. had been seeing before the accident.

Good Lord Almighty, I'm a slow learner, she said to herself, dropping the spent hydrangea blossoms into the can. I've been sick at heart for years that she wasn't more popular and successful in school and now just having her alive is a blessing.

She had had a long talk on the phone yesterday with M.J.'s psychiatrist. Dr. Feinberg was pushing for court permission to send M.J. on some kind of wilderness experience run by therapists in the Blue Ridge Mountains. Troubled kids learning to light campfires from wood and string, with psychologists at the ready to help them sort through their problems and build self-esteem. Frances wasn't sure it made sense, given all M.J. had already been through.

Frances had now worked her way back to Roberta Dawkins' rose garden and was taking out her frustration on the roses that were past their peak.

She had been insulted by Dr. Feinberg's implication that Frances herself might have a drinking problem. No doubt an opinion asserted by M.J. Always ready to blame her mother for everything. Sure, she wasn't perfect. But, God knows, she tried. She had two children to raise and nobody to help and, damn it, she did the best she could.

The sun had climbed higher in the sky, and Frances was starting to sweat, the bright cool morning dissolving into a hot Arkansas afternoon. She put away the garden tools, muttering to herself about life's unfairness and looking forward to a chilled Pimm's Cup on the back porch.

chapter fifty-eight

A week later Lee was organizing himself for the trip back to California. He would be leaving on the weekend, and his mother had talked him into sorting through some of his boxes stored in the attic. A storm was blowing in and that had cooled things off, enough to make the attic bearable.

It was dusty and dark as he found his way to the shelves in the far corner where he had stored odds and ends he didn't want to toss out just yet—photographs and papers, old yearbooks, championship trophies, mementos boxed up after graduation from Tulane and before he headed out to California for law school.

Growing up, Lee had spent many a rainy afternoon in the attic, playing hide-and-seek with friends or building model airplanes in the crafts room behind Grandmother Dawkins' old trunks. He and M.J. always kept a partially completed jigsaw puzzle on a folding table in that room. M.J. had loved their time together in the cluttered attic, even though she was absolutely forbidden to mess around with the models he kept on the work bench. She would find a doll, or a game or puzzle, and play quietly nearby while he worked on his projects.

Lee found a short stool, set it in front of the shelves and started to pull out boxes. He flipped through his senior yearbook, he and Annie together everywhere, looking much younger but every bit as much in love. Most Beautiful and Most Likely to Succeed—a storybook romance. *And they lived happily every after.*

He sighed. Things were tense between them now, both pulling away,

preparing for separation. Was this how divorce felt? He would miss her—tremendously. He could feel her distance now, maybe even her anger. But what did she expect? That he would propose? Maybe she *did* expect that. It had been a chaotic summer. The transition from school to law practice wouldn't be easy. They would work him like a dog for the first few years. He couldn't imagine space for her in his life right now. He knew they had to talk about it. She would expect that. But what to say?

He heard steps on the old wooden staircase, then M.J. appeared at the top of the stairs. "Can I help with anything?"

"Hi, Sis. Just going through old boxes. Mama wants me to clean out some of my stuff."

The shelves were packed with cardboard boxes that Frances had long ago tucked out of sight. M.J. pulled a box from the shelf, shuffling through pictures and working companionably beside her brother.

Occasionally one of them would find an old picture or newspaper clipping. "Look at this."

They remembered holidays and vacations, and laughed about some of the crazy mishaps of childhood.

M.J. found a picture of Frances and Trey with their two children at the Country Club, Lee and M.J. dressed in formal velvet and silk, all four of them looking fashionable, *happy*.

"Do you remember much about him?" she asked.

"Oh, sure. I was old enough when he left. I have some pretty nice memories from when I was a kid. A happy guy. Kind of the carefree type. Never really involved with me that much though. I don't remember throwing balls around or him reading books to me. Anything like that."

"I hardly remember him at all."

"You were only six."

"It must have been a terrible scandal. Mary Lou told me all about it a few years ago. Not that Mama ever particularly hid anything from us. I've just never felt comfortable talking about it with her."

"The girl was half his age. A hippie. The daughter of one of those tent revival preachers."

M.J. laughed. "I know. Mama must have been furious. I don't think it's funny really. Just such a weird thing to do."

"You know, I can see how that kind of affair could happen," Lee said. "Cute young chick. Exciting. I'm sure Mama was never easy to live with. But what I can't understand is his just walking out of our lives. A lot of people get divorced but are still parents to their children."

"He's supposedly out in California," M.J. remembered. "At least the last Mama heard. Do you think you might try to find him?"

"No."

"Hey, here's Grandmother and Granddaddy Dawkins."

Lee peered at the photo. "Talk about a fine-looking couple. They must have been going out to a ball."

"For sure," said M.J. "Now *she* was a beautiful woman."

"I've got a whole folder on them in that other box. Lots of newspaper clippings about the eminent Judge Dawkins and his socialite wife."

Lee was making piles by category: Keep, Toss, Read. M.J. had become engrossed in the old news stories from Lee's box. "Oh my gosh, Lee, look at this." The yellowing headline from the old newspaper read "Lawsuit Against Riverton Police Dropped." "Granddaddy was involved in the case having to do with Axel Jones' death. You know, Miss Etta's twin brother."

Corky Dawkins had come home from the war with a limp that he would have for the rest of his life. But he was happy to be alive. The U.S. economy was booming, while Europe lay in shambles. The population of young men in France, Germany and Italy had been decimated, its brain trust killed or immigrated to the United States, its infrastructure destroyed. Young Americans, returning victorious from the war to an intact country, geared up to provide manufactured goods to the rest of the world. Riverton, like most small towns and cities in America, welcomed back its war heroes with open arms. Many of the younger soldiers, raised on farms or in Ozark

hamlets and now able to better themselves with a college education paid for by Uncle Sam, moved to town after four years in college, ready to claim their share of the America dream.

Those a bit older and from affluent backgrounds like Corky Dawkins became community leaders in what would become the golden age of American life. Having already completed law school before the war, possessor of a stately home and a beautiful young wife and daughter, Corky Dawkins rose quickly from a successful law practice to an appointment to the bench. Judge Dawkins was soon a deacon at St. Bede's Episcopal, on the board of the Country Club and a prominent Riverton civic leader.

He didn't talk much about the horrors he had seen in Europe. Like most Americans, his recollections of World War II—the German atrocities, the American soldiers as saviors of freedom and symbols of virtue for the world—came to be shaped by what he saw in films rather than the ugly truth he had actually witnessed. He felt that he deserved the station in life he had achieved through individual effort and talent. He had done his part in Europe and didn't question the good fortune that he, his town and his country were enjoying. Corky would have liked a bigger family, but Roberta was done with childbearing, and she made that quite clear to him. And so they settled into a comfortable life.

When the newspapers reported that a black war veteran had been killed by police trying to break into a Riverton office building, Judge Dawkins just shook his head.

"Those poor boys," he said to his wife. "Such an adjustment for them coming back from the war. The country built up false hopes for the Negro by sending him off to fight alongside whites in Europe."

Like all respectable upper-class whites in Riverton, Corky was careful to pronounce Negro correctly. He had heard both whites and blacks use the derogatory mispronunciation of the racially descriptive term, but he considered it demeaning and crude. He would never have used the epithet himself, nor would he have heard it used by people in his circles.

Roberta was fascinated by the headlines. "Well, I'm sorry he was a veteran. But the colored people will probably revert to old habits. They are like children. No self-control."

"I can only tell you that the Negro units that fought near us in North Africa were as brave as any of us," Corky said.

They were sitting together in the sunlit breakfast room of the large Peach Street home. Upstairs the maid was dressing Frances and would then take her into the kitchen for breakfast before school.

Months later Judge Dawkins was assigned the civil case brought against the Riverton police by Mrs. Tanette Jones, mother of the dead veteran.

"A fool's errand," the ladies at the church had said to Tanette.

"Dangerous," her neighbors warned.

And so it was. The burning cross on their lawn, threatening letters, taunts from carloads of teens driving by the house.

Etta and Lovey would never forget the fear they felt or the fierceness of their mother's resolve.

"They can kill me, they can do whatever they want, I don't care. I am a citizen of this country too. My son fought for this country. They cannot get away with beating him to death for no reason. Over my dead body."

At the end of the day, of course, there was no justice. The police stuck to their story. Their friends and brothers in white sheets and pointed hats terrorized anyone in town who said a word against law enforcement. People at church said Tanette was hurting them all, stirring up trouble for the black folk.

It was Judge Corky Dawkins who would bear the responsibility for resolving the ugly dispute, he who would bring it to a conclusion and stop the stream of news that attracted prurient attention in newspapers as far away as Chicago. Corky Dawkins was a man of high ethics, a decent man. But he was also a realist. He was the one who had placed a personal call to Chauncey Miller over at the NAACP office, making it clear how the case was going to end, and the harm Miller would be inflicting on the local colored people if he continued to make an issue of it. It was Judge Dawkins who took the police chief out to lunch at the Club, threatening more trouble than any of them could contain if the Klan kept getting in the middle of this, trying to make him understand that there were currents afoot in the country, groups up north who were paying attention, threats to their very way of life.

Whatever he felt about it personally, not even Roberta would have known. He didn't talk about his cases at home.

Lee slipped the news story back into its plastic container. *Sins of the fathers…*, he thought to himself. "Etta talks about her twin brother all the time," he said. "Strange to think about Grandfather Dawkins being part of that."

"She's talked to me about it too," M.J. said. "Showed me a letter Axel wrote them during World War II."

"Whatever complaints we may have about Riverton today, you've got to admit things have improved for some people," Lee said. "What tangled webs were created in the building of this country. If we went back far enough, our ancestors probably owned some of Etta's people. Not to mention fathering their children. Those Washington kids are probably our distant cousins."

M.J. laughed. "Are you glad to be getting out of here?"

Sighing, he closed the box. "Might be if you tell me you're going to be okay."

"What's okay? Not killing myself? A year in jail?" She shoved a handful of newspaper clippings back into the box, angry to be reminded of how few options she could see ahead. "How do I know?"

"Well, *I* know. You *are* going to be okay. I promise." He was feeling no more anchored than she was, but was determined to be positive. "I'm going to miss you."

"Annie too, I imagine."

"Yep, Annie too." His plans for the fall, so compelling a few months before, felt empty.

"Lee, grab that article about Axel Jones. I want to take it down to Etta."

A breeze had sprung up, clearing the air for an afternoon storm. For the first time since spring, the wind felt crisp, a harbinger of the new season on its way. M.J. tapped softly on the screen door.

Etta smiled broadly at the sight of the girl, leading her inside with a hand draped over her shoulder. The herbs in the teapot smelled of ginger and peach as their heads bowed over the yellowed newspaper clipping. Neither of them could have said why, but there was a feeling of stillness and acceptance that enveloped the two figures seated at the small kitchen table. M.J. would have bristled at words like "God" or "Faith," but the space in that small room surrounded the two women with something sturdy and sacred that would not wilt before the forces of time or happenstance.

chapter fifty-nine

December 28, 2001

Dear Lovey,

Thank you, sister, so very much for the beautiful soft sweater. I opened it first thing Christmas morning and wore it to church with my violet suit. I wish you was right here beside me so I could love on you. But at least I can still pick up this pen and write to you (thank you, Jesus!) even if it is kind of shaky and scrawly.

I know it has gotten too hard for you to make the trip up here and Lord knows I'm too old to go to Dallas, but it has been too long since I've seen you. I can't believe it has been ten years since you spent that summer up here helping out with Ruby's kids. Time being what it is, I'm starting to wonder if I'll ever set eyes on you again in this life. I never thought I would live to be this old and sometimes I wonder why.

I took your advice about those bad dreams I was having. I laid down that burden before the Lord and now I'm not so jittery any more. I don't think it would have bothered me so much if I hadn't seen it all on TV. All those people waking up that morning thinking they was taking a trip to see they kids or going to work and those airplanes flying into buildings and blowing up and those huge skyscrapers just falling to the earth. Children and women, good people and bad people, burned up alive or falling through the sky. Sometimes in my dreams I started seeing Axel falling through the sky like that. I don't know. You just wonder why something like that would happen. Makes me think I've lived too long. But I've laid it aside now and I'm all right.

I did want to tell you I had a surprise visitor the day after Christmas. I was just setting by the window reading that Bible with the big print that Calvin gave me for my birthday. And guess who walked across my lawn and came up and knocked on my door? It was M.J. Addison, looking bright and happy and just beautiful really. I hardly even recognized her at first. Her hair is a little darker, kind of brownish-gold, and pulled back into a ponytail. She seems taller and thinner than she used to be. But healthy with good color in her cheeks. She's still quiet, kind of inward, but not angry or scared any more.

You wouldn't think being in jail could make any living soul better or happier, but somehow it seemed to work for that girl. Just getting her away from her mama for a while was probably a good thing. And I don't think she ever took a drop of liquor after she got out, not then and not now. Never married neither and that's kind of sad. M.J., I said, you need a husband and a houseful of children. She laughed at that. No thank you, Etta. When I need kids in my life, I just get on a plane and go out to San Francisco and spend a few weeks in Lee and Annie's house. That cures my longing for kids real quick.

Do you know, Lovey, that girl is living and working in the worst part of Houston. You couldn't pay me enough to walk around in the neighborhood where she works. And she's over at the Federal prison all the time, working with the people there. Lots of them black people. Legal Aid, she calls it. I wished Judge Dawkins could see that. His granddaughter. You know she earned her law degree while she was supporting herself waiting tables. I'm so proud of that girl. She took to me, you know, during her troubles. I don't know why. She would come down here just to get away from the house.

After her mother died and they sold the house, neither of those Addison kids wanted to come back here. Annie of course comes once a year to see her family, but I don't think Lee ever comes with her. That's where M.J. was staying, out at the Rayburns. She came because Tommy has been so sick. You know, Annie's brother, who is kinda retarded. I guess Lee and Annie and the three kids are coming in a few days. Maybe they'll come by to see me too.

I haven't seen Lee since that summer you was here, except for when his mother died. He did come down to see me then, but he was only here for a few days and left Annie and M.J. to finish cleaning out the house. I thought I knew Lee best of all of them. But he is so busy being a lawyer he can't seem to make time for anything else. Even when he's with you, he's not with you. He's on that little phone he carries in his pocket all the time or sending a message to someone important. Sometimes he has a whole bunch of people on that little phone all at the same time.

Don't know how I got mixed up with that family—Judge Dawkins' brood. What would Mama have said? I like to think she would have understood. Nothin' we could do would bring Axel back, would it Lovey? Everybody have they own kind of heartache.

Love,

Etta

acknowledgements

I owe a debt of gratitude to my first and best editor, critic and supporter Nat Sterling who patiently endured much grumbling and consternation and provided great insight and advice as this story came together. Without him I couldn't do much of anything, certainly not write.

My sister Lou Dye was the first person I trusted to read an early draft of the story without hurting my feelings, and she was warm and wise and supportive the way she always is.

I was assisted by a group of excellent readers who, because of their literary expertise and personal affection, provided thoughtful and valuable input on the manuscript as the story developed: Barbara Babcock, Melissa Brown, Julia Burfeind, Ann Dye, Patty Fisher, Julia Molise, Ellen Smith and Jennifer Sterling. And thanks to my brother Karl Kemp for input on Arkansas law.

I am grateful to my editor Lynn Stegner, a notable teacher and writer from one of California's eminent literary families, for her encouragement and advice.

Will Kiester provided invaluable expertise in his oversight of publication of the book, along with his outstanding network of designers, printers and editors.

Texarkana artist Thomas Hinton (1906 – 1975) captured the unique beauty of Arkansas as few artists have. My thanks to his niece Betty Miller Jones and her daughter Valorie Jones for letting me use the image of one of his paintings on the cover of this book.

Heather Olah at DesignOlah helped me create a fabulous website and has been ready to jump in whenever needed to make things look perfect.

Discussion Group Topics and Frequently Asked Questions may be found at www.MarciaKempSterling.com.